THE LEOPARDS OF NORMANDY:
CONQUEROR

DAVID
CHURCHILL

THE LEOPARDS OF NORMANDY:
CONQUEROR

Headline

First published in Great Britain in 2018
by HEADLINE PUBLISHING GROUP

1

Cataloguing in Publication Data is available from the British Library

ISBN 978 1 4722 1931 2

Typeset in Garamond MT by Avon DataSet Ltd, Bidford-on-Avon, Warwickshire

Printed and bound in Great Britain by Clays Ltd, St Ives plc

Headline's policy is to use papers that are natural, renewable and recyclable
products and made from wood grown in well-managed forests and other controlled
sources. The logging and manufacturing processes are expected to conform to the
environmental regulations of the country of origin.

HEADLINE PUBLISHING GROUP
An Hachette UK Company
Carmelite House
50 Victoria Embankment
London EC4Y 0DZ

www.headline.co.uk
www.hachette.co.uk

The Leopards of Normandy trilogy would never have been possible without the support, encouragement, advice and occasional stern commands of Mari Evans, Frankie Edwards, Flora Rees and Julian Alexander. And so this third volume is dedicated, with gratitude and affection to them all.

THE LEOPARDS OF NORMANDY:
CONQUEROR

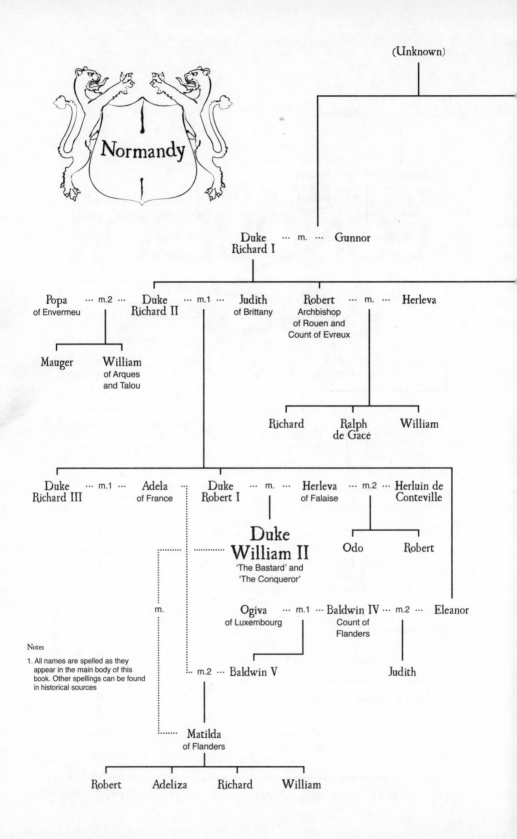

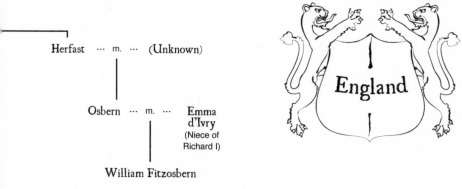

Herfast ··· m. ··· (Unknown)

Osbern ··· m. ··· Emma
d'Ivry
(Niece of
Richard I)

William Fitzosbern

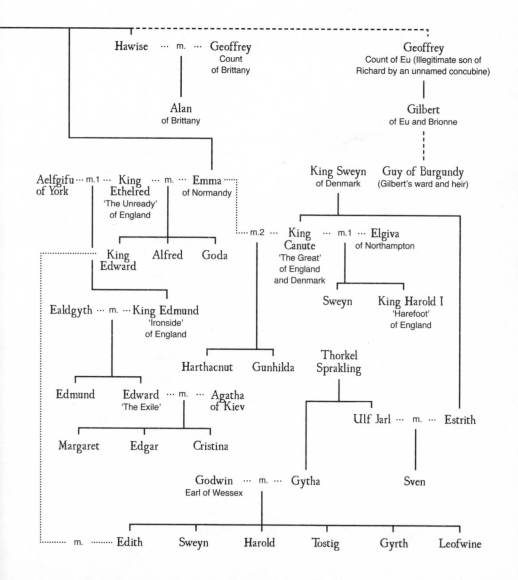

England

Hawise ··· m. ··· Geoffrey
Count
of Brittany

Geoffrey
Count of Eu (Illegitimate son of
Richard by an unnamed concubine)

Alan
of Brittany

Gilbert
of Eu and Brionne

King Sweyn   Guy of Burgundy
of Denmark   (Gilbert's ward and heir)

Aelfgifu ···m.1··· King ··· m. ··· Emma
of York   Ethelred   of Normandy
                     'The Unready'
                     of England

··· m.2 ··· King ··· m.1 ··· Elgiva
Canute   of Northampton
'The Great'
of England
and Denmark

King   Alfred   Goda
Edward

Sweyn   King Harold I
            'Harefoot'
            of England

Ealdgyth ··· m. ···King Edmund
'Ironside'
of England

Harthacnut   Gunhilda

Thorkel
Sprakling

Edmund   Edward ··· m. ··· Agatha
             'The Exile'   of Kiev

Ulf Jarl ··· m. ··· Estrith

Margaret   Edgar   Cristina

Sven

Godwin ··· m. ··· Gytha
Earl of Wessex

········· m. ········ Edith   Sweyn   Harold   Tostig   Gyrth   Leofwine

List of Characters

Historical Characters

Mauger, later Archbishop of Rouen; and William, Count of Arques and Talou (referred to as 'Talou'):	William's uncles
William Fitzosbern (referred to as 'Fitz'):	William's distant cousin, but closest friend
Roger of Montgomery:	the son of a rebel, but now another of William's inner circle
Hugh Montgomery:	his brother
Mabel, Dame of Bellême:	the daughter of William 'Talvas' of Bellême, a very pretty chip off a very nasty block
Gervais, Bishop of Le Mans:	Mabel's cousin
Robert of Champart:	former abbot of Jumièges, now Archbishop of Canterbury and confidant of King Edward of England
Lanfranc of Pavia:	a monk, scholar and William's envoy to the Pope
Herluin:	founder of the monastery of Le Bec
William Fitzgiroie:	a horribly mutilated monk
Arnaud d'Echauffour:	his son
Raoul de Tosny, Walter Giffard, William of Warenne, Robert 'the Bishop's Son' and Hugh de Grandesmil:	loyal followers of Duke William

Eustace, Count of Boulogne:	an opponent of the English and supporter of the invasion
Stephen FitzAirard:	captain of William's flagship, the *Mora*
Hugh Margot:	a monk and emissary to King Harold

The French and Flemish

King Henry I:	William's liege-lord and adversary, husband of Anne of Kiev
Odo Capet:	his younger brother
Theobald, Count of Blois:	an ally of the king
Geoffrey 'Martel', Count of Anjou:	an aggressive and ambitious nobleman
Hugh, Count of Maine:	a victim of Martel's ambition
Herbert of Maine:	Hugh's son
Count Enguerrand of Ponthieu:	a nobleman with land bordering Normandy
Guy of Ponthieu:	his brother
Baldwin V, Count of Flanders:	Duchess Matilda's father and (half) brother-in-law of Tostig Godwinson

The English

King Edward:	later known as 'the Confessor'
Queen Edith:	his wife, the daughter of Godwin of Wessex

Prince Edward 'the Exile':	the son of King Edmund 'Ironside' of England, husband of Agatha of Kiev
Margaret and Edgar:	their children
Prince Edmund:	Edward the Exile's brother
Earl Godwin of Wessex:	the richest, most powerful man in England
Gytha Thorkelsdottir:	his wife
Sweyn Godwinson:	their eldest son and black sheep of the family
Harold Godwinson:	later Earl of Wessex, and later still King of England
Edith 'Swan-Neck':	Harold's mistress and common-law wife
Gunhild and Gytha:	Harold and Edith's daughters
Ealdgyth of Mercia:	Harold's wife, in a marriage of convenience
Tostig, Leofwine and Gyrth Godwinson:	Harold's younger brothers
Judith of Flanders:	Tostig's wife and (though younger than her) Duchess Matilda's aunt
Copsige:	Tostig's faithful lieutenant
Stigand, Bishop of Winchester:	a friend to the Godwins
Edwin and Morcar:	the sons of Aelfgar, Earl of Mercia, and brothers of Ealdgyth
Gospatric:	a Northumbrian nobleman

Robert FitzWimarc, Sheriff of Essex:	a loyal supporter of King Edward

The Norsemen and their women

Harald 'Hardrada' Sigurdsson:	husband of Elisaveta of Kiev and King of Norway
Ingegerd and Maria:	their daughters
Tora Torbergsdatter:	Harald Hardrada's second wife
Magnus and Olaf:	their sons
Sven Estrithson, King of Denmark:	Harald's perennial adversary
Ulf Ospaksson:	Harald's right-hand man
Skule Knofostre:	a fiery young Viking
Ostein Orre:	Tora's brother, one of Harald's best men, in love with his daughter Maria
Pal Thorfinsson, Earl of Orkney:	Harald's host

Named Fictional Characters

Agnes:	Mabel of Bellême's maid, and more . . .
Jarl the Viper:	a professional poisoner, also known as Jamila
Hervé of Abbeville:	a henchman of Talou
Martin:	a poacher in Duke William's service

Henrik the Dane, Big Jan and Torf Stoneheart:	three Norman soldiers employed on a grisly task
The Reverend Mother:	abbess of Wilton
Maud of Tytherly:	a mean girl
Arne the Red, Leif Carlsson and Erik Magnusson:	three Norsemen serving the Emperor in Constantinople
Johans of Perpignan:	a brothel keeper
Eudo:	chamberlain of Arnaud d'Echauffour (a fictional name given to an anonymous, but actual historical figure)
Aldred Kimballon:	captain of the *Stormrider*
Niblung of Montreuil:	a petty landowner on the northern coast of France
Reavanswart and Amund:	captains of Tostig's housecarls
Eldred of Buxted:	a vociferous thegn
Etienne of Brix:	a nervous Norman
Haimo:	a master carpenter and shipwright

Prologue:
A Handful of Princes

The palace of Yaroslav the Wise, Kiev, 1044

Five of them there were: five young men all born within a couple of years of one another, all exiles, all with claims to the thrones of their native lands. They lived in the royal palace of Kiev under the protection of Grand Prince Yaroslav the Wise. Far from home, but protected by a powerful and generous host, the five considered themselves both cursed and blessed by Fate. Though they might be bereft of their rightful inheritances, they had at least survived when so many around them had perished.

The oldest of the group was called Levente. He and his brother Andras, cousins of King Stephen of Hungary, had had to flee their native land after their father Vazul was murdered on the orders of the king's wife, Queen Gisela. Her men tore Vazul's eyes from his face and poured molten lead into his ears.

In Kiev, Levente and Andras met Edward and Edmund, twin sons of Edmund Ironside, the short-lived king of England. Their father had lost his kingdom to Canute the Dane and his life to an assassin who stabbed him while he was sitting defenceless on the privy with his hose around his ankles and his sword belt undone. Having seized the throne, Canute had no intention of letting any claimants to it survive. He ordered the boy princes to be killed. But before that murder could be committed, the twins were spirited away as far from danger as possible, to Kiev.

The fifth of the exiles was Harald Sigurdsson, self-styled Prince of Norway. He had been only sixteen when he arrived in Kiev a dozen years earlier, but he was already battle-hardened, and he swiftly became more so in Yaroslav's service. Within a few years, Harald left Kiev to seek his fortune in Byzantium. Today he had returned, and the entire royal family, including all six of Yaroslav's sons and all four of his daughters; every nobleman and woman of the grand prince's court; every rich trader and his wife; every servant who could find an excuse to be absent from their duties had gathered in the great hall of the palace to witness his homecoming.

'By God, I swear he's even bigger than he used to be,' Andras whispered to Edward as they watched the Norseman stride through the cavernous chamber, while the crowds gave way before him.

Harald stood a full head higher than the mightiest of Yaroslav's warriors, so that even the most fearsome of them looked like mere children next to him, and their weapons were as toys compared to the monstrous double-bladed axe that hung from one side of his belt and the mighty war sword scabbarded on the other.

'He's putting on quite a display,' Edward replied. 'I wonder if it'll work.'

Andras grinned. 'Well, if it doesn't, it won't be for the want of trying. Just look at those brutes!'

Behind Harald came twelve Bulgar slaves, purchased in the market at Constantinople and selected for their strength. Their oiled muscles were so bunched and swollen that they resembled a team of prime oxen, yoked to the plough as they strained and struggled to bear the weight of the three great chests that were suspended from thick oak poles carried upon their shoulders. There were four slaves to a chest, two to the front and two to the rear, and just as the farmer stands behind the plough, driving his beasts forward with shouts of encouragement and stinging lashes of the whip against their haunches, so a driver walked beside the slaves, commanding them, beating them when necessary, always maintaining their steady march across the hall.

As he completed his progress Harald stepped aside and let the slaves walk past him until they stood before the thrones where the Grand Prince and his wife Ingegerd sat, their faces expressionless at the drama playing out before them. Harald had beseeched Yaroslav to allow him to address the prince's eldest daughter Elisaveta in person, and so she was enthroned beside her parents, while her siblings looked down from the royal gallery.

The slaves lowered the chests to the ground, bowed deeply to the king and were herded away, to stand to one side in mute immobility.

Harald selected a black iron key from the three that hung from a ring in his hand and turned it in the lock clasping the heavy iron chain that secured the lid of the first chest. The lock snapped open, Harald loosened the chain. He threw the lid open with a sweep of his tree-trunk arm and a gasp went up from the crowd of people staring at the scene, standing on tiptoe, craning their necks and elbowing their neighbours to get a clearer view.

The chest was entirely filled with gold and silver cups, plates, goblets, crosses, candlesticks, gilded icons painted in colours so iridescent that they made rainbows seem drab and monochrome: ornaments of every sort, many studded with precious stones, looted from cathedrals, palaces and the treasuries of the dead and defeated.

Harald stood up straight. He looked towards Yaroslav, Ingegerd and Elisaveta, searching out any sign of reaction in their eyes or expressions, but they remained regally impassive.

The giant nodded to himself, found a second key and opened

the next chest. Now the gasps of astonishment were mixed with a higher-pitched tone: the sighs of a hundred women as they gazed, bedazzled, upon a myriad jewels, a cornucopia of pearls, rubies, diamonds, garnets, turquoise and lapis lazuli, all formed into rings, chains, necklaces, bracelets, brooches, earrings and headpieces. The gems and trinkets filled the chest to the very brim: enough to bedeck every concubine in Christendom. Ingegerd could not help herself. She raised one hand to her mouth. But if Elisaveta saw anything in the chest that took her fancy, she gave no sign of it.

Finally Harald opened the third chest, the biggest of them all. And now even Yaroslav could not help himself. He leaned forward, just a fraction, and his eyes widened – imperceptibly, perhaps, to a casual observer, but not to Harald's eagle eye. For long though Yaroslav had reigned over the two principalities of Kiev and Novgorod, and vast though his territory was – stretching from the limitless steppes of Kiev, along the banks of the Dnieper and the Don, and then north and west, past Novgorod to the shores of the Gulf of Finland, and further yet to the frozen waters of the White Sea – still Harald doubted that he had ever seen the like of this. The chest was entirely filled with gold coins. There was enough money here to commission the finest masons and craftsmen that Byzantium had to offer to build a palace fit for the Emperor himself; enough to equip an army so vast and well armed that no enemy could resist it. Yet as Harald well knew, neither of those possibilities explained Yaroslav's very evident hunger.

I know what you want, you greedy old goat, he thought. And you shall have it . . . just so long as I get what I want, too.

The master of the Kievan Rus was not the audience for whom Harald's drama had been performed. His true target was Elisaveta, and now he turned his full attention to her.

The princess was as delicate as Harald was massive, as graceful

4

as he was powerful. When first he looked in her direction, her great blue eyes were soft and modestly lowered. Yet as she raised them now to meet his unabashed examination, they did not flinch, for she came from Viking stock, and Norsewomen had no fear of looking men straight in the eye.

'Thirteen years ago, almost to the very day, I came here to Kiev, a mere boy of sixteen, fleeing for my life from the battlefield where my brother, King Olaf of Norway, lay dead, his body a feast for the crows . . .' Harald began.

'He always fancied himself as a poet,' whispered Edmund of England, but his brother Edward did not respond. His attention was all on Elisaveta.

'Your half-brother,' she said, with a sweetly gracious tone. 'On your mother's side, so that his royal blood was not yours.'

The twins both winced at the princess's dismissal of Harald's pedigree. But the Norwegian was not beaten.

'Aye, but I have king's blood of my own, for I can claim a direct line of descent from Harald Fairhair, first king of all Norway, through my father Sigurd Syr,' he retorted, barely breaking his verbal stride before continuing, 'I came here to Kiev, and wishing to show both my gratitude and loyalty to your sagacious and regal father . . .' he paused a second to bow towards the Grand Prince, 'I enlisted in his army and swiftly rose to the rank of captain, for in his great wisdom, His Majesty saw that I possessed not only the lineage of a fighting prince, but the warrior spirit too.'

The eyes of the crowd turned towards their ruler and Yaroslav gave a little nod of the head to show that he had accepted the truth of those words.

Harald added, 'I also had the hot red blood of a young man in need of a woman.'

He spoke the words with an intensity that drew sighs from

some of the more susceptible women around him, but nothing whatever from Elisaveta.

'I saw that in all the land of the Rus there was no maiden more beautiful than you. Your eyes glow like the shining lights in the northern sky on the nights when God and all his angels reveal their glory to us mere mortals. Your hair is like spun gold, more lustrous than any treasure in these chests. In my dreams I run my hands through those fair tresses like a warm wind through a wheat field.'

Harald accompanied those last words by sweeping his bear's paw of a right hand across his body in a slow, surprisingly delicate rippling motion that suggested it might be as capable of pleasing a woman's body when tenderly applied in the bedchamber as of splitting a man's skull in two when grasped around an axe on the battlefield. Having established his fundamental physical intent, as a dominant male confronted by an irresistible female, he moved his argument onto higher ground.

'Yet your beauty, resplendent though it may be, Princess, is perhaps the least of your virtues. For there is surely no lady more gracious, nor more educated in all the womanly virtues than you. If all this were not enough, you ride as well as any man, and though your hunting bow may not be as sizeable or as stiff as mine . . .' that clear message was not missed by any woman in the hall, 'still your eye is as sharp and your aim as true.

'And so, fair Elisaveta, when first we met, all those years ago, I dared to plead my case to you. I kneeled before you and begged for the gift of your hand. In artful verse, I listed my eight notable accomplishments. I stated – and this was no boast, but a simple recital of the truth – that I possess the ability to shoe a horse, and to ride it. I can ski on snow and swim through water. I can shoot an arrow and throw a javelin. Finally I am a skilful harpist and I pride myself that I can match any poet in his art.

'But in my blazing ardour and my barely bridled passion I forgot the cold, unfeeling truth. I might be the brother of a king, but I had no crown, no land, no fortune, while you, the daughter of a mighty prince, surely merited a match with a husband of equal standing. So how could I object when you told me that I had to earn the right to ask for your hand?

'"Go away," you said, "and come back when you are rich."

'So away I ventured to mighty Constantinople, the city of a million souls. Like so many Norsemen before me, I served the Emperor Michael as an officer in his Varangian Guard, the most trusted and most feared of all regiments. I fought in his service in every corner of the Empire. I went to war against the Saracens who had dared to invade Sicily, Norman rebels who rose up against the Emperor in southern Italy, marauding Pechenegs in Anatolia, rapacious Arab pirates in the waters of the Aegean and the Caliph's armies on the banks of the Euphrates. Eighteen great battles I fought, and countless minor skirmishes besides. I even battled for our divine Lord in heaven, driving the heathen out of the Holy Land so that the land of God might be returned to Christendom once again. I bathed in holy Jordan and was not sparing in my gifts to the churches that stand on the holiest places in Jerusalem.

'Yet the Emperor for whom I'd fought showed scant gratitude for my services. He betrayed me and imprisoned me on the pretext of foul lies and base slander. But I escaped and had my revenge, for it is the custom among the Byzantines to render a traitor helpless by blinding . . . and I blinded the turncoat Michael with these very hands.'

A tremor of horror, fear but also fascination, passed through the watching crowd as Harald held his hands before him and slowly squeezed his fingers into two fists, as if popping an eyeball in each one. Then he let his hands and arms relax as he said, 'Thanks to my service, and that nose for profit that all those of Norse blood surely possess . . .' there were nods and grunts of agreement, for the Rus of Kiev took pride in their merchant skills, 'I was able to make my fortune.'

Harald bowed before Yaroslav as he went on, 'And thanks to the generosity of your great and noble Majesty, and in return for intelligence that I was only too happy to pass on, concerning the strength and dispositions of the Emperor's forces on land and sea, I was able to send much of what I had earned back here to Kiev, to be stored in the Grand Prince's own vaults. What you see before you is but part of a still greater hoard. Blessed Princess, I can bestow upon you silk from Damascus and linen from Egypt, that you may wear gowns so fine and so light that they will feel as though they were sewn from the very air itself. I have scents from the furthest Orient to surround you with intoxicating aromas of jasmine, sandalwood and rose. I have mirrors whose reflection of your beauty will seem like the work of magicians rather than glass-blowers.

'All this I lay before you. All this I offer as my tribute to you. And so I kneel before you . . .' Harald got down on one knee, although he was still as tall as half the men there, 'and beg you for your favour, plead for the promise of your hand and ask you one simple question. Am I rich enough for you now?'

Absolute silence fell upon the throng, as if no one in the hall dared even to breathe, so great was the tension and so strong the expectation as they all, men and women, young and old, waited for their princess to give her assent and the celebrations to begin. The four exiles were as caught up in the moment as anyone else, for Harald was their friend and they knew that none of them could have given a better account of themselves than he had done.

'Come on, Elisaveta . . . give the man what he wants,' Levente murmured, and the others nodded in support.

Finally, Princess Elisaveta rose to her feet. Now there was a collective intake of breath, a craning of necks and standing on tiptoes as the crowd leaned forward to claim the best possible view.

'Well spoken, Harald Sigurdsson,' she began, in a voice that was soft and calm, but so clear that all could hear her. 'I salute your courage and your fortune . . . but I fear that neither has served your purpose as you hoped.'

A breeze of whispers and murmurs eddied about the great hall as the onlookers turned to one another at this unexpected turn of events. Grand Prince Yaroslav frowned. But Elisaveta had not finished speaking yet. Perhaps she was merely teasing Harald a little, making him sweat before she surrendered herself to him.

'I may have said, many years ago, that your fortune was not great enough to win me. I do not recall that particular conversation, although I clearly said something that left a great mark on you. But even if you had appeared here with thirty treasure chests, or even three hundred, my response would have been the same.

'For all your fine words, you have not come here to woo me, but to buy me. Though you paid me many elaborate compliments, you ignored the one that would have most impressed me. If you had respected and trusted me enough to present yourself to me with no battleaxe or golden hoard, but only your good heart and true love, then I might have given you my heart and my love in return. Instead, you asked me to sell myself, and there is simply no price for which I will do that. So I say no to you, Prince Harald. But please do not be downhearted. I have no doubt that there will be many a maiden younger and more lovely than me who will be only too happy to strike her bargain with you.'

With that, the ungrateful princess turned on her heel and, surrounded by her ladies-in-waiting, made her way back to her private quarters, closely followed by her distraught mother.

It took Yaroslav a moment or two to regain his senses, and then he leaped to his feet, pausing for a second with his head turned to follow Elisaveta's swiftly departing figure.

By God, you deserve a good spanking, he fumed to himself. And you shall have it yet, I swear. But Yaroslav had another, more urgent issue to consider.

Just a few paces away, on the floor of the hall, Harald was drawing himself back up to his full height.

'Don't do anything stupid, Harald!' Andras called out, though his friend could not have heard him over the hubbub of conversation that had broken out among the aghast onlookers.

Even the Grand Prince trembled at the thought of how a man as proud as Harald might react to a humiliation as absolute and public as the one his wilful daughter had just delivered.

Setting his royal dignity to one side, Yaroslav clambered down off the dais and walked towards Harald with a rueful look on his face and his hands held wide in supplication. 'Please accept my deepest apologies,' he said. 'Elisaveta's ingratitude and discourtesy were unforgivable.'

Harald said nothing. But his jaw was tight, a vein was standing out from the centre of his forehead and his breath was as heavy as if he had just carried one of the great chests in single-handed. This was a man on the very brink of an eruption of violent fury.

'Lock the chests,' Yaroslav said. 'I will make sure that no one so much as touches them. Then come with me. We must talk.'

Harald looked at the Grand Prince, who was uncomfortably aware that his life was in the giant Viking's hands. He did his best to return the stare in a way that was unyielding without being in any way provocative. The people had given way, leaving the two princes standing alone, like two wrestlers in the ring, though the captain of the royal guard was trying to force a way through the crowd, for he too could see the danger that Yaroslav was in.

Harald took one last deep breath, then exhaled slowly, heavily, letting the tension seep out of his shoulders as he did so. He rolled his head round in a circular motion, causing the bones in his spine to crack loudly enough for Yaroslav to hear them. Then he looked towards the captain of the guard, who had just pushed his way out of the crush of onlookers and was advancing towards them. Harald held out a hand, palm up, to halt the man in his tracks. Then he closed the chests one by one and locked them, causing one or two groans of disappointment as the spectators lost sight of the riches they contained.

When he straightened up again, he looked back at Yaroslav.

'Very well then,' he said. 'Let us talk.'

The four exiles gave great sighs of relief and looked at one another, shaking their heads, all stunned by what they had witnessed.

It was Levente who broke the silence. 'Ale,' he said. 'I don't know about you men, but I have a powerful thirst for ale.'

Harald lowered his prodigious frame onto a chair that was only just large enough to take it, and nodded his assent as servants offered him first a large goblet of rich purple-red wine and then a plate of honeyed pastries. He picked up the goblet, drained it in a single draught and held it out to be refilled.

'You can leave the pitcher here,' he growled. The servant looked at his master, and Yaroslav nodded his assent.

'Leave us now, all of you,' the Grand Prince said, once the flagon of wine had been placed on a table beside Harald's chair. The servants at once disappeared, but one or two of the most senior Kievan courtiers remained until their ruler gave an impatient wave of the hand, making it clear that the order applied to them as well.

'Once again, I can only say how sorry I am about this deeply regrettable misunderstanding,' Yaroslav said.

'Is that what you call it – a misunderstanding?' Harald replied. 'It does not seem like that to me. On the contrary, it is all very clear. We had an agreement. You assured me that your daughter would comply with it. She has chosen to disobey you and make a fool out of me. What have I not understood?'

'The misunderstanding was on my daughter's part. Evidently she did not grasp the need to obey my command. She will be reminded of that duty soon enough. You have my word on that.'

'And what about your people? Even now the story of what happened today will be spreading across the city, from tavern to tavern and house to house, and with every retelling, the account of the idiot Norseman's refusal by their beautiful princess will become more exaggerated, his clumsiness and failure made more grotesque while her disdain becomes all the more cutting.'

'Do you really believe that?' Yaroslav asked, and there was a note of genuine curiosity in his voice, for it had never occurred to him that a man who appeared so impregnable should actually doubt himself so much. But then again, he had more than once noted surprising contrasts between the way a man was seen by others and the way he saw himself, while many a beautiful woman saw only the flaws in her own appearance. Am I any different? he asked himself. The people call me

Yaroslav the Wise, though I agonise over every decision and remember my many mistakes far more clearly than my few successes.

'Yes,' the Grand Prince answered his own question, 'I can see that you do. But you may rest assured that the tale you recount is not the one my people will be telling. They will be calling my Elisaveta a fool for turning down so fine a husband, and me an even bigger fool for letting her get away with it. You must surely know that other men see you as mightier and deadlier than them, and women . . . well, have you ever had trouble persuading them into your bed?'

Like the sun hiding behind a cloud but piercing it with the occasional beam of light, something approaching a smile threatened for a second to break out on Harald's face. 'No,' he admitted. 'Not until now, at any rate.'

'Very well, then, so you must know that every woman in that hall, though they might have envied Elisaveta, will have raged at her for being so arrogant as to discard you. The truth is, this has hurt me as much as it has hurt you, and I can only regain the ground that my family and I have lost by helping you rebuild your own position.'

'So our deal still stands?' Harald asked, reaching over to pick up a pastry.

Yaroslav gave an inward sigh of relief. If Harald was thinking about food, his temper must be lifting.

'Of course. I need those thirty ships you promised to build me. I lost an entire fleet, little more than a month ago. We were taken by surprise.' He looked more pointedly at Harald. 'My spy failed me.'

'I could not have known that the Emperor would use Greek fire,' Harald retorted, for an outnumbered and apparently helpless Byzantine fleet had destroyed the great host of Kievan vessels by shooting burning arrows and other projectiles, whose flames could not be extinguished no matter how much water was used to douse them.

'We lost fifteen thousand men,' Yaroslav said. 'In all my years, I've never seen anything like it.'

'Well, you need not worry about the Byzantines now,' Harald assured him. 'They're too busy fighting one another to be able to follow up their victory. It will be a miracle if the whole empire does not fall. Even so, you shall have your ships. But I need your daughter. And her acceptance must be public and ungrudging, so that everyone may see it.'

Yaroslav nodded. 'Agreed.'

'And tell her this, if what she really cares about is my heart and not my purse. I was not lying when I said I fell in love with her when I first arrived in Kiev. I loved her from the moment I saw her, and my love only deepened with every moment I was in her company and every little bit more that I knew about her. All those years I spent fighting . . . they were not in the Emperor's service, but in hers. Everything I did took me closer to being able to return to her, and be worthy of her love.'

Yaroslav shook his head in wonderment. 'My dear boy, why didn't you say that to her when you had the chance? Listen . . . I'm not going to order Elisaveta to accept you. Even if you wed her, she would never love you. Her pride wouldn't allow it. But I can ask her to come to dinner tonight and listen with an open mind to what you have to say. If you choose to express yourself in the verse of which you are so proud, so be it. But remember this. It won't be your clever wit, your subtle rhymes or your fancy words that win her. It will be what is in your heart. Show her that, and then, Harald, then you may truly win her heart too.'

So it was that Harald Sigurdsson, prince of Norway, spoke a second time before Grand Prince Yaroslav, Elisaveta and the nobility of Kiev, not to mention his four very drunken friends. He entertained them with a poem of his own composition that began as bawdy self-mockery, portraying himself as the clumsy buffoon quite incapable of melting the icy heart of the lovely Russian princess. The whole court roared with laughter, and the exiles shouted out their own words of encouragement, for Harald's jokes were funny and his willingness to lampoon his own failure only made them like him all the more. Elisaveta did her best to resist, but soon even she was joining in, and the sight of her smile and her sparkling eyes gave Harald hope that he might win the battle yet.

Then, like a commander who has feinted with an attack on one flank, only to mount his real assault on the other, he switched the tone of his ballad from comedy to romance and retold the story he had first recounted that morning, when standing by his treasure chests. Now the bombast and boastfulness had disappeared, and he confessed to Elisaveta what he had told Yaroslav: that it had all been for her; that all he had ever wanted was to make himself good enough that she could begin to imagine him as her equal and perhaps her husband. His sincerity was so evident, the words he used so direct, the catch in his voice so unforced that no one could doubt the love he felt for Elisaveta.

And so, once again, Harald stood before her and asked for her hand, and once again silence fell upon the multitude.

Elisaveta rose to her feet. She was blinking rapidly. She tried to speak and then stopped, for she did not trust herself to do so without losing her composure.

The air in the great hall was heavy with tension. Surely she could not refuse Harald twice? And yet, if she really did not love him, what good would mere poetry do?

The silence stretched out, every second seeming infinitely extended.

Harald waited patiently to hear his fate.

And then a woman near the back of the hall, unable to restrain herself a moment longer, yelled, 'Oh for God's sake, Your Highness, if you don't take the poor man, I will!'

The whole hall erupted into laughter as the tension was suddenly released. And it was then, when very few people were actually paying her any attention, that Elisaveta walked over to Harald, took his huge hand in her slender fingers and, feeling dwarfed by his godlike stature, looked up into his eyes. 'Yes, Harald, I will be your wife.'

Harald and Elisaveta were married within the month, and great was the rejoicing in Kiev, not least among the shipwrights on the Dnieper river, who had more work than they could handle, thanks to the orders placed by Grand Prince Yaroslav and paid for by his share of Harald's treasure.

As for the bride and groom, they blooded the sheets of the wedding bed, as custom demanded, and took great pleasure in doing so. Afterwards, as they lay entwined in the dark, Harald said, 'We must soon leave for Norway, my darling. My gold could not buy you, but my gold coins and the steel of my axe will surely get me the crown. You are a princess here in Kiev. But in Norway I will make you a queen.'

He was as good as his word. Within three years he was king of Norway. Meanwhile, Yaroslav and Ingegerd matched two more of their daughters, Anastasia and Agatha, with their choice of the princes exiled at their court.

When Hungary descended into rebellion and anarchy, the sons of Vazul returned there, and Andras emerged from the chaos as king, with Anastasia of Kiev as his queen.

Edmund and Edward accompanied their friends to Hungary. Edmund died in the fighting, but Edward survived and went to live with Agatha at Castle Réka, an estate in the Mecsek mountains, close to the border with the duchy of Croatia. Soon after their arrival a daughter, Margaret, was born to them, and a few years after that a son named Edgar.

In the same year that Edgar first drew breath and cried, the fourth of Yaroslav's daughters, and his favourite, Anne, left her homeland to make the long journey across the whole breadth of Christendom to marry yet another monarch, King Henry of France.

Thus the Grand Prince and Princess of Kiev had placed their daughters on three thrones.

But they had little chance of securing a fourth: the throne of England. For though Prince Edward had by far the strongest blood claim to be the next king, and though the current monarch, his uncle and namesake King Edward, had no sons of his own, the prince's very existence was still unknown to the English court. He had, after all, disappeared more than thirty years earlier. Everyone assumed that he was dead. And so the king had another successor in mind.

This candidate for kingship was a dozen years younger than Edward the Exile. There was not a drop of Saxon blood in his veins, nor did he speak a word of English. He had never, in fact, set foot on English soil. And far from being the legitimate scion of the line of English kings that stretched back to Alfred the Great, he was the illegitimate offspring of a short-lived affair between a duke's younger son and a common village girl.

Members of his own family considered him unworthy of any honours or titles whatsoever.

That was why they called him the Bastard.

Book One:

The Promised Crown

March–November 1051

1

The Castle of Tours, France

'Good morning, Bishop, how are you today?' said Geoffrey, Count of Anjou, peering through the fetid gloom at the captive who lay chained and shackled to the wall on the far side of the dungeon cell beneath the castle of Tours.

His enemies had given Anjou the nickname of Martel, which meant 'the Hammer', partly because he was a formidably powerful, dangerous opponent, but also because he was a crude, unsubtle bludgeon of a man. He accepted the nickname, and both reasons for it, proudly. So far as he was concerned, his simplicity was a virtue. Someone had once told him of Julius Caesar's line: 'I came, I saw, I conquered.'

'I like that.' Martel had replied. 'But I like "I saw it, I smashed it, I took it" even better.'

He had spent the past five years trying to take the entire county of Maine, which lay immediately north of Anjou. But for all the destruction he had wreaked upon it, Maine was not yet his. Nor would it be so long as the fortress of Chateau-du-Loir held out against him and, a hard day's ride to the north, the county's main city, Le Mans, remained in the hands of its ruler, Count Hugh IV. So Martel's desires had been frustrated, a situation he never enjoyed. Still, he had enjoyed one piece of good fortune.

Although Chateau-du-Loir had stood firm for more than two years, despite many of the buildings within its walls being burned down by flaming arrows shot by the besiegers, it had done so without its owner, Gervais, Bishop of Le Mans. When Martel had swooped on the castle he had surprised Gervais and a number of his knights in open country before they could take shelter within its walls.

Like many bishops, Gervais was not a priest but an aristocrat, a scion of the House of Bellême, which controlled a sizeable territory in the borderlands between Maine and Normandy. Once he had occupied Maine, Martel was intent on taking the Bellême lands too. So it suited his purposes to keep the bishop alive, for his family could afford a handsome ransom. Even if he did not fetch any money, his mere presence in Martel's keeping would discourage his Bellême relatives from trying any rash counterattacks. Gervais could be killed a great deal faster than they could possibly rescue him.

The bishop, however, was not taking his captivity well.

'How am I?' Gervais rasped, so malnourished and exhausted that he could barely make himself heard above the clatter of rusty iron chains as he struggled up from a stone floor strewn with filthy, rotting straw made even more damp and malodorous by bodily waste, both his own and that of the rats with whom he shared the cell.

He came closer to Martel to see his jailer better. 'How dare you even ask me that question?' he asked. The exertion of standing and speaking brought on a spasm of reedy, hacking coughs. 'You know precisely how I am, for you have chosen to treat me in this insufferable, inexcusable way. Don't you care that I am a man of God? It is a mortal sin to imprison me, and your mistreatment only compounds the offence.'

'Man of God, my arse,' growled Martel. 'I captured you in battle, fair and square, no different to any other fighting man, so that's how I'm treating you. You've got water to drink, food to eat . . .'

'A crust of stale bread and a bowl of gruel so vile I would not give it to my dog.'

'It's food. You can eat it. That's all that matters. Tell you what, I'll get you an old wine barrel to crap and piss in. I'll even get my lads to chuck in some fresh straw while we're at it. You'll think you're right back in your bishop's palace.'

'Do you not have a shred of conscience, Anjou? One day, I swear, His Holiness the Pope will hear of this assault on the Church, and then he will make you sorry for your defiance.'

'You mean he might excommunicate me?'

'He might well do just that, and with God's blessing too.'

Martel laughed. 'He already has, almost a year ago. Didn't I tell you? That's right, Pope Leo himself kicked me out of the Church. So no Mass for me, no confession, no church services of any kind.'

'For God's sake, man, repent your sins. If you should die while excommunicated, I fear for the fate of your immortal soul.'

'Oh, I think I'm past worrying about my immortal soul. The things I've done, the Devil got me long ago.'

'And you don't care about that?'

'Not really. I'm no worse than anyone else, just more honest about it. There'll be plenty of priests and nuns and men who pray three times a day joining me in the fires, I've no doubt of that.'

'I had hoped . . . I prayed again and again that the Holy Father would rescue me, but now I can see that I was wasting my time. All hope is gone . . .'

Gervais' words hung unanswered in the stinking air, and then, his defiance all used up, he asked, 'How much do you want?'

'To set you free, you mean?'

'What else would I pay you for?'

'I don't know. A gold coin or two might buy you a good square meal.'

'Yes,' Gervais said, 'to set me free.'

'Hmm . . .' Martel pondered the question as if it were an entirely new concept to him. 'I'll have to think about that. I'll come back in a day or two when I've got an answer for you.'

Gervais' hands reached out in supplication. 'No, please, tell me now, I beg you. Tell me . . .'

Martel shook his head and turned towards the door.

'Please,' begged Gervais. He tried to run after Martel, but jerked to a halt as his chain stretched tight against its shackle. 'I can't stand another day!'

Martel opened the door. For a second Gervais caught a glimpse of the torchlit corridor outside the cell, and it seemed like a vision of paradise.

'Please!' he cried again, but before the word had left his lips the door had slammed shut, the bolts outside had been slid into place and he was alone again in the impenetrable darkness and absolute silence of the grave.

Two days later, Martel returned to the cell. 'I have an answer for you.' He chuckled to himself. 'Had it the moment you asked how much I wanted, truth be told.'

'Then why didn't you tell me?' Gervais asked, in a pathetic, pleading whine.

'Oh, I don't know. I thought it would be more fun to make you wait.'

'So how much is it, then? I have gold, tapestries, some fine horses . . .'

'That's not what I want.'

'So what . . . ?'

'I want the Chateau-du-Loir. Bloody thing's been standing there for the past two years, thumbing its nose in my face. Give

24

it to me, with everything in it and all the land around it, and you can go free.'

'But that's my whole estate!' Gervais pleaded. 'I can't give you my whole estate . . .'

'Suit yourself,' Martel said, and the next thing Gervais knew, he was alone again.

Another week passed. Martel occupied his time by leading a raiding party right up to the walls of Le Mans. There he dared Count Hugh to come out and face him like a man. A messenger called down from the battlements to say that the count was feeling unwell, but that as soon as he recovered he would face and beat the Angevins, as the men of Anjou were known, wherever they chose to fight.

Greatly cheered by the prospect of a battle that he felt sure he would win, Martel rode south again. He spent the night with his forces outside Chateau-du-Loir, and then made a further day's ride down to Tours. The city was dear to him, since it was one of the first he had captured, eight years earlier, at the start of his empire-building campaign. He spent a few days hunting, a few evenings feasting and a few nights fucking his second wife, Grécie, a fine, broad-hipped, big-breasted woman whose only failing in Martel's eyes was that, like her predecessor, she had failed to provide him with an heir.

Finally he paid a visit to Bishop Gervais, finding the man stripped of all resistance, or even the slightest shred of personal dignity. He was willing to offer Martel anything he wanted. 'Just let me out of here, please, dear Count, I beg you.'

'Very well,' Martel replied. 'I am going to take you up to your castle, still in chains. I am going to let everyone see the state you're in and make it clear that unless they do exactly as you command them, I'll throw you right back in this cell.'

'I'll say whatever you want, I swear it,' Gervais assured him.

'Good. You're going to gather together all the people who live and work in Chateau-du-Loir and inform them that I am their new master, the castle is mine, and you are going into exile.'

'Exile? Where?'

'Nowhere in Maine, that's for sure. Aside from that, I really couldn't care less.'

Gervais hesitated for a moment and Martel made as if to go to the door.

'No-o-o-o! Please . . .' Gervais begged, and Martel could hear the tears in his voice. 'I'll go into exile. I will, I swear!'

'Good. You may take a servant or two, but no fighting men. You may also take one mule. Whatever clothes and other possessions you can get on the donkey, you can take with you. But nothing valuable; no coins, no jewels, nothing precious. That's all mine, along with those horses you were telling me about, the castle servants, the men-at-arms. Mine, the lot of it.'

Gervais collapsed on his knees in front of Martel, reached out and wrapped his matchstick arms around his captor's tree-trunk legs. 'I will say all that, give you whatever you want,' he wheezed, 'but please, I beg you one solitary favour.'

'What is that?'

'I cannot walk far. May I have a cart to carry me into exile? And please, a beast to pull the cart . . .'

Just to tease him, Martel pulled his legs away, let Gervais fall to the floor and played the 'pretending to leave the cell' trick again. The bishop's despairing cry, cut short by another burst of coughing, was enough to have him doubled up in mirth.

'Oh, that was priceless, haven't laughed so much in ages,' he gasped. 'Forget the cart,' he added. 'You get a donkey. You can sit on it, or you can stick baggage on it and walk. Your choice.'

And so Martel took Chateau-du-Loir, while Gervais rode off to exile on the back of his donkey, saying that he would seek the hospitality of the Duke of Normandy. A short while later, Count Hugh of Maine died, having never recovered from his illness, whereupon the people of Le Mans opened their gates to Martel, preferring a swift surrender to the inevitable lengthy siege.

Thus Martel was the master of Maine as well as Anjou. And so he looked north once again, and fixed his eyes on the lands of Bellême.

2

Alençon, capital of the county of Bellême

Bishop Gervais had not planned on spending any time in Le Mans, for he knew Martel and his army would soon be descending on the city and he had no intention of falling into that callous monster's grasp for a second time. But Count Hugh was dying and the bishop could hardly refuse to administer the Last Rites or conduct the funeral service at Le Mans cathedral. By the time he was finally ready to make his escape, Martel and his men were less than half a day's march away and it was a very relieved man who finally passed through the city gates into the open countryside and set his course north towards Rouen.

Hugh's widow Bertha had allowed Gervais to take a decent sword and a coat of mail from the late Count's armoury and replace his donkey with a pair of good strong horses from his stables, so he was now able to make good speed. His spare mount was lightly laden with a small amount of baggage, which included his robes, mitre and other badges of office along with the gold plate and chalice he used to celebrate Mass at the cathedral. A few days of freedom, proper beds and decent food had done a little to improve his physical state, but he was still painfully thin, easily tired and far from strong. Should he fall upon thieves or outlaws on the road to Rouen, he would be incapable of resistance. But that should not, he reasoned, be an insuperable problem.

His cousin Mabel, the Dame of Bellême, had inherited all the estates owned by her father William 'Talvas' of Bellême and,

28

following the sudden death of her brother Arnulf, was now mistress of the family's castle at Alençon. Gervais had never met Mabel, but he felt sure that once he explained the gravity of his situation and the wrong that Martel had done not only to him but also to the honour of the House of Bellême, she would supply him with the escort he needed to take him safely to Rouen and Duke William.

She'll be delighted to meet me, Gervais told himself. The poor woman's really not much more than a girl. She's lost her father and her brother. Now she's all alone, without a husband to look after her. She'll be only too glad of a male relative to give her advice, tell her what's what. I'll give her a blessing. Young women love that. It makes them feel as though God is looking after them with extra special care.

One other thought, however, had occurred to him: I'd better not go into too much detail when I tell her about my time in Martel's filthy, stinking dungeon. A sweet, delicate young noblewoman would be shocked to hear what that was like.

Mabel of Bellême's cool, heavy-lidded grey eyes examined with languid indifference the man who had introduced himself as Gervais of Chateau-du-Loir, Bishop of Le Mans. She had long since accepted the fact that the great majority of men she met tended to stare at her with a look of lustful hunger that was at best poorly disguised and at worst embarrassingly blatant. She wasn't bothered in the slightest by this attention. She just found it amusing that they made their lack of self-control so pathetically obvious.

This man, however, was different. He had looked at her with surprise when they were first introduced, as if she did not quite conform to his expectations. But once the introductions were complete, he paid far less attention to her than to the plate of warm, sweet, freshly baked pastries that had been sent up to the chamber in which she was passing the afternoon with her maid Agnes.

Christ, he's practically drooling! she thought. Look at the pathetic wretch, he's nothing but skin and bone. His face is as white as a corpse's shroud and his filthy hair looks as if it would come out in clumps if I gave it a good tug. He reminds me of someone, but who . . . ?

And then it suddenly struck her. Father! He looks just like Father after I'd finished with him. He's got that same whipped-dog look around the eyes. Maybe I should throw stones at him too, the way I did at my darling Papa.

Mabel just about suppressed the giggle that overcame her at the memory of her father squealing in pain and scuttling away in fear as yet another large, well-aimed pebble hit him on the backside, or shoulder or head. But she could not keep the smile from her face.

'My lady?' said the bishop hopefully, as if asking to be let in on the joke.

'Oh, nothing,' Mabel replied. 'A memory just came to me.'

'A happy one, I trust.'

'Oh yes,' she said, giving him her most charming smile, the one that never failed to make men her slaves. 'Very happy.'

She poured herself a little wine and helped herself to another pastry, deliberately not offering one to the bishop, waiting to see how long it would be before he gave up and asked, or preferably begged her for one. 'So,' she said, 'you were about to explain how we are related.'

'Oh yes, yes, of course, well . . . let me see now . . . My mother, Hildeburg of Bellême, was the daughter of Ivo, the first Seigneur of Bellême, who founded our family's dynasty. I, how-ever, was mostly brought up by my mother's brother, Avesgaud of Bellême, who was my predecessor as Bishop of Le Mans. Now Avesgaud and Hildeburg had an older brother, William . . .'

'William . . . of Bellême?' asked Mabel, just to tease.

'Oh yes, absolutely.' The bishop gave a nervous little laugh to show that he had a sense of humour too, and then went on, 'Anyway, it was that William of Bellême who inherited his father's position and became Count of Bellême, and two of his sons were your uncle Ivo, the Bishop of Sées, and your late father William, who was known as "Talvas", I believe.'

'That's right,' said Mabel. 'So, if I understand you correctly, my father and your mother shared a grandfather, which made them first cousins . . .'

'Exactly so.'

'. . . and I am one generation down from you. So you and I, Bishop Gervais, are first cousins once removed.'

'My dear, you are as intelligent as you are beautiful,' the bishop said, and it occurred to Mabel as he gave her a grin that was clearly intended to be dashing that he must once have been quite a handsome man and, still having that picture of himself in his head, did not fully understand just how ghastly he looked now.

'Thank you,' she murmured and lowered her head demurely so that she looked at him through upturned eyes. 'But, you know, I can't really be so intelligent, because I'm still unable to work out what it is you want from me.'

'I'm sorry, I'm not quite sure I know what you mean.'

'Oh, come now, Bishop,' Mabel said, sitting upright again and regarding him with the haughty condescension that was her natural expression. 'You turn up here, out of the blue, without sending any message in advance. I have never in my life heard of a bishop who stints himself at the dining table, yet you look as starved as a beggar. If you were anything like the other men in my family, Uncle Ivo included, you would not let your church duties get in the way, but spend your days out hunting, with the sun and the wind on your face. But you have the pallor of the grave. So clearly something has happened to you. And you are here, rather than in the cathedral or the bishop's palace at Le Mans . . . the bishop does have a palace, I presume?'

'Yes . . . yes, I am blessed with a fine establishment.'

'Clearly it is not so fine that you want to be there. Why not? What or who are you running from, Cousin Gervais?'

People had always said that William Talvas of Bellême was a cold, calculating and plain wicked man. Though he was by no means the eldest son of the Count of Bellême, he had schemed and plotted to ensure that he emerged with all the family's possessions, while most of his many brothers lay rotting in their graves. He had murdered, tortured and schemed without a trace of mercy or scruple. Now Gervais began to believe that the young woman in front of him was every inch her father's daughter.

Oh, Mabel was as lovely as a princess in a minstrel's *chanson*, but those ravishing eyes regarded him with the merciless, predatory indifference of a cat toying with a captured mouse. And every time she took a little nibble from one of the sweetmeats beside her, he knew that she did so to taunt him, seeing how thin and how famished he was.

When Gervais began the story of his confinement by Martel of Anjou, he decided not to spare Mabel's feelings, but to throw in all the most repulsive, pustulent, faeces-encrusted details. He had hoped to shock her out of her cold-blooded detachment, but to his horror he discovered that he had succeeded only in amusing her. He could see her gloating at the pathetic, heart-rending descriptions of his loneliness, the ghastliness of the endless silence and bottomless darkness.

And when he told her of how Martel had taunted him by walking out of his cell without warning, or reducing him to cowering terror by pretending to leave, she giggled. Just like

Martel himself. Oh, she put a hand in front of her mouth and apologised for her rudeness. But he knew that to be an entirely fraudulent gesture of apology, and the fact that she had made it, rather than simply laughing in his face as Martel had done, merely showed that she was not only vicious, but deceitful too.

Eventually Gervais left his story unfinished. 'I see no point in continuing my tale, madam, for whatever my purpose was in coming here, it assuredly was not to be an amusement to you.'

'So you do have some balls left after all,' Mabel said. 'Very well, then, tell me what you want, and why I should give it to you.'

'I want good food and comfortable lodging for the night, to which I am entitled, just as any traveller of noble birth who arrives at your castle would be, by the laws of hospitality – none the less real for being unwritten – by which all civilised people live. Since I am a blood relative, and a close one at that, I have every right to make a further request for assistance, to wit: the provision of an escort of, say, half a dozen mounted men to accompany me to Rouen, where I will seek the assistance of Duke William.'

'We Bellêmes don't have much of a history of assisting family members,' Mabel replied. 'Certainly not on my side of the family. You will have to give me a better reason than that, if you want me to help you out.'

'Very well then, I have knowledge that will save your pretty little neck and prevent you and your wench here from being raped by a conquering army – though God knows you might be improved by such an experience, and she looks like she would enjoy it.'

Mabel laughed aloud at that. 'Well spotted, Cousin Gervais! My darling Agnes was born to be a whore, weren't you, little one?'

'It's true,' the servant giggled. 'I just can't help myself.'

'But I,' Mabel went on, turning her eyes back to Gervais, 'am not inclined to make myself a pincushion for strangers' pricks. So I will promise you your escort . . . provided that the information you give me makes my generosity worthwhile.'

'Very well then, Cousin, listen to this: Geoffrey of Anjou is now in possession of Le Mans. I know this for sure, since the people were already talking in the streets when I left, having agreed that they would open the gates to Martel and his men in the hope that he might take mercy on them.

'I know the man. He will spend a short while there, looting, drinking and finding young women like your servant to satisfy his carnal lusts. But he will not delay long, for he has his eyes set on another prize: the county of Bellême. He wants your land, your castles, your manor houses and your towns. Above all he wants the prize of Alençon.'

'I see, so—'

'Wait!' Gervais snapped, surprising Mabel into silence with the forcefulness of his voice. 'I have not finished. I am going to be frank. I have heard enough tales of your father's behaviour to know that he was a hateful individual. Wasn't he thrown out of this city, and his own county, by his son, your brother Arnulf? And did this young man, having acquired as bad a reputation as his father, not meet a sudden and untimely death?'

'Yes, he did,' said Mabel, thinking: because I poisoned him.

'Now you are here, without a title and thus without any power over the city and its people other than your wealth and the men-at-arms your money buys you. I am guessing you are rather more subtle than your brother . . .'

'It would be impossible to be less subtle than him.'

'Quite so, but I doubt you have inspired much love in your people, even so. You may be a delight to look at, and clever, too, and I dare say you can be charming enough when it suits you. But your heart is cold and vicious and in the end that shows. So you cannot expect the people of this town, or anywhere else in the county, to defend you. Indeed, they may welcome Martel as a liberator.'

'And where does that leave me, pray?'

'In exile. Load whatever you can take with you onto as many ox carts as you can find. Surround yourself with men you know to be loyal and put as much distance between yourself and Martel as you can manage. You will, I feel sure, encounter one another. But my advice is to wait until you both find yourselves in the inferno of Hades, for that is where you will assuredly end up.'

'So I should just turn my back and run, without the slightest show of resistance?'

'You should do what is most prudent.'

'You are aware, presumably, that my family built a castle at Domfront.'

'Of course.'

'Then you will also know that it stands on a hilltop above the town, with a single approach to the gatehouse, which has two strong towers on either side?'

'I've never seen the place, but that is what I have heard, yes.'

'Well then, you are a man. You know more about these things than me. Would that not make it very difficult indeed to capture?'

'Yes . . . if the occupants want to resist the attack. But if they do not, the doors will open at the first knock.'

Gervais watched Mabel as she digested what he had said. She had not, he noticed, protested the suggestion that her people did not love her. But neither did she seem possessed by the kind of alarm and distress that any normal woman would surely have displayed when informed that a notoriously brutal warrior was leading his men towards her. Nothing seemed to disturb her icy, calculating demeanour.

35

'I fear I cannot give you any more than two men as escorts,' she finally said. 'If what you say is true, I will need every man I can get to defend me. In the meantime, do stop being so rude to me, Cousin, and so superior, too. After all, if we come from the same family, we share the same blood. And if my blood is tainted, then yours may be too. For all we know, you're just as wicked as you say I am. You just don't know it yet.'

As Gervais pondered that appalling possibility, Mabel blessed him with her most ravishing smile yet. 'Oh, by the way, could I interest you in a pastry?'

3

Mabel did her duty as mistress of Alençon castle and took the place of honour at the high table for dinner that evening, with her cousin Gervais seated at her right hand. But as soon as she had completed her meal, she left the table, telling him, 'I'm sure you and the other men will feel much happier being able to talk frankly without having to listen to a woman's foolish chit-chat.'

She was, of course, about as foolish as a snake, and he knew it, though he was not aware quite how venomous and deadly a serpent she could be if the fancy took her. But it was as good an excuse as any, and it allowed her to retire to her quarters to decide how to react to the news that Martel was intending to invade the county of Bellême.

Is that scrawny old cleric right? she asked herself. Will the people really surrender Domfront and Alençon rather than fight on my behalf?

As she walked from the dining hall, she caught the eye of Agnes, who was sitting at the servants' table, and summoned her with a flick of the wrist, not even bothering to look back, so sure was she that her command had been obeyed.

When she reached her chamber, Mabel sat before her dressing table, contemplating her reflection in her polished silver mirror as Agnes unpinned her veil and started loosening her hair.

'Tell me,' she said, 'all these men you lie with . . . do they love me enough to go to war if I tell them to?' She felt her maid's fingers fumble nervously with her braids.

'I . . . I wouldn't rightly know, your ladyship,' Agnes said.

Mabel sighed. The silly girl was too frightened to tell her the truth. She stood up, stepped away from her chair and turned to face Agnes. 'Come here, little one.'

Agnes walked up to Mabel, wrapped her arms around her back and laid her head on her breast. Mabel kissed the top of the girl's head and then began gently stroking her hair. Agnes sighed contentedly and snuggled even closer.

'Don't be afraid, little one,' Mabel said. 'I'm not going to hurt you. Just tell me exactly what you've heard. Will you do that for me?'

Agnes nodded her head.

'Very well then, what do they say?'

Agnes looked up at her and Mabel kissed her forehead, just to encourage her.

'They don't hate you,' Agnes said. 'Not like they hated your brother, or your father, or his father before him. And they think you're beautiful.'

'You mean they want to bed me?'

'Well, yes . . . though they aren't as polite as that, not most of them, anyway.'

'But do they love me enough to fight?'

Agnes bit her bottom lip.

'Tell me the truth,' Mabel said sternly. And then, more softly, 'I told you, I won't hurt you. Not unless you lie to me.'

Agnes shook her head. 'No, I don't think they do.'

'Why not?'

'It's not just you, my lady, it's more the House of Bellême. It's never done anything for them, that's what they say. They say you've all got lots of money, but no one's ever done anything to help them. No one feeds the poor when they're hungry, or gives them fuel when the winter's cold.'

'Am I really supposed to do that sort of thing? My father never did.'

'Exactly, that's the point. And it's not even like you *have* to help the poor. It's just that if you want them to risk their lives for you . . .'

'Then they want something from me. I understand.'

Mabel looked away at the tapestries on the walls, not really seeing them, nor paying any attention to the girl in her arms.

'My lady?' Agnes asked.

Mabel gave a little shake of the head as her mind returned to the here and now. 'What?'

'Would you like me to finish your hair?'

'No, don't bother with that.'

'Would you like me to stay with you? I can help you relax. You'll sleep so much better if—'

'No. Go. I need to think. Just go.'

Alone in the room, Mabel considered the possibility of accompanying Gervais to Rouen, but only for the merest instant. The prospect of his pathetic, whining company was unendurable, all the more so since his progress would be slowed to a crawl by his entirely self-inflicted infirmities. She took the view that the bishop would never have been in Martel's hands to begin with had he not stupidly allowed himself to be caught unawares in open country, within sight of his own castle. More fool him if that carelessness should land him in a dungeon for the next couple of years.

Even if I don't travel with him, maybe I should go to Rouen anyway, she thought, as she paced up and down. Gervais wants William of Normandy to come to his aid, and so do I. Maybe we could both plead with William; we might have more chance convincing him together than either of us would alone.

No . . . that won't work. Everyone knows the duke only

listens to his closest cronies and doesn't trust another living soul. I've never even been introduced to the surly brute and I'm sure Gervais hasn't either. Why would he listen to us? I need someone else, someone closer to him.

And then Mabel stopped in her tracks and her lips widened a fraction into the barely perceptible hint of a smile as a single word filled her mind: Montgomery!

She thought back several years, to the days when she and her father were on their travels. They had paused in Paris to visit Roger of Montgomery, a Norman noble who had been exiled there.

Roger had defied the authority of the young Duke William so flagrantly that a ducal court, supervised by William's steward and most loyal supporter Osbern Herfastsson had confiscated all his lands and banished him for life. But his sons remained in Normandy. One of them had later murdered Osbern and been killed in his turn for the crime. But another of the Montgomery boys, also called Roger, had made peace with William, served him loyally and become one of his closest confidants. He had even recovered some of the Montgomery family lands, though he was still a relative pauper compared to other young aristocrats at the ducal court.

Bearing all this in mind, Talvas had paid a call on the exiled Montgomery and explained that he owned a great deal of land but his son had stolen it all from him. Meanwhile Roger had a son with barely a single farm to his name. Talvas had therefore proposed a solution to everyone's problems. 'I will settle all my land on Mabel. I will also give her to your lad in marriage. Once he has her, he can go and kick my son out of Alençon, and leave him bleeding in a ditch, for all I care. All I ask is that he provides me with an agreeable place to live and the means to keep myself in a reasonably comfortable style.'

This was a spectacularly good deal for the Montgomery

family, and if Roger had possessed a single iota of good sense, he would have taken it in an instant. But he was almost as devious, unscrupulous and belligerent as Talvas, and thus felt certain that there had to be a catch somewhere: he just could not for the time being work out what it was. The fact that Talvas seemed unusually eager to reach agreement only heightened Montgomery's suspicions.

There was a good reason for Talvas's desperation. With every day that passed, it was becoming more obvious that Mabel was even more of a danger to him than Arnulf had been. She was only a slip of a girl, but she seemed able to bend him to her will. Talvas honestly believed it was some kind of sorcery.

Montgomery knew none of that. He just saw an offer that was too good to be true. So the agreement had never been made, though Talvas had made the foolish mistake of mentioning it to Mabel. 'Just remember, girl, I can dispose of you whenever I see fit, and give you to anyone I choose.'

Mabel had absolutely no intention of allowing that. Luckily for her, Talvas's very meagre resources had prevented him being able to stay long in Parisian lodgings. The two of them had been forced out onto the road and he had never had any further contact with the Montgomery family. Even so, the logic of his proposal still held true. So far as Mabel knew, the younger Roger of Montgomery was still unmarried and in need of greater wealth. And unlike her father, she could keep her side of the bargain.

Mabel left her room, and strode up the narrow, winding stone stairs to the attic where Agnes slept. She shook her awake. 'Get up! Pack all my best gowns and every veil, girdle, jewel and pretty little shoe that I possess. We're going hunting.'

Agnes rubbed her eyes, then smiled as her mind cleared and she understood what the prey would be. 'Ooh, are you going to bag a fine young stag, my lady? Or a big strong bull?' She

41

giggled cheekily. 'I hope you don't end up with a smelly old wild pig!'

'Enough insolence, or I'll whip your back so hard you won't be able to lie on it for a month . . .'

'Sorry, my lady.'

'I should think so. We will be leaving first thing in the morning. I expect everything to be perfectly packed away in my travelling chests by then. If there is the slightest delay, I will hold you responsible. Do I make myself clear?'

Agnes got to her feet. 'Yes, my lady.'

'Aah, don't look so downcast. When we get to Rouen, I'll have much nicer work for you to do at night, I promise.'

Agnes smiled contentedly. 'Can I get started, my lady?'

'Of course . . . but before you go, there's one last thing . . .'

Mabel kissed Agnes, driving her tongue into her servant's mouth and making her give little whimpers of pleasure before she let her go.

'There,' she said when she had taken her fill. 'Does any man ever kiss you like that?'

'No,' said Agnes, and went dreamily on her way.

4

The ducal palace, Rouen, Normandy

Agnes bobbed before Roger of Montgomery. 'Please, sir, I have a message from my mistress, Mabel of Bellême.'

'Mabel of Bellême?' replied Roger with a frown.

One of the group of men with whom he was talking in the shade of a cloistered courtyard laughed. 'Have you been keeping a secret mistress, Montgomery?'

'My mistresses are none of your damn concern, Fitz,' Montgomery replied. 'But this Mabel isn't one of 'em. I've never even heard of her before today.' He paused, frowning in concentration. 'No, wait, I think that name does sound familiar. Tell me, girl, is your mistress the daughter of William Talvas?'

'Yes, my lord.'

'That's right . . . I remember, now. My father wrote to me about her a few years ago. Her father had been kicked off his own land.'

'That's right,' said Fitz. 'Talvas was a ghastly man. Don't you remember, he had his first wife killed? She must have been this Mabel girl's mother. Then, on the day he married his second wife, he had William of Giroie, who'd been his loyal vassal for years, mutilated – and I mean really horribly – for no good reason.'

'Ouch!' winced Montgomery.

'Giroie's a monk somewhere now, I believe,' Fitz went on, 'but his brothers wouldn't let Talvas get away with it. They went on the rampage through Bellême, tore the whole county

43

apart. They ended up outside the walls of Alençon castle and challenged Talvas to come out and fight like a man. He refused, so the Giroies had to go away, cursing him to high heaven. But then Talvas's son, I can't remember his name . . .'

'Arnulf, your lordship,' Agnes said.

'That's the one. He booted his father out.'

'And that explains why Talvas ended up in Paris, trying to fob his daughter off onto me in exchange for a nice little estate for him to live on,' Montgomery said.

'Didn't the girl inherit all Talvas's land?' another of the men interjected. 'The son, Arnulf, died, so it came to her.'

'All of Bellême?' Roger asked.

'I believe so. If this Mabel's the one I'm thinking of, she's the mistress of the whole county. She has some damn fine castles too: Alençon for a start, and Domfront, too.'

'I wonder what she wants with you, Montgomery,' Fitz asked. 'I think you'd better find out . . . Don't you agree, gentlemen?'

The others made it plain that they did.

'Very well,' said Montgomery. 'But I'll do so in private, if you don't mind. I'm sure Lady Mabel would prefer that.' He looked down at Agnes. 'Come with me.'

He led her away down the cloister until they were safely out of earshot of the other men. Now for the first time he gave serious attention to the servant wench who stood before him. The message the girl was delivering suddenly seemed a great deal less interesting than her liquid brown eyes, the full lips over which she was running her tongue, and the splendidly bountiful breasts that seemed to be straining to burst out of her gown.

A woman seeing this display might have noted that the girl's dress was altogether too artfully cut and laced to be any normal servant's attire. If her mistress chose to dress her so, it was for a purpose.

Roger, however, was far more interested in the gown's contents than its tailoring. With some effort, he dragged his mind back to the reason for their meeting. 'So, what's this message your mistress told you to deliver?' he asked, feeling glad that his surcoat covered the evidence of his mounting arousal.

'She asks, if it pleases you, my lord, would you consent to take a walk in the palace garden this afternoon?'

'Does she need an answer right now?'

'I shouldn't think so, my lord,' the servant said, looking up at Roger shyly. 'I mean, not *right* now. So long as I tell her within the next hour or so, I'm sure that will be quite satisfactory.'

'I see. And can you think of what might keep you from returning to her before then?'

'I'm sure I can't, my lord. But my mistress likes me to be obedient to all my betters. So if there is any way in which I can serve you, I am at your disposal.'

'Pray, what is your name?'

'Agnes, my lord.'

'Very well then, Agnes, come with me.'

'Oh yes, my lord, I certainly hope so.'

5

'I assume you found Montgomery,' Mabel said when Agnes returned to the inn where she was lodging.

'Yes, my lady. I had to ask around, but I met him all right in the end.'

'I take it he has agreed to meet me?' Mabel asked.

'Yes, he suggests that you attend afternoon prayers at the palace chapel. He will do the same and then you can both take a walk in the gardens. "For spiritual contemplation," he said.'

'Did he now? And was that what he offered you: spiritual contemplation?'

Agnes giggled. 'There was nothing very spiritual about it, my lady. It was much more physical, I would say.'

'And what did you make of Roger of Montgomery?'

'Hmm . . .' Agnes paused thoughtfully, for male physical condition and sexual performance was a subject on which she was a considerable expert, so her opinion would be taken seriously.

'Well,' she began, 'he's got a nice face, lovely brown eyes and he's very well built. Tall, broad shoulders, good chest.'

'Presumably he spends his time either hunting or going to war, so I take it he is in good condition.'

'Excellent, my lady. And he eats well, so he's got more bulk on him, in a good way, than a common man would have. Lovely strong forearms, too.'

'Hairy?'

'On his chest, yes, and legs. But not his back, thank God, I never like that.'

'And now the part that you've been dying to tell me . . . good news or bad.'

Agnes smiled. 'Good, my lady. Very good, in fact. He's not exceptionally long – not short, though – but he's really thick, so he feels very nice. And he's good, too. Someone's taught him properly because he doesn't just get it over with in a few seconds and then roll off without a by-your-leave, the way some do. He takes his time. I think he's the type that likes seeing a woman really loving it. I expect that makes him feel manly and powerful . . . which he is, I suppose, if he can do that to you. Anyway, you won't be disappointed.'

'Except when I compare him with you.'

'Well, I could say exactly the same thing . . . my lady.'

'I should certainly hope so. Anyway . . . did he have anything to say for himself?'

Agnes laughed. 'He asked if you had sent me with orders to seduce him. I said, would it make any difference if you had? And he laughed and said, probably not. I liked him actually, you know, as a man. I think he's decent, and you can trust him.'

'He's not weak, is he?' asked Mabel. 'I don't want someone who's feeble and eager to please. I'll never forgive him for that.'

'No, he's not that. Roger of Montgomery's definitely the ambitious type. Strong, and determined, and tough. He just wants to do it the right way.'

'How very interesting,' said Mabel, intrigued by such an entirely foreign idea. 'Would he bore me, though, do you think? You know, if I had to spend a lifetime with him?'

'Maybe, my lady. I don't think he's your match, not in the end. But I don't think many are.'

'Thank you, little one.'

'Well, it's true. But he's good enough. And anyway, he'll go wherever Duke William goes. He really, really admires the duke, by the way. He'll be loyal to him till the day he dies. But the thing is, he'll be away a lot, so you won't have to worry about putting up with him all the time.'

'An excellent point . . . So, now you had better help me plan what I'm going to wear to meet him.' Mabel gave a wry laugh. 'It just struck me that I have to make an even better impression on him than you did, and you've already slept with him. I've never slept with a man in my life.'

'No, but you've slept often enough with me, my lady. When the time comes, you'll know just how to keep him happy.'

6

The congregation in the palace chapel rose and every head turned to watch Duke William make his entrance and stride down the aisle to the ornately carved pews, the very closest to the altar, that were reserved for the ducal household. Tall, heavily built, with his red hair shaved up the back of his neck to make his head slip more smoothly into a helmet, William was still not twenty-five, but he possessed an aura of strength and dominance that verged on belligerence.

He walks into prayers as if he's marching off to war, Mabel thought. She examined him more closely. His neck was thick and his face was as strongly built as the rest of him: heavy-browed, square-jawed and fleshy. But then she caught a flash of his hard blue eyes and imagined what it would be like to have the full force of his personality turned upon her. It struck Mabel that this might be the first man she had ever encountered whom she knew, right from the instant that she saw him, had an even stronger, more implacable will than her own. He was no beauty, that was for sure. But he was the prime bull in this herd. He had the strength, the power . . . She felt a sudden stirring of desire. Calm yourself, woman. You're not here for him.

Beside the duke strode a small, very obviously pregnant woman whom Mabel took to be Duchess Matilda. She was dwarfed by her husband's physical stature, and while his appearance was sturdy and combative, she carried herself with regal grace. Her dress was simple, but made of finely woven fabric. She's a Flemish girl; naturally she has the best cloth,

Mabel thought, admiring the quality of the embroidery around the neckline and the hem of the sleeves, and the translucence of the veil, held in place by a golden coronet, through which Matilda's long dark hair could be seen.

Ah, but look at her eyes! She holds her head high and still, but her glance is as sharp as a jackdaw's. Mabel smiled to herself. I must remember never to underestimate her.

Behind the couple walked a small knot of men, all of William's generation.

'That's Roger, there,' said Agnes, nodding towards the nearest member of the group of courtiers. 'I think he's the hand-somest of the lot.'

Mabel did not dignify the remark with an answer, but Agnes wasn't wrong. Roger of Montgomery was good-looking in precisely the way that William was not. His jaw, his cheekbones and his long but elegant nose were all so finely carved that no sculptor could have improved upon them. His features were even, and the way he smiled at something one of his companions had whispered as they walked up the aisle suggested a man at ease with himself and his friends.

Then he looked in Mabel's direction and she knew at once why he had been smiling. Someone had spotted Agnes, recognised her and realised that she could only be present if her mistress had brought her. Mabel met Montgomery's eyes and gave a cool, unsmiling nod of acknowledgement, not giving anything away just yet.

Mabel was not given to envy of other women. With the very occasional exception, such as the teacher from whom she had learned skills that made her as deadly as any of the sword-bearing men in the chapel, and possibly Duchess Matilda, towards whom she felt an instinctive, if grudging respect, she regarded her fellow females as a feeble, gutless, pathetically submissive lot. But for this one moment she wished she could be an empty-headed maiden, for Roger Montgomery was just the kind of beau that a girl like that would swoon over. Mabel, however, had other requirements of her man. She was prepared, purely for expediency's sake, to wed him now and secure Bellême; then, if completely unable to face another moment of married life, make a corpse of him and a widow of herself. The exercise of her skills was always a pleasure, and she had so few opportunities to try it. But even if she did in the end decide to rid herself of her husband, she would, on balance, prefer one who would actually interest her first, for a while at least.

As the clergy made their entrance, she spotted the figure of Bishop Gervais, looking a little the better for his journey. His skin had acquired some colour, his hair had been cut and he must have been keeping himself well provisioned, for he seemed marginally less emaciated than when she had last seen him in Alençon. He sensed her looking at him and glanced up, catching her eye and immediately looking away again without the slightest acknowledgement.

So much for a united front: if she wanted to save her estates in Bellême, Mabel would have to see to her own salvation.

As he left the chapel, Montgomery caught Agnes's eye. He nodded in the direction of the woman next to her, raised an eyebrow as if to say, 'Is that her?' and received a fractional nod of the head in return. He had wondered whether the mistress had sent her servant girl to seduce him as a compensation for her own shortcomings. But that was far from the case. Agnes was a saucy little commoner with whom a man could pass an extremely pleasurable hour or two. But Mabel of Bellême was a ravishing young noblewoman fit to grace the arm of a king.

He cursed his father for not snapping her up the moment old Talvas made his offer. *I could have been nailing her for*

51

years by now! Well, if the chance comes again, I'm not going to miss it a second time.

He manoeuvred himself so that he and Mabel arrived at the chapel door side-by-side. As she passed him, he murmured, 'Go to the rose bower, I'll see you there.'

She turned and examined him with cool grey eyes. 'I won't wait long,' she replied.

Montgomery felt a sudden stab of alarm. She means it. Damn that old monk for turning up out of the blue!

Within the past hour, he had been told that Robert Champart, the newly appointed Archbishop of Canterbury, had appeared quite unexpectedly in Rouen, while on his way to Rome to be formally installed in his office by the Pope. Champart was a Norman by birth and had been abbot of Jumièges, one of the duchy's grandest abbeys. Naturally, he had felt it appropriate to break his journey and pay a visit to the duke. Now William expected his closest advisers to be present for the occasion.

'Your Grace, may I beg your indulgence for one moment?' Montgomery asked William. The duke nodded, then turned to his wife. 'Go on ahead with the others. If the archbishop is already there, tell him I am on my way. And win him over. We need him on our side in Rome!'

He turned back to Montgomery. 'Well?'

Montgomery had long ago learned that one had to be totally honest with William of Normandy at all times if one wanted to get and keep his trust. So he told the simple truth. 'Mabel of Bellême has requested a meeting with me. She is the heiress to all the lands of the Count of Bellême. And she has no husband.'

William gave a sardonic half-smile. 'Well, I can see why she might interest you. But watch yourself. There's bad blood in the House of Bellême. Her father was a wicked man. Her brother wasn't much better.'

'So I gather.'

'Still . . .' Montgomery could see William's mind working through the pros and cons of a marriage between him and Mabel. 'If I knew that Bellême was safe in your hands, that would secure our frontier with Maine.'

'Provided Martel doesn't take it first. Gervais of Le Mans seems convinced that it's only a matter of time before the Hammer falls on Bellême.'

'I know, he won't stop pestering me, trying to get me to interfere.'

'And will you?'

'Not as long as Martel confines himself to Maine. But I can't let him walk into Bellême without doing something about it.'

'If we don't fight him, he'll just keep coming.'

'Precisely. Bellême is Normandy's underbelly. If I were Martel, I'd stab into it, as deep as I could go.'

The duke slapped Montgomery on the shoulder. 'Go then. Talk to this lady of Bellême. And let's pray you can get her land before that bastard Martel does.'

'Thank you, Your Grace. I'll do my best.'

Montgomery hurried away to the garden, praying that Mabel of Bellême would still be there to meet him when he arrived.

7

'I was just about to leave,' Mabel said, gratified by Montgomery's inability to hide his relief when he saw her waiting for him. Good, she thought. He knows what's on offer and he wants it badly. Now let him work for it.

'I apologise. I had pressing business with His Grace Duke William.'

Mabel supposed she should be impressed by that. But she said nothing, forcing Montgomery to fill the silence.

'It is my great good fortune that His Grace counts me among his closest advisers.'

'That is fortunate, I agree,' she said. 'For you, I mean. Do you suppose it is fortunate for the duke?'

'I hope so. He knows he can count on my loyalty at all times.'

How extraordinary, Mabel thought. He really means it.

'That's how I feel about Agnes, my maid. The one I sent to you today. I can always count on her to do exactly what I ask.'

'Can you now?' said Montgomery with a wry amusement that suggested he was starting to gather his wits.

'Absolutely.'

Another silence fell. Again Montgomery filled it.

'It strikes me that we have something in common, you and I,' he began, with the air of someone giving a speech that he had previously rehearsed. 'We are both the offspring of men who fell from grace. Our fathers found themselves exiled from their own lands. I imagine you don't want to end up with a husband who suffers the same fate.'

'No man who was my husband would ever find himself in that position.'

Montgomery paused a second to consider the possible meanings of that remark and then continued with his recitation. 'So let me reassure you that I learned a lesson from my father. He lost everything he had because he defied the House of Normandy. I intend to regain my family's fortunes, and lift them to a level my father never even dreamed of by supporting that house. I have known Duke William since we were small boys. As I say, he trusts me.'

'Even though your father defied him . . .'

'His Grace does not judge anyone by what their parents, brothers, cousins or anyone else did. He judges them by their own actions. My father could have been the finest, most upstanding, virtuous vassal that any duke ever had. But that would do me no good if I were treacherous. Likewise, my father might have betrayed the duke and my brother murdered his beloved guardian Osbern in front of His Grace's own eyes, but that has not harmed me because he knows that he can count on my absolute fidelity to him.'

'That's very interesting,' said Mabel, quite genuinely, for she found the duke's reasoning commendable. 'And if you broke that trust?'

'Then I would have to be ready to go to war against him and fight to the death, because he would never forgive me or show me the slightest mercy.'

'His Grace is quite right. Mercy would be a sign of weakness. You know, I've never met Duke William. In fact, the first time I set eyes upon him was just now, in chapel. So tell me all about William of Normandy. What kind of a man is he? Apart from merciless.'

'Have you really asked me here to quiz me about the duke?' asked Montgomery. 'I did not come here to betray my lord's confidence.'

'I know exactly why you came here, sir,' Mabel replied. 'And my interest in the duke is entirely reasonable. I saw him today. I formed a very strong impression of him. Since I may be seeing a great deal more of him, I would like to know whether that impression is correct.'

'So what was this impression?'

'That William of Normandy is as strong and determined and masterful a man as I have ever seen.'

Montgomery gave a little nod of acknowledgement. 'Very good, madam, your intuition serves you well. But you omitted one crucial quality from your description. His Grace is a hard, hard man . . . that's the first and most important thing to know about him. He's always been that way. Perhaps he had no alternative.'

'Why so?'

'God . . . Fate . . . I'm no philosopher, I can't tell you for sure. But I know what I've seen and heard, and I've known Duke William since we were small boys. In those days he lived at the palace here in Rouen with his father, Duke Robert. His mother lived in Conteville with her husband. William missed his mama terribly; it was obvious, but he'd never admit it. He forced himself not to care. Then Duke Robert went away on his pilgrimage and never came back, and William was all on his own, just a boy, surrounded by men no better than wolves who all wanted to get their teeth into him. I suppose my father was one of them; yours too, I dare say.'

Now it was Mabel's turn to give an ironic smile. 'Oddly enough, William was one person he never plotted against. But I dare say he'd have done it eventually, if he'd had the chance.'

'You seem to have precious little regard for your papa.'

'Let's not talk about that now. Finish what you were saying about William.'

'Well, he had to be very hard to survive, so that's one thing about him. The other is that he could never rely on anyone. It wasn't just that he had so many enemies, it was that the men who were supposed to look after him kept dying: his father, obviously, and Osbern the steward, but also the guardians that his father had entrusted with his care. They were all killed. So His Grace learned that in the end, the only person he could really trust was himself. And then, just to cap it all, he was illegitimate.'

'Ah yes, William the Bastard . . .'

Montgomery looked around nervously to see if anyone had overheard her. 'Don't ever let him hear you calling him that,' he hissed. 'He never forgives anyone who even mentions that he's illegitimate, or insults his mother's memory by mocking her background.'

Ah, so that's his weakness, Mabel thought. 'Then I shall do neither. So, the duke is strong, he is hard, but he is extremely sensitive about his background. But who, apart from you, can he trust? Whom does he love?'

'His wife, for a start. William and Matilda truly love one another.'

'A man who loves his wife.' Mabel laughed. 'Now there's an extraordinary thought!'

'Let us hope that you and I are able to follow their example . . .' Montgomery left the sentence unfinished for just long enough for its meaning to be apparent, and then added, 'When we each find our respective spouses.'

'Yes, let's,' replied Mabel flatly. So now he wants to get to the point, she thought. But I am going to make him wait just a little bit longer.

'Who else does William count upon?' she asked. 'Apart from you, of course.'

'Well, there's Fitz – William Fitzosbern, the son of Osbern the steward. He's probably the duke's closest friend. Then there are his brothers . . .'

'I thought Duke William was an only child.'

Montgomery held up his hands in apology. 'My mistake, I should have said his half-brothers, Odo and Robert. They're his mother's sons with Herluin of Conteville.'

'And he trusts them? Even though they are the most obvious threats to his position?'

'On the contrary, they're the perfect allies: brothers who have no ducal blood. Without William, they'd just be a pair of minor provincial seigneurs. But thanks to his patronage, Rob is now the Count of Mortain and Odo is Bishop of Bayeux.'

'That really is brotherly love,' said Mabel, knowing that the Bishop of Bayeux was second only to the Archbishop of Rouen in the church hierarchy of Normandy.

'I think it was his reward for helping William woo Matilda.'

'Really? I can't believe he needed assistance. That seems very out of character.'

'Not in the end, no, he didn't. It's a long story.' Montgomery hesitated, waiting to see if she was interested.

'Then tell it.'

'Well, William went off to Flanders with Odo and Fitz to ask for Matilda's hand. It was purely a formality, because it had been arranged in advance that he would be betrothed to her . . . except she wasn't having any of it. She didn't like the look of him, and she flatly refused to accept him.'

'He must have hated that,' Mabel commented, 'seeing how he can't bear anyone making a fool of him.'

'You might say that. William left Bruges at once. He was halfway to Normandy when he suddenly said, "The hell with this," turned around and rode right back again. When he arrived at the count's palace, he was told Matilda was just about to go for a ride, so he went round to the stables and there she was on her pony. William got off his horse, marched over to her, pulled her off the pony, put her across his knee, smacked her thoroughly and then rode straight out of the palace and away back to Normandy.'

'Oh . . .' said Mabel, genuinely surprised.

'Oh, indeed,' said Montgomery, obviously pleased that he'd finally scored a point. 'Count Baldwin went berserk. He was literally on the point of declaring war on Normandy when Matilda walked in and said she'd changed her mind and wanted to marry William after all.'

Mabel nodded, 'Yes, I can understand that.'

'You can?'

'Of course, it makes perfect sense. William was not interested in Matilda until she defied him. Matilda was not interested in William until he showed her his passion and his strength. After that, each knew that the other was worthy of them.'

Montgomery made his move. 'So are we worthy of each other?' he asked.

Mabel rebuffed him. 'The man who is worthy of me does not have to ask.'

'The woman who is worthy of me does not have to beg.'

'Is that what you think I am doing?'

'Let's get down to business, you and I,' Montgomery said. 'We both know why we're here. You need me. I'm the best means you have of securing your land. I have Duke William's ear, and, as you have made plain, you don't know him from Adam.'

'Tell me, have you discussed our assignation with the duke?'

'I was obliged to, in order to explain my absence from his audience this afternoon.'

'And did he approve?'

'Yes, of both my absence and the reason for the meeting.'

'So he should. My land would not only make you rich, it would secure William's border with Maine.'

'That was the very reason he gave. You clearly have a gift for strategy, madam.'

Mabel gave a dismissive little pout. 'Not really. Bellême has always been a gateway to Normandy. Any duke would want it to be well guarded. So, you want my land, and the duke wants you to have it. But what do I get in return?'

Montgomery leaned closer and lowered his voice. 'I have plenty to offer you, fair lady. Or did your little servant girl not tell you?'

Mabel raised a dismissive eyebrow. 'She was not entirely uncomplimentary. I trust she was as flattering to you about me.'

'She was indeed.' Montgomery stepped back again and examined Mabel from top to toe, lingering at all the usual spots in between, with undisguised, unfeigned admiration. Mabel was surprised to discover that she quite enjoyed it. She waited for the little speech that men felt obliged to make at this point, the one in which they suddenly discovered an undying love for her and sang the praises of all her feminine charms, wondering if Montgomery would manage to think of a single word she had not heard a dozen times before.

This time, however, it was Montgomery who let the silence linger. He looked right at her and this was not a wooing but a challenge, a test of wills. It struck Mabel that this man understood her, had realised that he could not possibly succeed by charming her, but only by matching and – this thought occurred to her for the first time in her life – besting her. She found herself becoming more interested, not to say aroused by the tension between them. She had to force herself not to call out: *Say something! Do something!*

And then Montgomery moved. With the speed of a sword-fighter he crossed the space between them, and before Mabel had time to react, let alone fend him off, he had taken her in his arms and planted his mouth firmly on hers and was kissing her with a passionate intensity that robbed her of the power to do anything but give in to the swirling, tingling, melting surge of pleasure inside her. Somewhere in the distance she thought she heard a woman give a soft, sweet moan and was aghast to discover that it was her own voice, and that she was unable to prevent it moaning again. And then, without any warning, Montgomery let her go, leaving her dizzy and struggling to stand upright, with a voice in her head screaming, *Don't stop! For God's sake don't stop!*

'I believe that concludes our negotiations,' he said, with maddening calm and self-control. 'Can I take it that we have reached an agreement that is satisfactory to both parties?'

Mabel had by now recovered sufficiently to draw herself up to her full height and fix Montgomery with her coolest, most haughty stare. 'Certainly not, if you ask me like that.'

Montgomery laughed. 'You are as tough as Duke William. But mark my words, so am I. Do not mistake my loyalty to my liege for weakness or subservience. I have made a cold, calculated decision, based on my own self-interest. If I defy William, he will destroy me. But if I make myself indispensable to him, he will give me riches and land and power beyond imagination. William of Normandy is another Caesar, another Charlemagne. He can conquer the world. I will be there beside him. So my question to you is, do you want to be beside me?'

He placed his hands on Mabel's shoulders and looked into her grey marble eyes. 'Will you marry me, Mabel of Bellême?'

Mabel found herself possessed by another unfamiliar emotion. Could this possibly be what happiness feels like? she wondered as she answered, 'Yes, my lord, I will.'

8

'You, William of Normandy, will be the next king of England.'

Robert Champart, Archbishop of Canterbury and emissary of King Edward of England, smiled happily as he stood in front of the massive wooden chair, worthy of a royal throne, on which the young duke sat. He glowed with the smug pleasure felt by someone who, having been in possession of a piece of wonderful news for some time, finally had the chance to pass it on to an entirely unsuspecting recipient. He had, after all, just told a young man still barely in control of his own duchy that he would one day ascend to the throne of one of the most prosperous, stable kingdoms in all Christendom. Now he stood back with an ingratiating smile on his well-fed face and prepared for the outburst of gratitude, excitement and joy that would surely follow.

He would, he felt confident, be called upon to take part in a service of thanksgiving, to pay homage to God for the blessings he had bestowed upon the House of Normandy. And once that duty was complete, a celebratory feast would certainly be in order. Robert was a Norman born and bred, and having been forced to eat Saxon slop for the past fifteen years, the thought of some proper food, cooked the way he liked it, had him salivating in anticipation.

Distracted as he was by the image of a spit-roast suckling pig with a Cambremer apple stuffed into its mouth, followed by some soft, creamy cheese thickly smeared onto warm, freshly baked bread, it took Champart a second or two to realise that William's reaction was not at all what he had expected.

The young duke was not punching the air in youthful jubilation or crying out in delight. Instead, he regarded Champart without a trace of pleasure on his face – his jaw set, his eyes a cold, steely blue – and when he spoke, his voice was heavy with surly scepticism. 'You say that the nobility of England were commanded to give vows of support to the king's wish that I should succeed him?'

'Absolutely, Your Grace. They greeted the announcement as joyous news, as I am sure you do too.'

William looked as joyless as a newly sealed coffin. 'I see,' he said. 'Tell me, Archbishop, was Godwin, Earl of Wessex, among their number?'

'Oh yes, absolutely. He was one of the most enthusiastic supporters of the king's wishes.'

'And Earl Godwin is the king's father-in-law . . .'

'Yes, his daughter Edith is bride to the king and thus our gracious queen.'

William grunted thoughtfully. 'Huh. You know, if I were Godwin, and I'd married off my daughter to the king, I wouldn't want the throne going to anyone but her child.'

'Sadly, Her Majesty has been unable to furnish the king with an heir.'

'Yes, but if I were Godwin, and I thought about the number of children my wife had given me . . .' William paused. 'I am right, aren't I, that Godwin and his wife have a lot of sons and daughters?'

'Yes, the good Lord has blessed their union with many children. Ten, I believe . . . possibly more.'

'Exactly. So Godwin must surely think that if he and his wife can produce that many babies, his daughter, being their child, must surely be capable of delivering at least one. Presumably he blames the king . . .'

'Really, Your Grace, I must protest. You are, if I may say so, demonstrating scant respect to a monarch, particularly one who has shown you such favour.'

'He's not my monarch,' William countered, without the slightest attempt at diplomacy. 'And we have yet to establish what favour he has shown me. I have never met Earl Godwin, but I know his reputation. No man in England is as powerful as him . . .'

'Aside from the king, possibly not.'

'I was including the king. And a man like that would not stand by and let his country be handed over to a foreigner. Not when the Queen of England is his own daughter and he has plenty of children of his own that might sit upon the throne.'

'But they have no blood claim to the crown.'

'Mine is hardly a strong one. King Edward's mother is my great-aunt.'

'But Godwin's sons have no claim whatever!' Champart protested. He was beginning to regret ever setting foot again on Norman soil, let alone making this journey to the ducal palace. William really was a singularly unpleasant young man. He had no wit, no grace, barely any manners to speak of.

Champart was well aware that the young duke had already established a formidable reputation as a warrior, and he imagined that he fought in the same way that he talked, landing one brutish, thudding blow after another until his opponent died, surrendered or ran away. He was wondering whether to claim a sudden need to return in haste to England when the duke asked: 'The Godwinsons have some claim, surely. Aren't they related to Canute the Great?'

'Distantly, and only by marriage, not blood.'

'That's enough, and Godwin would never approve of anyone who got in their way.'

'You are assuming that his power remains as great in the future as it appears to be now,' Champart observed.

'You say that as though you knew otherwise.'

Yes, I do, thought Champart. You've underestimated King Edward, young William. And so has Godwin, as he will discover. The archbishop gave a casual shrug, but said nothing.

William looked at him, eyes narrowing in suspicion. Then he nodded to himself, drawing his own conclusions from Champart's silence and seeing there was nothing to be gained by pursuing that matter, and returned to his original point. 'So, did the king make the nobles swear an oath?'

'I believe His Majesty required some sort of response of them,' Champart replied, 'but I could not say exactly what.'

'That's hardly the action of a man who really meant what he said, is it? Do you remember when my father made me his heir? You must have been at Jumièges in those days . . .'

'I was the prior of the abbey of Jumièges in Duke Robert's day, that is correct. I became abbot there shortly after your father's sad passing.'

'Then you will recall that my father ordered every lord in Normandy to Fécamp, told them that I would succeed him and made them swear fealty to me before the rest of the assembly and in the sight of God. Then he issued a charter that asserted his desire, and my right of succession, signed and sealed so that there could not be the slightest doubt about his wishes. Has King Edward signed any such charter?'

'His Majesty has not yet done so, but when it pleases him, I am sure he will attend to it.'

William gave a short bark of laughter. 'Oh yes, I'm sure he will. And when he does, will Sven of Denmark or Harald of Norway feel bound by it? Both claim England through Harthacnut, son of Canute.'

'There was some talk of that, at the very start of the king's reign . . .'

'Some talk? The English were shitting themselves that the

Norwegians or Danes would invade, that's what I heard. Luckily for them, Sven and Harald have been too busy fighting one another for either of them to bother with England.'

'Your Grace seems well informed,' said Champart, finding it all but impossible to maintain his polite demeanour in the face of this boorish young man's refusal to behave with appropriate decorum.

'I'd be a pretty poor Duke of Normandy if I didn't make it my business to know what was going on around me. I'd have to be a deaf duke, too. The number of Norsemen who pass through Rouen – and Englishmen too, come to that – it doesn't take long for news to reach us here.'

William was about to say more but then stopped himself for a second and frowned. 'Hmm . . . Come to think of it, I don't recall any of them mentioning King Edward wanting me to be his heir. A story like that, well, you'd think it would spread like wildfire, wouldn't you?'

Champart had had enough. 'I must protest, Your Grace! I have come here in good faith to deliver news of the utmost gravity, but also of the greatest good fortune for you and your successors. For reasons that I confess I cannot comprehend, these glad tidings appear to have offended you. Am I to tell His Majesty that you are refusing his offer of the throne?'

Now, at last, William smiled. But that only unnerved Champart all the more, for it was the smile of a predator that knew that its prey was trapped and helpless. 'Absolutely not. I'm not sure that I believe a word of your story. I doubt very much that Godwin has any idea that you have come here to visit me. If he did, he'd have found a way to keep you in England, by force if necessary. From what I know of my cousin Edward, he lacks resolution. What he says one day he may contradict the next. His promise, even if he made it, is therefore worthless. But . . .'

He leaned forward on his throne and regarded Champart with an intense gaze that made the seriousness of his words all too evident.

'I am not like your king. When I say something, I mean it. When someone gives me their word, I hold them to it. And even if they change their mind, I do not change mine. So . . . you have come here and passed on the message that I am to be the next king of England. The man who gave you that message is likely one day to send another messenger to another man bearing the same promise. Even if he does not, the men who stand to lose by my ascent to the English throne will do their best to prevent it. The rulers of other lands who believe that England should be counted among their dominions will fight with me for the prize.

'But so far as I am concerned, the King of England has named me his successor. I will take him up on that offer. And I will kill any man who tries to stop me.'

As William leaned back in his chair, Champart recalled the first time he had seen him at a ducal audience. He had only been a boy then, barely fifteen years old if that, but already he had possessed an aura of purpose, intensity and dominance over others. Now that he was a man, those characteristics had developed to the point where this Duke of Normandy, though he might only be lord of a relatively modest province on the western fringe of Christendom, was as powerful and frightening as any king. He really means to take England, the archbishop thought, and a shiver ran through him as he imagined what would happen to anyone who stood in William's way.

'Are you all right, Archbishop?' the young duke asked. 'You must be hungry. Please, join me for dinner. I spoke to the palace chamberlain and he assures me that we are in for a treat this evening. The cooking fires have been lit. I'll bet the pigs are already roasting on the spit.'

9

Matilda, Duchess of Normandy, had regretfully decided that she was too tired to attend dinner this evening, and since she was bearing his son and heir – for he refused even to contemplate any other possibility – William had raised no objection to her retiring early. Now he sat on the edge of her bed and looked at the woman he loved, propped up against a heap of silk- and linen-covered pillows.

'What are you thinking about?' she asked, smiling, intrigued by the uncharacteristic warmth in her husband's eyes. His guard was lowered and it made her love him more than ever to know that there was no one else in the world who would ever see him this way.

'Oh . . . just how beautiful you are, and how lucky I am to have you,' he said, and then smiled back at her. 'And also that my mother was right about you.'

'Really? What did she say?'

'That she was sure you would be pretty because your grandmother Constance was the most beautiful women she had ever met.'

'My mother says I get my dark colouring from her.'

'She also said that your grandmother was the most frightening woman she'd ever met!' William laughed. 'That made me curious . . .'

'Of course . . . it would.'

'So then Mama told me how Constance married King Robert of France and then had his previous wife, Bertha, murdered because she feared he still loved her. I think she was hinting that you might be a bit like Constance in that way, too.'

'You never know, I might be,' she said, gently teasing him. 'Think about that if you ever fancy bedding another woman.'

'I will never bed another woman. Never.'

Matilda reached a delicate, thin-fingered hand out to touch William's face and stroke away the fierceness that had been fixed upon it as he said those words. 'Another young man might have been frightened if his mother had said that about the girl she wanted him to marry,' she said. 'But not you.'

'I've never been frightened of anyone in my life,' said William. The words were not a boast, just a statement of fact.

'I know, my darling, and I love you for it. But your courage also makes me worried. Sometimes it pays to be fearful. It stops a man doing something rash, without thinking of the danger.'

'The only rash thing I ever did was to ride back to Bruges for you. It's a good thing I wasn't fearful then.'

Matilda laughed happily at the memory. 'Isn't it just!'

She felt William's mood change, knew the thoughts that were running through his mind and basked in his desire like a cat in the warmth of the sun.

'I want you, now,' he said.

Matilda gave him a sly, smug smile. 'Well, you can't have me. I'm not feeling well and you are supposed to be in the great hall, playing host to the Archbishop of Canterbury.'

'Damn the Archbishop of Canterbury.'

Matilda giggled. 'You can't say that! He's a man of God. You'd better say a dozen Hail Marys, immediately, or your soul will be damned.'

A look of genuine concern crossed William's face, for his faith was profound and he regarded hell as an all-too-real place, of which even he was afraid. 'Do you really think so?' he said.

She placed a hand on one of William's huge paws. 'Don't be

silly. I was only teasing. Just mention it at confession on Sunday and I'm sure all will be well.'

William gave a little grunt, nodded, and set the matter to one side. 'Since you mention the archbishop, I wanted to ask you about something.'

He told her about the promise of the throne of England that Champart had conveyed from King Edward, and how he had responded. 'Do you think I did the right thing?'

Matilda considered the matter and William made no attempt to hurry her, for he knew that her insights were well worth any wait.

'Well, I'm sure you're right that you can't trust King Edward,' she began. 'It's just not in his nature to make a commitment and stick to it. I mean, just think of what happened when he and his brother Alfred both went to England. I remember when his mother, Queen Emma, was living in Bruges. I was only a very young girl then, but I can just picture her, very tall and majestic and still beautiful, even though I thought she was terribly old. Emma used to go on and on about how Edward had let her down, because he had taken one look at the English soldiers on the shore then turned his boats around and gone right back to Normandy.'

William laughed. 'I remember that too! No one could believe that he hadn't even tried to put up a decent fight.'

'Yes, but Edward lived and Alfred, who did go ashore and tried to march across England to meet his mother, well, he had his eyes gouged out by mad King Harold and died.'

'At least he died like a man.'

'What difference does that make? He's still dead and Edward is alive, that's the point. Edward's not as strong as you, or as brave. Men won't follow him into battle the way they follow you. So he has to rely on cunning and deceit.'

'But I can still act as if he meant what he said, can't I?'

70

'Naturally. You were made a promise. You should expect that promise to be kept.'

'Good.' William nodded and then looked into Matilda's eyes. 'There's something else . . . I didn't tell the Archbishop of Canterbury about it, because it was none of his business, but I'll tell you—'

'Because everything about you is my business,' Matilda interrupted.

'Yes, it seems to be.' William paused. 'I wish you had met my mother. You would have liked her so much and she would have loved you. Ah well . . .'

'What were you going to tell me?'

'Something else about Mama . . . On the first night she lay with my father – she swore it was the night I was conceived – she had a dream, and in it she saw my rule spreading across the water, like the shadow of a great tree. And the tree was the dynasty that I would found . . . that *we* would found, my darling. When Champart told me of King Edward's promise, I thought of that tree and I realised that the land across the sea, that I would rule one day, was England. So I don't care if he means it. I am going to take his country, whether he likes it or not.'

Matilda knew that this was no idle boast, for William never said anything unless he meant it – a quality she greatly valued since it meant that she could absolutely rely on his words, whether she liked them or not. She was about to tell him that she would follow him wherever his fate might take him, but before she could speak, there was a knock on the door and even as William was calling, 'Enter!' the duke's half-brother Robert of Mortain was walking into the room.

Robert's father, Herluin de Conteville, had been the closest, most trusted companion of Duke Robert of Normandy, after whom he had been named. Herluin had a decent, trusting, cheerful nature and he had passed it on to his son. Known as Rob by all those close to him – though William referred to him as Mortain in formal situations, to avoid any suggestion of family favouritism – he was a much sunnier soul than his elder brother. He had none of the latter's inner rage or need to master others, possessing instead a boundless enthusiasm and eagerness. But though they were very different, William loved and trusted Rob, and was worshipped by him in return.

'Excuse me, Your Grace,' Rob said, with a formal nod towards Matilda.

'What is it?' William asked.

'A messenger from Alençon,' Rob replied. 'The Hammer has sent his men into Bellême. They've taken the castle at Domfront and were advancing on Alençon itself when the man set out.'

'He rode hard, all the way here?'

'Yes: two full days and a night, non-stop. He practically fell out of his saddle and the horse wasn't much better off. He said it was the third he'd worn out.'

'So, we have to assume Alençon has fallen by now.'

'In that case, there's not a moment to lose,' Rob said, barely able to contain his eagerness, for he had yet to be bloodied in a serious battle and was desperate for the chance to prove his worth. 'Do you want to march tonight?'

'No,' William replied. 'I have an archbishop to entertain at dinner. But that'll work out nicely, because my uncle Talou will be there and so will Fitz and Roger Montgomery.'

'Well, *he'll* certainly want to fight! I heard he's betrothed to Mabel of Bellême. So that's his land now and he'll want it back.'

'She made quite an impression at chapel this afternoon,' Matilda said. 'All the women of the court were talking about her afterwards.'

'What did they say?' William asked.

'That she was utterly ravishing and made the rest of us look quite dowdy.'

'You could never be dowdy, my love.'

Matilda smiled, 'Why thank you, my lord. We also agreed that there was something about her that was, well . . . dangerous. She's like a very beautiful cat, with very, very sharp claws.'

'Well, let's see if Montgomery can tame her, eh? Now, Rob . . .' William got back to business. 'I'll summon the senior barons to a council after dinner, work out a plan and give them three days to gather their men and be ready to move. Then we'll all head down to Bellême as one force. I don't want the Hammer picking us off piecemeal.'

'What can I do?'

'Go to the kitchen and tell the cook from me that he's to give you a cut of his best pig and a large slice of bread. You're going to need food in your belly.'

Rob grinned. 'Why's that, brother?'

'Because you're going to take a company of men from the palace garrison and go on ahead of us. I want you to find out what's happening down there. I need to know if Martel has committed his entire army. I'll bet he hasn't. If he's got half a brain, he'll wait for us to respond to his opening move and then counter whatever we do. But I have to know what I'll be facing. So keep your eyes peeled, find out as much as you can. And under no circumstances engage with the enemy. Do you hear me?'

'I can't just let them march into our land,' Rob protested.

'Yes you can. And you will. I need you to give me information and you can't do that if you're dead. Got that?'

'Yes, Your Grace.'

'Good . . . Meet me a week from now in the forest south of Argentan.'

'Why not Argentan itself?'

'I'm staying away from towns if I possibly can. The fewer people who see where we're going, the better chance we have of taking Martel by surprise. Once you've delivered your intelligence, we can decide whether to move on Domfront first or Alençon.'

'Then I'd better get going,' said Rob. 'And I swear I won't get into any fights until I have reported to you. But after that . . .'

'After that, you will be in the thick of the battle,' said William. 'You have my word on that.'

10

For the young nobles who were William's closest confidants, the prospect of him becoming king of England was an enticing one. True, the weather was said to be appalling and the food worse, but England was rich, its land was fertile, and judging by all they had heard from the Normans who had followed Edward across the Channel, it was a relatively calm, peaceful kingdom. There were, to be sure, the usual squabbles over land and royal favour, and the marches along the Welsh and Scottish borders were prone to raids and skirmishes. There was always the threat of invasion by the Vikings, too, though the best part of forty years had passed without such a thing. And a weak or wicked king might still lash out at his subjects. But by and large the English had somehow learned to settle their differences without the almost constant warfare that plagued Normandy and the surrounding counties and duchies of France. In England, men of noble birth were not required to pass their days in endless battles, sieges and rebellions, constantly worrying that they might be murdered at any moment. Instead they ran their estates, attended the king at court and spent the rest of their time out hunting.

It was, the young men agreed, a tantalising prospect. But to another, somewhat older generation, the very idea of William wearing the crown of England was just one more blow to their pride, one more threat to their ambition, one more drop of bitter gall added to their simmering stew of discontent.

The duke's uncles, Talou and Mauger, were the legitimate

sons of Duke Richard II of Normandy by his second wife Papia. They had only been boys when their father died and his place was taken by their oldest half-brother Richard III. A year later, Richard had been succeeded by Robert, their father's second son. The circumstances in which Robert had inherited the duchy had been deeply suspicious, and many held him responsible for his brother's sudden death. Even so, Robert was older than Talou and Mauger. He therefore had more right to rule Normandy than either of them.

William, however, was different. Not only was he a small boy when he became duke, he was illegitimate, too. As true-born sons of a duke of Normandy, Talou and Mauger bitterly resented being passed over for a bastard. In an attempt to buy their loyalty, they had both been richly rewarded. When the old Archbishop of Rouen died, Mauger was installed in the role, becoming the most senior churchman in Normandy. Talou had been given a great deal of land and the right to build a mighty castle at Arques. But this well-meant generosity had created the opposite result to that intended. The more Talou had been granted by William, or those acting on the boy duke's behalf, the more he'd been reminded of his unfairly subordinate position. He, after all, should have been the one doing the granting, while William had no right to any land or title at all.

'And now the little shit is in danger of becoming a king!' Talou exclaimed.

He had waited after dinner while Mauger made sure that Champart, the bearer of such bad news, was settled in a luxurious chamber at the archbishop's palace. Then the two brothers had retired to Mauger's private study to talk in peace over a flagon of wine. In the days when their uncle had been archbishop, the room had been decorated with Persian rugs, whose rich colours and complex patterns were a thing of wonder; fine Saxon tapestries showing biblical scenes and a Byzantine icon of the Virgin and child that glowed with gold leaf. Now the room was bare. It was not that Mauger was particularly holy or ascetic. He simply did not notice, let alone care about, his surroundings.

'This is a disaster for us,' Talou continued. 'How can that fool of a king possibly consider naming the Bastard his heir? He always was a pathetic little man, Edward, hanging around in his nasty old clothes, pretending that he was somehow more pious than the rest of us when we all knew what a bitter, twisted coward he was. How in God's name did he ever become king of England? What in God's name made him suddenly pick on William? And why the hell, dear brother, didn't you nip this in the bud years ago?'

Mauger's face twitched and his bony shoulders squirmed beneath his cassock. From his earliest boyhood he had been a thin, nervous, decidedly odd creature, but with every passing year, his eccentricities became more pronounced and his oddness more difficult to distinguish from something close to madness.

'Don't know what you're talking about,' he said in his high, reedy voice. He gave a little peck of his head and giggled to himself. 'I don't nip buds. That's a gardener's job.'

Talou took a deep breath, followed by the long sigh of an angry man doing his best to control his temper. 'By Christ, you're even worse than Edward. You're the archbishop, shit-head. You were supposed to get the Pope to excommunicate William and stop him marrying that Flemish bitch. You were supposed to ruin his life.'

'I tried,' Mauger whined, clasping his hands together and hunching his body as if Talou's words were physical blows. 'The Pope tried. We both tried very hard. The marriage was banned. Can't try harder than that.'

'Banned? Banned?! Well, if it was banned, how do you explain the fact that William and the bitch are married and that she's carrying his brat?'

'William doesn't do what he's told, never has done.' Mauger nodded in agreement with himself. 'Yes, that's it. William is a very bad boy.'

'Yes, and he's a bad boy who seems to get what he wants, all the time. He got the title, and now . . . now the wife that he wasn't supposed to have is about to produce an heir, a legitimate heir, and he, that bastard son of a common tannery girl, is in line to become king of England. And what do you propose we do about that, brother, eh? Any bright ideas come to that addled head of yours?'

Mauger smiled beatifically. 'Think about the Kingdom of Heaven, that's what I do. Ruled by God. No one else, just God. That's where I'm going one day . . . off to the Kingdom of Heaven. Happy, happy day . . . you should think about that day, too.'

'I'll think about the Kingdom of Heaven the day I'm lying on my deathbed,' Talou retorted. 'Until then, I'll concentrate on the Duchy of Normandy.'

There was a loud knocking on the door to the chamber. 'Yes! What is it?' Talou called out. It did not occur to either brother that Mauger, whose palace this was, after all, might answer the knock.

A junior priest came into the study. He gave a cursory nod to his archbishop then spoke to Talou. 'My lord, word has just come from His Grace the duke. He requests your presence in the council chamber.'

'Did he say why?'

'No, my lord, simply that it was a matter of the utmost urgency and seriousness and his most trusted nobles are being called to attend upon him.'

'Most trusted nobles, eh? Well, in that case, who am I to refuse his call?'

The dukes of Normandy were descended from Rollo, a giant among men known as 'the Strider', for it was said that there was no horse strong enough to carry him. The massive wooden chair upon which they sat when conducting their councils had been constructed in keeping with their physical stature as well as their ducal status. When he had first inherited the title as a small boy, William had been as dwarfed by the chair as he had been by the dukedom itself. Now, however, he was a grown man, in full command of his land, and when he sat on the ducal throne, he was more than man enough for it.

His council of war was brief and to the point. William gave a straightforward account of Geoffrey Martel's invasion of Bellême, his seizure of Domfront castle and the likely fall of Alençon. The overwhelming impression he gave was not of a man alarmed by the very obvious threat to his duchy, but of a leader whose sole focus was on dealing with an unexpected difficulty as swiftly and decisively as possible.

'The danger to Normandy is very real, but we can see it off,' he told the assembled nobles. 'The key thing is to move with the utmost speed and take the Hammer unawares. If we can surprise him before he has time to prepare his defences, we can kick him back into Maine and retake Domfront and Alençon in a matter of weeks. But if he has time to install his own garrisons, get Domfront properly provisioned and secure Alençon's defences . . . well, you all remember the siege of Brionne.'

'Oh dear God, not another three years spent up to our necks in mud and shit outside some godforsaken castle!' said Fitz in a tone of mock anguish that provided the first light-hearted moment of the council.

'Not if we get there early enough. But we absolutely have to move fast. My brother Mortain is already on his way to Bellême to find out precisely what Martel is up to and how his forces are disposed. We will meet him in Argentan. My lords, I expect you all to leave here at once, ride directly to your lands and muster as many men as you can.'

Montgomery had been doing his best to maintain the earnest expression of a man being called to arms, but it had not been easy. William was taking Normandy to war to win back land that would soon belong to the united houses of Montgomery and Bellême. This campaign could make his fortune.

Talou, on the other hand, had not bothered to disguise his sour expression, nor the griping tone in which he commented, 'Summer will soon be upon us. Men won't want to be taken from their fields.' Yet even as he spoke, he was already beginning to wonder whether there might, after all, be an unexpected advantage to be gained from Martel's attack, so that he was barely even paying attention when William replied.

'Then pick men who aren't farmers. You all have plenty of knights and vavasours who owe you their allegiance. Call on them. Their wives can administer their estates perfectly well without them. Now go. There is not a moment to lose!'

11

Argentan, Normandy

William reached the Argentan forest just before sunset on the fifth day after leaving Rouen with his hastily gathered force of barely five hundred men. He found a glade in which to pitch his tent and those of his commanders, and set up the horse lines for their mounts. The bulk of his men were left to bivouac as best they could among the trees, while sentries were posted around the perimeter of this makeshift camp.

His half-brother Rob met him there as ordered. William was barely off his horse before he drew Rob to one side for a private conversation.

'So?' he asked. 'What's Martel been up to?'

'He's taken Alençon,' Rob replied. 'The people opened the gates to him without a fight. They didn't have anyone there to lead them, and from what I hear, they've got no love for the House of Bellême anyway. Martel's left about fifty men to watch over the place.'

'I don't know Alençon. What are the defences like?'

'The town itself is walled. It stands on a bend in the River Sarne. There's a bridge across the river. Martel's men are building a fort to guard the far end of the bridge, on the bank opposite the town. It's only wooden, but it looks sturdy enough.'

William took in what Rob had said, then nodded to himself. 'What's Martel's strength?'

'His main force is pretty evenly matched with ours, I'd say, not including the men he's got on garrison duty.'

'So the reports we heard were right – he's definitely taken Domfront?'

'I'm afraid it fell as easily as Alençon. There was hardly any garrison there to speak of, and by the time Martel arrived at the castle, the gates were wide open, the place was empty and he walked right in.'

'Tell me about the castle. From what I've heard, it sounds like an impressive sort of place. Is that your opinion too?'

'Absolutely. It's very strong, all stone. Reminds me of Falaise, the way it's built on top of a steep hill, with a massive gatehouse guarding the only way in. If there had been twenty good Bellême men willing to fight for the place, they could have kept Martel at bay for weeks.'

'So is Martel himself at Domfront?'

'No, he's taken most of his men off raiding. They're laying waste to the whole county.'

'Montgomery won't like that,' William remarked drily.

Rob grinned. 'Yes, Martel's playing havoc with Mabel's dowry. But he's done us a very big favour.'

'How come?'

'Because the last I heard, he was heading off towards Sées. He's left hardly any of his men at Domfront, and the ones that are there are too busy drinking their way through the contents of the castle cellars to organise any sentries or even close the gates. I was half tempted to take the place myself.'

'Why didn't you?'

'Because I was under orders not to get into any fights, but report back to you. And I couldn't report to you if I was stuck inside Domfront castle.'

William nodded at the logic of that.

'But you could take it now, William,' Rob urged enthusiastically, and then remembered whom he was talking to and went on more nervously, 'I mean, Your Grace might take the castle . . . if it pleased you to do so.'

'It might well please me to do so. And if I do, you shall come with me. I did promise you a fight, after all.'

'Thank you!' Rob beamed.

'No, thank *you*,' William said, laying a hand on Rob's shoulder. 'You did exactly what I asked and told me what I need to know. Good work, well done.'

A short while later, William's tent was pitched and he was addressing his key lieutenants: Rob, Fitz, Montgomery and Talou. He outlined the situation as Rob had described it and concluded: 'The key to beating Martel is to take Domfront. Rob, how far are we from the castle now?'

'At least a day and a half's march, if you're going at the pace of the foot soldiers and the baggage. But if you were riding hard, you could do it in a day, just . . . or overnight, if you didn't mind riding the horses into the ground.'

William's eyes lit up. 'You mean we could be there by tomorrow morning?'

'You'd be hard pressed to get there by dawn. But if you left now and allowed even two or three hours for the men and the horses to rest and eat en route, you could make it well before noon.'

'By God, that would give them the surprise of their lives!'

Talou coughed. 'If I might make an observation, Your Grace . . .'

'Yes, Uncle,' William snapped with evident impatience.

Talou made a visible effort to retain his temper. 'I was merely going to mention that while I appreciate the strategic benefit to be gained by holding the strongest castle in the region, and the benefit of moving as quickly as possible, you would surely not wish to arrive there in the full light of day. Even if the men Martel has left at Domfront are as careless as young Mortain suggests, it would only require a single man keeping watch on top of the keep to see us coming, giving the Angevins time to close the gates. All they would then need to do, if the castle is as well fortified as has been suggested, is wait until Martel comes to their aid. And we would not want to be caught between Martel's forces on one side and the castle on the other.'

'Well, thank you for pointing out the problem,' William said acidly. Once he'd set his mind on a particular course of action, he never took well to being told that it was impossible.

'I'm just saying that it would seem to make sense to arrive at Domfront under cover of darkness, whether at sunset or in the middle of the night or shortly before dawn. I would tend to favour the latter option. It would mean one could approach unseen, but then fight in the light of the day.'

'Yes, I can see the sense in that,' William admitted grudgingly. 'Rob, do you have any reason to believe that Martel knows we've reached this far?'

'No, I'm almost sure he doesn't. The last time I saw the main body of his force, which was yesterday evening, they weren't acting like men who were getting ready to face the enemy in battle. They were looking for the next village to ransack.'

'And our scouts haven't come across any sign of Angevin troops, Fitz?'

'No, Your Grace. I've had men riding ahead of the column, and to either side, as you commanded. They heard a lot of stories from the locals about all the terrible things Martel's men are supposed to be doing – raping women, stealing everything they can get their hands on . . .'

'The usual,' William remarked.

'Exactly. I've had a couple of reports of men seeing smoke in the distance, which might have come from fires Martel's lot started. But they didn't actually see any Angevins in the flesh.'

'So we have a little time to play with,' William said, half

talking to himself. 'But not a lot . . .' He sighed and let his head droop, his eyes closed, deep in thought.

His men waited while their duke mulled over everything he'd heard, knowing from experience that he would soon come to a conclusion. William of Normandy was not a man given to dithering.

Sure enough, it was not long before he snapped back up straight. 'Very well then, this is what we will do. There is no point trying to extend the march this evening. The men are tired and so are the animals. We will remain where we are overnight. In the morning we will march on, but stop a little earlier than usual, let us say halfway between here and Domfront. I want everyone well rested, fed and watered.

'Tomorrow night, my brother Mortain and I will take fifty of our best men and ride hard for Domfront. We will attack, as you suggest, Uncle, at dawn, or just before. Forget the gates. If they don't see us coming, we can be up the hill, have ropes over the battlements and be up them and into the castle before those drunken Angevins even know we're there.

'Uncle, you are the next senior man to me, so I am placing you in charge of the remainder of our force. Have the men up early and march for Domfront. And I know how much you like a good meal, so I'll have the cooks hard at work to provide a hearty supper for you all when you get there.'

Talou nodded in gracious acknowledgement of the favour that was now being shown him.

William punched a fist into his palm. 'Gentlemen, we have been handed a marvellous gift from God, a chance to beat our enemy with a single well-placed blow. Once Martel knows we're in Domfront, he'll see at once that he's in serious trouble. We'll be in his rear, with a base he can't hope to capture, able to strike from there, cut his lines of communication and leave him completely stranded. My guess is he'll march straight back the way he came and pray to God that he can get back to Maine before we block his road home.'

He looked around the tent at each man in turn, then clapped his hands and called to the servants waiting just outside, telling them to bring wine and goblets.

'Come, let's drink a toast to our good fortune,' he said once each man had a drink in his hand. 'Raise your glasses . . . to God and Normandy!'

'God and Normandy!' the men echoed. Their goblets were emptied and then the meeting dispersed as each of the nobles returned to his own company.

Talou lingered a little longer than the others, just to talk through William's plan so that he knew exactly what would be expected of him when he was in command of the bulk of the Norman forces. Then he respectfully bade his nephew farewell and went to the area of the camp where his own men were congregated.

Over the past week he had been thinking about how best to manipulate the current situation to William's disadvantage and his own benefit. Now he was ready to act. He sought out a knight by the name of Hervé of Abbeville. 'Geoffrey, Count of Anjou . . .'

'The Hammer,' Hervé murmured.

'Yes, exactly . . . I want you to go to him.'

'Isn't he our enemy?'

'He's the duke's enemy. He has caused me no offence.'

'Very well, my lord, but where should I find him?'

'In the region of Sées. Leave the camp once darkness has fallen; it won't be too long now. Make sure no one sees you go. Then ride hard. It's absolutely imperative that you reach the count as soon as possible. D'you understand?'

'Yes, my lord. What am I to tell him when I get there?'

'Tell him that the castle of Domfront, which his men

currently occupy, is in grave danger. William of Normandy is planning a surprise attack. He will strike at dawn, two mornings from now. If Count Geoffrey wishes to keep the castle, he must make sure that it is properly defended when that attack takes place.'

'Very well, my lord.'

Talou made Hervé repeat his orders. 'Don't you worry, my lord,' the knight said after he had done as his master asked. 'I'll make sure he gets the message. You can count on that.'

'Excellent . . . and Hervé?'

'Yes, my lord?'

'Get someone to bring me some wine.'

'Of course, my lord.'

Talou waited until he was alone again before adding to himself, 'I want to drink to the downfall of William the goddamned Bastard.'

12

The castle of Domfront, in the county of Bellême

The ride to Domfront had gone according to schedule. William and Rob had set off under clear skies and a full moon that lit the paths on which they rode as clear as day. They took with them a company of fifty men, hand-picked from the best of William's ducal guard, along with men from his stepfather's estates near Conteville whom the two brothers had known all their lives.

Among them was Martin, the poacher who had helped William gain entrance to Falaise castle several years earlier, when he had fought his first engagement, and won his first victory too. Martin had an uncanny way of being able to move across even the most exposed terrain without being spotted. If the men at Domfront were as undisciplined as Rob had suggested, they would have no idea that he was there until they heard a faint chink of metal against stone. Even then someone would have to identify it as the sound of a grappling hook locking onto the parapet, work out where the sound was coming from and get men to that spot. And by that time, William was planning to be over the wall himself, right behind Martin, with another three men behind him whose job was to reach the gate tower, lower the drawbridge and open the gates to Rob and the rest of the Normans.

The raiding party stopped a league short of Domfront to rest, eat and take care of their horses. In the grey half-light before dawn, between the setting of the moon and the rising of the sun, Martin, William and the three other soldiers slipped out of the woods and made their way across a patch of open ground to the foot of the bluff on which the castle stood. They wore no more than their tunics, hose and boots, for they wanted to move as quickly, nimbly and silently as possible. But each man carried both a sword and a dagger, for, just as Martin and William had done at Falaise, they would have to hold their own against the castle guard until Rob and his men could come to their rescue.

Martin stopped and signalled for total silence, and the five men waited in the shadows, listening for any sound of movement, as cautious as deer in a wood filled with wolves, ready to fly at the slightest threat. But there was no hint of any danger, so he led them up the steep incline, finding a path where none of the others could see one and guiding them to the base of the walls.

Again the poacher paused. He looked around, listened, sniffed the air, calling on all the senses and instincts developed during a lifetime spent stealing game from under the noses of well-armed foresters. At last he looked at William and nodded: it was safe to proceed. William returned the nod and pointed a single finger upwards. Martin stepped back from the walls, swung the hook round and round on a lengthening line and then threw it up into the air.

The hook flew perfectly between two battlements. Martin pulled hard on the line. It held firm. Without waiting for further orders, the poacher started scampering up the wall, his feet walking up the vertical stonework while his hands worked their way along the rope. Within seconds he was halfway up the wall and William was following him, his feet scrabbling for purchase at first until he got the feel of it and began his own smooth ascent.

Above him he could see Martin almost at the level of the battlements.

Then he heard a shout from up above: a command that was followed by the sound of rushing feet and shouting men, the sight of torches flickering all along the top of the wall and the sudden flash of an axe being swung over a man's head, like an executioner beheading his victim.

But the blade was aimed not at any human neck; rather at the rope from which Martin and William were suspended.

William felt the rope shudder as the first strike of the axe cut into it.

He saw Martin hesitate, uncertain whether to keep climbing or to try and get back down. The axe swung again and suddenly the rope had been severed and Martin's scream of terror filled William's ears, and then he was shouting too and falling and hitting the ground with an impact that winded him, and in the same instant, Martin's body smashed into the turf just a whisker away from him, and there was a terrible cracking sound as his bare head smacked against a boulder protruding from the grass.

William knew without even looking that the poacher must be dead. But there was no time to mourn the loss of the man who had nursed him through that first blooding of his sword in combat, for now there were Angevin men peering over the battlements and bows being drawn, and William was scrambling desperately back down the face of the bluff with his men around him, jumping the last few feet and then racing across the open land, jinking from one side to the other to throw off the aim of the archers, who were surely aiming for his defenceless back.

He heard a scream and a man shouting, 'My leg! My leg!' William stopped, turned, ran to where the man was writhing on the ground, ignoring the fluttering sound of arrows flying past him and the thud as they hit the ground and buried themselves in the turf. He picked up the soldier and flung him across his shoulders and started running again. Ahead he saw the other two men practically throw themselves between the trees as they reached the edge of the wood. He could make out the rest of his company, and Rob too, standing in the shadows, shouting encouragement to him, though he could barely hear them over the incoherent screams of the wounded man.

The men in the woods were waving their arms at William as if they could somehow pull him towards them, and their presence gave him hope and strength and put speed into his legs. Still the arrows kept flying, somehow missing their mark. A moving target, from a wall atop a hill, into a crosswind: that's a damned hard shot, William told himself. And then there was a thud between his shoulder blades, an impact whose force knocked him so hard that he almost stumbled, and his first thought was: I'm hit! But there was no pain and he could still move and then he realised that the moaning had stopped and the man on his shoulders was completely still, and he suddenly understood: The arrow hit him. The poor bastard was my shield.

He let go of the body and sprang forward as the weight was released from his shoulders, and before he knew it he was in the woods, arrows thudding harmlessly into the first line of trees, and Rob was running towards him, crying out, 'Thank God you're all right! You had me worried there.'

As William felt his brother's arms embrace him and realised he was safe, he was filled not with relief, but a sudden over-whelming rage. 'You fool! You incompetent idiot!' he shouted, pushing Rob away. 'Two good men are lying dead out there because of you. It's a miracle I wasn't killed too. You told me the castle was undefended. What do you call that then? Eh? Undefended, my arse!'

The men-at-arms drew back as William glared at his brother with murderous fury in his eyes. His voice dropped to a venomous growl as he stabbed a finger towards Rob. 'Did you make it all up, is that it? Trying to prove to big brother that you were old enough to be treated like a man? Or was it deliberate?

Did you lead us here knowing I'd go in first, knowing they were waiting for us? Did you betray us to that Angevin bastard Geoffrey Martel, eh? Eh?!'

Rob said nothing. He seemed stunned by the hatred in William's voice, the bitterness of his accusations. And then he did something that surprised every man there. He sprang forward and with one mailed fist – for he and his men were fully armoured – he grabbed the front of William's tunic, just below his neck, while he drew the other fist back, ready to strike.

One of the soldiers made to step forward from the rough circle that had formed around the duke and the young count, but another, older man held him back and shook his head. This was a family matter, two brothers, and it behoved no man to come between them, no matter how exalted they might be.

'I told you what I saw,' said Rob, and the men now saw what had somehow not been apparent before: that though he was less heavily built than William, he was just as tall, and though he had always carried himself with a steadfast good nature that the Conteville men knew came from his father Herluin, he had fire in him too. 'And I told you true. I would never lie to you. I would die rather than betray you. And if you doubt my loyalty, then fight me and kill me, for I'd rather die than live with that dishonour.'

William looked his brother in the eye. Then he took him in his arms. 'I'm sorry. I'll never doubt you again.'

The men clustered between the trees relaxed as they saw that all was well, though the failure of their mission meant that none of them had any inclination to cheer at their lords' reconciliation. William, as was his way, wasted no time brooding. He gave brisk orders to half his men to establish a perimeter around the castle, out of range of the archers. The other half he would hold in reserve, ready to greet any attempt by the Angevins to sally out of the castle.

That task accomplished, he turned to Rob.

'Those men didn't just happen to be waiting for us on the walls. They knew we were coming, and when, too. Which means someone got word to Martel that we were coming.'

'Fitz would never betray you,' Rob said. 'He's as much your brother as Odo or me and loves you just as much.'

'I agree. And Montgomery's too clever to be disloyal. He knows his best interests lie in serving me, marrying Mabel and becoming the new lord of Bellême.'

'Do you think he's that cynical? I'm sure his loyalty to you is heartfelt.'

'Then if I have his heart and his head I certainly have no need to fear him. No . . . there is only one man who would have the malice to do this, and the desire to gain from it: my beloved uncle Talou.'

'What will you do? You could have him tried and executed for treason. No one would think ill of you if you did.'

'No one who was already on my side, perhaps. But what of those who aren't? I don't have any proof. My enemies could say I killed my own uncle just to make myself more powerful. And Uncle Mauger may be half mad, but he's still archbishop of Rouen and the last thing I need is him appealing to the Pope for yet another reason to excommunicate me. No, all I can do is watch him like a hawk and be ready to move the moment he shows his hand. So we do nothing, we say nothing. We just wait.'

13

William may have decided to do nothing about Talou, but he still had plenty to keep him occupied.

Four years earlier, he had defeated a revolt led by his cousin Guy of Burgundy. Guy had fled from the battlefield where the rebel army had been slaughtered, crossed a river choked with the bodies of his men and fled to his castle at Brionne. It had taken William more than two years to prise him from his fortress and banish him from the Duchy of Normandy, but he had learned a great deal about siege warfare in the process. So as soon as the main body of his troops arrived at Domfront, he had them piling up earth and rocks to build three mottes, exactly like those on which castles were often constructed. Then they were set to work chopping down trees and fashioning great siege towers to be placed on these mottes. Atop these he sited ballistas, catapults that looked like giant crossbows that could fire bolts heavier than any spear, or even small rocks, directly across at the castle battlements. These war machines could not breach a castle's walls. But they could wreak havoc among any men foolish enough to come within their range.

A camp was set up and men were sent out across the surrounding countryside to scour it for the food and ale they would need to sustain them. The Normans paid less for the supplies than they were worth, but they did not steal them, nor harm the farmers and peasants who provided them. The siege might go on for months and food would be as much of an issue for the Normans outside the castle as the Angevins defending it.

It was best, then, to maintain good relations with the people who would feed them.

The siege had been in place for two weeks and the men's morale was still high, for the weather had been warm and dry and they still had plenty of building and foraging to keep them occupied, when word came in that Martel and his men had been spotted heading towards Domfront.

William dispatched Fitz and Montgomery to meet them. 'Go and speak to Count Geoffrey. Tell him that he has caused great damage to the county of Bellême, and done harm to its people. And since I am their liege lord, he has done harm to me too and damaged what is mine. I expect fair recompense, starting with the return of Domfront and Alençon to my care. If he wishes to surrender the castle, I'm happy to hear his terms. If he's calling me out to fight, I will be happy to oblige, either with my army or in single combat; it is all the same to me. If he asks me to withdraw, my answer is that I will never, ever take a backward step by choice. But if he wants to force me to do so, then he is more than welcome to try.'

'Do you want us to count how many men he has?' Montgomery asked.

'Of course, that's always useful to know. But however big or small his army, it makes no difference. My terms remain the same. Now go! I'm curious to find out what the Hammer has in mind.'

There was plenty of silver hair among the black on Geoffrey Martel's head, and in the week's worth of stubble that covered his heavy jaw and his thick, fleshy neck, and he didn't take kindly to the way in which the two Norman whelps delivered their bastard master's terms.

He glared at Fitz and Montgomery and stepped so close to them that they could smell his breath. 'I was already a man, with blood on my sword and enemies in their graves, when your duke was just a squealing, puking, shitting babe in arms – aye, and you too, by the looks of you. Maine has fallen to me, and now Bellême, and you have the damned insolence to stand here before me, in front of my men, and tell me that I should pay recompense to Duke William of Normandy? If you took a silver penny and cut it into eight, I would not give him one single piece of it.'

'That is just as well, because he wouldn't take it,' Fitz said, not looking away or conceding any ground to Martel.

'Wouldn't he now?'

'No, my lord. But he will accept the return of the castle of Domfront and the town of Alençon, and he will give your men there safe passage if they lay down their arms and surrender.'

Martel grinned and turned to his knights, who were massed around him. 'Did you hear that, lads? The tanner's boy wants me to surrender our castle and our city to him. Now why would I want to do that?' He fixed his eyes once more on the two Normans. 'Well . . . why?'

'Because they are not your castle or your city; they are rightly held by Mabel of Bellême, by the grace of the Duke of Normandy,' Montgomery replied.

'Not right now they're not. Your duke is camped outside my castle and he's the one who should lay down his arms and go.'

'He will never surrender to you, or any other man on this earth.'

'Then I shall just have to kill him. Tell your master that I do not fear him. No man has ever bested me and he will soon find out why. I challenge him to single combat. I'll ride to Domfront tomorrow and he won't have any trouble spotting me because I'll be riding a white horse and carrying a shield of gold.'

Now it was Fitz's turn to laugh.

'Do I amuse you, boy? By God, I swear I will make you

smile tomorrow, with my sword . . . right here.' Martel reached out with his index finger and swept it across Fitz's neck.

Fitz bridled, and Montgomery reached out a hand to restrain him.

'You will be wasting your time if you ride to Domfront tomorrow,' Montgomery said. 'For Duke William of Normandy will be ready to fight you at dawn. And he will do it right here.'

Martel dismissed the Normans and then set his squires, grooms and armourers to work. He wanted his sword and armour polished, his shield freshly gilded, his saddle and reins in perfect condition and his horse brushed till its coat was as dazzling as snow in the sun when he rode out to kill William of Normandy.

He ate well and drank sparingly and was preparing to retire for bed – for he always slept like a log before battle – when a messenger burst into his tent, without bothering to ask his permission. The man's face was caked in dust and sweat. He was so tired he could barely stand.

'What is it?' Martel snapped.

'My lord,' the messenger gasped, his chest still heaving with the exertion of his journey, 'I bring news from Anjou. King Henry of France has invaded the county at the head of a mighty army and is bearing down on Tours. Without you, we are defenceless. If you do not return now, he will take the city and all Anjou will be lost.'

Martel said nothing. He could not back out of the combat against Duke William. Men would think he had been too frightened to face him. The dishonour would be intolerable. But what alternative did he have? Henry had been trying for years to cut him down to size. Now, by the very extent of his conquests, and the distance they took him from home, Martel had given the king the perfect chance to strike at the homeland he had left behind. I'd do the same thing if I were wearing his crown, he thought.

The longer he waited, the greater the chance that Henry would succeed. 'Damn, damn . . . damn!' he cursed.

The messenger was shattered and his horse would be in an even worse state. There was no point sending him back to Anjou. Martel summoned one of his best men. 'Ride to Tours. Ride as if the hounds of hell were on your trail. If you meet any of our men along the way, tell them to march back the same way. I want the gates closed and every grown man armed. Tell them King Henry must not get into the city, not at any cost. Tell them I will be on my way to save them. I will have the whole army on the march within the hour. However fast you go, we will not be far behind.'

'But my lord, what about William the Bastard?'

'The hell with him. Domfront will not fall, but Tours might. I must deal with my own land now. There will be plenty of time to deal with Normandy later.'

The following morning, William led his men to confront Martel and the Angevins. But when they got to their camp, the tents were empty, the fires had all burned low and the enemy had gone.

Deflated and frustrated, they returned to Domfront. A week later, news came in that explained Martel's disappearance. For the foreseeable future, he would be tied down by his squabble with King Henry. So William and his men settled down to wait until the garrison of Domfront was too hungry, too thirsty, too sick or too disheartened to resist any longer. And wait, and wait . . . and wait.

14

Southwark, England

Godwin, Earl of Wessex, sat in the manor house of his estate at Southwark, on the Surrey bank of the River Thames, hard by the bridge that led to London, and wondered how he had made such a glaring series of entirely avoidable mistakes. He, of all people, had miscalculated the balance of power. He had allowed himself to be outmanoeuvred by King Edward. It was inconceivable, and yet it had happened.

If England were a chessboard, Godwin was staring at a position in which he was checked, and most probably mated. It was not a sensation to which he was accustomed.

He had started, almost four decades earlier, with a small patch of land in Sussex and turned himself into the richest man in England, whose estates exceeded even the Crown's in size and value. Through the lives of five kings he had never failed to emerge more powerful and prosperous at the end of a reign than he had been at the beginning. The throne had been held by Englishmen, Danes and now, in King Edward, a man who was half Norman by blood and had spent more than half his life as a guest – little more than a poor relation, if truth be told – at the court of the dukes of Normandy. Yet Godwin had remained a constant presence at the king's right hand, whoever that king might be: proffering advice, remaining steadfastly loyal (until his interests demanded a change of allegiance), manipulating events to his own advantage. His two eldest sons, Sweyn and Harold, were fully grown men, of thirty-one and twenty-nine respectively. Godwin had successfully petitioned the king on their behalf and they had been granted the earldoms of East Anglia and Hereford in their own right. His daughter Edith was the Queen of England, married to Edward at Godwin's behest.

That had been his first miscalculation. Edward was a cold and bloodless husband. Godwin had always known that the king had hated his own mother, Emma of Normandy, the wife of both his father, King Ethelred, and then Ethelred's conqueror and successor, King Canute. What he had not realised, however, was that Edward's hostility had somehow grown into a loathing of all women. He refused to consummate his marriage, leaving Edith as virginal as a wife as she had been as a maiden. Had the king's preference been for the sweet round buttocks of young boys, or the rough hands of burly soldiers, Godwin might have understood the reasons for his daughter's mistreatment, even if he would not have found it any more forgivable. But the king seemed uninterested in men or women, and equally incapable of finding satisfaction with either. He dressed his impotence up as chastity, born of deep religious principles, and no one put on a better show of piety and devotion than Edward. But in truth he was as cockless as a eunuch in a Saracen harem.

For a man like Godwin, who took a hearty delight in the pleasures of the flesh and had eleven sons and daughters, all born of his wife Gytha, to prove it, Edward's absence of virility made him contemptible.

'Maybe that's why I underestimated him,' he murmured to himself.

'Because you're not as clever as you think you are,' retorted his eldest son, Sweyn, loudly enough for Godwin, Harold and the third of the Godwinson brothers, Tostig, to hear.

Godwin darted a furious glance at Sweyn. The young man was drunk, and as usual, wine was acting like the Devil on his shoulder, driving him on to cause trouble, making him hunger for violence. Harold and Tostig very deliberately said nothing and avoided their brother's eye. Men who confronted Sweyn Godwinson when his rage was upon him had paid for it with their lives. Even the brothers' own cousin, Bjorn Estrithson, had been murdered by Sweyn out of misplaced grievance. For that, and other offences almost as heinous, Sweyn had twice been exiled. He had since been pardoned but his conduct had scarcely improved. How could it as long as his nature remained unchanged?

For now, Godwin ignored his delinquent son and heir and returned to brooding over the cause of what he feared was his imminent downfall. And to think that it had all arisen from such a little thing, just a minor act of insubordination.

Count Eustace of Boulogne, who was married to Edward's sister Goda, had come to England to visit his brother-in-law and reaffirm their friendship and political alliance. When he had landed at Dover there had been some minor trouble – barely more than a skirmish – between his men and the townspeople. On their return journey, en route to the port where their ships lay waiting, the soldiers of Boulogne had put on their chain mail and helmets, unsheathed their swords and decided to punish the citizens of Dover for their impudence. The townsfolk had fought back and around twenty people on either side had died.

So far as Godwin was concerned, that was a sort of rough justice. Both sides had behaved badly and both suffered equally for it. If Eustace had been any kind of a man, he'd have seen it the same way. But instead he'd gone running back to Edward, demanding retribution for his lost men.

A strong king would have laughed in Eustace's face, told him to be more careful next time he picked a fight with the good men of Kent, and sent him on his way. But Edward had taken his guest's side against his own subjects and ordered Godwin to go to Dover and teach its people a lesson they would never forget.

'Your Majesty, I beg you to reconsider,' Godwin had pleaded. 'Ten years ago, when Harthacnut was king, I was ordered to go with Leofric of Mercia to punish the people of Worcester. We obeyed the king's command—'

'Then you can obey my command too,' Edward snapped in that petulant way of his, like a cross little girl stamping her foot.

'I could, sire, yes . . . but not in good conscience. Not if I have your best interests at heart. Worcester was a terrible business. We ravaged the city and slaughtered its inhabitants, men and women, young and old. I have fought in many a battle, but I have never seen anything to match the carnage of Worcester. And the people never forgave the king for what he had commanded.'

'Why should I care what the people think? I am their king and they must obey me. Their thoughts are of no concern to me.'

'Your Majesty, you surely recall that Harthacnut was king in name alone from then on. His grip on the crown was loosened. Had he not died, he might have let it go completely.'

'Then I should have become king all the sooner, for there was no one else whose claim matched mine.'

Tell that to the kings of Denmark and Norway, thought Godwin, but he kept the words to himself.

So why, he now asked himself, did you open your mouth to say something worse? For when Edward had repeated his command, Godwin had made a fool's mistake. He had not stopped himself from saying what he actually thought (the most cardinal of all errors!) and had replied, 'No, Your Majesty, what you ask would be a sin. And I cannot commit it.'

Even then, he did not think his position was endangered. The king accused him of treason and summoned the greatest nobles in the land to a council at Gloucester. Godwin raised a small army in Wessex. Sweyn and Harold brought fighting men from their respective earldoms. Together they marched on Gloucester. Godwin's plan was to rally support among his fellow nobles, for none of them could bear Edward any more than he could. Furthermore, Leofric was bound to support Godwin's position, for he had been equally horrified by the carnage inflicted on Worcester.

But Godwin had not allowed for the resentment his own power had set festering in so many breasts. The king was weaker as well as poorer than the Godwin clan. So, of course, were all the other earls of England, individually. But together with the king, men like Leofric, Siward of Northumbria and Edward's nephew Ralf of Mantes – or 'Ralf the Timid' as he was known – could form an alliance of the weak that could overpower Godwin, Sweyn and Harold.

Godwin and his followers arrived at Gloucester to discover that the king had managed to cobble together precisely such an alliance. If the earl went to trial, he would be found guilty, and if he picked a fight, he would lose that too. So he, his sons and their men had retreated to Southwark. Edward and the other earls had pursued them and were now encamped in London, on the far side of the river. Godwin had dispatched Stigand, Bishop of Winchester, a man whom both he and the king trusted, to find Edward and plead his case. Until Stigand returned, however, there was nothing for Godwin to do but contemplate that imaginary chessboard and try somehow to escape his inevitable defeat.

15

Hours passed as the earl ran through every possible move he could make, and every counter with which Edward and his allies might respond. Sweyn drank himself beyond the point of belligerence into a bitter stupor. Harold and Tostig were playing dice. Harold, the elder of the pair, approached the game in the same way he did his whole life, with an easy confidence born of his natural optimism. Life had taught him that things tended to work themselves out in his favour, and so he rolled the dice with faith in his own good fortune: cheering with delight when the numbers he needed came up, and dismissing his failures with a relaxed, easy-going smile. So far as Harold was concerned, life was there to be enjoyed

If Harold was handsome in an effortless, smiling, sunny way that reflected his personality, there was a darker, more brooding cast to Tostig's face. The black fire in his eyes betrayed a troubled soul, driven by a hunger for money, power and status that he could never satisfy. Tostig was not prone to the same rages or sudden, barely provoked flashes of violence that plagued his oldest brother Sweyn. But he took nothing for granted and assumed that he would have to scheme and fight and bargain to get what he wanted. So he cursed the failed throws of the dice and, though they were playing for mere pennies, scooped up his winnings as voraciously as if they been golden guineas.

As they played, the brothers talked about women. 'Did I tell you the new name the people have given my Edith?' Harold asked. 'She's been "Edith the Fair" all her life, but now they're calling her "Swan-Neck". I heard it from a farmer, and when I asked him why he said, "'Cause she's as beautiful and graceful as a swan, me lord.'"

'Are you sure it's not because she paddles her feet and lives off pond weed?' Sweyn quipped, evidently not so drink-sodden that he couldn't aim a barb at his brother.

Harold ignored the malice that underpinned Sweyn's humour and laughed the insult away. 'I've not seen her do either of those things,' he replied. 'And she can't lay eggs or fly, either, so I think it really must be her looks. By God, she's a beautiful woman. I look at her sometimes and can't believe my luck.'

'So why don't you marry her?' Tostig asked.

'There's no need. We love one another. There's no one else that either of us wants. She's already borne me little Godwin, and he will be my heir. We will always be together, so why do we need a priest to tell us what we already know?'

'Because that's the law,' Tostig replied.

'It's the custom now . . . yes. But it wasn't always. Canute never married Elgiva of Northampton, did he, Father?'

Godwin roused himself momentarily from his reverie. 'What was that?'

Harold repeated what he had said and Godwin agreed. 'No, they never made church vows. Nor did your mother and I, come to that. People didn't see the need for it back then, not unless the woman or her father demanded it.'

'Well, I want to marry,' Tostig insisted. 'I want to know that my wife is mine, and I want the world to know it too.'

'I suppose it just depends on what you think the point of it all is. I'm with Edith because I love her and she loves me. That's all we care about.'

'That, and the several thousand acres of land that she's due to inherit from her father,' Sweyn said.

Again Harold brushed the words aside with an easy smile. 'I hardly need any more land; it's all I can do to manage what I've already got.'

'There's no such thing as too much land,' Godwin growled. 'By God, Harold, you should have learned that by now.'

'Maybe, but it's not the reason I'm with Edith.'

'You're with Edith until I find a better wife for you than her, boy, and don't you forget it.'

'Speaking of that, Father,' said Tostig, 'what's going to happen to my betrothal to Judith of Flanders?'

'What do you mean, what's going to happen?' the old patriarch growled. 'You're betrothed. That means you'll marry her. Baldwin and I have done the deal. The papers are signed, witnessed and sealed. There's no going back on it now.'

'I'm not going to go back on it. I know exactly why it would be good to have the Count of Flanders as my father-in-law. I just mean that, you know . . . in our present situation . . .'

'What "present situation"?' Godwin barked. By prompting him to defend himself, Tostig's doubts had served to revive the earl's fighting spirit somewhat. But perhaps he was trying to persuade himself as much as his sons as he continued, 'A bunch of idiots who don't know their best interests from their backsides have sided with the king against us. What difference does that make? We've still got more money, more land, more men than any of them. Even if they have the advantage now – and I'm not saying they do – they won't keep us down for long. You can take my word for that. And you can rest assured that Baldwin knows it too. The Flanders girl is yours. I bought her and I'm taking her.'

'There you go, Harold,' said Sweyn. 'Listen to our dear old papa and learn the facts of life. Fuck love. Women are just another asset to be bought and sold, like farms, or horses, or cattle for the slaughter.'

'Watch your tongue, Sweyn,' Godwin warned.

'Why? I'm not saying anything but the truth. At least Mother is honest about it. She made her fortune – made yours too, for all I know, the start of it at any rate – flogging Saxon slave girls to randy Norsemen.'

'Leave your mother out of this, or by God I'll . . .'

The words died in Godwin's mouth as his attention was distracted by a commotion outside the hall – shouting, scurrying footsteps – and one voice above it all calling out in what sounded close to desperation, 'Stand aside! I insist on being admitted!'

A second later the oak door to the hall crashed open and Stigand of Winchester walked in, a look of utter exhaustion on his face. He looked around, searching for somewhere to sit.

'Tostig, give the bishop your chair,' Godwin commanded. 'So . . . what happened? What did the king say?'

Stigand took a moment to gather his thoughts. 'First, Sweyn is outlawed from this moment on. He is to leave the country and never return.'

'The old bastard!' Sweyn shouted. 'How dare he?'

'Because he is the king,' Stigand replied. 'You committed an act of murder when you killed Bjorn Estrithson, or caused him to be killed by your men. And His Majesty now regrets that he ever pardoned you. He says his conscience will not allow him to let you go unpunished any longer.'

'That's not fair!' Sweyn protested.

'Yes it is,' said Harold, in a voice that suggested that the brightness of his disposition was like sunshine glinting on steel: dazzling, but with a sharp edge beneath it. 'You killed Bjorn. You should pay for it.'

'That's a minor matter,' said Godwin. 'The bigger question is, what did Edward have to say to me?'

Stigand lowered his head into his hands with a sigh of

despair. Then he raised it and said, 'The king commanded me to tell you that you would have his favour once again . . .'

For a second there was a glimmer of hope in Godwin's eye, but Stigand dashed it as he went on, '. . . when you return his brother alive and well to him, along with his men and all their possessions.'

'But that's impossible!' blurted Tostig. 'His brother's dead!'

'Thank you so much for telling us that,' drawled Sweyn. 'I'm sure none of us got the point by ourselves.'

'Shut up, both of you!' snapped Godwin. He looked at Stigand imploringly. 'How can he say that? I've already stood trial for Alfred's death. It was established that I was obeying Harefoot's orders and that I had no idea that pathetic excuse for a king was going to gouge Alfred's eyes out and leave him in the middle of Ely marshes to die. I was cleared, for God's sake. I was innocent!'

'So I'm not the only one who's had his pardon revoked, eh?' said Sweyn. 'Doesn't seem like a minor matter now, does it, Papa?'

Godwin said nothing. He ignored everyone around him, retreating deep into his own thoughts. Eventually he spoke. 'We must leave – now! Harold, take all the money we have with us here and make your way to Ireland. The rest of us will go to Flanders. Tostig, ride as fast as you can down to Bosham. Tell your mother to get some ships ready, as many as she can, and load them with everything we've got that Edward could steal from us. Tell her the rest of the family need to be ready to embark the moment I get there. I'll be following you.'

Tostig hesitated. 'What about Edith, Father? Who's going to look after her if we've all gone?'

'Her husband, I should damn well hope.'

'But if he thinks we're betraying him, won't he take his revenge on her?'

Godwin was about to give Tostig a short, scathing reply, but stopped himself just in time. 'Look, son, I know that you and your sister are very close, have been since you were barely more than babies. But look at it this way: isn't it better for Edith if we're out of the country, instead of staying here and fighting the king? She's a good wife. She will stay loyal to Edward, and so she should. And even he wouldn't dare to do harm to his own queen. People wouldn't stand for that. It's against his best interests. Now, off to Bosham with you.'

As Tostig departed at a run, Harold asked a question of his own. 'Is it wise to split up? Won't that make us weaker?'

'Possibly,' Godwin admitted, 'but it also makes it that much harder for Edward to stop us. He has to send forces in two directions, and knowing him, he'll spend so long dithering, we'll be at sea before a single one of his men has left London.'

'And he'll have to watch both ways afterwards, because he won't know if we're coming back from the west or the east,' Harold said, quickly picking up his father's train of thought.

'Exactly.'

'What about me? Which way do I go?' Sweyn asked.

'With me, to Flanders,' Godwin said. 'I want you where I can see you. I don't trust you to stay out of trouble otherwise.'

Sweyn was about to reply with his usual sarcasm, but something got the better of him: a realisation, perhaps, that this was not the time for petty point-scoring. He put a hand on Harold's shoulder. 'I keep a ship in Bristol harbour, crewed and ready to sail at any time.' He gave a wry smile. 'You know me – never know when I might need to leave the country fast. The captain's a Dane, Havard Johansson. He's a good man and he doesn't ask questions. Just tell him you're bound for Dublin and he'll get you there faster than any other skipper around.'

'Thanks, Sweyn. I appreciate it. Here . . .'

Harold held out his arms and the two brothers embraced.

When they stepped back, Sweyn said, 'Good luck.'

Harold nodded. Then he hugged his father and other brother in turn and left the hall, shouting out for his groom and firing orders at his personal guardsmen.

'You too,' Godwin said to his other sons, and they followed. Now the Earl of Wessex and the Bishop of Winchester were left alone in the room.

'What shall I tell the king?' Stigand asked.

'Tell him that I apologise for leaving without bidding him farewell in person, but I had to catch the tide. Assure him that I remain his most loyal and trustworthy servant and that it saddens me that, for now at least, I cannot provide him with my best advice and counsel. But let him know that I will return. He will see me standing before him in person soon enough.'

16

The royal palace, Winchester

When she heard that her family had fled the country, Queen Edith was quick to stand before the entire royal court and assure her husband of her absolute loyalty and devotion, as both a subject and a wife. 'I must apologise on my father's behalf, Your Majesty,' she said, having meekly bowed her head when she came into Edward's presence. 'I am sure that there has been a misunderstanding of some kind, and with your permission I will do everything in my power to remedy the situation.'

A loving husband might have sympathised with the impossible position in which Edith found herself, torn between her loyalties as a daughter and sister on the one hand and a wife on the other. Such a man, appreciating that his wife was sincere in her protestations of loyalty towards him, might have reassured her that she had nothing to worry about and thanked her for her offer, even if he did not wish to take her up on it. Edward, however, regarded the beautiful woman kneeling in supplication before him with a look of revulsion on his face, as if her proximity to him, or perhaps that of any female, were so repellent that it was all he could do not to step away in disgust.

He spoke as if having to fight back his nausea. 'There is no misunderstanding, my dear. Your father disobeyed me, thereby committing an act of treason. Rather than face a fair trial by his peers, and lacking even the courage of an honest traitor to confront me in battle, he has fled the country. You may take it from me that I will never, under any circumstances, give him permission to return.'

'But my lord, the Earl of Wessex has served you well, and your predecessors before you. I am sure that when he has time to reflect on what he has done, he will wish to do whatever is required to win back Your Majesty's trust and favour.'

'Oh, but I told him what he could do,' said Edward with a smirk. 'I told him all would be well just so long as he returned my brother Alfred alive and well, along with all his men and their equipment. I thought that was very reasonable.' He gave a simpering little giggle. 'Wouldn't you agree, Archbishop?'

'Oh yes, sire, most reasonable indeed!' replied William Champart, who had recently returned from Rome formally installed as the Archbishop of Canterbury. He pursed his lips in vindictive triumph and flashed a contemptuous look at the queen.

'That being the case,' King Edward continued, 'the question now is what are we to do with the traitor's daughter?'

'Mmm, that is indeed a matter worthy of serious consideration,' the archbishop agreed, ostentatiously stroking his chin, as if deep in thought.

It took a second for Queen Edith to realise that they were talking about her. Even by Edward's standards this was an extreme degree of vindictiveness. She could see Ralf the Timid and his gang of toadies sniggering like schoolboy bullies enjoying the sight of a classmate being tortured by their tutor. It occurred to her that they had all – the king, Champart, the whole rotten gang – been looking forward to this moment. And the sense that she was an unwitting player in an already written drama was only heightened by the absurdly exaggerated, theatrical manner in which Edward asked the assembled company, 'Well, does anyone have a suggestion?'

'May I make so bold, sire?' Champart piped up.

'You may indeed, my dear archbishop. Pray tell me the fruits of your profound ruminations.'

'Well, Your Majesty, I believe a period of penitence is called for.'

'Penitence, eh? I like the sound of that. It seems to me that this deceitful jade has yet to appreciate the guilt that naturally attaches to her as the daughter of a man who has betrayed the King of England.'

'But Your Majesty . . . Edward . . . I would never do anything to betray you,' Edith pleaded.

'Silence, woman!' Edward snapped. 'You see, my dear Champart, they're harpies, conniving harpies, all of them. We must never forget that.'

'Oh no, sire, not for an instant. And that being the case, perhaps the best thing to do with this sinful woman would be to remove her to a place of confinement, so that she no longer offends the eyes of your decent, law-abiding, loving subjects with her disloyalty, nor teases their ears with her conniving, deceitful speech, nor revolts their nostrils with the stench of her treachery.'

'Do you have any such place in mind?' Edward asked.

'I do indeed, sire. You may be aware that the sinner before us spent some years as a pupil at the nunnery of Wilton . . .'

'I believe she has mentioned this to me on occasion, yes.'

'Very well, then, I propose that she should be sent back there. But this time, let her show her penitence by an act of abnegation. Let her set aside her queenly pride and serve in the kitchens and dining hall as the most menial of scullions, humbling herself before her betters, seeing all as her superiors and acting as an example, through her abject debasement, to any young women who may be tempted to give themselves airs, or betray their duty as loyal, obedient wives to their lords and masters.'

As the full extent of the humiliation to be inflicted upon his wife simply for the sin of being her father's daughter became clear, Edward could barely contain his glee. He clapped his hands in delight, thrilled by the thought of Edith being humbled and debased.

For her own part, Edith of Wessex, the crowned Queen of England, said nothing as her punishment was declaimed. Nor did she let her feelings show upon her face as her husband declared before the whole court that he was fully in agreement with the archbishop and wished his wife to be taken away at once, so that her act of penance might commence as soon as possible.

Only when she had left the hall in which the king and his courtiers were gathered and was being led away to have her head shaved before being taken in a donkey cart, her hands bound with rough rope, on the three-day journey to Wilton did she finally break down and let the pain of her husband's cruelty and malice reduce her to a torrent of helpless tears.

17

Domfront and Alençon

William, his jaw clenched and his brow furrowed in simmering, pent-up frustration, picked his way across a camp that autumn rains had reduced to a quagmire of mud, horse dung and human sewage. Across its surface was scattered all the rubbish and rotting food scraps that a force of several hundred men was bound to accumulate. Four months had passed, but the siege of Domfront was no closer to success.

Every day the ballistas flung their rocks against the walls of Domfront, or sent rotting animal bodies into the castle itself in the hope that the vile humours rising from the bodies might spread disease among the men inside. The defenders had little hope of being relieved, for Martel was still distracted by the presence of King Henry's troops on his borders. Their campaign of occasional raids and skirmishes posed no serious threat to the Angevins, but they kept Martel pinned down and unable to turn his attention back to the invasion of Normandy.

Even so, the men inside Domfront had not surrendered, and their discipline and morale remained high. The Norman besiegers, meanwhile, were beset by the widespread sickness, low morale and increasing arguments and fights among the men that were the inevitable accompaniment to any prolonged siege.

'By Christ, Montgomery, we're going to a lot of trouble to secure your wife's dowry,' William grumbled.

Montgomery, whose distaste for the filth around him was

even greater than his duke's, did his best to lighten the mood. 'I have to get my wife first, Your Grace. She insists that there's no purpose in marrying me unless her land is recovered.'

'Spoken like a typical member of the House of Bellême.'

'Oh, she's nothing like her father,' Montgomery insisted, praying to God that he was right. 'And I don't think she really means it. I've held enough women in my arms to know when their passions are aroused. That woman desires me. I know it.'

'Huh,' William grunted. 'Well, what I desire is to see my son and heir.'

A week had passed since news arrived from Rouen that Matilda had given birth to a son. William had sent word back to congratulate his wife and instruct her that the boy was to be named Robert, in honour of his grandfather.

Toasts had been drunk to the latest scion of the House of Normandy, with one lord after another raising his tankard and finding new words with which to call for more wine to be drunk. Eyes were dulled and wits slowed, and no one really noticed that Talou, who was now one more step removed from the ducal throne, was barely able to summon up even the most insincere enthusiasm.

Robert of Mortain, however, was genuinely delighted to hear of his new nephew's birth, and even more pleased that they shared the same name. 'Go to Rouen, brother,' he said, letting the wine get the better of his manners as he laid an arm across William's massive shoulders. 'You have to see young Robert, and Matilda too. Don't worry, we'll make sure that the siege is maintained until you get back.'

William had removed Rob's arm and rejected his offer. 'I can't ask my men to leave their families while I go straight back to mine. I'm staying here.'

Still, Rob's words had resonated in William's mind over the following days. Whatever he might say, he longed to see his son

116

and lie with his wife again. And this endless siege was trapping him as badly as the men inside the walls. There were things to do, a duchy to be run. He had to do something to break the deadlock. And then an idea struck him and he ordered Rob to undertake another scouting expedition.

'Go to Alençon,' he said. 'Just take a couple of men and don't tell them or anyone else where you're going. I want to know what the Angevins there are up to. They've been there for months. Nothing has happened. They know that we are stuck here. Do they have their guard up? I doubt it, but I need to know. Oh, and one other thing: I want to know the quickest route from here to there.'

Rob knew better than to ask William what he had on his mind. It was much better to do what he was told and let the whys and wherefores take care of themselves.

Three days later, he returned. 'You were right, Your Grace. The Angevins are good soldiers. They've not turned into a rabble. But it's obvious, if one watches them carefully, that they've become slack and somewhat undisciplined. Careless, you might say.'

'You could be describing our men here,' William said ruefully. 'Very well, how many of them are there?'

'No more than a hundred, split evenly between the fort and the city itself.'

'Ah yes, I remember you said they were building a fort. Tell me about it.'

'It stands, as I say, by the bridge that leads across the Sarthe to the gates of Alençon. There are a few peasant cottages next to it, little more than shacks, that have sprung up since I was last there.'

'That'll be the servants and whores.'

'Exactly. That aside, the land is mostly flat and quite open.

Even at night it would be hard to achieve complete surprise. On the other hand, the fort itself is a far less imposing structure than the one here at Domfront. It's a basic wooden palisade, mounted on a low motte, with a stone gatehouse. The motte makes up a little for the lack of any natural height, but it's not so big that we can't rush up it. And the wooden walls aren't as high or as strong as stone would be, though the pointed tips of the logs are always a problem.'

'Good,' said William. 'I mean to take that fort, and Alençon with it, the same way we should have taken this place. Damn it, we *would* have taken this place if we hadn't been betrayed. There was nothing wrong with the basic plan. So we're going to give it another try. Two nights from now, you, Montgomery and I will take eighty men—'

'Against a hundred of them?'

'Yes, but we are Normans,' William grinned, adding more seriously, 'Any more would weaken us too much here. I don't want the Angevins breaking out when my back is turned; don't want any more traitors passing information on to Martel from our camp, either. So far as the men are concerned, I'm going to visit my son. I'll tell them they can all have an extra ration of wine to toast the good health of their next duke and promise them that I will be back before they know it. Then we'll ride through the night for Alençon. If I can take the city, that will leave Domfront isolated and the men inside will lose heart. Martel's got his hands full dealing with King Henry, so they know he's not coming to their rescue. I'll promise them safe passage if they surrender, and they can all be home with their families by All Saints' Day.'

'As can our men too,' said Rob.

'A damn sight sooner than that, if I've got anything to do with it.'

* * *

Just after dawn, William and his men emerged from the woods on the south side of the Sarne. Ahead of them they saw the hamlet that had grown up by the bridge to Alençon and beyond them the fort that had been erected to guard it. William slowed their advance to a walk, held his reins in his left hand and lifted his right up to his face to shield his eyes from the low rays of the rising sun. As he took in the scene, he began to formulate a plan of action. He turned to Rob, who was riding beside him, and, like a teacher quizzing a pupil, said, 'Well, you described the fort well enough. So what would be your plan of attack?'

'To attack,' said Rob, with a grin. 'I mean, I wouldn't wait. The sooner we hit them the better.'

'That's the spirit. I was about to—'

William stopped in mid-sentence and frowned. 'What the hell are they doing?'

The Normans were now about two hundred paces from the fort and their approach had provoked the defenders into activity. Some of them were hanging hides over the sides of the wall on either side of the gatehouse. That was perfectly normal. The hides would be soaked in water to prevent any fire arrows setting the wooden walls alight. But there was something else. Some of the Angevins were banging the hides with wooden paddles while others were leaning through the gaps between the logs that formed the palisade and shaking their fists at the approaching Normans, or giving them the finger.

'They're shouting something,' Rob said. 'I can't hear it.'

William turned an ear towards the fort and grimaced as he tried to work out the words he was hearing. Shaking his head in frustration, he rode on between a few peasant shacks until he had cut the distance to the fort by about half. Then he held up his hand to stop the column and quiet the noise of the horses.

Now he could hear. Now every man in the column could hear the Angevins chanting, 'William the Bastard, come and get your skins!'

Now they understood why the men were hitting the animal hides, for that was what tanners did when they were curing them. Every man knew what that referred to, but even if they had not, the Angevins were about to make it plain. 'Tanner's boy! Tanner's boy!' they shouted.

William felt the rage rising within him like a living force, a beast demanding to be released. But even as the berserker spirit of his Viking forefathers took hold of him, there was a part of his mind that was still calm, still calculating.

There aren't many of them, he was thinking. The rest must be asleep. So I've got time, but not much, before they're up and armed. As for this lot, they sound drunk. They've been on the wine all night. They'll be tired, their reactions will be slow. I'll never have a better chance.

'Rob, go and get the ram, and a dozen men to carry it. And tell the men to have the scaling ladders ready too. Montgomery, I need a distraction. Take your men and ride off over to the left.' He pointed to where he meant. 'D'you see? Just there, where that field is, right in front of the wall. Ride around, make a noise, make them think you might just be crazy enough to charge the fort.'

A sardonic grin crossed Montgomery's face. 'I can actually charge it if you want, Your Grace.'

'No, don't. I want you all in one piece. And keep a very close eye on what I'm doing. Because when we breach the gate, I want you and your men to charge right in behind us.'

William waited while Montgomery gave his men their orders and moved off towards the field. All the while he was listening to the insults, the jeers, the mocking taunts about his background and his illegitimacy. Then one of the Angevins shouted, 'William the bastard, William the bastard, his grandad's a tanner, his mother's a whore!'

The men around him took up the chant, repeating it as more men joined them on the walls and added their voices too. Then they got bored of that and went back to their first idea: 'Come and get your skins! Come and get your skins! Hey, tannery boy, come and get your skins!'

'I will make you pay for that,' William growled, too low for anyone else to hear. Then he repeated the words at the top of his voice, shouting at the fort, 'I will make you pay!'

He turned around to face his men, gave the order, 'Dismount!' then leaped down from his horse.

'Squires, take the horses. Guard them with your lives,' he commanded. He took his shield, emblazoned with the golden leopards of Normandy, off his back. Then he looked around, scowling. 'Mortain! Where's that godforsaken ram?!'

'Here, Your Grace,' Rob said, slightly out of breath as he jogged towards William, followed by eight men, in two lines of four, carrying the ram between them on leather slings. Four more men came behind them, ready to replace any who fell in the fighting.

William ordered his men into place, so that those carrying the ram were surrounded by others, all bearing shields, forming a human wall around them. Then he held up a hand for silence. The men on the fort were still shouting their insults.

'Do you hear that?' he asked the Normans. 'Those Angevin scum are insulting me, insulting my mother, insulting my family. Would any of you stand for that if it was your loved ones they were mocking?'

'No!' the men shouted, but not loudly enough for their leader.

'I said, would you stand for that?' he repeated.

'NO!' the men roared back.

121

'Now think of your mothers, think of your families, for in mocking me, they mock you too. They mock Normandy, and they'll take Normandy too, if they get the chance. But I'm not going to give them that chance. I'm going to charge that pathetic little excuse for a castle, and smash down its gate. And when I get inside, I'm going to ram those words right back down their fucking throats.'

The men looked at William and they saw the mood he was in, the fury that gripped him and the craving for vengeance that was driving him on. They knew that he meant every word he said. They knew, too, that he would lead from the front and place himself in more danger than any of them, for he never hid from the enemy. Instead he made a point of daring them to attack him.

William unsheathed his sword and held it aloft. 'For God and Normandy!' he cried.

'For God and Normandy!' the men shouted back.

And then he shouted, 'Charge!' and ran full tilt towards the castle as if he could smash down its walls with nothing but the power of his own unstoppable will.

18

Chaos. Pandemonium. A deafening cacophony of battle cries; the shouts of commanders; the screams of the wounded; the pounding of an iron ram-head against the studded oaken planks of a fortress gate. The smell of sweat, and blood, and human waste, and burning pitch, flung down from the ramparts. The howl of a man as the thick brown-black liquid rained down on him, and his clothes caught fire, and his skin and hair burned, and his eyeballs disintegrated.

William realised that he'd made a terrible mistake. By charging all at once, instead of sending the ram and a small covering force up ahead, he had simply crammed all his men into a small space, pressed together like eels in a barrel, squeezed up against the wall. They raised their shields above their heads to protect themselves, but still they were easy targets for archers and crossbowmen and the hellish pitch.

If they could not soon find room to move, the crush alone would kill them, for it was becoming harder to breathe, or move, and any man who slipped was trampled beneath his comrades' feet. But there were only two ways to go: over the walls, or through the gate. Some men had tried to clamber up the ladders, and a ragged cheer went up as one of the attackers reached the top, skewered an Angevin soldier and threw him down from the battlements. But a second later, the Norman too found a blade in his guts and was tumbling from the top of the ladder to his death on the ground below. Other brave men followed him up, but the spiked wall impeded them and the defenders beat them off. Now no one could move until the gate was breached.

Desperately though William's men strove, smashing the ram into the massive doors time and again, digging great chunks out of the wood and sending splinters a handspan long flying like arrows through the air, still that gate would not give.

Three of the ram crew fell and were replaced. But when a fourth went down, the man who should have taken his place was nowhere to be seen. With one member of the crew missing, the man opposite him was rendered useless, standing helplessly with one end of their leather sling in his hand. The blows of the ram were losing their power and rhythm. In the havoc all around him, William had no time to select another man and order him onto the ram. He would have to do the job himself.

He pushed and punched and fought his way through the mayhem and picked up the leather sling. Then he glared at the other seven men. 'We open this gate, or we die.'

The men looked back at him, their chests heaving from their exertions, but gaining new hope and resolution from the presence of their duke.

'So let's smash the bugger!' he shouted, and as an arrow buried its head among all the others clustered like hedgehog bristles along the wooden shaft, he started a swinging motion, sending the ram back and forth, gaining in pace and momentum until finally he yelled, 'Now!' and they stepped forward as one and piled the ram into the door. It did not budge.

William kept going. He was as big and as strong as any man beside him, and more determined than all of them. He drove them harder and harder, pounding the ram against the wood again and again.

All around him men were falling. But others, seeing their duke at the point of greatest danger, rushed to protect him and the rest of the rammers, holding their shields up to create a wall and roof around the ram. And slowly the door began to give. A hole had been pinched right through it now, and all that was keeping it from opening was the wooden cross-beam that held the two doors in place.

But with every second that passed, the casualties among the Normans increased, and still barely any of them had laid a sword on an Angevin soldier.

William could sense that his men were losing faith. If just one of them gave up and ran, the rest would soon follow. But there was nothing he could do except swing the ram, and shout encouragement to the men around him, and act as though the very possibility of defeat had never entered his mind, for all that a cold, dead pool of fear was settling upon his guts.

And then, from one blow to the next, the cross-beam cracked and fractured and folded back. It was not broken yet, not quite, but it was only a matter of time, and the sight of the yielding timber twisted their parched, gasping lips into manic smiles and the men on the ram heaved and swung and pounded once more . . . twice . . . and the third time, the beam gave way, the gate swung open and they were through.

With a roar of desperation and relief as much as triumph, William let go of the sling, drew his sword and hurled himself through the gap in the gate. He carried no shield and wore no armour but his helmet and gauntlets, but there was an aura about him, a sense that he would not, could not be defeated. He swung his sword through his enemies' defences like a scythe through corn. The first man he met was standing with a look of bafflement on his face, as though he could not believe that the fort had been breached, nor that it was the Duke of Normandy himself who was coming towards him, his face smeared with grime and sweat. The Angevin barely had a chance to raise his own sword before William had thrust his blade deep into his abdomen, ripped it back out and turned to face another man coming at him from the side. He, too, was dispatched, with one cut to his sword arm that left it hanging broken and useless and a straight jab that sent William's swordpoint right into his throat.

Even now, though, the battle hung in the balance, for the fort's commander had rallied his men well, forming a line across the castle yard, all on foot, while his archers still fired down from the ramparts of the walls and gate tower alike.

But there were Normans on those ramparts now, climbing up the ladders and over the palisade or clambering up the inside of the fort. Yet though the danger from above was gone, the Angevins down below were still holding firm. And then there was a thunder of hooves from outside the fort and William hurled himself to one side to avoid being trampled underfoot as Montgomery and his mounted knights, each with his lance at the ready, charged through the gate and hurled themselves at the Angevin line.

As the first of their comrades fell beneath the spears of the knights and the hooves of their mounts, the other Angevins dropped back, desperate to escape to the shelter of the wooden tower at the centre of the fort that served as a castle keep.

But Montgomery sent his men to either side of the fleeing defenders, first outflanking them and then forcing them to huddle together, rounded up like sheep, surrounded by the mounted knights.

It was clear to every man on either side that there was no point in fighting on, and the noise of battle that had been so deafening fell away so that the only sound in the fort was the snorting of the horses, the rasping breath of men exhausted by combat and the occasional howl of pain from the wounded scattered across the muddy, blood-drenched ground.

William forced his way between Montgomery's knights and stood before the Angevins. He said nothing. His presence alone

– the hostility that seemed to emanate from him, the sight of him spattered with other men's blood – was enough to put the fear of God into the very men who had not long before been mocking him.

The Angevin commander cracked. He threw down his sword and tore the helmet from his head. 'We yield!' he pleaded. 'God in heaven have mercy upon us. We yield!'

19

'Your Grace! Your Grace!'

It was a boy's voice, not yet fully broken. William turned to see one of the squires leading his horse across the yard of the fort. He nodded in acknowledgement and mounted, then rode at the walk across to Montgomery.

'That was good work, well done,' he said. 'And not a moment too soon, either. The battle was still in the balance. Now, I have another task for you . . .'

'Of course, Your Grace,' Montgomery replied, evidently pleased by his duke's faith in him. 'Anything.'

'Ride across the bridge under a flag of parley. Summon the town's burghers. Tell them that if they value their lives, they must stand atop their walls and look across the river. Then they will see what kind of enemy they face.'

'Do you want me to demand their surrender?'

'No. Just tell them to watch.'

Montgomery frowned, paused a second as if about to question William further, then thought better of it and rode away.

One of William's men, a tough old campaigner called Henrik the Dane, came across to him. 'What do you want us to do with the prisoners, Your Grace?'

'How many of them are there?'

'About thirty, Your Grace, maybe a few more.' Henrik had served under three previous dukes and had the scars, and the broken nose, and an ear that had been sliced in two, to prove it. In his hand he carried Dragonfang, the battleaxe that had been his weapon of choice since before the current duke was born. 'I've taken a look at them,' he added. 'Their captain's good for a decent ransom, I reckon. Don't think the others are worth keeping.'

'There'll be no ransoms,' William said, making Henrik frown in puzzlement. Everyone knew that was the way battles worked. Any prisoners who were rich or of noble blood were held as captives until a ransom was paid. The commoners gave up their weapons and were sent back whence they came.

'So what should I do with them?'

'Make nooses for all of them. Use rope, horses' reins; use their own hose, I don't care. Just make sure that each man has a noose around his neck, nice and tight. Then line them up and tie the loose ends of the nooses to the man behind, so that they're all tethered together.'

'Like animals, you mean?' Henrik asked.

'Yes. They behaved like animals, let them be treated like them too.'

When he got back to where the Normans were keeping the prisoners, Henrik passed on the duke's orders and made sure they were carried out. Then he went to have a word with his closest comrade, a fellow Norseman known to one and all as Big Jan.

'I don't know what the Bastard's going to do to that lot, but it's not going to be pleasant,' he said.

Big Jan looked up at Henrik, for he was a tiny, wiry indi-vidual, though as tough and strong as any soldier in Normandy, with the combative nature and relentless energy of a rat-catcher's terrier. 'Serves them right for calling him names, if you ask me. And that stuff about the Lady Herleva, there was no need for that.'

'Yeah, she was a proper lady, that one, even if she did come from common stock. But that son of hers . . . There was something about the way he spoke to me just now, like he was still eaten up with anger but keeping it all under control. I don't mind admitting, it scared the shit out of me.'

'I know what you mean. You can see it in the way he fights. His dad was never like that, his grandad neither. His uncle Richard, mind, he had a temper on him.'

'Yeah, but he was just a drunken bully. This one's different. He's the best general you and I ever served . . .'

'Wouldn't argue with you there.'

'. . . but I thank Christ I'm not his enemy. Hold on . . .' Henrik narrowed his eyes, then strode across to where one of the men, a pimply youth on his first campaign, was making a poor fist of tying up an Angevin.

'What the hell do you think you're doing?' he barked at the hapless lad, who dropped the rope in sheer panic at Henrik's approach.

'Just watch me, you useless little weasel. You put the rope round his neck, like so. You tie it . . . like so. You pull it good and tight, like so. Then you take the end and tie it to that piece of shit back there. Got that?'

The boy nodded.

'Well, get a fucking move on and do it! And you can wipe that smile off your face and all,' Henrik snarled at the prisoner. 'You've got no reason to be happy, believe me.'

While Henrik was off supervising the tethering of the prisoners, William had been giving more orders. 'Take down one of those,' he told one man, pointing at the pointed logs that comprised the palisade, 'and cut me two sturdy logs, good and thick, both long enough that they reach a man's chest.'

'Yes, Your Grace.'

'Then take them down by the riverbank, close by the bridge.

Drive one of the logs into the ground, far enough that it can stand upright. I want it nice and solid. Then lay the other flat along the ground beside it. Did you understand all that?'

'Yes, Your Grace.'

'Then repeat it back to me.'

The man did so, to William's satisfaction, and went off to carry out his orders.

To another of his soldiers William said, 'Get me a pot of that burning pitch they were throwing down at us. Make a fire by the river, close to where the logs are. Then hang the pitch pot over the fire and keep it good and hot.'

A short while later, Montgomery returned from his mission.

'Well, are they going to do as I commanded?' William asked.

'They claimed that they were men of Bellême and did not have to take orders from you.'

'Did they now?'

'I told them that they would regret it if they defied you and asked them to consider how fast you had taken the fort that was supposed to be guarding their bridge. That made them think. One of them asked what it was they were going to see from the walls.'

'What did you tell them?'

'That they would see whatever His Grace the Duke of Normandy cared to show them.'

'They will get a show all right. Be in no doubt about that.'

Henrik the Dane returned to Duke William. 'The prisoners are bound as you commanded, Your Grace. What shall I do with them?'

'Line them up in a column. Make sure you've got plenty of men to guard them, with spears and swords at the ready. Don't give them a chance even to think about escape.'

'Oh they won't escape, Your Grace.'

'Good, and Henrik . . .'

'Yes, Your Grace.'

'I have need of your axe. I should like to borrow it if I may.'

'Your Grace . . .' A look of anguish crossed Henrik's battered face, for his weapon was as precious to him as a child to its mother.

'Fear not, I will treat your Dragonfang well, and feed it too. And I will reward you handsomely for the loan.'

Henrik grinned, for he knew that the duke would keep his word. He handed his beloved axe up to William, who laid it across his lap.

'Tell the men to follow me,' the duke said, kicking his horse into motion and walking it towards the ruined gate.

William, with Rob and Montgomery riding beside him, led the prisoners and the half-dozen men guarding them out of the fort and onto the field beside the river. The other Normans hurried after them, for they were curious to discover what their lord had in mind. Across the river a crowd of people could be seen scurrying to and fro along the battlements atop the walls of Alençon as they searched for a vantage point, just as Montgomery had commanded them.

The two logs had been set up as William had specified: one standing upright, the other lying flat on the ground, with the iron pot containing the pitch suspended above a fire close by. He stopped just beyond them, then looked towards the men guarding the prisoners and called out, 'Line them up along the riverbank, so that all may see them.'

The prisoners were shuffled forward, each one obliged to stay in perfect step with those behind and in front of him if he did not want to feel the noose tear into his throat and throttle him.

132

William jumped down from his horse with Dragonfang in his hand and went to stand by the upright log. 'Cut the first man free and bring him here,' he ordered.

Henrik did as he was told. The Angevin prisoner followed him like a dog on a lead. He seemed nervous, but not unduly apprehensive. The Angevin dialect was not the same as the Norman, but he understood enough to know that he had not been accused of anything, or threatened with any punishment.

Now the duke addressed him. 'Roll up the sleeves of your tunic.'

The Angevin looked at him with a puzzled expression, for he had not understood the command.

William gave a short, sharp sigh of irritation. 'You do it,' he told Henrik, 'and then place his hands on that block, wrists up.'

Now the Angevin was worried, for the log, whose purpose he had not been able to fathom, suddenly looked very much like a chopping block. He struggled against Henrik for a second, but when William took a single step towards him with an expression of murderous intensity on his face, the Angevin did not dare resist any further. He placed his hands very tentatively on the block. Henrik turned them over so that the wrists were facing upwards. The Angevin was trembling now and moaning to himself. William heard the Blessed Virgin's name and understood that the prisoner was praying.

He realised he was going to need another man. 'Henrik, stand behind him and hold him still. Big Jan, you come here. Take his hands and hold them down hard.'

William stepped back, holding the axe in both hands. Then he turned towards the far bank. 'Let the whole world see what William of Normandy will do to any man that mocks him!' he shouted.

Whether the words carried across the river, no one could say. But a silence fell, thick and heavy with apprehension, for they all knew that their duke had some terrible punishment in mind. And as they looked at the logs and the pitch and the merciless, implacable expression on William's face, they were beginning to understand what it might be.

The prisoner searched frantically for the words that might save him. He cast desperate, pleading eyes at William. 'No . . . no . . . please . . . So sorry . . . please . . . No!'

And then his words were lost in a scream of unspeakable agony as the battleaxe, swung with every last bit of William's power, sliced into his wrist like a butcher's chopper into a joint of beef. It cut through skin, flesh, sinew and bone and hit the wood beneath so hard that William had to pull hard to free the blade.

One hand had been cut off completely and was being held by Big Jan, who was looking aghast at the flaccid, dead fingers and the bloody stump.

William swung again and the other hand was separated from the prisoner's arm. It fell limply to the ground, for Big Jan, who had seen horrors aplenty in his time, but few as brutal as this, bent double and threw up on the ground at his feet. The prisoner howled and thrashed and his comrades lined up beyond him shouted in rage and fear, their individual words lost in the raucous babble.

William marched across to Jan and grabbed him by the scruff of the neck. 'Stand up. I'm not done yet.'

He looked at the writhing prisoner, whose arms were now spurting blood in pulses from their severed wrists.

'Lie him on the ground and place his ankles on the other log.'

Even Henrik looked shocked by what he had seen, and what was now very obviously being proposed. 'Your Grace . . .'

'Are you questioning my order, Henrik the Dane? I'll kill you with your own axe if you are.'

'No . . . no . . . of course not, Your Grace.'

'Then do it. Now!'

The prisoner was easier to handle now. His movements were much weaker and his screams had been reduced to whimpers. He barely protested as he was laid upon the ground, though the clamour from the other captives was growing even louder.

'We need more men,' William said to Rob, whose face was ashen with shock. 'Twenty at least, with lances and clubs. Keep the prisoners under control.'

Rob nodded, as if uncertain that he could keep the contents of his stomach inside him if he opened his mouth, and broke into a run, desperate to escape the butchery.

Now William strode to the very edge of the river and glared across the water at the townspeople on the walls. There were a number of armed bowmen scattered among them, and the sight of William confronting them so defiantly provoked a ragged volley of arrows, but they all fell short of where he stood, landing harmlessly in the river or burying themselves in the bank beneath his feet.

William had not moved a muscle as the arrows came towards him, though several of his men had cowered in alarm. He simply stood and watched them, then fixed his gaze upon the walls for a moment before turning back to the prisoner, who was lying on his back with his legs draped over the log, his feet gripped by Big Jan. As battle-hardened and accustomed to violent death as Jan was, his eyes were closed and his head was turned away.

William approached the log. He stood with one leg almost touching the wood, while the other was stretched out behind him. He flexed his knee and lowered his body, then laid

Dragonfang on the lower part of the prisoner's exposed shins, just above the ankle.

The clamour from the other prisoners subsided, as if their horror at what they were about to witness had driven the air from their lungs. Somewhere in the distance a raven cawed. A horse whinnied and scuffed at the ground with one of its hooves.

William raised the axe. The sun caught it and glinted on the blade.

And then Dragonfang came flying down, cutting an arc through the air, gathering momentum. William strained himself even more than he had done on the previous strokes, grunting with effort as he sent the honed steel smashing into the prisoner's shin bones. They splintered with an audible crackle that was immediately drowned by a high-pitched wail as the prisoner writhed and cried out again. There were deep cuts, welling with blood and lined by torn shreds of skin, across both legs, but neither had yet been severed.

William swung again and the two incisions deepened, but still there was enough muscle and skin remaining to keep the feet attached to the legs.

The third blow did the trick. The prisoner's feet came off in Jan's hands and were dropped as if red hot to fall upon the ground, one leaning against the other like a pair of discarded boots.

William was breathing heavily, his chest heaving.

He turned to Montgomery who was standing slightly off to one side, his jaw set, his eyes fixed determinedly on the half-dead, mutilated prisoner. William looked at him and rasped between breaths, 'Get me something to drink.'

Then he turned his attention to Henrik and Jan, who were standing on either side of the log, with the prisoner's twitching body between them.

'Seal his wounds with the pitch,' he said.

The two men picked up the prisoner between them, with what was left of his arms over their shoulders, and dragged him towards the fire on which the heavy iron pot containing the pitch was bubbling away like a noxious black soup. Only when they reached it did they realise that they lacked any means of applying the pitch to the prisoner's stumps.

'Hold him,' Jan said, and ran back to the fort. When he got there, he looked around until he spied a wooden club that had been discarded by one of the tower's defenders. He grabbed it and tucked it into the belt from which he hung his sword. Then he pulled the woollen hose from one of the corpses that lay where the fighting had been, tore off a strip of fabric and wound it around the end of the club, tying it tight.

He returned to the riverbank to find the prisoner lying unconscious on the ground.

'Probably just as well,' he muttered to himself.

Behind him, one of the Norman troops called out, 'Bet you a quarter silver penny he dies.'

'Done!' another man instantly replied, and there was a ripple of nervous laughter from the watching soldiers, grateful for any relief from the savagery before them. They had all attended executions, but this was much worse, for there was not a man among them who would not have preferred a quick death to the hellish existence that awaited this poor wretch, assuming he even survived.

Jan dipped the cloth into the boiling pitch, picked up a dollop and applied it to one of the man's leg stumps. There was no reaction from the victim, but right up close to the body, even over the reek of pitch, the soldier caught a pork-like waft of cooked meat and skin.

Three more dollops saw to the other leg and the two fore-arms. The prisoner moaned when the first arm was cauterised, but immediately passed out again.

William watched the whole rigmarole in total silence. Only when it was finished did he call out, 'Bring me the next man.'

The prisoner at the end of the line tried desperately to scrabble away from the men who came for him. Shouting and crying and pleading for mercy, heedless of the ever tighter grip of the noose around his throat, he tried to hide himself among his friends. But then one of them pushed him towards William's men, and others joined in, willingly sacrificing him in the hope that they themselves might be spared.

The man was kicking and lashing out with his hands as Henrik and Jan came for him. He bucked and squirmed and twisted his body in a desperate bid to escape his fate as he was carried towards the blood-soaked logs. He yelled so loudly that William grimaced and said, 'Shut him up.' A filthy rag was tied across the man's mouth, pulled tight between his teeth and tied behind his head.

Henrik held his body and Jan his outstretched hands, not needing instructions now, and William repeated the whole grisly process. This time, because the screams were muffled, or perhaps because everyone's senses were numbed by what they had already seen and heard and smelled, it seemed to be a less nauseatingly brutal spectacle. Yet still it was accompanied by shouts and yelps as the prisoners fought their captors – ready to risk death now to avoid the fate of mutilation – and were rewarded for their pains with a club to the head or the prick of a lance jabbing into their skin to keep them in their place. And the outcome was the same as well: another barely breathing cripple with blackened stumps, lying half-dead on the ground beside the first. There were more arrows from the town walls, but yet again William ignored them, even though one shaft buried itself almost to its feathers in the soft turf by his feet.

He went to the water's edge once more and confronted the

townspeople. His arms hung by his sides, the axe held loosely in one hand, daubed in blood and stippled with scraps of meat and bone, for it had feasted well.

'Well?' he shouted. 'Do you understand me now?'

He was not sure if they could hear him, but they surely comprehended his intent as he jabbed a finger in the direction of the other prisoners, then looked back and glared furiously at the walls of Alençon.

He could see that there were people behind the battlements gesticulating at one another. They were arguing, unable to decide what to do. Well, I had better help them make up their minds, he thought, and turned towards where the bulk of his men were massed. 'Where are you, Torf Ironheart?'

A man got down from his horse and walked towards the duke. He said nothing and his face was blank. But then it was always blank, for Torf was a man devoid of emotion. In battle he felt no fear, no matter how desperate the odds, but also no exultation, no matter how sweet the victory. He knew neither love nor hate. It was as if his soul had already been taken from him, and because of this, his comrades and his enemies alike regarded him with superstitious dread, for although he walked and, very occasionally, talked, it was as if he had already died and so could not be killed again.

'Finish the job,' said the duke, throwing Torf Ironheart the axe. 'Keep chopping until I tell you to stop.'

Torf nodded and took up his position beside the wooden blocks. Henrik crossed himself and Jan, seeing him, did the same. 'God forgive me,' Henrik murmured to himself, and then looked at Jan. 'Come on, let's get the next poor bastard.'

The next Angevin victim, who was no longer a soldier but a desperate, howling wretch, was halfway to the logs when he soiled himself in his terror. Henrik and Jan recoiled in disgust, almost letting go of him. Torf just watched blankly, then lifted his axe, rolled his shoulders and neck to loosen up his muscles and got down to work.

A dozen men had been mutilated, cauterised and laid out on the riverbank, when one of William's knights, still mounted on his horse, shouted, 'I can see the town gates, Your Grace. They're opening!'

A few seconds later, the truth of his words was made evident, for everyone could see the gates opening to reveal a group of townsmen, who proceeded to walk over the bridge towards William, with a flag of truce before them.

'You did it, Your Grace,' said Montgomery.

William shrugged and spat on the ground in front of him.

'It's just a pity you were obliged to, ah . . .' Montgomery, politically aware even in these grisly circumstances, searched for the most tactful word and concluded, 'deal with those prisoners.'

William wiped the back of his hand across his face. 'I'd have chopped the hands and feet off every last one of them if that was what it took. Now, let's talk to the good people of Alençon.'

Not bothering to remount his horse, he strode off towards the deputation, who were now reaching the end of the bridge. As he got closer to them, the leader of the group fell to his knees, immediately followed by the others, and held out his arms in supplication. 'Please, Your Grace, have mercy upon us, we beg you! Do not punish us for the actions of others! We surrender!'

William let him continue in the same vein for a little while longer and then held up his hand for silence.

'People of Alençon,' he said. 'You have seen how I punish those who mock or defy me. But now I will show you how I punish those who do not. I will lead my troops into the city. If you do no harm to me or my men, I promise you that I will treat you with mercy. Your people and your property will be untouched. But if anyone should even consider an act of resistance . . .'

The leader of the deputation did not wait to hear the rest of William's threat. 'They will not resist, I swear it!' he called out. 'The gates are open, noble prince. Alençon is yours.'

William gave a curt nod of acknowledgement, then turned and walked back to where his horse was waiting. He remounted and turned to Montgomery. 'Right then, let's go and see what Mabel of Bellême has to offer you.'

20

They rode into the town to find themselves greeted as liberators by townspeople overjoyed to discover that no harm would befall them. William supervised the rounding-up of any stray Angevin soldiers, then they and their surviving comrades from the fort were sent off down the road towards the border with Maine. William was not bothered if they ran into the rest of Martel's army along the way: the more enemy soldiers who were filled with dread by tales of what he did to his prisoners the better. Just to underline the point, the half-dead victims of his act of calculated savagery were lying in a line of mule carts, strung out at the back of the Angevin column. Their severed hands and feet, however, were gathered up in a large sack and went with the Normans, bound for Domfront.

After they had been on the march for an hour or so, Rob approached William and asked if he could have a word with him in private. They rode on ahead of the rest of the men.

'Well?' William said. 'Out with it, brother. Say your piece.'

Rob looked uneasy, more like a nervous schoolboy than a fighting man as he chewed his lip and screwed up his face, trying to find the best way to say what he had on his mind. All he could come up with was 'Did you have to?'

'They insulted our mother. Would you allow that to go unpunished?'

'No, of course not . . . But what you did, it was . . . I don't know . . .'

'Brutal? Cruel? Excessive?'

Rob said nothing, but his expression made it plain that those were exactly the sort of words he'd had in mind.

'Yes, it was all those things,' William said. 'Word of what I did will spread, and with each telling the story will grow, so that I did not mutilate twelve men, but twenty, or thirty, or hundreds, perhaps. But each time the story is told, the moral of it will be unchanged: William of Normandy is merciful to those who obey him and cruel beyond measure to those who do not. And that is a good lesson for people to learn, is it not?'

'I suppose so, but—'

'But nothing, Rob! Grow up. Consider what happened today . . . or, more importantly, what did not. Alençon did not resist. There was no siege, no storming of the city, no burning buildings and raped women, no dead men on either side. A dozen men suffered, but many more did not. And this is not just about Alençon. What happened here today will get us into Domfront in a few days' time, just you wait and see.'

They rode on a little further in silence, until William said, 'Look at me, brother . . . do you understand why I did it?'

Rob nodded. 'I think so. But I thank God that I don't have to do such things myself.'

Their progress back to Domfront was more leisurely than the ride to Alençon had been, so it was two full days before William led the bulk of his forces up towards the castle.

'Now let's take the place, shall we?' He grinned at his younger brother, his smile broadening as he saw Fitz riding towards him. William held up his hand in greeting. 'I bring good news,' he called out. 'Alençon is ours.' But then he saw Fitz's tense, almost downcast expression.

'What's happened?' he asked, instantly on the alert.

'It's Talou, Your Grace. He left the encampment while you were at Alençon, taking all his men with him. He said he refused to accept you as his liege lord any more. He wants to be Duke of Normandy himself.'

Fitz sat nervously astride his horse, knowing full well that a messenger was often blamed for the news he brought.

William, however, wasted no time or energy on recriminations, but focused at once on what Fitz had said. 'So now we know. Talou wants the duchy for himself. Well, it's hardly a surprise. He's resented my existence all my life. Sooner or later it was bound to come to this. But we can see him off easily enough. Now, let's take this castle. I promise you, gentlemen, we will be dining in its hall tonight.'

'How—' Fitz began, but Montgomery grabbed his arm.

'Don't,' he muttered, too low for William to hear.

Fitz looked at him questioningly.

'You'll see soon enough.'

When he reached his tent, William sent for a priest, telling him to bring ink and a parchment. 'Write me a note, addressing it to the captain of the garrison of Domfront. Say, "These belonged to your friends. If I have to take the castle by force, I will do the same to you too."'

'These what, Your Grace?' the priest asked. 'I mean, what was it that belonged to his friends?'

'Don't worry, Father, that will be obvious.'

William signed the finished note, poured some wax onto the parchment beneath his signature and pressed his ducal seal into it. Then he had the note pinned to the sack of severed hands and feet. It had not been opened since his return to Domfront, but word had already gone round the camp about its gruesome contents.

The sack was placed on a ballista, where a rock would normally go, and was catapulted into the castle.

Barely five minutes later, the gates were opened.

'There,' said William to his companions. 'What did I tell you?'

21

The ducal palace, Rouen

'He's very small,' said William, looking down at his son as he lay in his cradle.

'That's a fine way to greet the future Duke of Normandy,' Matilda replied. 'Of course he's small. He's three months old. Babies are meant to be small.'

'I wasn't. Mother always used to say that I was more like a calf than a baby. My old nurse, Judith, told me that my grip was so strong she had a hard time opening my fists. She said I once grabbed my father's sword and—'

'Stop it! For pity's sake, William, stop going on and on about how big and strong and mighty you are and for once in your life think about someone else!'

William felt the familiar surge of temper rise inside him, that instant reaction to anyone who defied his will. Then, just in time, he caught the pain in Matilda's voice and saw the anguish in her face and the tears in her eyes. The next thing he knew she was sobbing, and he suddenly realised that while he had seen her cry with joy before, and sometimes with anger – though she more often stood up for herself without any resort to tears – this was the first time he had ever seen her truly unhappy. And he, of all people, had been the cause of it.

'Oh my darling, I'm so sorry,' he said, taking her in his arms, utterly mortified by his own stupidity. 'I didn't mean to say anything bad about our beautiful little boy. I just—'

He stopped as it struck him, in the nick of time, that any

attempt to justify what he had said would only make matters worse. 'Well, it doesn't matter. The main thing is that you have been a perfect, wonderful, brilliant wife and given me a fine, healthy baby, and I'm sure that he will grow up to be a great man and a wise ruler and . . .'

He paused, uncomfortably aware that Matilda had not replied to anything he had said, or reacted at all come to that.

'Was that the right thing to say?' he asked.

She kept her head buried against his chest, but at least she nodded.

'And was it what I should have said in the first place?'

There was another nod.

He kissed the top of her head and then, very gently, prised himself a little apart from her and with great care lifted her chin so that she was looking up at him, realising as he did that this was a completely new side to her that he was seeing, much softer and more fragile than he had ever known before.

He looked down into her lovely dark eyes and saw a vulnerability there that made him want to protect her, and keep her safe from all the dangers of the world in which he lived. 'I know I'm no poet or minstrel who's good with fancy words. I'm crude and stupid and I say the wrong things . . . but I love you with all my heart. I think you've done a wonderful, magical thing. And I love our little boy. And . . . What are you doing?'

The look in Matilda's eyes had changed. Now they were wicked and teasing, and a smile was playing around the corners of her mouth. William could feel her breath getting heavier and her fingers were undoing his sword belt, which fell with a clatter to the floor. Then her hand was feeling its way inside his hose and she was giggling and saying, 'Oh, hello!' as it closed on its target, which was suddenly a great deal easier to find.

'I've missed you so much,' she said. 'I can't bear it when you're away.'

'Oh God . . . I miss you too,' William said.

Then he picked her up and carried her to their bed, and they made love twice in quick succession: once with the desperate, animal need to feel their bodies joined as one after far too long apart, and the second time for the sheer pleasure each took in the other.

Afterwards, as they lay side-by-side, basking in contentment, William felt Matilda tense a little. A moment later she giggled again and said, 'Robert slept right through it. What a good little boy.'

'What a good big boy,' William corrected her.

'Just like his papa,' Matilda said, turning towards him

And then she gave her husband his due reward for saying just the right thing.

Book Two:

Rebels and Murderers

August 1052–August 1057

1

Wilton Abbey, Wiltshire, England

'Edith!' The sharp, high-pitched shout cut across the gentle murmur of the convent refectory, causing several of the nuns to look up from their food, and the abbess to cast a look of tight-lipped disapproval towards the table where the young ladies who had been sent to be pupils at Wilton Abbey were taking their breakfast.

Edith of Wessex, Queen of England, scurried at once to answer the call, for she knew that the young lady who had uttered it, a local landowner's daughter called Maud of Tytherly, had a sharp temper and did not like to be kept waiting. Arriving at the girls' table, she gave a respectful little bob, her eyes suitably cast down. 'Yes, miss?'

'This porridge is cold. You should know better than to serve cold porridge, isn't that so?'

'Yes, miss. Sorry, miss.'

'And I like a great deal more cream on my porridge. You should know that by now.' Maud held out the offending bowl. 'Get me another portion, at once!'

'Yes, miss.'

Edith took the bowl, bobbed again and walked away as fast as she could without breaking into a run, which was strictly forbidden. She heard a burst of semi-suppressed laughter behind her as the other girls tittered at Maud's daring. They had all been told that Edith was to be treated as a servant, but even so, it was one thing to know that her royal status had been stripped from her by order of the king, and quite another to be spoken to as if she were a menial peasant.

Ten months had passed since Edward had banished Edith. Autumn had turned into a cold, unforgiving winter. Spring had given way to the height of summer and now the dog days of August were drawing to a close, the swallows were leaving, the apples hung heavy on the boughs and a new autumn would soon be stripping the leaves from the trees. And in all that time there had been no word from her husband.

Perhaps I am dead to him, she thought. Perhaps this is all I have left until the day I die.

The kitchen was in a separate building, detached from the refectory and living quarters, for there was always a danger of the cooks' fires getting out of control. It meant that the moment Edith was out of sight of the nuns, she was free to pick up her skirt and run. In the kitchen, she quickly ladled a helping of hot porridge into an earthenware bowl, poured a generous helping of cream over the top, ignored the curses of the cook, who couldn't decide if she was more cross with the hoity-toity young madam who had demanded a fresh helping or the incompetent scullion who had failed to give her a good enough one to begin with, and dashed back to the refectory.

'I got you warm porridge, miss, as you ordered, and some nice fresh cream,' Edith said when she returned to the table.

Maud looked at the bowl with an air of utter disdain. 'I suppose it will have to do.'

'Thank you, miss.' Edith turned to go but was stopped in her tracks.

'Wait!' Maud commanded. 'I haven't dismissed you.'

Edith heard a little gasp from one of the other girls, who could not believe Maud would have the nerve to take things further. She turned back towards the table. 'Sorry, miss,' she said.

'Tell me, Edith, did you have porridge for your breakfast?'

'No, miss.'

'What did you have?'

Edith told herself not to scream in fury and frustration. She wanted to grab the arrogant little minx by the throat and throttle her. But there was nothing to be gained by an act of disobedience, or any trace of the sin of vanity. Besides, it would only make Maud happy to know that she had succeeded in causing pain. So she just said, 'Some bread, miss.'

'Was it stale bread?' Maud asked, putting a special emphasis on 'stale'.

'Yes, miss.'

'Left over from our supper last night?'

'I should think so, miss.'

'Would you like some nice hot porridge?'

Edith said nothing.

'And some lovely thick cream?'

Still Edith remained silent. Every girl watching her knew what her answer to the questions would be. But to admit it would be to lose whatever tattered shreds of dignity and self-respect she still possessed.

'Well?' Maud insisted. 'I have asked you a question. And when a servant is asked a question by her mistress, she must answer it. So . . . would you like some porridge?'

Edith felt overcome by a sense of confusion that amounted almost to panic. She didn't know what to say or where to turn. 'I . . . I . . . don't know.'

'You don't know? You don't know if you want some—'

'That is quite enough!'

The sound of the abbess's voice stopped Maud of Tytherly dead in her tracks. The other girls, who had all been leaning forward, hanging on her every word, tittering at her cleverness and courage, recoiled into guilty, downcast silence.

'I will not have the servants being treated in this manner! We are all God's children, and even though God has put us all in our places, still He loves us equally and is equally hurt when we suffer. I will deal with you later, Maud. In the meantime, Edith, please come with me.'

'Yes, Reverend Mother.'

The abbess led the way to her private chamber. She closed the door then turned to Edith with her arms held open. 'Come to me, my child.'

Edith did as she was told, for unquestioning obedience had become a matter of course to her now. She felt the abbess's arms wrap around her. It had been so long since she had been treated with any kindness, or felt the warmth of another human body, that her first instinct was to recoil, like a whipped dog that snarls at a hand that just wants to pet it.

But then she heard the gentle voice of the abbess saying, 'Hush now, my child,' and let herself relax against the older woman's warm, sheltering embrace. Tears came to her eyes and she sniffed hard, not wanting to mark the abbess's robe. Still keeping her hands on Edith's shoulders, the abbess stepped back and looked into her eyes. 'It must be so very hard for you, my child, to be brought so low when you have always been raised so high.'

'Yes, Reverend Mother,' Edith said, so used to responding as a servant that it did not occur to her to do anything else.

'You may talk to me freely. I will not judge you. Nor will anything you say go beyond these four walls. Just tell me this . . . how have you been able to bear it?'

'I—' Edith stopped herself and looked at the abbess, still not quite sure if she really was free to speak her mind.

'Please . . . do continue.'

She drew herself up, only realising as she did so how cowed she had been all these months. In a voice she hardly recognised any more, she replied, 'I don't think I *can* bear it.'

'Is there really nothing you can learn from this experience?'

Edith frowned as she considered the question. 'I suppose that in some ways life has become easier. I used to have to make so many decisions: what gowns to wear, what orders to give my household, what to say to His Majesty the king when next I saw him, what gifts to make to this or that church or monastery. There was always someone wanting to know my wishes, so that they could obey them. But now I have no choices. I wear the same robe every day, whatever the weather. I carry out the same tasks. I do whatever I am told. It is a much simpler existence.'

'I quite understand,' the abbess said. 'I am responsible for everyone in this abbey. Their physical and spiritual welfare is my concern. And then there is the upkeep of the buildings and the management of the estates, and the collection of rents and donations and goodness knows what else. Sometimes I think life was so much easier when I was a simple novice, with nothing to do but pray to God and obey my superiors.'

She looked into Edith's eyes. 'Do you see God's purpose in any of this?'

'I try to. I do my very best to accept this as His will. I tell myself that He wishes me to learn what it is like for those less fortunate than myself – or less fortunate than I was, at any rate. I pray that if I should ever be returned to my former station, I will be kinder and more considerate to my servants and the workers on my estates, and more charitable to the poor and needy. For I have learned what it is to be hungry and cold and helpless in this world.'

'That is very good, my child. And perhaps that was the king's purpose, too. For God was surely working through him. Perhaps Our Lord wished you to be a better, more humble, more loving wife to your husband.'

'I have tried, Reverend Mother. I tried so hard, but . . . but . . .'

Edith could no longer hold back the river of tears. Her body shook with sobs and the abbess had to hold her once again and stroke her like a child until she was calm. Edith wiped her face against the rough, grimy wool of her sleeve. 'There is nothing sinful about the act of love between a husband and a wife, is there?'

'No, not if its purpose is the procreation of children.'

'Then why will His Majesty not touch me? Why does he recoil from me?'

'His Majesty is a very devout man,' the abbess said. 'Some even think of him as saintly. Perhaps it is no wonder that he renounces the acts of the flesh.'

'But must he renounce love, too?'

'Have you ever considered that perhaps he does love you very much? This act of penance you are now enduring is so extreme that it must surely pain His Majesty's heart.'

'Do you really think so?' Edith looked up at the abbess. 'May I say anything to you, as I would in confession, knowing that it is for your ears and Our Lord's alone?'

'Of course, my child.'

'I fear that His Majesty takes pleasure in reducing me to this state. He . . . he clapped his hands and laughed when he condemned me to come here.'

The abbess sighed. 'There are indeed times when all of us have difficulty in understanding God's plans for us. But let me ask you this, would you say that you have learned humility during your time here?'

Edith lowered her eyes, bowed her head and, like the servant she was, answered, 'Yes, Reverend Mother.'

'Very well, now, look me in the eye and answer this question. Do you think you have learned that through suffering one can acquire strength?'

Edith frowned. 'I don't understand.'

'Consider this, then. Maud treated you very cruelly just now, did she not?'

Edith nodded.

'And yet you withstood it. Think of the example Our Saviour set us. He is the Son of God, and yet he was betrayed by Judas and sentenced to crucifixion by Pontius Pilate. He walked to Golgotha, carrying his cross, with a crown of thorns around his head, mocked by the crowds, brought as low as the most common criminal. He suffered. He was treated with unbearable cruelty. He died in agony upon the cross. And yet where is He now?'

'In heaven, Reverend Mother.'

'Yes, child, Our Saviour is in heaven, with all the hosts of angels around Him. He turned suffering into triumph. Perhaps you can follow in His footsteps.'

'But how?'

'By making your suffering your strength, and pain your path to redemption. Let your humility exalt you. Love your husband more deeply, even when he turns from you. Devote yourself to being his queen, even when he casts you out. Then perhaps one day you will sit beside him in glory once again, just as Our Saviour sits beside the Father.'

Edith felt herself filled with hope, as if there might still be a chance that she would be freed from this servitude. She was about to thank the abbess for all she had said when there was a hammering on the door so loud and forceful that it could only have been made by a male fist.

Sure enough, the door opened to reveal a tall, fair-haired man, closely followed by a nun who hurried in after him, protesting, 'I tried to keep him out, Reverend Mother, I tried!'

The man looked around the room, his gaze passing over the abbess until it settled on the half-starved, hollow-eyed figure in a filthy hessian dress that was little more than a sack with sleeves. He stared at her, aghast, until he finally gasped, 'Edie!'

'Harold?' Edith replied uncertainly, for she could hardly believe that her brother was in England, let alone at Wilton Abbey. 'What are you doing here?' There was uncertainty and even fear in her voice, for the bitter experiences she had endured over the past twelve months had taught her always to expect the worst.

'I've come to take you back to the king.'

Harold stepped a little closer, his eyes still wide in shock. Edith presumed that he'd expected to find her dressed in a nun's habit. The sight of her in a servant's filthy rags, with the marks of tears still fresh on her unwashed face, had brought a look of horror-struck pity to his face, followed by a fierce anger.

He turned his attention back to the abbess. 'What have you done to her?' he asked furiously. 'How dare you mistreat the Queen of England in this way?'

'My lord, please, I meant no harm . . .' the abbess began.

Edith ran to Harold and clung to his arm, as if afraid that he might raise it against the abbess. 'It wasn't her fault,' she said. 'She was only obeying the king's commands. Edward said that I was guilty of treachery, just for being Father's daughter. He asked the Archbishop of Canterbury how he thought I should be punished, and it was the archbishop who said that I should be sent here, as a penance, to work as the most lowly servant in the abbey.'

'Well, he'll rue the day that thought ever crossed his mind, I can promise you.'

'Hush, Harold, don't say that . . .' Edith paused and stepped back a pace from her brother, though she still held his right hand. 'Just tell me, what are you doing here? Is Father back in England too?'

Harold looked around the room at the abbess, the nun who

had tried to deny him entry and a third who had followed her in. They were all watching in rapt fascination, for they were as keen as Edith was to discover what had happened to bring the once-disgraced Harold Godwinson, son of the treacherous Earl of Wessex, back to England and into their own small rural nunnery.

Sadly for them, however, Harold had no intention of sharing his news with anyone but his sister. 'If you would be so good as to leave us in peace, Reverend Mother, I need some time alone with Her Majesty.'

'But my lord, this is my personal—'

'Get out . . . please, and take your sisters with you.'

The nuns left the room. It was a simple whitewashed chamber, lit by a single window. On the wall there was a crucifix and a small painting of the Virgin Mary with the infant Jesus. The only furniture consisted of the abbess's bed, with a thin blanket upon it, the desk at which she worked and a pair of plain wooden chairs.

Harold arranged the chairs so that they were opposite one another. 'Sit down, Edie, for heaven's sake. I can't bear to see you like this. I'll make Edward pay for what he's done to you, by God I will.'

'No, please don't,' Edith replied. 'The last thing we need is even more conflict between our family and the Crown. You forget, he's my husband. I've sworn a vow in the sight of God to love, honour and obey him. It tears me in two when my own father and brothers are fighting him. And I'm the one who pays the price . . .'

Harold nodded thoughtfully. 'You're right. You have suffered for what we have done. I just never thought Edward could do anything like this to you. None of us did . . .'

'Well, it's done now, and perhaps it's for the best.' Edith was suddenly struck by a sharp twist of resentment in her heart. It struck her that she felt it not towards Edward, but Harold. It made no sense to her. Why would she suddenly feel bitter and even angry towards the brother who had come to rescue her, rather than the husband who had caused her distress in the first place?

It was not a question she could answer for the moment, and so she did her best to brush the whole thing to one side. 'Tell me, what have you all been up to?'

Harold grinned. He was completely unaware of Edith's feelings.

Why would he be aware? a voice inside her said. He never cares about anyone's feelings but his own.

She forced herself to concentrate all her attention on Harold as he said, 'It's a long story, but the gist of it is that I went off to Ireland and Papa went to Flanders with Sweyn and Tostig.'

'Are they back too? I can't wait for us all to be together again!'

'Tostig is . . . and with his new wife, Judith of Flanders.'

'Is she nice? Is Tostig happy with her?'

'Funnily enough, I think he is. It turns out Judith is a perfectly sweet girl. She seems to cheer Tostig up. Makes him less irritable. So that's a blessing.'

'Good, I'm glad they're happy. And how about Sweyn? I know he's done terrible things, but I worry about him. I sometimes think he must be possessed by a demon, the way he behaves. It must be awful for him to have a creature like that inside him.'

'Well, he might not be possessed by demons any more. Believe it or not, Sweyn has gone off on a pilgrimage to Jerusalem.'

'No! I don't believe it! When did that happen?'

'Pretty soon after they all arrived in Bruges. Sweyn just announced he was walking barefoot to Jerusalem. It was completely out of the blue. One day he was his usual self, getting drunk in taverns, picking fights, causing trouble. The next he was off to the Holy Land in search of forgiveness and redemption.'

'I do hope he's found them.'

'Well, we're pretty certain he reached Jerusalem. A couple of Flemish merchants who had been in Constantinople had word of him passing through the city, and then a priest who had been on a pilgrimage of his own came back to Bruges with stories of Sweyn giving splendid donations to the church that stands on the site of Our Lord's crucifixion.'

'The Church of the Holy Sepulchre,' said Edith. 'The Saracens destroyed it but it's recently been rebuilt. It's supposed to be quite magnificent. I envy Sweyn for seeing it. We should pray for his safe return home.'

'Yes, we should, but let me tell you what happened first. I sailed to England from the west and Father came from the east and we met up at Portland, in Dorset. From there we sailed along the south coast, from west to east, picking up more ships and men as we went until we came around Kent and into the Thames. Just like last year, we made our camp in Southwark. But now the people were with us, and they led us over the bridge into London. Soldiers were coming from all over the country, rallying to our cause, and this time Edward was on his own. Leofric and Siward refused to support him against us. They stood aside and left us to it. So he had to back down. Our exiles have been revoked. All the accusations against Papa have been dropped and his earldom and lands have been returned to him.'

'But how is the king? Is he well? Is he still safe upon the throne?'

Harold frowned in puzzlement. 'How can you ask after him like that, after all he has done to you?'

161

Even as he asked the question, Harold must have realised it was a foolish one, for Edith had already told him that her marriage vows were still sacred to her.

She said nothing, and in the silence that fell upon the room it was as though something changed inside her. The feelings inside her crystallised, like the moment cold water turns to ice, and at once she understood why she felt this sudden acrimony towards her brother. She was furious that she, who had always been loyal to the king, had suffered so terribly for the treachery of her father and brothers. And all the time she had been locked away, in miserable servitude, they had been gallivanting around without a care in the world. Now Harold had turned up with that same blithe confidence that everything would turn out exactly as he wanted it (how that casual arrogance must have driven poor Tostig mad all these years!) and had found her reduced to the state of a helpless, cringing, weeping wretch. And that, Edith now saw, was the thing that she hated most of all: his pity.

In her bitterness, she also understood why Edward was filled with such bile, for he must always have felt exactly as she did now, towards the Normans upon whose hospitality he had relied, and the Godwins who, though his subjects, were so much richer than him. She felt a new communion with her husband, a sense that she would now find it much easier and more fulfilling to be his wife. And it struck her that, for all that had happened, her marriage had not been dissolved, which meant that her rank still applied.

Edith looked at Harold with a new resolve in her eyes. She sat straighter in her chair, squared her shoulders and raised her chin. 'Is that the sort of question a subject should ask of his queen?'

'No,' said Harold, and then, realising that more was expected of him, added, 'No, Your Majesty. It is not. Please forgive my impertinence.'

'Very well then, can you tell me where the king is presently residing?'

'At the palace of Winchester, Your Majesty.'

'Then please be good enough to escort me there at once. His Majesty has plainly been obliged to endure a trying few months. At a time like this, he needs the unfailing support of his loyal and loving wife.'

2

A brothel in Constantinople

Sweyn Godwinson leaned somewhat unsteadily against a marble pillar in what claimed to be the finest whorehouse in all the Byzantine Empire. He surveyed its human merchandise, who were draped almost naked over an assortment of divans, large cushions and intricately patterned rugs, like a starving man confronted with half a dozen plump, juicy, well-basted roast chickens rotating before him on a spit.

He had been travelling for the best part of a year now, all the way from the damp, boggy climes of Flanders to the dust and heat of Jerusalem. By completing his pilgrimage and donating very generously to a number of churches and religious institutions in the holiest of cities, he had attended to the care of his immortal soul. Now, though, it was time to satisfy the urges of his mortal flesh: first a good long drink of wine – several long drinks, in fact – and then a night of rampant fornication with as many of the women currently giving him come-hither looks as he could fit onto a very large bed.

Sweyn was about to take a few steps towards the houris, for the purposes of closer investigation, when he saw the women's eyes dart towards a door that had opened to reveal the brothel's proprietor, a bald-pated, desiccated old goat called Johans of Perpignan, leading three more men into the hall. They were all much taller than any natives of the city, broad-shouldered and bearded, with blue eyes and long fair hair. Plainly they were Norsemen, and from their red cloaks, tunics and trousers, all richly embroidered in gold, not to mention the swords that hung from their belts, Sweyn realised they must be Varangian guards.

The largest and most lavishly costumed of the three, whose cloak was held by a jewelled gold clasp that even Sweyn, heir to the greatest fortune in England, could not help but admire, looked around the room. He caught Sweyn's eye, grinned, held up a hand in greeting and then dismissed Johans before marching across the room in Sweyn's direction.

Sweyn racked his brain. Did he know this man? Had he offended him at some point? God knows he'd made enough enemies in his time. But even he had not had the chance to spark up any fresh antagonisms in Constantinople. He'd only been to the city once before in his life, on the outward journey to Jerusalem, when he had been on his very best behaviour, like a true penitent pilgrim.

In any case, the Varangians all seemed cheerful enough, more like old friends than long-standing adversaries. Sweyn turned to meet them, thanking God that he was a well-built man himself and could look them right in the eye.

The first Varangian stopped, frowning almost as if he was embarrassed. 'Excuse me, sir, but are you by any chance Sweyn Godwinson?'

He spoke Danish, a tongue in which Sweyn was fluent, for his mother was a Dane and he had spent time in that country.

'Yes,' Sweyn replied cautiously. 'And who is addressing me?'

'People call me Arne the Red. I am a captain in the emperor's guard, and these are my comrades, Leif Carlsson and Erik Magnusson.'

'Well then, good day to you, Arne the Red, and to your comrades, too.'

Hearty handshakes were exchanged and then Sweyn said, 'Might I ask how you knew who I was?'

'Ach, we all know about the exploits of Sweyn Godwinson. Good God, man, you are a legend among us Varangians. We all enjoy tall tales about wild men who drink and fuck and fight. And who has done more of any of those things than you?'

Sweyn could not help but feel flattered. 'I have done my share, it's true. And now, if you will excuse me, I'd like to fuck one, or possibly several of these young women . . .'

'Ha! I'm sure you would, you old dog!' Arne laughed. 'But stay and talk a while. Then I will have Johans prepare a steam bath for you, so that you can sweat the dust of the road from your skin. When you come out, one of his girls will attend to you – one of the good ones, the Circassians, the loveliest women in all the Empire. She will oil your body and scrape away the sweat and filth. She will massage the fatigue from your legs and back and shoulders and neck. Then she will lead you to a pool, and when you feel the shock of the cold water, your whole body will be filled with energy and desire. My friend, you will be as hard as an Egyptian obelisk and you will nail this beauty, and a dozen more just like her, and you will know pleasure like none you have ever experienced.'

'Sounds good. Now show me you mean it. Get me some wine, and ask one of these Circassians to bring it.'

'Of course,' Arne said. He turned to his two men. 'Leif, go and have a word with Johans. Tell him we had better have the very best he has to offer, or I will personally slice off his balls and offer him to the empress for service as a eunuch.'

When Leif Carlsson returned from his errand, two women were walking beside him, both completely naked. One carried a silver tray on which stood a jug filled with deep purple-red wine. The other held an identical tray bearing four crystal goblets. A Moor carrying a wooden table accompanied them.

He placed the table next to Sweyn. The women, moving with the grace of proud princesses, put the jug and glasses on the table, handed their trays to the servant and then stood in front of Sweyn, offering themselves for his inspection.

They were each perfect, but in delightfully different ways. The one to his right was fair in colouring, slender and sleek, with long legs, boyish hips, small but pert inviting breasts and a beautifully formed face, with high, delicate cheekbones, a neat upturned nose and a cool, haughty mouth, with lips of the palest pink. She was looking at Sweyn with a detached, superior expression that made him want to show her who was master.

You'll heat up soon enough once the ice is broken, won't you, bitch?

The second Circassian, to his left, was a much more willing proposition. She was built for pleasure, with a nice big rump to hold onto and full breasts to squeeze and slap and suck. And the way her eyes were half closed and her full lips were slightly parted made it obvious that she was already hot and wet and ready for action.

Sweyn grinned. 'Tell you what, Arne, you were damn well right about Circassians. I'm getting hard just looking at them. So forget the conversation and the bath. I'll just find a room and show these two what an Englishman is made of.'

Arne smiled. 'Not so fast, Sweyn Godwinson. You can have these women. And I'll make sure that Johans doesn't charge you for them, or this wine, which, by the way, I insist you sample . . .'

He barked out a few words in a language Sweyn did not understand, and the cool, slim girl poured Sweyn some wine and handed it to him.

'Mary, mother of God, that is delicious!' Sweyn exclaimed. The heady perfume of the wine rose from the glass and its taste was soft and filled with the flavour of fruit and spice.

'Drink more, relax,' said Arne, sounding like the perfect solicitous host. 'These lovelies will be yours for the taking soon enough. But not just yet.' He gave them another order and they walked away, allowing Sweyn a delicious view of their departing rumps.

'So,' said Arne, 'there is something I have to ask you.'

Sweyn gave an amiable shrug. 'Be my guest.'

Suddenly all the good humour drained from Arne's face and his eyes were as cold and blue as the Arctic sky. 'Why did you kill Bjorn Estrithson?'

Sweyn looked as startled as if he'd been slapped. He gave a half-hearted laugh. 'Whoa! What did you say?'

Arne remained calm but forceful. 'I said, why did you kill Bjorn Estrithson? He was your cousin, your own blood. Why did you kill him?'

A defensive, almost resentful tone entered Sweyn's voice as he asked, 'What is it to you?'

'Bjorn was my cousin too. We are all related: you, Bjorn and me. We all had the same grandfather, Thorkel Sprakling. Bjorn's father was Ulf Jarl, Thorkel's oldest son. My father was Eilaf Thorgilsson, the second son.'

'And my mother is Thorkel's daughter Gytha, wife of Godwin of Wessex,' said Sweyn. 'You should have given me your real name, Arne Eilafsson, told me that we were family. It would have saved a lot of time.'

'Maybe, but I am a fair man. I wanted to give you a chance to show me that you were anything other than a drunken, lecherous, violent shit.'

Sweyn did his best to retain his habitual devil-may-care attitude. 'I object to being labelled a shit, but the rest I'll admit. Anyway, it's not so long ago that you were praising me for all my drinking, fucking and fighting. Why be such a pompous prick about it now?'

'There is a difference between fighting fairly, like a man, and killing a member of your own family in cold blood,' Arne said. 'What happened between you and Bjorn?'

A bitter, malicious sneer crossed Sweyn's face, revealing the true man beneath his jovial exterior. 'The two-faced little shit betrayed me, that's what. While I was away, my old man gave half my estates to my brother Harold, and the other half to Bjorn. And when I say "my estates", I mean a stretch of land that ran right across five shires, all the way from the Berkshire Downs to the furthest edge of Herefordshire, up on the Welsh marches.'

'So you killed him over some land?'

'Partly that.' Sweyn reached for the wine jug, saw that it was empty and threw it away in disgust. It smashed on the stone floor. He threw his glass after it. 'Are you a priest in disguise?' he asked Arne. 'This is meant to be a whorehouse, not a confession box.'

The Dane said nothing, just kept looking into Sweyn's eyes as if he were boring into his very soul.

Sweyn stared back for a moment and then looked down, breaking the contact, conceding defeat. 'Very well, then, I'll tell you. A few years back, I fucked a nun, the Abbess of Leominster, to be precise. People said it was rape; total nonsense. That bitch was hot for it, believe me. Anyway, that dickless old misery-guts Edward packed me off to exile. I went for a while, and then I came back, but without the king's permission. So I needed someone to go to him, plead my case. And I asked Bjorn to do it.'

'And did he?'

'Like fuck he did. That slimy shit said I had no right to return to England. And . . . I don't know, I was just angry. Me and my men took him prisoner on my ship. And I killed him. Nothing fancy. I just got out my sword, and before he had time to pull his from its scabbard, I'd stuck him deep in the guts like—'

'This,' Arne said, reaching for his own sword.

Sweyn sprang back, away from Arne, trying to escape. But the other two Varangians were blocking his way. They grabbed his arms from behind and pulled them backwards and to the sides, so that his chest and belly were opened up and defenceless as Arne the Red stabbed his blade four times deep into Sweyn's guts, ripping his intestines, slicing into his liver and skewering one of his kidneys.

Sweyn had screamed in pain and terror as the first cut was made, but by the fourth he was silent, hanging limp and lifeless in his captors' grasp.

Arne nodded to Carlsson and Magnusson to let go, and the oldest son and heir presumptive to the Earl of Wessex fell dead on the tavern floor.

Arne summoned Johans of Perpignan. 'Clear up this mess,' he instructed. Then he led the other two out onto the street. They were Varangians, and neither Johans nor any other man in Constantinople would breathe a word against them. Not if he valued his life.

3

The ducal palace, Rouen

Talou's power seemed to spread across the duchy like a thorny bramble climbing unstoppably up and around the branches of a tree. His lands stretched from the small fishing village of Dieppe, on the furthest northern shore of Normandy, all the way down to the forest of Brotonne, which lay on the southern banks of the Seine, to the west of Rouen. He made no secret of the fact that he was establishing his position as the lord to whom all the lesser nobles of the region – bar a few who still remained true to William and the Duchy of Normandy – owed their loyalty. That he was a threat went without saying. What William could do about him, however, was another matter.

'Everything Talou's got, he owes to our family,' he told Matilda bitterly. 'Some of it he inherited from his father. A lot of it he was granted by my guardians, to keep him sweet. But it's all ducal land. I could take it back and be entirely within my rights. That damn castle of his, too . . . he was given the right to build it and live in it by the duchy. But it's not his, not really. I could stick my own men in there as the garrison and he couldn't object.'

'But he would object, wouldn't he?' Matilda replied.

'Yes, he would.'

'And then what would you do?'

William sighed. 'I know, you're right. There's no sense provoking a fight with him.'

'It will come soon enough, I'm afraid. But you mustn't be

the one who starts it, because whoever starts it will be in the wrong.' Matilda paused, and William watched her while she thought something through. He knew it would be worth waiting for.

'I love watching you,' he said. 'I know that you're dreaming up something much more cunning than I'd ever think of.'

'Ssshhh! Don't distract me!' she hissed, though he could see she was pleased by his compliment.

Finally she said, 'Right . . . now I know what to do.'

'And?'

'And it's very simple. You wait until you are ready to start the war, or when you know that if you don't start it soon, your uncle will be too powerful to beat.'

'Yes, all right. Then what?'

'Then you make him start it.'

'I'm sorry, I don't understand.'

'That's because you don't think like a woman. Every mother teaches her daughters, "You can make your husband do exactly what you want, but only if he thinks it's his idea."'

William laughed. 'You don't do that. You make it perfectly plain that it's your idea.'

'Yes, well, I'm different.' Matilda smiled smugly. 'Anyway, you have to play that game with your uncle Talou. When you think the time is right, send a company of men up to occupy his castle. That's your right, after all. Let him know that he is still free to live there, so he can't complain that he's been kicked out. Just say that for reasons of . . . oh, I don't know . . .'

'Security,' said William. 'I can say that for the safety and security of the people of Normandy, I want my men up there to defend against any attacks from the counties of Ponthieu or Picardy. They're just across the border from Arques.'

'What about Flanders?' Matilda said. 'Aren't you afraid of my father invading?'

'Why should I be?' William grabbed her round the waist. 'I'm keeping his daughter hostage.'

'Oh, is that what I am? And there I was thinking I was your wife.'

'You are my beloved wife, and I will happily take advantage of that fact very soon . . . but not before you've finished explaining your plan.'

'It's very simple. You move in your men. You give a reason Talou can't quarrel with. Then you wait until he can't stand it any longer . . .'

'And he kicks out my men, which is a hostile act, so I have to respond, but he has started it, so I am in the right. Well done!'

'Thank you, my lord. Now, do you wish to take advantage of me?'

'I do . . . but I have one other question.'

'I may not be able to answer it. I'm just a feeble woman, after all,' she said, and William felt her fingers moving over him and knew that very soon he would be unable to control himself. He grabbed her wrist. 'Wait, you wicked little harlot.'

'That's right, I'm a harlot,' she murmured throatily, 'kept as a hostage by an evil duke, but I'm just so wicked, I can't stop myself . . .'

'Oh the hell with it,' William said.

Some time later, Matilda reminded him, 'You had a question, I believe . . .'

'Mmm, yes,' he said, running his hand down the curve of her back and over her perfect little rump. 'It was about your uncle, King Henry.'

'Why are we always talking about uncles?' she enquired frivolously. 'Why are they such trouble?'

'I have no idea, but yours has suddenly become best friends with Geoffrey Martel of Anjou.'

'I thought they were at war. I liked that. The longer they were at war, the longer we were at peace and you didn't have to go off to fight, and the more time you could spend with me instead.'

'I know, but I have a feeling it's about to end. I've had reports that Henry and Martel have made peace. They're even witnessing charters jointly. I don't like the sound of that. It makes me nervous, makes me wonder if they're uniting against me.'

'It would make sense,' said Matilda. 'I'm sorry to say that, but it's true. You have to remember one thing about the kings of France – they have less land under their direct control now than at any time since their kingdom was founded. I know because my mother never stops talking about it. The whole family is obsessed with the legend of Charlemagne and his empire that covered all Christendom, and how low they have sunk since then. You know how you feel about your uncle Talou, that he only has his land because your family let him have it?'

'Yes.'

'I bet that's exactly what Henry thinks when he looks at Normandy. I'm sure he thinks of old King Charles giving all the land between the River Epte and the sea to Rollo the Viking, and then he thinks, "I want it back."'

'You know my family's history very well,' said William.

'That's because it's my family's history too!'

'I suppose it is . . . So now what?'

'Go to the king. Assure him of your devoted loyalty. Tell him you have a problem with the Count of Talou.'

'Won't that put ideas into his head? He might think of becoming allies with him too.'

'He already has!'

'Become Talou's ally?' William was genuinely alarmed at the idea.

'Not necessarily, not yet . . . but he's certainly thought about it, because everyone knows what Talou is doing and what he wants in the end.'

'I can see what the agreement between them would be; it's so obvious. Talou keeps Upper Normandy, north of Rouen. Martel takes Bellême and maybe the Hiémois or the Cotentin. The king takes back everything in between. I'd go for that if I were in their shoes. And I'm not sure I can persuade the king not to do it, if he's already got his mind set on taking back Normandy. Even if I were to try to make an agreement with him, I'd have to give away so much, the duchy would barely exist. And it would be so weak, it would be swallowed up in no time – every one of our neighbours would want a bite of the pie.'

'You're right, my darling. You can't stop Henry or Martel or Talou from doing what they want to do. But if you speak to the king, at least you'll be able to get some sense of what he's up to. And maybe . . .' She let the word hang in the air.

'Yes?'

'Maybe I could come with you. I am His Majesty's niece, after all, and he does have a new wife, Anne, who's come all the way from Kiev, so the least I can do is welcome her to the family. Henry may not tell you everything you want to know. But I'll find it all out from Her Majesty the queen. You can count on me.'

'I know,' said William. 'I do. Always.'

4

Falaise, Domfront and Alençon

The first time William of Normandy travelled to meet the King of France it was as a small boy. The second time it was as a desperate young man of nineteen. But the third time it was as Duke of Normandy, and when he journeyed south to King Henry's hunting lodge, half a day's ride east of Orléans, it was more akin to a royal progress than a vassal going to meet his sworn liege lord.

Before William left Rouen, he gave orders for a company of his own men to replace those of Talou on the battlements of the castle of Arques. Then he rode out of the city at the head of the column, with Rob and Fitz to either side of him. They were joined by his other half-brother, Odo, Bishop of Bayeux, whom William considered a more appropriate, not to mention less embarrassing, representative of the Norman clergy than Talou's brother Mauger, Archbishop of Rouen.

Baby Robert had been left behind at the ducal palace with his nurse, but although Matilda was joining William on his visit, she was once again with child, so a carriage had been provided for her. As the hours and days went by, however, and the sun beat down upon the carriage roof, the atmosphere within became increasingly hot and airless. The ride was bumpy, too, and it bored Matilda to sit with a pair of her female attendants, who talked about nothing but gowns, jewels and other fripperies, and the attractions or otherwise of the knights whom William had selected as their escort. So from time to time she mounted her palfrey, which she had insisted on bringing with them, tethered to the carriage, and, ignoring the women's fretful warnings of what this might do to her womb and its new inhabitant, rode up the column to be with William and his companions.

The summer weather was warm, the countryside was looking at its best, and wherever they went the peasants working in the fields would stop whatever they were doing and run to the side of the road to see their duke and his duchess go by. As long as they were in Normandy, there was always a castle in which they could spend the night, where the local lord would make a great show of loyalty, feeding them with the finest produce from his estate and often giving up his own marriage bed so that William and Matilda might have it.

They passed a night in Falaise, where William had been born, and he took great delight in telling the story of how his father had first seen his mother Herleva when she was dancing with her friends and asked her to join him for dinner that very night.

'He wanted Mama to enter the castle through the postern gate, round the side where no one would see her, but she refused. She wasn't having people saying she'd sneaked in, as if she had something to be ashamed of. She insisted on coming in through the main gate, with her head held high. I remember Papa, before he went off to Jerusalem, saying how proud he'd been of her, how she carried herself like a duchess right from that very first night.'

William introduced Matilda to his uncles Osbern and Walter, Herleva's older brothers, who still lived in the area. Both men had done well out of their family's unlikely association with the House of Normandy, but their new-found wealth and status had not changed the men they were at heart: uneducated and unsophisticated, yes, but also tough, decent, honest and

177

straightforward. They did not say much, but they meant what they said, and meeting them made Matilda realise how important and valuable William's common blood was to him. He might be a duke, but he had the physical strength, the rugged constitution and the blunt honesty of a peasant.

They stopped at Domfront, where the mound on which William's siege tower had stood was still visible, though the timbers for the tower itself had been carted away and placed in storage for future use. William showed Matilda the place where Martin the poacher had lost his life trying to scale the walls, and where he himself had taken a nasty fall. They walked arm-in-arm across the field between the castle and the woods and he told her how he had stopped his pell-mell dash for the cover of the trees to go back for his wounded soldier. A little way on, he stopped and looked back at the castle, then forward to the woods. 'I was just about here, I reckon, when that poor man took an arrow that was meant for me. If I hadn't been carrying him, it would have hit me right between the shoulder blades. I'd have been stone dead, just like that.'

He gave a casual flick of his fingers, but Matilda pulled him closer. 'Don't, please . . . don't talk like that. I can't bear to think of you being killed, me being alone, Robert growing up without a father. All this fighting . . . and over what? This is just another castle.'

'Every castle in Normandy is just another castle,' William said. 'But at any one time, any of those castles might hold the key to the whole duchy, and defending a castle I already have, or taking one that I don't have, might make the difference between me still being Duke of Normandy and losing my title, my land or even my life. That's what it's like for people like us. You know that, my darling.'

'I do know that, but sometimes I wonder why it has to be like this. My father fought with my grandfather for control of

Flanders. My uncle Henry fought with his father and his brothers for the throne of France. Then you all have to fight to stay where you are. What's the point of it?'

William shrugged. 'The Lord God has his plan for all of us, and we just have to accept what is in store.'

'Mmm . . .' Matilda replied non-committally, and there the conversation ended, though it remained on her mind through the three days she and William spent in Alençon as guests of Montgomery and Mabel. Matilda found them a fascinating couple. For all the mutual benefits that their union provided, this was very clearly more than just a marriage of convenience. But they made such an unlikely pair of lovers. Montgomery was a pillar of decency and rectitude, determined to mark himself as different from his rebellious father and murderous brother. Yet he had married a woman who, for all her ravishing looks and undoubted charm, seemed more obviously dangerous, not to say wicked, than anyone Matilda had ever met. She wondered whether Mabel's beauty and wealth had simply blinded her new husband to the defects of her character – in which, from all that Matilda could gather, she was following in a family tradition that was even more reprehensible than that of the House of Montgomery. Or was that, in fact, the reason why he had fallen in love with her? Was it her very wickedness that had drawn him into her web?

These were not questions that Matilda put to William. So far as he was concerned, the joining together of Montgomery and Bellême was entirely beneficial to his interests. He would not appreciate that judgement being questioned. Nor was there any reason to do so, for Matilda had not detected any desire, even on Mabel's part, to undermine William or challenge his dominion.

In any case, there were other subjects she wished to raise with her husband: other topics to which to return. They had stopped one night at a monastery and were taking a stroll in the cloisters when Matilda said, 'I've been thinking about your mother. You know, since we were at Falaise . . .'

'Me too,' William replied.

'Did she always love your father?'

'Always, till the day she died.'

'But was she happy, in the end, when she went to live in Conteville with Herluin?'

'Oh yes.'

'It's so strange, your father giving the woman he loved to his best friend.'

'I suppose if you put it like that, yes. But Herluin is the nicest, most decent, most loyal man you could ever meet. He was always kind to me. He loved Mama very much and she loved him too. Not in the same way she loved Papa, maybe, but she loved him for being so kind to her and because he was such a good father to Odo and Rob.'

'Is the Conteville estate a nice place?'

'Very. It's just on the south bank of the Seine, close to the sea, so there are woods to hunt boar and deer, or you can go fishing and wildfowling in the marshes along the coast.'

'I can see why your mother was happy. What woman wouldn't be? To live in a beautiful place, with a man who loved her, her boys to look after and all the business of the estate to fill her days. It sounds like bliss.'

'Ah well, you will just have to make the best of the task God has set you, to be duchess of Normandy and one day queen of England. Your sons and grandsons will be kings and dukes in their turn, and your daughters will marry princes.' William smiled down at Matilda, 'It's not such a bad life really.'

'No,' said Matilda. 'But our uncles and their allies want to take it all from us.'

'And that, my darling, is why we have to fight.'

5

The royal hunting lodge, Vitry-aux-Loges, France

The moment she stepped down from her carriage, took her place by William's side and curtseyed before the King and Queen of France, Matilda knew that this trip, far from helping relations between Normandy and France, would only make them worse. William was too commanding a presence, so physically dominant that King Henry could only seem smaller and inferior by comparison. The contrast was echoed by their retinues. The Normans were altogether younger, more handsome, more richly dressed and armed than their French counterparts. They were young bucks laying down a challenge for which their French elders would surely resent them.

Matilda had not realised until then quite how wealthy Normandy was. William's entire life had been consumed by the struggle to hold onto his dukedom and establish his rule in the face of opposition from within his own family, from other Norman families and from rival houses in neighbouring lands. Yet the gathering of taxes, tolls, import duties and the various payments that had to be made for the right to farm, hunt, cut wood or catch fish had somehow carried on unceasingly through all the apparent anarchy.

The royal domain of France, however, seemed to have provided far less wealth for its monarch. Or perhaps it was just that the cost of being king, paying an army, keeping up appearances was just much greater.

For her part, the queen was clearly of Nordic blood, for she was a strapping, broad-shouldered, big-breasted creature, with thick flaxen hair, bright blue eyes and a broad, sensuous mouth, and even William, faithful as he was, was casting glances in her direction. Her gown was made of a beautiful patterned silk that must have come from a Saracen loom, for no weaver in Christendom could have fashioned it. But that, Matilda felt sure, had travelled with Queen Anne from Kiev. King Henry could never have bought it for her in France.

'So, young Normandy, I gather your cousin King Edward of England has promised you his throne,' Henry said as they walked into the royal lodge.

Damn! thought Matilda. If Henry thinks William might be king of England one day, all the more reason to nip him in the bud before that happens.

'So I am led to believe, Your Majesty,' William replied.

'You sound strangely sceptical. Have you any reason to doubt His Majesty's promise? It is the word of a king, after all.'

'I doubt every man's word when I have not heard it from his own lips, nor had proof that it is meant.'

Matilda gritted her teeth. She knew that her uncle was bound to take William's words as a personal affront. It was all she could do to stop herself grabbing her husband by the arm and telling him to stop talking, now, before he made matters even worse.

'But, Your Majesty, while I may not trust a man's word, I still hold him to it. He may be speaking dishonestly, or he may change his mind. But he had best be aware that so far as I am concerned, his word still stands.'

'I see . . .' said King Henry. He smiled as he spoke, but there was not a shred of amusement in his eyes. 'Am I to take it, then, that so far as you are concerned, you are the heir to the throne of England, no matter what King Edward or anyone else may say?'

William was not stupid, Matilda knew that. But she also knew that he either could not or would not play the diplomatic game of fine words, flowery protestations of devotion and friendship and promises that blew away in the air like the seeds of a dandelion. Maybe that was the peasant in him too.

'If King Edward produces a son, then of course I would consider relinquishing my claim,' William said. 'But Your Majesty surely knows that Edward has no interest in fatherhood, and he can hardly sire an heir if he keeps locking his wife away in a convent every time they fall out.'

King Henry gave a little chuckle that was at least partially genuine. 'Indeed not, whereas you clearly have no such lack of interest. My congratulations, Normandy, on the birth of your son.'

'Thank you, sire. My wife is bearing a second child. I am certain that will be a son too.'

The king beamed. 'My dear Matilda, please accept the heartiest congratulations of a loving uncle. What a clever girl you are, producing all these heirs to the Duchy of Normandy.'

'Thank you, Your Majesty,' said Matilda as Henry enfolded her in his arms. And what a fool you have been, William, she was thinking, giving the king yet more reasons to fear you.

6

Queen Anne had barely said a word when she and Henry had met their Norman visitors, and when Matilda was invited to attend upon her in her private chamber while the men got on with their discussions, she understood why. Anne's command of her new country's language was still unsophisticated, and her husband's Frankish courtiers, steeped in arrogance and condescension would be only too tempted to mock her for it.

Once they were alone, Matilda suggested that she might prefer to converse in Latin, but Anne insisted not. 'I am a France queen, so must speak like France people, no?'

'That is very wise of you, Your Majesty, and, if I may say so, very brave as well,' said Matilda, meaning it, for she could not imagine how she would have coped if she'd been packed off to a husband in Kiev.

'Thank you,' said Anne. She cleared her throat, visibly collected her thoughts and then embarked on what Matilda swiftly realised was a prepared opening gambit to their conversation. 'I am favourite child of father, Yaroslav the Wise One, Grand Prince of all the Rus, yes. But my sister Elisaveta is also a queen. Once she have very pretty face, now I don't know. Since many years she is wife of Harald, King of Norway, who has other name Hardrada, which means, ah, same as . . . how you say word in Latin, "*durus*"?'

'Hard, Your Majesty.'

'Ah, yes, hard, and "*rada*" is his people's word for "council".

So this is hard man in council. He gets what he is wanting . . . even if it hurt other person very much.' Anne's face fell.

'In what way?' asked Matilda.

'Elisaveta very good wife to Harald. She love him, advise him very well how to keep his people happy, though he is often not listening, also obey him as wife should, and is giving him two beautiful daughters.'

Matilda sighed. Any woman of noble birth understood what that meant. 'But no son,' she said sympathetically.

'No.' Anne shook her head disconsolately. 'So now Harald take second wife. Is custom in his country. I think they are not true Christians there, still keep way of old gods.'

'Who is she, this second wife?'

'Name is Tora. Is from powerful family in Norway.'

'That would be helpful to Harald politically, of course.'

'Yes, and also she have two sons, very quick, just like . . .' Anne clapped her hands twice.

'I'm so sorry. That must be terribly hard for Elisaveta.'

'Yes. But she is strong. She knows Harald still love her most and she not let Tora be number one wife. She is a daughter of Yaroslav. She is very very strong.'

That thought seemed to cheer Anne up, so Matilda took the opportunity to move the conversation on. 'Do you have any other sisters?'

Anne beamed. 'Oh yes, my sister Anastasia. She is also queen.'

Matilda was very conscious that she was representing Normandy, and William, and therefore had to put on the best possible show. She clapped her hands in delight. 'How remarkable! Three sisters and each one has married a king. Your mother and father must be so proud.'

'Yes, all queens. Anastasia she marry King Andras from

185

Hungary. And yes, my parents are happy for daughters to be queens, that is normal, no? But still if you take all these kingdoms of the husbands, all together, they are not comparing to my father's lands of Kiev and Novgorod. When I come to Paris, I say, "This is like little village next to Kiev."'

Matilda laughed politely. Evidently encouraged, Anne went on, 'And France is so small, I cannot believe! I tell King Henry, you can ride one side of kingdom to other side in, shall we say, one week. For a man to ride right across lands of Kiev and Novgorod, this is one year he is taking. One year!'

'Incredible!'

'Yes, yes!' Anne gave a little giggle of her own. 'I am saying to Henry, "Your Majesty is need more land!"'

'Oh, that's too funny!'

'I know! Always I say this, "More land! More land!" King Henry, he is laugh and laugh. He tell me, "My best I will do, I promise."'

Matilda made a show of joining in with the hilarity. When it had finally subsided she said, 'It sounds as though you and King Henry are very happy together, Your Majesty.'

By this point Anne had clearly decided that she had found a new bosom friend. 'Oh yes,' she said. 'His Majesty is very nice, very kind, though . . .' she leaned forward conspiratorially, 'I must be telling you, I not like the other ladies in France. They are, I don't know . . .' She grimaced as she struggled for the right words, then sat up straight with her nose in the air. 'Like this, you know? Like I am not as good as them, even being queen and daughter of great prince. But you are not like them, no. So I can tell you, two women talking, I am not with man before I marry, of course.'

'Absolutely. Nor was I,' Matilda replied. Except for all the times William and I lay together, she added silently, but since he was the man I was going to marry, and would have married much sooner if Mauger and the Pope hadn't made it so difficult, that doesn't count.

If any of Matilda's inner thoughts showed on her face, Anne had not noticed. She was clearly longing for the chance to share her experiences with someone sympathetic.

'First time, on wedding night, I am thinking, this is not good. Hurt so much. But I remember Mother say, if you have luck and man is good then it is not so bad next times. And Mother is right! Next time is very good and so we are doing it more times and now we have baby, like you, and is also a boy, Prince Philip, for being King of France.'

'I hope he brings you as much happiness as Robert has brought me.'

'Oh yes. But you are already making second baby. So,' Anne giggled again, 'I am thinking it is good for you too. Though, please excuse, I am rude, but Duke William, he very big man and you so small. Is he hurting you?'

Matilda laughed, with genuine amusement this time, and settled down to talk to Anne about babies, men and all the unexpected delights, but also burdens, of motherhood. Anne was actually a perfectly nice woman, if one simply paid no attention to her references to all the things that were bigger and richer and better in Kiev than in France.

When Matilda complimented Anne on her dress, she discovered that her assumption had been correct: the fabric had been one of the gifts bestowed by the Emperor Constantine on her family when they had paid a state visit to Byzantium.

'It is now since three years I go to Byzantium with my father, Grand Prince, and mother Ingegerd, who is daughter King Olof.' Anne's face fell. 'Now Mother is dead, since month before I leave Kiev for come France.'

'I'm so sorry,' Matilda sympathised.

'Yes, very sad. She very good woman. The people, they call her a saint.'

Anne fell silent.

'You were going to tell me about your trip to Byzantium, Your Majesty . . .'

Anne's face lightened. 'Ah yes! We sail down Dnieper river, which is so long is impossible to say, and wide like a sea.'

'Fascinating . . .'

'Yes, and then come to Black Sea and sail across to Byzantium. Oh my God . . .' Anne crossed herself, 'Byzantium is . . . I don't know words . . . is . . . most best city in world, I am sure.'

With a little help from Matilda, and occasional excursions into Latin, Anne told of the huge churches, magnificent palaces and beautiful broad streets of the capital of an empire that dated back to Ancient Rome. She described fountains playing in gardens; water that came out of pipes inside buildings, so that it did not have to be collected from a well but was available whenever one wanted to drink or wash; magnificent bath houses with both hot and cold pools; staterooms heated by fires that burned under the floor but were sealed so that they gave warmth but without any smoke in the air; and countless other wonders that Matilda thought Anne might be making up, except that how could one possibly even imagine such things?

The time passed very pleasantly and Matilda was happy for her uncle that the bride who had come all this way to marry him should have turned out to be so comely and so companionable.

But when their conversation was done and the two women retired to be with their respective husbands, the words that still echoed in Matilda's head were 'More land! More land!'

She was wondering about the best way to raise the subject when William beat her to it. 'You were right,' he whispered, when they were alone in bed together. 'Henry's after my land, I'm sure of it. And I'd wager that he's making alliances with Martel and Talou as well.'

'What makes you think that? What did he say?'

'It's what he didn't say. I mentioned the threat that I felt Martel still posed to my southern borders, even after we've secured Bellême, and how I looked to the Crown, as master of us all, to maintain the safety of our counties, and he just said he was sure that Count Geoffrey felt that he too was acting within his rights. So then I mentioned Talou and how I suspected he was plotting a rebellion, and Henry just went, "Pah! You are still very young. You worry about everything. I was just the same at your age. Then I learned not to concern myself with trifles." I felt like telling him that it didn't feel like a trifle to me when Talou deserted the siege of Domfront, set himself up in his damn castle and started lording it over most of Upper Normandy.'

'Tell me you didn't actually say that.'

'No, even I wasn't that stupid. I told the king that I thanked him for his advice and I was sure that he was right . . . and I did my very best not to sound sarcastic when I said it, too. But I know he doesn't really think Talou's opposition to me is a trifle.'

'He'll think it's an opportunity.'

'Quite. But let's look on the bright side, my darling. You were, as always, entirely correct to tell me to come and visit the king. Now I know that we were right to be suspicious. He's up to something, for sure.'

'But do you know what, exactly?'

'No, but I don't have to. I just have to wait, and watch, and be ready to move like lightning when there's the first sign of trouble. And that'll do for now.'

* * *

Elsewhere in the lodge, King Henry of France had summoned his chaplain, with orders that he should bring quills, parchments and ink.

'I have two letters that I wish inscribed and dispatched with the utmost urgency,' the king declared. 'In a moment I will dictate a message to William, Count of Arques and Talou. But first, this is to be sent to Geoffrey of Anjou . . .'

7

The port of Hedeby, Denmark

The nickname Hardrada suited Harald of Norway well. He had indeed become hard, but it was the hardness of ice: cold and unfeeling.

He stood now and looked out across the devastation he had wreaked, at the charred, skeletal ruins of buildings, at the corpses strewn and piled about the ground like dead autumn leaves beneath a great tree. And he felt . . . nothing. Absolutely nothing.

It should have meant more than this.

Yesterday, Hedeby had been one of the finest towns in all the kingdoms of the Norse. It lay at the southernmost point of Denmark, hard by the border with the Holy Roman Empire, its prosperity arising from its position at the head of an inlet called the Slien. The Slien was roughly ten leagues long and opened onto the Baltic, thus providing access to Denmark, Sweden, Pomerania and the lands of the Rus. But just a few leagues inland, close enough that ships could easily be rolled on logs across the flat, low-lying countryside, lay the Trenen river, which flowed into the Eider and thence out into the North Sea. From there merchants, slavers and Viking raiders could make their way down the coast to Holland, Brabant, Flanders and all the various Frankish duchies, or sail west to England, Scotland and Ireland. By cutting across the Jutland peninsula from one sea to the other, sailors avoided the long and often dangerous journey up and around its coast.

Hedeby was thus the meeting point of travellers going in either direction: a place for mariners to restock their provisions, trade their wares and indulge their hunger, their thirst and their lust. It was a place where men worked hard, hauling ships out of the water and loading them onto the logs that would roll them across to the Trenen, or taking the vessels that had come the other way off the logs and back into the water.

The harbour and the city were one and the same thing. Every street, each with its tightly packed crowd of small houses, converged on the waterfront. There was a small church, but this was still a pagan place where animals were sacrificed to the old gods and impaled on posts outside the doors of houses to signify the religious devotion of the inhabitants within. Slender, dark-skinned Arab traders from al-Andalus and North Africa, used to a life of incomparably greater sophistication, civilisation and cleanliness, looked on in appalled fascination at the massive Norsemen and their equally well-built woman and noted how both sexes used paint to enhance their eyes; how the women were able to divorce their husbands, but men could not leave their wives; how the drinking songs were low and rumbling, so that they seemed more like the barking of dogs than anything that could possibly be called music.

Or so it had been in Hedeby yesterday. But then, in the dawn light of this particular morning, a mighty fleet, led by King Harald of Norway in the largest and most elaborately decorated of all the longships, had emerged out of the morning mist, sailing down the fjord barely a league from the city. For several years now, Harald had attacked Denmark every summer, so that the sight of his ships on the horizon had become as reliable a marker of the season as the first flocks of swallows flying up from Africa. But never before had he ventured this far south, nor picked such a significant target.

Hedeby possessed no fortifications. None had ever before

been required. So there was no way that Harald and his seaborne army could possibly be kept at bay. The only hope was to flee. But where?

A few ships took to the waters of the fjord, hoping that the ravaging Norwegians would ignore them. But they were like rabbits trying to run from a sky filled with hawks. The fleet just swallowed them up and then passed on, leaving burning, looted ships and their freshly killed crews bobbing in its wake.

Others tried to take the other way out, overland. But there were too many captains trying to get their ships onto too few logs, and soon fights began to break out as the crews battled for the chance to escape. As men stopped fighting with fists or wooden clubs and reached instead for their swords, they did Harald's work for him, slaughtering one another with such abandon that by the time the Norwegians came ashore, the ships held more dead sailors than living.

Not that it would have made any difference, in any case. Harald and his men were hardened by years of fighting against his former ally, Sven Estrithson, King of Denmark. They could not possibly have been defeated.

Harald had brought fireships with him: vessels he was willing to sacrifice by setting them alight and sending them into the harbour. They set ablaze the ships still clustered on the water and beside the jetties, and the flames then spread onshore and feasted on the houses built of birch and pine.

The Norwegians watched while fire consumed Hedeby. They saw the people of the town desperately trying to extinguish the myriad blazes, then, when that task proved impossible, clustering in those few places the flames hadn't reached. Harald smiled. By gathering together like that, they just made themselves easier to slaughter.

When the conflagration had died down a little, Harald sailed his ships right up to the foreshore, jumped into the shallows and ran up the beach with a thousand yelling, whooping, axe-wielding Norsemen hard on his heels.

There were men and women from many lands in Hedeby that morning. Their rulers had no quarrel with Harald. They should have been left in peace. But it was no more possible to tell the ravaging Norsemen to kill one man but not another than it would have been to expect a swarm of locusts to leave a few ears of corn standing as they destroyed an entire field.

Harald was at the head of his men and the heart of the fighting: massive, unflagging and seemingly invulnerable. He wore his favourite chain-mail shirt, which he had christened 'Emma', and swung the same sword that had seen him through all the countless battles he had fought across the Byzantine Empire, in the principalities of the Rus and now in the Norse lands.

Beside him his standard-bearer carried the Raven Banner, the triangular pennant decorated with an embroidered black raven, the symbol of Odin. Harald might be a Christian in times of peace, but when he stepped onto the battlefield he wanted the support of the pagan gods of war.

When it was done, and the houses were just smouldering ruins and all their people dead, Harald and his men went to work collecting whatever valuables had survived the fire and loading them into the one or two merchant vessels that were still intact.

Now the raid was over and Harald was taking one last look at what he had done, trying to understand why he felt so little sense of triumph. Soon he would set his fleet to sea again, return down the Slien and thence back home to Norway. His annual raids were less part of a coherent plan to conquer Denmark than a way of torturing Sven with the knowledge of his own impotence, endlessly reminding him that Harald could come and go as he pleased, ravaging and pillaging without constraint.

But then, just as he was about to turn his eyes away from the ruination of Hedeby and return to the boats, one of his men came running up to him. 'Sire! Sire! A messenger has arrived from Sven of Denmark. He says his master spotted your fleet a week ago and sailed down the coast with his own army. He is camped by the shore of the Slien, less than half a day's march from here. He challenges you to battle on the morrow.'

Now Harald felt his blood grow warm at last. 'Where is this messenger?' he demanded, and was led through the ruins to the outskirts of the town. Three men were waiting there, standing by their horses.

'Which one of you is Sven's errand boy?'

The middle of the trio, a man almost as tall as Harald himself, heavily bearded, with a crest of black hair rising from a tattooed, half-shaven scalp, stepped within a head-butt's range of Harald and looked him right in the eye. 'I am the king's messenger. Will you accept his challenge?'

'Oh yes, your king will have his battle all right. But he need not wait till tomorrow. I'll be coming for him today.'

Harald was as good as his word. His men force-marched along the Slien until they reached the place Sven had chosen for his battle. He had camped atop a low hill that rose from an area of marshland cut through by countless small streams so that there was very little dry ground along which anyone who wanted to seize the hill could advance. With a proper degree of preparation, with pointed stakes set as an obstacle behind which the defenders could take up their positions, it would have been a hard place to assault.

But Sven had not completed his preparations. There were no stakes. There was not even a properly ordered formation of defenders. There was simply a mass of men scurrying around the top of the hill while their commanders desperately tried to get them into good enough order to fight today the battle that had been planned for tomorrow.

Harald's men did not break step. They arrived at the foot of the hill and just kept marching right up it. The men at the top took one look and started fleeing with as much abandon as the merchants at Hedeby had done. Harald could see Sven desperately trying to make his men stand and fight, but it was too late. Panic had seized them, their minds had lost all reason and all they could think of was to run away as fast as possible.

But there was nowhere safe to run.

By the time Harald reached the top of the hill, the Danes were all desperately wading through the streams and marshes below. Wherever he looked, men were falling into the swamp, weighed down by their armour, thrashing about in the water and mud until they finally went under and drowned.

A handful were able to pick their way along the few dry paths that threaded through the marshes to the shore, where the Danes' boats were drawn up. Harald saw Sven being led by a man who seemed to know his way through the maze.

'Do you want us to go after them, sire?' one of Harald's earls asked him.

'No, the water will kill them as well as we ever could, and it would kill us too if we went down there.'

The earl laughed. 'Well, that's the easiest battle I've ever fought. Not a scratch on any of us.'

'That's the way I like them,' said Harald, laughing too as he slapped the earl on the shoulder. 'Now, let's take the men back home.'

As the earl strode away, barking orders for the march back to Hedeby and their ships, Harald was left alone once again with his thoughts, but once again there was no exultation in his triumph.

Sven had escaped to fight again . . . and again. There seemed no end to the constant struggle between them. Sven could never defeat Harald, but neither could Harald secure a victory so conclusive that it would win the war and with it the crown of Denmark. It seemed a poor return for the lengths to which he had gone to become King of Norway, and a poor legacy for his young sons to inherit.

He shook his head ruefully. The conflict at home was no closer to resolution than the one between him and Sven: Elisaveta and her girls on the one side, Tora and her boys on the other. Of the two women, his first wife was his true love, but the second had given him what he needed. He did not want to rid himself of one and could not afford to dispose of the other.

He had climbed all the way to the top of the mountain, only to find that when at last he got there, he did not even like the view.

8

The Old Minster, Winchester, April 1053

Godwin of Wessex was dead. He had been taken ill, very suddenly, while attending a feast given by the king at Winchester Palace and died soon afterwards, with Harold, Tostig and the fourth of the Godwinson brothers Gyrth at his bedside. But though the moment of Godwin's passing was unexpected, the sense that his life was ending had been evident to his family for some time.

'I don't believe he ever got over the news of Sweyn's death,' Harold said to his mother, Gytha Thorkelsdottir, as they stood in the Old Minster, where Godwin was to be buried, looking down at his body lying in an open casket so that the people of Wessex could pay their respects to their lord.

Gytha wiped an uncharacteristic tear from her eye. 'Your father loved all of you, of course he did, and I know that he was particularly proud of the way you have turned out. But a man places all his hopes for the future in his eldest son, that's just human nature. From the day he is born, the firstborn is the one who will carry the family name. Of course Sweyn made your father despair sometimes, the way he behaved. Poor Godwin . . . he used to get so angry, he must have sworn he was going to disinherit Sweyn a thousand times. Still, he always hoped he could be made to grow up and accept his responsibilities. So when he died, that was the end of all those dreams.'

'It can't have helped seeing Edith suffer so much at the king's hands.'

'No, that was awful. You father blamed himself, of course, any father would. He knew the king was, well . . . odd, I suppose you'd say. But he couldn't possibly have predicted that Edward would turn to Edith on their wedding night and say, "I'm never going to sleep with you as long as I live."' Gytha gave an affectionate little chuckle. 'That, I can assure you, is one thing your father would never, ever have said. We never had any problems in the bedchamber, he and I.'

Now it was Harold who grinned. 'And I've got the brothers and sisters to prove it.'

'Aye, and they're your responsibility now. You must get to work on the king. Tostig needs an earldom, Gyrth and Leofwine too.'

'Four earldoms for one family? That's asking a lot.'

'The king won't say no, he can't afford to. Oh, he'll complain and whine and feel sorry for himself, the way he always does . . . I'm sorry, Harold, but that man is no kind of man at all. When I think of Canute, mastering an empire that stretched from the south coast of England to the frozen north of Norway, and then compare him to Edward . . .' She sighed at the thought of the gulf between the two kings. 'Anyway, the point is, he'll give you what you want in the end. And the way to make sure that he does is to act from the very start as if there is no possibility of any other outcome. Don't go begging, "Oh please, sire, could you be so very kind . . ." Just say, "I think Tostig should have Northumbria, and Gyrth should have East Anglia, and Leofwine should have Kent."'

'You sound as though you've given this some thought, Mama.'

'A little, perhaps. But do it, Harold . . .' Gytha looked down at the body of the man she had loved for more than thirty years. 'Do it for your father's sake.'

9

From the Cotentin peninsula to Arques,
Normandy, October 1053

Summer had given way to autumn and William was on a hunting trip on the Cotentin peninsula when the storm finally broke. A messenger found him in the forest, standing with the nobles who had accompanied him as they looked at a wild boar that William had stuck with his lance before getting down to finish it off with a knife. The man brought news that Talou had kicked the Norman soldiers out of his castle and replaced them with his own men. 'Your Grace, he has summoned his liegemen and their followers all across his territory, from Rouen to the sea. There are said to be more than a thousand men massing inside the castle of Arques. And, Your Grace, there is more . . . There are rumours that his lordship has been in contact with Enguerrand, Count of Ponthieu . . .'

'Enguerrand?' William was surprised by the news. Ponthieu was a county on Normandy's northern border, but not one that had troubled him before, and Enguerrand had always been a friend to the House of Normandy. But then he remembered that Talou was married to Enguerrand's sister, and what were marriages between noble houses for, if not to ensure that one always had at least one ally in times of trouble?

The messenger continued, 'Count Enguerrand has been promised a great measure of land in return for his support.'

'I see,' said William, snapping out of his private thoughts.

'So my uncle is already giving away parts of my duchy. Well, we'll see about that.'

'Your Grace, there is one more item I must report . . .' The messenger's voice faded away. It was as if he dared not say any more for fear of the reaction it might provoke.

'Come on then, out with it!'

'My lord, there are rumours . . . none yet certain, but men are saying . . .' The messenger made a final effort to screw up his courage and then blurted, 'They say that the Count of Arques and Talou is in league with the King of France, and that the king and his army are even now marching to his support.'

'Then we have to beat him to it.'

William looked at the nobles around him. Fitz was away supervising the building of his new castle. Montgomery was in Alençon and his brothers Odo and Rob were off managing their diocese and estate respectively. But there were still good warriors close at hand.

'Gentlemen, there's no time to waste. We have to move now, this minute, or my uncle will be in Rouen, raising a toast to King Henry, while we're still sitting on our backsides here in the Cotentin. It's absolutely essential to take the castle and Talou with it before Enguerrand and the king arrive.'

William had expected his words to be met with a hearty cheer and immediate action. Instead, the general attitude was cautious, not to say pessimistic.

'Are you sure that's wise, Your Grace?' one knight asked. 'If the count really has a thousand men at his back, we'll need at least as many to beat him. It'll take time and planning to muster a force of that size. And there's the French to consider, too.'

'Less haste, more speed,' another agreed. 'Rush now and you could lose everything, Your Grace. Patience and preparation, that's what we need.'

The remarks were greeted with nods and grunts of approval

and William was becoming worried that for the first time in his life he had been unable to inspire his men into action. But then a voice cut through the low, dispiriting buzz of negativity.

'I cannot believe what I'm hearing. I thought this was a hunting trip for proud Norman men. But you all sound like a bunch of feeble old women. "Oooh, we don't have enough men" . . . "Oooh, we need months to get ready." By God, my father and brothers must be turning in their graves. They were proper soldiers. They never backed down from a fight in their lives, and I for one have no intention of betraying their memory.'

The speaker was Raoul de Tosny. Like Montgomery, he was the son of a man who had once defied William. Fifteen years earlier, Tosny's father Roger, a tough old soldier who'd just returned from fighting the Moors in Spain, forced his way through a packed congregation at Rouen Cathedral to speak to his young duke. Even as a small boy William had realised that the man standing in front of him was very obviously drunk. Roger de Tosny made it perfectly plain that he would not swear allegiance to William on the grounds that he was far too young to be duke, and he stuck by that assertion. But he also assured William that he would never lift a sword against him, and unlike some of those who did swear to be true to their duke, he stood by that promise too. William always respected that honesty, and when Raoul de Tosny declared that he would be honoured to be his vassal, his offer of support was accepted and he had taken his place among the young nobles who clustered around their duke.

'Thank you, Tosny,' William said now. 'And you're quite right, your father never backed down. Not even from the Duke of Normandy.'

That got a laugh, because every man there knew the story of Roger de Tosny's refusal to recognise William as his lord.

Raoul's words had hit home. William could tell that the mood around him had changed, but the men still weren't ready to take the fight to Talou. He needed someone else to state the case for action. And then his eyes lit on just the man.

Walter Giffard, lord of Longueville and a distant cousin of William's, was a man of an older generation. It wasn't his style to make a display of himself. So it had taken William some time to recognise that this taciturn individual, with his grey-speckled beard and his determination never to say two words if one, or preferably none at all, would do, was one of the most steadfast, reliable lords in all Normandy.

'What do you say, Giffard?' he asked. 'Do we make a dash for Arques right away, or do we take it slow and steady?'

Giffard said nothing. He cast his eyes slowly round him, taking in his fellow knights and nobles, then looked directly at William. 'I'm with you, Your Grace,' he growled. 'I say we ride. And if it's just you, me and young Tosny, we'll still beat that treacherous snake Talou.'

By Giffard's standards, that was a lengthy oration, and it worked just as well. He'd challenged the others' courage, their honour and their manhood, and no one could now back down without being branded a coward.

An hour later they were on the move, with messengers sent racing to every corner of Normandy to issue calls to arms and rouse the duchy – or those parts of it, at least, that Talou had not already subverted – to their duke's defence.

During his days in Brother Thorold's classroom, William had been fascinated by the Greek myth of Sisyphus, the ancient King of Corinth. The gods had punished him for his sins by making him roll a huge boulder to the top of a steep hill, only for it to roll back down to the bottom. Sisyphus rolled that rock up and saw it fall back down again and again, without ceasing, for all time. In the early hours of his ride to Arques, William felt some sympathy for him.

Six years earlier, he had ridden this exact way: down from the Cotentin peninsula and then along the coast, around the Bay of Veys, across its four river estuaries and on towards Bayeux. He grinned to himself as he remembered Bloodfang, his beloved stallion – now spending his time at pasture, eating grass and covering mares – who had carried him on that ride. On that occasion he'd not been galloping to fight rebels, but to escape them. His enemy, Guy of Burgundy, was also his kinsman, just like Talou, and a childhood friend to boot. He'd been in the same classroom as William and heard Thorold tell the same stories. But neither blood nor friendship had prevented him going to war against the duke.

How many times will I have to make this ride? William wondered. How many rebellions will there be? Tell me, dear Lord, please: will I ever rule Normandy in peace?

One day of frantic riding rolled into another, and another again. At night, William allowed his men and beasts to snatch a few short hours of sleep, but he had them up before the dawn and moving, always moving, until long past the sun had set and the moon sat high in the night sky.

After a while even William felt almost drunk with fatigue. His brain was befuddled, his reactions slow, his senses dulled. Again and again he found himself drifting off to sleep in the saddle, and it was only with a huge effort that he was able to rouse himself before his eyes closed tight and he fell unconscious from his mount. But still he pressed on. Men joined them along the way and slowly the column that trailed behind him lengthened. But even as they came within sight of Arques the force at his disposal was barely a third of that available to Talou, possibly less.

As he saw the castle looming up ahead of him, William

suddenly realised the scale of the task he had taken on. Brave words were all very well, but they would not smash down those high walls, nor kill the men within them. Perhaps the doubters were right: he should have taken his time, built up his army and only confronted Talou when he was certain of victory. But then his natural, combative nature reasserted itself.

The hell with that. We're here. We can't just turn around and go away. So we might as well win.

10

The castle of Arques itself stood on a long, narrow ridge that rose just high enough to make climbing it an issue for any attacker. The fortifications followed the line of the ridge so that the castle was shaped like a massive bottle, much longer than it was wide and narrowing to an even thinner neck. At the end of this neck, like the cork in the bottle, stood a massive gatehouse flanked by two huge towers that protruded forwards, ahead of the gate, so that anyone trying to enter did so between the walls of the towers, in plain sight of the defenders on their battlements and in point-blank range of their arrows or cross-bow bolts.

William was still several hundred paces from the castle when he saw the gates open and a large company of mounted knights trot out under the banner of Talou. They rode beyond the two towers, more and more of them in an apparently endless stream, and assembled across the ridge in front of the castle walls, looking more as if they were preparing for a parade than a battle. William instinctively searched for his uncle in the place he himself would have occupied: at the front and centre of the formation, where both his men and his enemies could see him. But there was no sign of Talou. At last William spotted him safely tucked away in the midst of his troops.

That's no way to win a battle, he thought. No, wait . . . does he even want a battle at all?

It struck him that Talou, knowing that he possessed a huge numerical advantage, wanted to put on such a show of force that he could persuade William to give up without a blow being struck.

You should have spent more time fighting beside me, Uncle, he said to himself. You might have learned how to fight against me.

He leaned across to Giffard, just behind him. 'Ride back along the column, tell them to form up six abreast and be ready for my signal to charge. But don't make a show of it. I don't want the enemy to know what's coming.'

Giffard nodded and turned his mount, and gradually the line, without any obvious orders or effort, reshaped itself from a ragged string of riders into a rough approximation of a column of fighting cavalry.

The imminent prospect of battle had revived William's spirits more than any amount of sleep could have done. His nerves, which had recently been so numb with exhaustion, were suddenly humming with energy, his reactions and perceptions pin sharp.

He kept trotting on until he was less than a hundred paces from Talou's mass of men, stretched out in front of him across the entire field of his vision. He rode on. Now he was close enough that he could have called out to his uncle, so close that when Talou, sitting stock still on his horse, gave him a mocking wave, he was able to answer with one of his own.

He kept his hand in the air for a second longer than was strictly necessary, and then, without the slightest warning, swept it down, shouted, 'Charge!' and kicked his horse into a gallop. His lance was raised beside his head, ready to be thrown; his eyes were fixed on his treacherous uncle. If he could only fight his way through the men protecting the Count of Talou, he could end his life, and the rebellion with it.

He did not once look around to see if his men were following him. He took it for granted that they were, and if they were not, it would serve little purpose to turn and watch their retreating backs. He heard cheers break out around him and knew that all was well: the charge was on and the enemy were taken completely by surprise.

Crammed together in a tight mass, Talou's knights were unable to move forward to meet William's advance. If Talou had been a true general, he might have seen that his best hope was to hold the enemy's charge in the centre of his line and then sweep his wings forward in a pincer movement, hitting the Norman column in the flanks and cutting it to pieces.

But Talou was no soldier. He saw the light in his nephew's eyes as he skewered the first man he faced with his lance. Then William drew his sword and began cutting his way through men who were still reaching for their own weapons, while their horses whinnied and reared in panic. In that instant, Talou understood for the first time what kind of man the illegitimate whippersnapper he had so long held in such contempt really was. He knew that William possessed an inherent, instinctive quality of dominance that he could never match. He also knew that if his nephew should ever get within a sword's length of him, he would be a dead man.

He pulled at his horse's reins, trying to turn it around, but the press of men and animals around him was so tight that it was impossible to manoeuvre.

'Retreat!' he screamed in high-pitched panic. 'Back to the castle! Retreat!'

Barely any of his men heard their commander's desperate shriek. No one budged. William was getting closer, killing and trampling on anyone who stood in his way.

Talou turned to the captain of his guard, who was stationed to his left, to protect his blind side. 'Get me out of here!' he shouted. 'Cut your way through if you have to!'

The captain hesitated for a moment as he took in what his

lord was ordering. Then he glanced at the duke and saw the terrifying air of controlled fury with which he was slaughtering anyone who stood before him, and the way that the Bastard's men seemed to have been caught up in their leader's killing frenzy. He muttered, 'The hell with it,' and lashed out with his sword. Ignoring the looks of horrified surprise in the eyes of the men, his own men, that his blade was striking, shutting his ears to their pleas for mercy and their curses on his soul, he forced his way through the mob, with the petrified Talou close behind him.

When their lord turned and ran, so did his men. Within seconds the entire area between the gate towers was jammed with desperate soldiers trying to escape the battle.

William found himself briefly exposed as the men he had been fighting fled. He looked around and saw the crossbowmen massing on the battlements. As long as the two armies had been locked together, the archers could not shoot for fear of hitting their own men, but now their enemies were much more clearly defined. William's immediate instinct was to solve the problem by closing with the enemy again, but that would mean advancing between the towers, and when the last of Talou's men was safely inside the castle and the gates closed behind him, the men of Normandy would be caught in the deadliest of traps.

He knew what he had to do, but hesitated a fraction, for it was so against his nature. But then the first volley of crossbow bolts was fired from the walls and two of his men's horses were hit and fell screaming and kicking to the body-strewn ground, and now William had no option. 'Go back!' he shouted, waving his men away from the castle. 'God knows we beat them, but we have to go back.'

Over the days that followed, more contingents of fighting men arrived to stand with William against Talou. The duke began operations with the practised confidence of a man now well versed in the business of bringing a castle's inhabitants to their knees. Siege towers were erected and ballistas hauled up them to train upon the enemy. Guards and lookouts were posted around the castle and across the local countryside, searching for the first sign of King Henry and Count Enguerrand marching on Arques to relieve the siege.

Once those essential preparations had been concluded, however, William was for once uncertain how to proceed. He could hardly allow the French to ride straight past him and free Talou from the blockade that now entrapped him. But on the other hand he was reluctant to go to war against the king to whom he had sworn loyalty.

Tosny was as forthright as ever. 'If Henry marches into your duchy, you are entitled to stop him, and by any means necessary.'

'Are you sure?' William replied. 'After all, he can say that Normandy is really the Crown's and I only hold it by his grace. In any case, how can I ever complain about anyone who rebels against me if I have rebelled against my own liege lord?'

'But you haven't rebelled! He has broken his oath to you. A lord can't go to war against his vassal any more than a vassal can fight his lord.'

The arguments swayed back and forth without any conclusion. In the end it was Giffard who settled the matter, though not by any masterful debate.

One day, while leading a patrol in the vicinity of a village called Saint-Aubin, just a league or so south-east of Arques, he came upon a force of soldiers, some from Ponthieu, others the king's men, led by Count Enguerrand. To judge by the half-dozen heavily laden carts that were trailing in its wake, this raiding party was hoping to get supplies to the castle's defenders.

Count Enguerrand gave the order that started the fight, but

it was Giffard who finished it. He was not the kind of man given to sudden brilliant inspirations that turned a battle on its head, but he was a supremely tough, competent soldier who kept his nerve under pressure, led by example and knew how to organise his men. He met Enguerrand's attack, held it, repulsed it, and then led the slaughter that ensued when the enemy broke and ran. Enguerrand himself was killed in the action.

William gave orders that the count's body should be mounted on a bier and sent under guard, flying a flag of truce, back to the French encampment. When the king saw the mutilated corpse, he decided that Talou was not worth the loss of any more fine noblemen and retreated back to France. William also sent word to the castle to inform the Countess of Talou that her brother was dead. He was later told that the men on the siege tower could hear her cries of anguish when she learned the news, so desperate was her grief.

From that moment on, William knew that victory was only a matter of time, and not a great deal of time, either. For the great number of men that Talou had recruited was a significant disadvantage in a siege, when every man and his horse needed feeding and watering. Nor did those men have any great desire to starve themselves in Talou's service, having seen what he was willing to do to their comrades to save his own neck.

When the surrender came, William ordered Talou into exile, telling him never to return, under pain of death. He left Normandy a crushed and beaten man, with an embittered wife who blamed him for the loss of her brother. One look at the two of them, hollow-eyed and hunched, as if the weight of the world was upon their shoulders, was enough to tell William that he need never again give his uncle a moment's thought. Another opposing piece had been removed from the chessboard.

The castle of Arques now became William's personal property. His first act was to arrange a service of thanksgiving for the victory. His second was to host a feast of celebration for all the men who had served him so well. He made a particular point of thanking Walter Giffard for his service. 'I will never forget your part in this, Giffard. Without your fine words I would not have been able to lead us here so fast. And without your brave action, King Henry would not have been sent on his way and the castle might not have fallen.'

Giffard managed a mumbled word of thanks, which provoked the men around him into ironic calls for a speech.

'And thanks to you too, Tosny,' William went on. 'You were the first to support me and you fought well here too, even if you would have me be a traitor to my king.'

'Well, it doesn't matter now,' said Tosny, raising his tankard as yet another toast was called by one of the knights gathered at the duke's table. 'Good old Giffard saw him off and he won't be coming back.'

'Oh, I think he will,' William replied. 'And one of these days he'll bring the Hammer with him.'

11

Alençon, January 1054

Hugh Montgomery emptied his goblet, not for anything like the first time, and leaned towards his brother Roger. It was the twelfth day of Christmas, and in the great hall at Alençon the final feast of the season was coming to its end. The women had long since retired and the men had been unrestrained in their talking, singing, drinking, belching and vomiting.

'Something I want to say . . . as your older brother . . .' Hugh began, with the fierce, frowning concentration of the profoundly drunk.

Roger asked himself for the thousandth time what in God's name had made him offer the hospitality of Alençon castle to his wastrel brother. All these years I've worked to make the Montgomery name respectable, and this buffoon could wreck it in an instant.

'What is it?'

'Your wife . . .' Hugh began. Then, seeing his younger brother bristle, he held up his hand. 'Wait! I know what you're thinking: what right do I have to say a word against your wife? Fine woman, given you a son and heir . . . and a daughter too, obviously. How is the lad, incidentally?'

'Very well, thank you,' Roger replied. Four months had passed since Mabel had given birth and passed the baby to the wet nurse. The boy, whom they had christened Robert, seemed well enough. He was waited on hand and foot, as was his older sister, Matilda, who would be two in the new year. Mabel, meanwhile, paid her children almost no attention, preferring to concentrate her energies on her husband. Montgomery had no complaints about her priorities. 'What about my wife?'

'Well . . . I don't know how to say this, to be honest, don't want to say the wrong thing, but . . .'

'Get on with it!'

'Then to hell with it. Roger, your wife is a damn witch. There, I said it.'

Roger said nothing. The silence extended. Hugh looked around as if seeking support, but there was none to be found from any man there.

'The woman's got you under her spell,' he said, as if he could somehow prove his point by making matters even worse. 'She just has, don't care what you say, it's the truth.' He looked around again furiously, 'And you all agree with me, don't pretend that you don't.'

Roger gave a tight, forced smile. 'Please excuse my brother, gentlemen. He doesn't seem to hold his drink as well as he used to. It makes him foolish. He talks nonsense. Says things he shouldn't. Well . . . who doesn't have an embarrassing relative in the family, eh?'

There was a ripple of nervous laughter.

Roger stood up and the others leaped to their feet. 'I bid you all goodnight. Feel free to sleep here in the hall. We ride for Rouen in the morning. Duke William believes the duchy may be in danger and wants good men to stand beside him. We will answer his call.'

As he walked out, he passed Hugh, who was doing his best to walk in a straight line across the hall. He put an arm across his brother's shoulder. 'Never, as long as you live, talk about my wife like that again. Believe me, big brother, I won't let you get away with it a second time.'

He gave Hugh a friendly pat on the back, for the benefit of

anyone watching them, and walked away to the chamber where Mabel was waiting for him, already feeling himself harden in anticipation of what was to come.

Childbirth had left Mabel with much fuller breasts, a slightly rounder, softer stomach and buttocks that his hand took even greater pleasure in stroking, kneading and spanking. When he reached their chamber, he found her in one of the nightgowns that she purchased from merchants who carried them all the way from the bazaars of Araby. The stuff from which it was made was so fine that he could clearly see her nipples pressing against it, and the shape of her body was both concealed and yet tauntingly suggested.

She smiled as he closed the door behind him and advanced towards her, but just as he reached her, she gently placed the fingertips of one hand against his chest to stop him.

'Wait,' she purred. 'I have something for you. I made it specially.'

Montgomery groaned softly in anticipation and his breathing came faster as he watched her take the cork stopper from a small glass flask and pour the contents into an equally diminutive goblet. 'Here,' she said, 'drink.'

He took the glass from her hand and drained the contents in one. He felt the taste of the rich, thick liquid on his tongue, a delicious combination of bitterness and sweetness at one and the same time that was unlike anything else he had ever known. Very soon, he knew, the drink would work its magic upon him and he would be more of a man than he had ever known he could be and experience pleasure beyond his wildest imagining. And then, much later, when he lay on the bed, bathed in sweat, his heart pounding and his penis lying limp, drained and exhausted against his leg, she would come to him again with another little bottle, and he would drift away on a soft, warm cloud of blissful ease and sleep as deeply as the dead.

For Hugh had been quite right. Mabel practised arts that might as well have been witchcraft. And her enslaved, enchanted husband was utterly under her spell.

12

Le Bec Hellouin, Normandy, and Rouen

'Thank you so much for coming, my son.' Abbot Herluin, the founder of the monastery of Le Bec, watched as Arnaud d'Echauffour dismounted from his horse. Herluin was an old man now, and the sparse hair that ringed his tonsure was pure white, yet he still maintained the upright bearing and long, brisk stride of the soldier he had been before God called upon him to exchange his sword for a prayer book. 'I know your father will be so pleased that you are here. He does not have long now, but with Our Holy Lord's blessing he will surely take his place in heaven when his time comes to depart this earth.'

Arnaud steeled himself as he was led along a passage to the abbey's infirmary. The plain whitewashed room contained eight beds, arranged in two lines of four, with an aisle between them. Abbot Herluin walked between the beds, dispensing a smile or a brief word of greeting to any patients well enough to acknowledge his presence, until he came to the final bed, pressed into the far left-hand corner of the room. 'Brother William, your son Arnaud has come to see you.'

Herluin stepped aside, and now Arnaud had an unimpeded view of the ruin of his father's face. There had been a time, and not so many years ago, when William Fitzgiroie had been a handsome man, with a broad, engaging grin that spread to his bright blue eyes. Arnaud treasured the memory of seeing his father smile when he came back home after time away serving the House of Bellême, for whom he had been a good and loyal soldier; or when he was pleased by something that Arnaud had done; or just because he loved his boy and was always delighted to see him and share a joke.

But there were no eyes now, just the livid pink scars that lined the sockets into which William Talvas's men had stuck a red-hot poker. And there were just two holes in the middle of his face, for those same men had cut off William's strong, proud nose, with its bump where it had been broken in a boyhood fight. They'd taken his ears too, so that all that was left on the sides of his head were two semicircular ridges of scarred gristle. All these wounds inflicted when William had been a guest at Talvas's wedding, a loyal follower assaulted and abused for no good reason, accepting his lord's hospitality, justifiably expecting his protection.

Talvas's conduct had been far beyond the boundaries of acceptable behaviour. Not a man in Normandy would disagree with that.

But this was not a time to debate the rights and wrongs of the issue. Arnaud was here to say farewell to the father he loved.

Don't cry! You mustn't let him hear you cry.

'Your father can hear you,' Abbot Herluin said, as if reading Arnaud's mind. 'Come close to him, but don't speak too loudly. He finds it very frightening.'

Arnaud knelt by the bed and took his father's hand. It felt as frail and desiccated as an old leaf that would crumble into dust with a simple clench of his fist. He tried not to think of how safe he had felt as a boy, putting his little hand into his father's strong, warm grasp.

'Hello, Papa,' he said. 'It's Arnaud.'

He felt a flutter against his palm that he realised was his father attempting to squeeze his hand, and saw a tremble at the corner of the old man's lips that he took to be a smile.

'Marie sends her warmest regards, Papa, and so do our boys,

218

Fulk and little William. We named him after you, of course. I take them hunting and fishing just like you used to take me. Do you remember?'

Once again Arnaud sensed the faintest tremble of his father's hand against his, so he went on, 'Fulk is older, so he's much bigger and stronger and faster, but Willie's got the brains in the family. He's more patient and crafty. I think we may have a little soldier and a little priest.'

He talked a little more about his family, trying to maintain a cheerful air, as if he were not talking to the mortally sick relic of a once strong and cheerful man whose death was close at hand. But then he paused, unable to maintain the pretence any longer. 'I'm so glad you're here, Father, with all the other monks around you, in the sight of God. He will bring you peace, I know He will. He will take you to be with the angels. He will restore you and you will have your sight again so that you can see God's glory, and your ears so that you will perfectly hear the angels sing their hosannas, and—'

A rasping sound emerged from between his father's lips, and Arnaud stopped in mid-sentence. The old man was trying to say something. 'What is it, Papa?' he asked. 'What do you want?'

Again there was a hoarse, dry whisper, but Arnaud thought he could detect a single word: 'Here.'

'I'm coming, Papa,' he said, and leaned forward so that his ear was directly above his father's mouth.

With one final effort, summoning up the last scrap of energy in his body, William lifted his head a fraction from his pillow. 'Avenge me.'

Then his hand stiffened in his son's grasp and his head slumped back, and the body of William Fitzgiroie was fixed like a statue in the absolute stillness of death.

* * *

Arnaud of Echauffour remained at Le Bec for long enough to see his father buried. He gave a donation to the abbey to pay for Masses to be sung in William's memory on the anniversary of his death. As he prepared to leave, Abbot Herluin came to him.

'Don't hurry away,' the old man said. 'There is something I must say to you before you go.'

'Of course, Father,' Arnaud replied. 'I would be very grateful indeed for any words of comfort or advice that you could give me.'

'Thank you, my son. Here, sit beside me on this bench . . .'

It was a cloudless day and Herluin tipped his head back for a moment to bask in the feeble rays of the winter sun, then he sighed and turned to Arnaud. 'You were struck from the same metal as your father, and like him you have a good heart. You are more inclined to love than to hate, to forgive another man than to hold a grievance against him.'

'You are too kind, Father, but I am no less of a sinner than anyone else.'

The abbot smiled. 'The very fact that you say that rather proves my point, don't you think? But I have fought enough wars, on enough battlefields, to know that there are times when even the kindest, most decent of men can be moved to hatred.'

He looked straight at Arnaud, and his gaze was so piercing that it seemed to see inside the younger man, as if it could somehow gauge the content of his heart, his mind, even his very soul.

'Listen to what I am about to say, Arnaud of Echauffour, and mark my words well. No mortal man who loved his father could have looked upon him as you did, in the final moments of his life, and not wished ill upon those who disfigured him so cruelly without the slightest provocation. Your heart must have cried out for vengeance. It would take a saint to feel forgiveness for the perpetrators of such a crime.'

Abbot Herluin paused and then said very quietly, 'I'm right, aren't I?'

Arnaud nodded. He could not trust himself to speak, for there was a part of him that wanted to shout out, 'My father demanded vengeance!' and he knew that it would be an act of betrayal to give his dying words away.

The abbot took Arnaud's hands in his. 'Trust me, my son, no good can come from hatred. That is the Devil's currency, and he plants hate in men's souls so that he can have dominion over them. He wants men to be angry and vengeful, for then they will sin, and every sin committed is like a blessing for the Devil. If you free yourself from hate, you free yourself from the Devil too. Do you understand this, my son?'

Arnaud nodded. 'I do. But what am I to do? I must have some form of restitution.'

'That is true. And though Talvas is no longer with us, his family would help themselves and the fate of their immortal souls if they made some act of penance. Might I make a suggestion?'

'Of course.'

'You cannot avenge yourself against Talvas of Bellême, the man who ordered your father to be so horribly mistreated, for he has gone to meet his master in hell. I do not have to tell you that his only surviving child is his daughter, Mabel. I am sure that you also need no telling that no man who valued his honour, let alone his immortal soul, could punish a weak and defenceless woman for her father's sins.'

'Of course not,' Arnaud agreed. In truth it had been bothering him that Mabel was the only obvious target for an act of retribution, and he no more approved of a man attacking a woman than did the abbot. 'What then do you suggest?'

'Mabel is a married woman. Her husband is therefore responsible for her, and she must obey his commands. I hear good reports of young Montgomery. Unlike his father and most of his brothers, he seems to be honest, decent and conscientious – much like you, in fact.'

'I know him well. We have served together in His Grace Duke William's campaigns.'

'Then you know the true measure of the man. Now, I gather Montgomery is currently in Rouen, at Duke William's court. Go to him there. Talk to him. Tell him that I suggest that a small chapel might be added to the church here at the abbey, where your father's remains could be reinterred in a fine stone tomb. That would make a fine setting for those Masses for which you have so generously provided. If Mabel of Bellême were to fund the building of the chapel and pray for your father's forgiveness at its altar, then I think his suffering would be honoured, and her family's sin might be expiated. And you, my son, could be sure that you had done your duty.'

'Thank you, Father,' said Arnaud, falling to his knees before the abbot. 'You have taken a great weight off my soul.'

'Go in peace, my son,' said the abbot. 'And let us all hope that it will not be long before we hear the sound of the masons wielding their hammers and chisels as they cut the stones for that chapel.'

13

Arnaud found Montgomery in attendance at William's court and explained the idea of founding a chapel in his father's honour. 'The abbot is a very wise man,' Montgomery replied. 'I know from my own family how important it is not to carry grudges over from father to son, or even brother to brother. I've often said that William Fitzosbern had every reason to hate me for what my brother did to his father. So did Duke William. Imagine how different it would have been at Domfront if we had all been fighting amongst one another.'

Arnaud grinned. 'It was bad enough dealing with Talou's desertion.'

'Exactly! And there's a perfect case of the damage bitterness can do. Talou spent all those years building up a grudge against His Grace, resenting him for his position, but now look at him. Exiled from Normandy, his lands forfeited, his life in ruins.'

'It's madness really. All he had to do was accept God's will and offer Duke William his loyal support and he would have been as blessed with land and wealth as any man could wish.'

'Exactly. And the same applies to us. I have no wish whatever for us to be at odds, and I'm sure Mabel would say the same. Your land is next to ours. We should be good neighbours. If we can help secure that friendship by an act of contrition for what happened to your father, well, what possible reason could there be for us to object? In any case, Mabel and I have been thinking about endowing a new monastery. So building a chapel, seeing how it's all done and so forth, would be a nice preparation for that.'

'Thank you, Montgomery. I was hoping you'd see it that way.'

'No need to thank me, my friend, it's you who is being generous and big-hearted. Listen, I have to stay here in Rouen. His Grace is concerned that King Henry may be back at any moment to finish off what he started with Talou, and he has asked me to support and advise him in that campaign. But there's no reason why you can't go to Alençon, with my blessing and my absolute guarantee for your safety, and speak to Mabel yourself. I'll have a monk write a letter explaining the situation and setting out what I think will happen. You can take it with you.'

'Are you sure she will agree?'

'Oh, I'm sure she will,' said Montgomery, as if there could be no doubt about it. 'What you're proposing is very reasonable, very reasonable indeed. And Mabel is an exceptionally astute and perceptive woman. She'll understand at once that this is the ideal way to put an old conflict to rest.'

Those words were enough to reassure Arnaud, but Montgomery failed to persuade himself. The longer he spent with Mabel, the more he understood that she had no interest in being reasonable. She could not care less about compromise or fairness. All that concerned her was power.

Montgomery was now all too aware that Mabel's need to control other people extended to him too. She used her potions to enslave him. He had explained his absence from the Arques campaign to William by saying that he was shoring up Bellême's defences against any future invasions. The truth was, he had barely left his bedchamber for weeks, so totally had Mabel reduced him to an intoxicated stupor.

When he had finally summoned up the strength and

willpower required to return to his duties, he had felt sick for weeks. He found himself racked with pain, shivering uncontrollably, unable to sleep and convinced that his friends, even William himself, were plotting against him.

'By God, Montgomery, you must love that wife of yours,' William had said once. 'You've gone to pieces without her.'

In time, however, the fever had subsided and he had returned to his old self. Everyone told him how well he looked and how glad they were that he was better, and the whole thing was soon forgotten.

Montgomery swore to himself that he would not fall back under Mabel's spell when next he saw her. But was he just deluding himself? Could he really resist the promise of her body, her sweet kisses and her wild, ecstatic lovemaking? Ah, but with that love would come those little glass bottles and their intoxicating, devilish contents, and the whole process would start all over again.

The hell with that, he told himself. I'm going off on campaign. Arnaud can deal with Mabel. And whatever happens, well, that's his lookout.

14

Alençon

'Build a chapel? At my expense? To the memory of William Fitzgiroie?' Mabel's voice rose in pitch and volume with every one of her rhetorical questions. 'The hell I will!'

She flung Montgomery's letter across her bedchamber, sending Agnes scurrying to retrieve it.

'What reason does his lordship give for his command?' Agnes enquired, picking up the letter and returning to her mistress.

'He says that some abbot has suggested it as an act of contrition.'

'But what sin have you committed against this Fitzgiroie, my lady?'

'None whatsoever. But I'm supposed to feel sorry for what my father did to that vile little man, who deserved everything he got.'

'And what was that?' asked Agnes.

'He had some men stick hot pokers in his eyes, so that he was blinded.'

'Ooh . . . how horrible!' said Agnes with relish.

'And they cut off his nose.'

'Ugh!' Agnes put a hand to her own nose and giggled at the horror of it.

That set Mabel laughing too as she added, 'They also cut off his . . .' She left the sentence dangling, and Agnes's eyes widened at the thought of how it might end.

'Ears!' concluded Mabel.

'Oh, I thought you were going to say something else.'

'I know you did, you filthy little slut.'

'So what had this man done to upset your father?' Agnes asked when their laughter had receded.

'He refused to obey a direct order.'

She neglected to add that the order in question had been for Fitzgiroie to murder Talvas's first wife, Mabel's own mother. Even as a little girl, Mabel had been fascinated by her mother's death, constantly asking her father to tell her all the details, as another child might want a favourite bedtime story to be repeated time and again, never for a moment feeling any loss at her passing. But the specific means by which Fitzgiroie had been rendered less than human, yet somehow kept alive, had intrigued her even more.

Agnes, meanwhile, had judged the time right to get a little closer to Mabel. 'I would never disobey you,' she said. 'I would do anything to please you.'

'And you shall, little one, you shall,' Mabel replied, giving her a peck on her forehead. 'But not just now.'

'Please don't make me wait too long.' Agnes pouted.

'I won't, never fear. But for now, there's something I have to do . . . by myself.'

Mabel of Bellême had a chamber in Alençon castle to which only she was allowed entry. There was but one key that would open its door, and she kept it on a chain around her neck that she removed only when she lay with her husband in bed: Montgomery used to say that he was 'unlocking' her when he lifted the chain over her head and put it carefully to one side.

Behind that door Mabel kept a range of powders, tinctures and concoctions, some derived from minerals, others from plants and even animal secretions, that no apothecary north of the Alps could have matched. Nor did any man possess, let alone have the knowledge to use, such an extraordinary collection of glass flasks, pipes, funnels and bottles, all differently sized and shaped, in which substances could be heated, transported, condensed and then stored.

Mabel's room was situated at the top of a corner tower and had windows, much larger than was common in a fortified building, that opened to the east, south and west, guaranteeing light at any time of day. She worked at a long table on which her equipment was arrayed alongside more familiar pestles, mortars and scales (albeit hers were of Moorish design and accuracy). Beside this table stood chests whose many small drawers contained the ingredients from which she brewed the draughts that made Montgomery her willing slave. Each drawer was marked in ink with lines, curves, circles and dots that would have made no sense to any Christian who looked at them, for they were the names of the substances that lay within the drawers, inscribed in Arabic.

Mabel had learned the script from the same person who had taught her the mysteries of creating potions that could alter a person's mood, arouse or kill their physical ardour, keep them awake and energised long after others were exhausted, or send them into a death-like sleep when they had been wide awake a moment earlier. She had likewise learned how to kill in a myriad ways designed to imitate fevers, turmoils of the guts and bowels, conditions of the heart or lungs; indeed all the evil spirits that could infest and destroy the human body.

Her teacher preferred to be known as Jamila, the name that her husband had bestowed upon her. In Normandy, however, she had gone by a man's name, Jarl, for it was in the guise of a man that she conducted her business as a murderer for hire. Years before, Mabel had heard of Jamila's skills, tracked her down to her new home in Narbonne and persuaded her that the former apprentice should turn teacher.

Thanks to Jamila, Mabel was now familiar with substances such as the beans that Arabs called *gahwa*. Roughly the size of peas and a pale-brown nut colour when dried, they turned a rich dark brown when roasted and, if powdered and then boiled with water, provided a remarkable increase in one's vitality and alertness. The *gahwa* possessed a bitter taste, but this was greatly improved by the addition of honey and formed the basis of one of Mabel's most effective love potions, whose other ingredients might at any time include *ashwaganda* powder from India, *ginseng* from China and a powder Jamila referred to as *tanqat ali*, which was said to come from Oriental lands beyond China. Certain forms of mint, celery, mushroom and even parsley could also be exploited for their aphrodisiac effects.

Mabel was always happy to stimulate her man's desires and stamina, both because she benefited directly from the results of her labours and because it increased her power over him. And if Montgomery had any qualms about a wife who knew secrets fit only for sorceresses, they had so far been swiftly allayed by Mabel's promise that if his lovemaking proved satisfactory to her, she would reward him with another magical dose from her little bottles.

One of these contained a substance called *afyun*, derived from the sap excreted by a particular form of poppy, which she mixed with the paste that Arabs called *hashish*, which meant 'grass'. This not only sent Montgomery to a state of bliss so profound he felt he had been transported to paradise, but also created a powerful craving for more. Since this craving could only be satisfied if he pleased her, it greatly assisted Mabel in her training process.

Yet Mabel was not entirely dependent on exotic imports from faraway lands for her substances. Some were taken from the flowers and seeds of plants that grew wild in the country-side, or were cultivated in her own flower garden. Foxgloves, daffodils, autumn crocus, buttercups, lily of the valley and of course deadly nightshade all harboured demons that could kill a man as effectively as any sword, if harvested, preserved and then employed by an initiate to the poisoner's craft.

Until now, Mabel had only actually disposed of a single victim: her brother Arnulf. In the years since his profoundly satisfying demise, she had yet to find another enemy worthy of her time and attention. The lack of opportunity to apply her skills frustrated her deeply and preyed increasingly on her mind. Now, however, she finally had a subject on whom to practise her craft.

15

Mabel spent some time at her work table, preparing her solution to the difficult situation in which she now found herself. Her stupid, presumptuous husband had made a decision on her behalf. He had then had the temerity to believe that she would be bound to comply with it, simply because she had sworn a marriage vow that contained a promise to obey him. Mabel had never willingly obeyed anyone in her life. She simply did not see how another person could have the right to prevent her doing what she wanted to do, as if she even cared about their opinion in the first place. And far from desiring a friendly, neighbourly relationship with Arnaud d'Echauffour, what she actually wanted was to find a way to seize his land. She didn't like the way his estates just sat there on the edge of hers, with some excellent forests, meadows and fields, when they would be much better off under her control.

So Arnaud had to die. This thought pleased and excited her, for the taking of life was the finest of all the ways in which one person might exercise power over another. It was clear to her, though, that she had to exercise some subtlety and even caution in the way she went about it. She felt sure that her husband wouldn't have been able to resist bragging to his beloved Duke William about how sensible and decent he and Arnaud had been (this thought particularly infuriated Mabel because she had been planning to use Roger to persuade the duke that Arnaud had been hatching plots against him, with a view to having Arnaud banished and the land given as a reward to

Bellême). That being the case, the whole of the ducal court would now know what had been agreed, and if Arnaud died while a guest at Mabel's castle, they might suspect that the daughter of Talvas, far from making peace with the House of Giroie, had simply continued the feud in defiance of her husband's will.

Or would they? Mabel reconsidered her position. If she were to make a great show of welcoming Arnaud and making him all sorts of promises in public, and then he died, it wouldn't look like murder at all. It would seem like a tragic end to what should have been a happy story – in the eyes of the stupid, pig-headed fools who populated Normandy, anyway.

But he can't die right away, she thought, with a drink still in his hand. That's too obvious. He has to die later. Unless everyone has seen me drinking too . . . And then a sweet, contented smile crossed her face. Of course. She knew just how to do it!

She opened a drawer in one of her chests that contained a green glass jar of arsenic in powder form. She took a very small spoon and filled it twice, placing the contents on a small square of parchment. This she folded over to form a little packet, which she tucked into the sleeve of the woollen shift that she wore beneath her gown.

Then she returned to her chamber and summoned Agnes. 'Please tell Lord Arnaud that I will be happy to meet him in the great hall. Tell him that I would be delighted to talk about the chapel he wishes me to build in his father's memory. And then ask the cook to prepare her finest honey pastries and instruct the cellarer to fetch some of our best wine.'

Agnes gave her a quizzical look, but she knew better than to question her mistress and simply said, 'Of course, my lady,' before heading off to run her errands.

* * *

A short while later, Mabel appeared in the great hall, looking particularly ravishing. A fair crowd of people was present: supplicants who had come to ask their liege lord or his lady for help in solving a dispute, or getting restitution for the losses they had suffered at someone else's hands; merchants hoping to sell their goods to the joint House of Montgomery and Bellême; passing travellers who had a right to hospitality; servants of the household. Plenty of witnesses, thought Mabel contentedly.

And, of course, there was Arnaud and his retainers, for he had not been quite so trusting as to enter the very castle where his father had been so cruelly mistreated without a squadron of strong, well-armed men to watch his back.

Mabel took her place at the high table and gestured to Arnaud to join her. She clapped her hands and servants came forward with plates piled high with delicious pastries, both sweet and savoury, and a carafe of wine.

She called the young man who had left the wine to come to her and then ordered him, 'Stand by the table. Watch the wine. The moment you see that it is running short, fetch some more. I do not want my guest to go thirsty.'

'Of course, my lady,' the servant said, and took up a position behind and to one side of his mistress, with his eyes firmly fixed on the carafe.

Mabel played the dutiful hostess, making sure that Arnaud had all the food he desired and personally pouring his wine, as any well-bred woman did at what was, after all, her husband's table.

When she was sure that he had everything he needed, she returned to her place opposite him and picked up her glass. 'My lord of Echauffour, and people of Bellême. Today marks a moment that will go down in the history of our county. For today, Lord Arnaud and I turn enmity into friendship, and hatred into forgiveness. Many years ago, my father, the Count of Bellême, did great wrong to Lord Arnaud's late father, William Fitzgiroie. Today I will do my humble part to right that wrong. I will pay for the building of a chapel at the abbey of Le Bec, which will house the mortal remains of William Fitzgiroie and stand for all eternity as a mark of my family's sincere contrition.'

Warm applause broke out around the hall and Arnaud looked genuinely moved, almost to tears, by Mabel's words.

'And so, I hope you will forgive me, a mere woman, for doing a man's task and calling for a toast. I ask you, Lord Arnaud, to join me in this toast . . . to good neighbours and good friends!'

'Good neighbours and good friends,' Arnaud replied, joined by a rumble of voices from the hall.

Then the conversation about the chapel began and Mabel tried her very hardest to feign the slightest bit of interest in all the talk of master masons and carpenters and quarries that were known for the quality of their stone. All the while, she made sure that her guest's glass was filled, and also that everyone saw her drink the very same wine too, albeit in smaller, more ladylike quantities.

Very soon the carafe was almost empty. Mabel was pleased to see the servant whisk it away and return it, fully replenished, just a moment later.

Perfect, she thought, reaching into her sleeve to get her handkerchief, which she used as cover for the little parchment packet that she removed at the same time. Just a few moments more and I won't have to listen to this ghastly, self-righteous non-entity talk about his blasted chapel for a solitary second more.

16

Hugh Montgomery missed the arrival of Arnaud d'Echauffour and his party at Alençon castle, nor was he present when Mabel made her toast to neighbours and friends. He had spent the whole day hunting wild boar in a forest beyond the town. He'd bagged a couple of decent-sized beasts, though the prize male that he'd been after, a hefty great brute that would have kept a normal family well fed all winter, somehow eluded him and his dogs.

Still, it had been a fine day's sport, with a good yarn or two to tell his cronies over dinner, and the two beasts he had managed to bag would look splendid roasting on their spits once they'd been hung for a while to get them good and gamey.

Damn, but that was thirsty work! Hugh thought, dismounting in the castle yard, handing the reins of his horse to a groom and walking up to the main entrance to the keep. I could make short work of a flagon of wine.

He strode into the great hall and looked around. There was that stuck-up, calculating little witch Mabel sitting eye to eye with a nobleman he vaguely recognised. He did not, however, waste any time wondering about the man's identity, for his eyes had lighted upon the carafe of wine sitting in the middle of the table. Perfect!

He set off at a good pace, pushing his way through the crowd without the slightest concern for the people he was barging out of his way. Up ahead, he saw Mabel stand and then make her way around the table towards where the nobleman was sitting.

What's she doing now? Hugh wondered. And then he realised, to his horror, that Mabel of Bellême, a woman he had never once seen pour her husband's wine, was about to come over all meek and compliant for this smarmy-looking newcomer.

Good God! The damned minx is making a cuckold out of my brother! Well, I'm not having that!

Hugh fought his way to the dais at the end of the room and leaped up onto it. Shoving past Mabel, he picked up the carafe and looked at the nobleman. 'Sorry, old man, but you're not getting your lips round my brother's property just yet.' He downed the wine in a single mighty draught, then reached across the table, grabbed a couple of pies and wolfed them down, and then a third for good measure.

He gave a massive belch and looked around. To one side of him, Mabel was watching him with cold, flat, hate-filled eyes that he found, frankly, terrifying. The nobleman – Arnaud d'Echauffour, that's his damn name! – wore an expression that mixed distaste with bafflement.

'Excuse me, good sir, but what did you mean by that vulgar remark? Are you insinuating that—'

But he never finished his question, because Hugh suddenly vomited violently all over the top of the table. Groaning in agony, he wrapped his hands around his stomach, then bent double and vomited again, spewing purply-red liquid all over the floor before collapsing in a writhing heap, racked by a pain more violent than any he had ever known. He felt a pressure building in his bowels and was quite unable to stop an eruption of liquid filth from his rear end. He'd wet himself too, and saw that the urine now staining his hose was a pinkish red. There was blood and sick and piss and shit coming from every orifice.

What a disgusting way to die, thought Hugh Montgomery. And then he did.

* * *

236

Mabel screamed. She had no need to, of course, but she assumed that it would be expected of her in the circumstances, and it was, at the very least, a way of releasing the fury and frustration she felt at the way her idiot brother-in-law had ruined her brilliant plan.

As the hours went by, her irritation only grew. Everyone had seen Hugh charge in, make a complete exhibition of himself gorging on pies and wine and then pay a terrible price for his gluttony. His arrival had been totally unexpected. Mabel and Arnaud had been enjoying a very civil conversation – Arnaud would be the first to bear witness to that – and both of them had eaten and drunk the very same pastries and wine as Hugh, but more slowly and in more modest quantities. So no one suspected foul play, still less thought Mabel had tried to kill Hugh. It was, in short, the perfectly crafted murder . . . except for a single flaw.

It was the wrong man who'd been killed.

17

*A military camp south of the River Seine,
Normandy, February 1054*

Geoffrey Martel, Count of Anjou, shivered, wrapped his cloak a little tighter to shield him from the bitter east wind and walked towards the burning manor house. As he came closer, he could feel the first heat from the flames against his cold, numbed face, contrasting with the flurries of snow that were still beating against his back.

'What did we get?' he asked the knight who came walking towards him still brandishing the torch that he had used to start the fire.

The knight shrugged. 'Not much, I'm afraid, my lord. They only had a couple of coins of gold and a few pieces of silver to their name. There were three woollen blankets and a fur rug – very old, all worn and patchy – and the wife had a bit of jewellery, nothing fancy.'

'Any food?'

'Couple of sacks of grain, one of flour, one of turnips. Aside from that, there's still about half a pig's worth of salted meat, a few chickens and four milking cows, two of them bearing calves by the looks of it.'

'Kill the animals and have them butchered.'

'Oh, and a barrel of that ale they make with apples,' the knight added, as if it were an afterthought.

'You weren't going to tell me about that, were you? Good thing you did. I'd have had you hanged for thieving if I ever found out you'd taken it.'

'Yes, my lord,' said the knight, eyes lowered in hangdog contrition.

'Share it out among the men. Make sure everyone gets some and no one has too much. I can't abide drunken soldiers.'

'Yes, sir.'

'You haven't told me about the people. I can't imagine the lord of a manor this poor is worth ransoming. Might have relatives who are richer, I suppose.'

'He's dead, my lord. Tried to stop us taking his money box.'

'He let himself be killed? Over pennies?' Martel gave a contemptuous shake of his head. 'Pathetic . . . What about the womenfolk?'

'The wife's getting on a bit.'

'She's still got a hole between her legs, hasn't she? Give her to the men. Any others?'

'Two slaves, both younger, rough faces and filthy as pigs, but they'll do, and one lass who's a bit better-looking. Reckon she's the daughter of the house.'

'Four cunts and a barrel of apple ale; what more could three score men of Anjou ask for, eh?'

The knight laughed at his master's wit. 'Will that be all, my lord?'

'For now, yes. But we march again at sunrise, and I want them all sober and ready to move when I give the command. I'll whip any man who isn't, d'you hear?'

'Yes, sir . . . and what shall we do with the women?'

'Use them, then kill them. There'll be plenty more for you to choose from soon enough.'

The knight hurried away and Martel stood for a moment looking at the dancing flames. Then he heard a voice from behind him, the girlish tones of a young squire calling out, 'My lord, my lord!'

Martel turned and grimaced as the snow beat at his face. 'What do you want?'

'The king has commanded me to summon you for a council of war.'

'Has he now?' Martel muttered beneath his breath, then replied more loudly, 'Very well. I'll get my horse. You'd better lead the way.'

The king's tent was crowded with some of the mightiest nobility in the kingdom. Martel caught the eye of Theobald, Count of Blois, and then grinned as Theobald turned away, unable to hold his gaze. Ten years had passed since Martel had fought, defeated and captured Theobald in a battle near a hamlet called Nouy. To win his freedom, Theobald had had to give Martel the county of Touraine and its principal city of Tours. He was hardly left homeless; he possessed huge holdings in Chartres, Sancerre and Champagne. But his humiliation still stung, much to Martel's delight.

Martel gave a more respectful nod to the Duke of Berry, who outranked him in aristocratic seniority, and to the commander of the contingent of men from Sens, who was a minor noble himself but was here under the banner of the Viscount Archbishop of Sens. Martel was well aware that his imprisonment of the Bishop of Le Mans had infuriated the senior churchmen of France, and though his period of excommunication was over, it was still unwise to cause more resentment among God's representatives on earth than one absolutely had to.

King Henry called the meeting to order and the men clustered around a wooden table on which a map, drawn on vellum, had been rolled out. 'My dear, true lords of France,' he began, 'I have good news to report. While we are marching into Normandy from the east and are now about here . . .' his finger stabbed at the map, hitting a point on the southern bank of the

Seine, about halfway between the Norman border and Rouen, 'my brother Odo, along with Count Rainald of Clermont and Guy of Ponthieu – whose brother, you will recall, was so cruelly murdered by Duke William's men outside the walls of Arques – is advancing south towards Dincurt, here.' Another stab, this time at a point just a few days' march north of Rouen.

'That much, of course, you already knew. But what I can tell you now is that their advance has been entirely successful. Though we have had reports of some local Norman barons banding together in an attempt at resistance, Odo's progress through Upper Normandy and the Vexin is encountering no more opposition than our march through Evreux. Our twin forces can now advance on Rouen, striking at Normandy's capital from two separate directions. Duke William will not know what to do. The moment he moves to attack one of our armies, he leaves his capital open to the other. And either one of our forces is larger than any he has ever put in the field. Together, they will be overwhelming.'

The king looked around at his commanders. 'We have him, by God, we have this bastard duke at our mercy . . . and there is absolutely nothing he can do to stop us.'

Hurrahs rang out among the nobles, but Martel remained silent. This kind of boastful overconfidence was not what he associated with Henry of France. The king was no great warrior, that was for sure, but he was a survivor. Every campaign he fought lasted just long enough to get to the point where he could extract some advantage from it, no matter how meagre. And the moment he felt that there was no longer any chance of victory, he retreated before he could face the certainty of defeat. The Arques campaign had been a classic case in point. Once Enguerrand and his men had been slaughtered, giving William the advantage, Henry had turned tail and left. He had conceded defeat, yes, but he had preserved himself and the bulk of his army. That was why he was able to return to the field again so soon.

Yet now he seemed to have forgotten all his natural caution. And he had forgotten his enemy, too.

Martel pondered whether to say his piece. No one would thank him for it. He doubted anyone would actually listen. But damn it, yes, he was going to speak up, if only so that he could say 'I told you so' if things went as wrong as he feared.

He waited for a lull in the sounds of mutual congratulation and cleared his throat. As the other men turned to look at him he said, 'Your Majesty, if I may . . .'

'What's the matter, Anjou?' the king asked, and then smiled broadly. 'No! You don't have to say a word. I can see with my own eyes. You have not been given a goblet, nor wine to toast our success. Chamberlain! Fetch wine for brave Anjou!'

'Your Majesty is too kind,' said Martel. I gave you one chance to listen, he thought, but you wouldn't take it. Why should I give you another? Ach . . .

'There was something I wished to say,' he pressed on. 'It concerns William the Bastard, Duke of Normandy.'

The king's smile vanished. 'What is it?' he asked.

'He's not attacked us.'

'Is that all? My dear Anjou, I believe we can all work that out for ourselves!'

Martel took a deep breath and tried to suppress the natural urge to punch the king's smug face as he let the sycophantic laughter subside.

'No, sire, there is more.'

'Oh well, I suppose we had better hear it. Go on . . .'

'I have no more love for William of Normandy than any other man here. Less, I dare say. He took Domfront from me, and Alençon too. And he mutilated my men while he was doing it.'

A frisson of disgust went round the room at the mention of Alençon. Every man there knew what William had done. They all regarded him as a bestial, cold-blooded brute. But they feared him too, every one of them.

'If there is one thing we know about Normandy, it's that he doesn't shy away from a fight. Nor does he wait for trouble to come to him. He goes looking for it, he moves fast and he strikes when his enemy does not expect it. He did that at Alençon, he did it at Arques, and he would have done it at Domfront too, if I had not been sent word he was coming. So why has he not struck at us or the northern army yet?'

'Because he can't, that's why,' said Theobald of Blois, relishing the chance to undermine Martel in the presence of the king. 'The Bastard has always been surrounded by enemies in his own duchy. Every time he puts one rebellion down, another one starts up. He's not marched against us because he has no men to march with.'

'He had men at Alençon, Domfront and Arques.'

'Not many. Not like we have now.'

'He has allies. I've met them. Cocksure little whippersnappers they are too. Young men like him: ambitious, greedy for wealth and power, wanting to make a name for themselves. They follow William like a pack of wolves follows its leader, because he will give them fresh meat to feast upon.'

'You sound mighty impressed by William and his whippersnappers, Anjou,' Theobald sneered. 'Sounds to me like you're scared of these Norman wolves. What's the matter? Is the Hammer not as hard as it used to be?'

'By Christ, Blois, if we were anywhere else, I would make you pay for those words. Your Majesty, I have been dishonoured and I will not stand for it.'

'Enough!' the king snapped. 'I cannot have my own lords fighting one another when they should be fighting our enemy.

Anjou, I think we have all heard quite enough about William of Normandy. You have said your piece; I wish to hear no more on the subject.'

Martel seethed, but he had no choice but to submit. 'Very well, Your Majesty.'

'As for you, Blois, I share your view that Anjou has an unduly admiring view of the Duke of Normandy, but you suggested that he was scared, and that I will neither believe nor tolerate. Withdraw the remark, if you will.'

'Yes, Your Majesty,' said Theobald, barely able to keep the smirk off his face. 'I withdraw my words, Anjou. I'm sure your Hammer is still rock hard.'

'Blois!' the king protested, though Martel could see he was trying hard not to laugh.

'I'm sorry, Your Majesty,' Theobald said.

Martel looked around the room at all the smug, pompous faces grinning at his expense. He knew that none of them would last a minute against him if they met on the battlefield, one man against another to the death. He knew that he had conquered more land, seized more treasure and fucked more women than the lot of them put together. And still they dared to look down at him.

Maybe that snivelling, bed-wetting Count of Blois is right, he thought as he stalked from the tent back out into the freezing February night. Maybe I am impressed by William of Normandy. Bastard or not, he's more of a man than those mincing Frenchmen. Martel chuckled to himself. Ah, William, I think we understand one another, you and I. Two of a kind, that's what we are.

18

Alençon

Mabel was toying with Agnes. She had discovered that a smaller dose of the same potion that sent her husband so blissfully to sleep reduced her servant to a state of helpless submission in which her lusts were if anything heightened, while her body was given over to utter abandonment. Mabel was thus able to play with her as if she were a toy, or at best a pet, utterly at her mercy and under her control. At this precise moment, Agnes was tied by her wrists to the bedposts in the master bedchamber of Alençon castle, with the three middle fingers of Mabel's right hand deep inside her. She was moaning softly and writhing, almost as if she wanted somehow to break free from the unbearable ecstasy by which she was pierced. But by pressing down with the heel of her palm, Mabel, who was kneeling alongside Agnes's squirming body, was able to keep her pinned in place, unable to escape.

Now Mabel raised her left hand and let it hover, the fingers fluttering speculatively as she decided what to do with them. The pleasure of moments such as this lay in the cool, detached consideration of how best to exercise her power. She thought for a second, much like a cook debating in her mind what seasoning to add to a boiling stockpot, and then lowered the hand over Agnes's right breast. Taking the nipple between her thumb and forefinger, she pinched it hard. A sudden shock surged through the helpless girl. Her back arched and she gave a scream of pain, yet Mabel could feel from the sudden flickering of flesh around her fingers, deep inside Agnes's body, that the scream was one of rapture, too.

She removed her hand and smiled as she heard Agnes groan and watched her lift her bottom off the bedclothes and tilt herself up and out in search of the fingers that had just deserted her. 'Like a baby chick blindly begging to have the worm put back in its beak,' Mabel murmured. She swung her leg across and straddled Agnes. Her left hand reached down and grabbed the hair on the crown of Agnes's head, clenching it tight and holding it still. Then she shoved her wet fingers into Agnes's mouth. 'Taste yourself,' she said.

As the other woman's soft lips and strong, warm tongue feasted on her fingers – a not unpleasant sensation in itself – Mabel leaned closer. 'Can you hear me, little one?'

Agnes did her best to nod but was brought up short by the hair still clamped in her mistress's hand.

Mabel noted the little wince of pain but also the unceasing play of the mouth against her fingers. She was a well-schooled creature, this one. She let go of Agnes's hair and used that same hand to stroke her forehead softly.

'Good girl,' she said. 'Now listen carefully . . . Do you remember when that fat fool Hugh died in the great hall?'

Agnes nodded again.

'Well, he drank wine that was meant for Arnaud d'Echauffour. So now I have to find another way to rid myself of him. Now, do you remember, when he visited us, that Arnaud had a chamberlain called Eudo?'

Agnes stopped licking and sucking just long enough to let a smile form at the corners of her mouth.

'I thought you would, a strapping young buck like that. Would you like to have him?' Mabel took her fingers out of Agnes's mouth. 'Well?'

'Mmmm . . .' Agnes sighed dreamily.

246

'Then you shall, and with my blessing, just so long as you give him a little bottle, from me, to be poured into his master's wine one night. You are forbidden on pain of death from lying with him until he has done that. I want him as desperate for you as you are for him. Once he has done what I need, you may each take your fill . . . but not until then.'

'I understand . . .' murmured Agnes, and from her smile it was clear that she was imagining Eudo's strength and vigour and hardness inside her, and that made Mabel intensely irritated, for she felt as though the insolent little strumpet had suddenly escaped her control. So she pinched both Agnes's breasts, even harder than before, and clenched her hair more tightly, and whipped Agnes's thighs and belly and sex with one of Montgomery's leather sword belts until the defenceless girl was crying in pain and frantically straining against the bonds that tied her hands as she strove to escape the punishment.

Finally Mabel had given the demons inside her the feast of cruelty they craved. She stopped, her own naked chest heaving with the exertion. Then she lay beside Agnes, took her head in her hands and spoke in the soft tones of a lover. 'You must never again think of anyone when you are with me.' Delicately she wiped a tear from Agnes's cheek. 'You only think of me. And all you think about is how best to please me.'

'Yes, my lady.'

'Would you like me to untie you now?'

'Only if it pleases you.'

Mabel smiled. 'Good girl.'

She freed Agnes's wrists and kissed them where the ropes had marked her skin. Then she lay back on the bed and held Agnes close to her.

'Does it hurt very much?'

Mabel felt Agnes's head nodding and the moisture of her tears against her skin. 'Tomorrow you will have welts across your legs and stomach where I beat you. I expect they'll still hurt, and every time your clothes brush against them it will be even worse.'

Agnes's body quivered at the thought of what was to come.

'But it will please me very much to think of your suffering, and the more it hurts you, the more you will be pleasing me. For now, I will release you from the pain, so that you can rest.'

She let go of Agnes and reached across to the little bottle by her bed. She undid the stopper and placed the open top of the bottle to the girl's lips.

'Drink,' she said.

It was not long before Agnes was asleep.

Mabel remained awake a while longer. Arnaud and his retainers had left Alençon as early as possible the morning after Hugh Montgomery's death, and there was no immediate prospect of their return. So it might take a little time for Agnes to find an opportunity to wheedle her way into Eudo's bed. Now she came to think of it, Mabel rather looked forward to the whole business of creating the circumstances that would allow her plan to come to fruition. Now she could commit a second murder when she had only expected one. In that sense, the fact that Hugh had drunk that damn poison was not such a disaster after all.

The main thing was that Arnaud d'Echauffour was already as good as dead.

And on that thought, she slipped contentedly into a deep, untroubled sleep.

19

Barely three leagues from King Henry's camp, William was also listening to news from the northern front, brought to him by a young knight barely old enough to shave called William of Warenne.

My God, there are men in armour ten years younger than me. I must be getting old, William thought. 'How far have they advanced?' he asked.

'Barely a day's ride from here, Your Grace. They are approaching the castle of Mortemer. And, Your Grace . . .' Warenne hesitated. 'If I may say something . . .'

'Go ahead.'

'The Franks are bringing devastation wherever they go. Men are seeing their homes burned down, their property looted. Women who cannot flee are being raped. Your Grace, we all want to know: when can we fight back? We can't stand and do nothing while these locusts plague our land . . . we just can't!'

The boy was impertinent, but that was just the passion and impatience of youth. William stepped up to Warenne and put a hand on each of his shoulders. 'Calm down, lad. You will never make a soldier if you lose your head at times like this. I do not like to see Normandy suffer, any more than you do. Now just answer me this, Warenne: are there signs of disorder among the Frankish ranks?'

'Yes, Your Grace. We have been spying on them as they march. I have heard Robert the Bishop's Son say that they look more like a band of drunken thieves than a proper army.'

'Good . . . and how quickly are they marching?'

'Slowly, Your Grace. Many of the men are weighed down by their booty, and there's a long line of carts, some pulled by oxen, others by the prisoners the Franks have taken. They're all piled up with loot, too.'

Far from being outraged at this report of mass larceny, William was oddly pleased by what he had heard. 'Excellent,' he said, patting Warenne's shoulder. 'So, are there many men of high rank among this robber band?'

'Oh yes, Your Grace, a great many. There are knights, vavasours and barons, even viscounts and counts, as well as the king's own brother.'

'Then they will soon provide you and your comrades with full recompense for all the damage done.'

'So what should we do, Your Grace? People are saying we should make a stand at Mortemer castle. If we hold that, we could slow down the French advance. They couldn't go any further if we were still sitting there behind them.' Warenne looked at William nervously. 'Well, that's what I've heard men say, anyway.'

William paused. His whole strategy depended on being able to destroy one column of the Frankish army, so that he could then concentrate all his men into a single force and destroy the second column too. But if the first engagement was not successful, the second could not possibly be. He had waited and waited for the perfect moment to strike. Was this it? But even if it wasn't, could he wait any longer?

He made up his mind. 'Listen to me carefully, William of Warenne, for the fate of the duchy may hang on what I am about to tell you.'

He watched the young man's eyes widen and saw him swallow hard. 'Don't be afraid,' he said. 'All will be well. Just carry this message to Robert the Bishop's Son and Walter Giffard. I have two orders for them. The first is that they are to abandon Mortemer and let the French have the castle. The second is this: remember the valley of Blavou.'

Warenne looked as though he could neither believe nor understand what he had just heard, and the expressions on the faces of the other men listening to the conversation, all of them among William's most trusted lieutenants, suggested that they felt the same way. As Warenne looked around them in silent desperation, it was Raoul de Tosny who came to his rescue. 'Forgive me, Your Grace, but did I hear you correctly? Is Warenne to tell his commanders to give up Mortemer without a fight?'

'Yes, that is exactly what I am saying,' William replied. 'And you, Warenne, may tell that to any man who suggests that you have mistaken my orders.'

'I don't understand, Your Grace . . .'

'You don't have to. But your commanders will. They both fought alongside my father when they were not much older than you are now. Ask them to cast their minds back to my father's actions at the valley of Blavou. Then do the same again at Mortemer.'

'But Your Grace, I don't know what that means.'

'Exactly. So if you should happen to run into a Frankish patrol and be captured, you will not be able to tell them what I have in mind.'

'Oh, yes . . . I see.'

'Then what are you waiting for? Be off with you. Go!'

Warenne went on his way at a furious gallop, though William doubted he ever rode at any other pace.

Roger Montgomery was among those who watched the young-ster set off on his mission. He had immediately answered

William's call when news came of the French invasion. He still felt the shame of having missed the Arques campaign and was determined that his duke should not be without him a second time. Nor was he the only baron to feel that way. Now that Talou had been defeated, no one could doubt that William was the master of his own duchy, and any man who wanted to maintain his standing in Normandy could not afford to ignore the duke's summons.

Montgomery waited until the others had drifted back to their own troops before he spoke. 'What did you mean by all that stuff about . . . what was the name of the place again?'

'Blavou,' said William. 'It was one of my father's greatest victories. Two of the sons of the old Count of Bellême had mounted a raid into the duchy, raping and burning and plundering their way across my father's lands, just as the Franks are doing now. My father tracked them, waited for the right moment and then destroyed them. He killed one of the Bellêmes with his own hands. The other died soon afterwards. That just left Talvas, your Mabel's father. In fact, my friend, now that I think of it, you owe your present good fortune to what happened that day in the valley of Blavou.'

20

Mortemer castle

'The valley of where?' asked Robert the Bishop's Son when he was given the duke's orders.

'Blavou,' said William of Warenne. 'His Grace thought you fought there once, under his father's command.'

'Well, he's wrong. I didn't. So what good is that to me? I have no idea what Duke William is talking about.'

'I do,' said Walter Giffard. 'I was there. And I know exactly what he means.'

Odo Capet was a scion of the family known as the Third Race of Kings, for the House of Capet had succeeded the Merovingians and Carolingians as the ruling family of the Franks. But had he been a man of lesser birth, he would not have been entrusted with the command of even the smallest detachment of fighting men, for he was so weak, so indecisive and so incapable of formulating a plan and sticking to it that many of those who served under him feared he was soft in the head. Guy of Ponthieu and his younger brother Waleran, who had accompanied him on the campaign against Normandy, had done their best to instil some order and discipline into the ranks, but they were still young men, with little experience, so the troops were disinclined to offer them more than token obedience.

From where he was standing, atop the palisade that crowned the motte on which the castle of Mortemer had been built, Guy

253

looked down on a scene of absolute chaos. The sun had all but set and there was sure to be a heavy frost, yet there were still not enough fires lit to warm the men and cook their food. Nor were there sentries patrolling the walkway to either side of him, or guards posted by the castle gates. It would, he reflected, be a pointless exercise even to try to find men who were able, let alone willing, to undertake arduous duties through the cold, dark watches of the night, for the castle gates were wide open and no one had the slightest interest in closing them. A constant stream of men, and the occasional woman – some there as a matter of professional choice, others as helpless captives – was passing to and fro between the castle and the fields outside.

The men had given themselves over to drinking, trading and fighting as they haggled over various items of booty, resorting to fists and even knives when agreements could not be sorted by words alone. Someone had found a set of pipes and was playing familiar folk tunes, to which men were singing, often adding obscene new variations to the familiar words that accompanied them.

Guy sighed helplessly. The army was falling to pieces and there was absolutely nothing to be done about it.

The Normans attacked Mortemer just before dawn, when the soldiers that King Henry was sure would help bring him victory were hung-over and half asleep. A force of mounted knights under Robert the Bishop's Son smashed through the unguarded encampment like a nailed warhammer through a fledgling's skull. The Franks were killed by lances, swords and horses' hooves as their fires were trampled, their tents were set ablaze and the stolen property over which they had been bargaining so intently was crushed underfoot.

Some of Robert's men had split away from the main charge and made for the castle gates. Guy of Ponthieu had been unable to sleep all night, so strong were his forebodings about the state of affairs that he had witnessed. So he heard the sound of the Norman's horses pounding against the rock-hard soil before their attack struck. It had only been a matter of seconds, but he had been able to dash from the castle keep, shout for help from the few sober men gathered inside the walls and slam the gates shut, just managing to lower the beam into its cradle to secure them before the first Norman horsemen arrived.

In so doing, he had secured the castle and saved both himself and Odo, who had also spent the night inside the keep. But he had condemned the men outside, who included his brother Waleran, for they were now fleeing pell-mell away from Robert's men and being scythed down as they ran. And it was then that the significance of William's orders became clear. For Giffard had remembered how Duke Robert had split his men at Blavou before another dawn attack. The first charge had been made by the duke's closest friend Herluin. But that had only been the means of driving the men of Bellême towards Robert and his men advancing from the opposite direction, so that the enemy was caught between one charge and another like a piece of iron between the blacksmith's hammer and the anvil.

Now Giffard led his men from the woods into which they had marched under cover of night, wheeled them towards the battle and charged straight into the terrified faces of the panic-stricken Franks. The slaughter was devastating. Here and there a knot of Frankish soldiers gathered by one of their comrades with more courage or fight in him than the rest put up some kind of resistance. The remnants of a company of archers were able to form a ragged line and loose two volleys that took down a handful of knights before they were swamped by the onrushing Norman tide. Giffard knew it would take some time to finish all these isolated nuisances off, but the battle itself could only have one ending.

In the castle, Guy of Ponthieu realised that the carnage that was all too visible and audible from the walls did at least give him the opportunity to save Odo Capet. The king's brother was dragged from the bed where he lay cowering and gibbering, placed upon a fast horse and surrounded by a small knot of mounted men all known for their bravery and loyalty. Guy waited until he judged that the Normans were so completely engaged in the business of destroying any resistance to them among the men in the fields that they had taken their eyes off the castle. Then he had the gates opened for just long enough for Odo and his escort to dash out, wheel away from the battle and race away into the woods. The men guarding Odo were under orders to head north and not on any account to stop until they were on the soil of Ponthieu.

Once the gates were secure again, there was nothing more Guy could do except wait. There would soon be another bout of haggling over booty. And he would be one of the items being traded.

There came a point when both sides could see that further slaughter was pointless. Walter Giffard accepted the surrender of the few men who had survived the twin charges and the fighting that followed, made sure that the prisoners were secure, then turned his attention to the castle. Giffard was tired. He had barely snatched much more than a nap between planning the battle with Robert and the other knights and then leading his own detachment into place. The sweat of combat was chilling against his skin, and though he had emerged from the fighting with little more than a few bruises and a shallow flesh wound – little more than a scrape, really – on his left thigh, still his joints and muscles ached and protested in a way they hadn't when he had first earned his reputation as a warrior back in

Duke Robert's day. Robert the Bishop's Son felt much the same, being of a similar vintage. So when they approached the castle and were greeted by Guy of Ponthieu calling down from the walls and offering terms for surrender, they were both happy to hear him out.

Guy did not bother to pretend that the situation in which he found himself was in any way better than it seemed. 'My lords, we all know that my men and I are in a hopeless position. If you were to attack, you would certainly take the castle. On the other hand, you would be sure to lose men in the process and you might even risk harm to yourselves. For my own part, I have lost a second brother in battle against Normandy. If I die too, the House of Ponthieu dies with me. I will therefore surrender this castle to you, along with my own person and those of the other men of high birth both inside this castle and without. That, of course, is on condition that the usual codes of behaviour in these situations are observed.'

The Normans understood precisely what Guy of Ponthieu was offering. Any battle was as much an economic affair as a military one. Men fought for self-advantage, and one of the easiest ways to profit from war was to take and ransom prisoners of noble birth. It was greatly preferable to capture rather than kill an aristocratic enemy. Lesser soldiers were valueless, which was why Guy had not bothered to mention them.

Giffard therefore accepted the offer. The captured nobles from the various counties of France were assigned to the Normans according to seniority, but even the lowliest knight who had ridden in the two charges was allotted someone to sell. Guy himself was reserved for Duke William to deal with as he saw fit. And so William's promise came to pass: the Franks recompensed the Normans in full for the damage they had caused.

* * *

When news of the battle reached William, he sent Raoul de Tosny off to inform King Henry of what had happened. When he came close to the place where the invading army was camped, Raoul clambered up a high tree and shouted out, 'Men of the Franks, I bring word from Duke William of Normandy.'

The camp fell silent, for when a herald was sent to deliver a message like this, it was invariably to summon an enemy to battle. They waited now to hear where and when the Bastard intended to fight. But the news they received was very different.

'My lord commands me to suggest that you should divert your march to the village of Mortemer, close by Dincurt. There you will find, strewn across a great plain, the bodies of countless brave men of France who have died at Norman hands. Your army is destroyed. His Majesty's brother has fled. Count Guy of Ponthieu and a host of other men of noble blood are now held captive in Normandy. Hurry now to bury your dead! Be quick, before the crows and foxes leave nothing to be placed in their graves!'

Raoul did not wait for a response. No sooner had the last words left his mouth than he was sliding and then jumping down from the tree, leaping back onto his horse and dashing to the safety of the Norman lines.

In King Henry's camp, Geoffrey Martel was equally decisive. He walked over to the Angevin lines and ordered his men to make ready to march at once. 'My lord, are you sure?' asked one of them. 'We can't desert the king.'

'We aren't deserting him,' Martel replied. 'We are anticipating his command. I know His Majesty's mind. He will soon be marching back to Paris. Why should we delay before returning to Anjou?'

Walter Giffard already had a perfectly good castle, and so had no objection when William gave Robert the Bishop's Son the castle of Mortemer as reward for his part in the victory. Robert was only too happy to receive his new property, for with it came the chance to rid himself of a burden that had long infuriated him. No longer was he to be known as the Bishop's Son. From now on his name was Robert Mortemer, and a great deal better it sounded too.

21

Alençon

Word of his brother's death reached Montgomery just as he was preparing to return to Alençon after the defeat of King Henry's invasion. He was, of course, upset by Hugh's passing, and in particular by the fact that he had not been able to say goodbye to him and pay his respects at the funeral. But over the many days that it took for him to ride home, he reflected that he and his brother had never really had much love for each other, and that Hugh would not have mourned his passing, and so his concern increasingly turned to Mabel. How awful it must have been for her to witness such a sudden and by all accounts violent death. She must, he realised, be very shocked. He would have to help her through the pain until she became her normal self again.

Yet to Montgomery's surprise, the emotion that seemed most apparent in his wife when he raised the subject of Hugh's death was irritation. For reasons he could not fathom, she seemed more inconvenienced by the whole business than shocked, let alone grief-stricken. But none of this stopped her from leading Montgomery straight up to the bedchamber. He followed with a keen urgency, for they had been far too long apart, and Mabel gave every sign of being just as desperately in need of the sheer physical relief of making love. After they had satisfied that raw hunger, and then spent rather longer, assisted by one of Mabel's potions, repeating the process with much greater care and attention, Montgomery waited till he had his wife lying sated in his arms before asking, 'What troubles you, my love?'

Mabel said nothing. It was not just that she was silent. She very specifically said nothing. Which meant that there was something she might have said, but didn't. Montgomery could tell.

'What is it? Come on. I know there's something on your mind. Tell me . . . please . . . I need to know.'

Mabel gave a long, heavy sigh. Then she turned over onto her side and propped her head up on her hand. 'Are you quite sure? You really want to know?'

'Yes, of course. We are husband and wife. There should be no secrets between us.'

Mabel looked at him with those predatory cat's eyes. 'Very well then, I'll tell you . . . I killed Hugh. I poisoned him with arsenic.'

'What? You killed him? Are you serious?' Montgomery tried to bring some order to the chaos Mabel's words had caused in his mind. 'But why? Why would you do a thing like that?'

'Well, I didn't mean to kill him, so there's no "why" about it. I meant to kill Arnaud d'Echauffour, that ghastly man, coming here and ordering me to build a chapel to his faceless father. And I will kill him too. Agnes, bless her, has seduced his chamberlain. I'll make sure he gets some more poison and—'

'You'll do no such thing!' roared Montgomery, leaping from the bed. 'By God, I ought to have you hanged for this.'

'I wouldn't do that, my darling,' said Mabel with wicked sweetness. 'My estates are all entailed on our son. If I die, you'll have to go back to being a poor little Montgomery. So calm down, you big cross man . . .' she patted the mattress where Montgomery had been lying, 'and come back to bed.'

'Bed? With you? I'd rather lie down with vipers.'

'Oh, don't say that, you know you don't mean it. Look . . .

I've got something for you, something you've been without for such a long time . . .'

She held up a little bottle, which glinted in the candlelight.

'How do I know that isn't poison too?'

She smiled. 'I knew you'd say that. It's only natural, really, now that you know what I can do. So I made a little more than usual and I will have the first taste, just to show you.'

She poured some of the thick, sweet liquid into the glass she kept for these occasions and sipped it all down. 'Mmm . . . that is so good. Oh, my . . . I think I've surpassed myself. You'd better come and get your share now, or I won't even be able to pour it for you.'

Montgomery hesitated for a moment, but eventually he cracked, as he was always bound to do, and shuffled back to the bed knowing that he had given in to her, painfully aware that he could not say no to that taste of paradise.

'There,' she said, scooping a spoonful into his mouth, 'that's better, isn't it?'

Her husband slumped down onto the bed, his eyelids growing heavy, and Mabel murmured in his ear, 'You won't hang me, you silly thing. You know you'd never find a better wife. And you never know . . . there may come a time when . . .'

She paused. Montgomery was lost to the world. The poor man, he really had no idea that from his arrival at the castle to her feigned discontent, the lovemaking, the conversation that had followed and his present helpless stupor, everything had played out precisely as she had planned.

Now she finished the sentence under her breath: 'When you need somebody poisoned too.'

22

Varaville, near the coast of Normandy, summer 1057

Henry, King of the Franks, had spent three years brooding over the twin humiliations that William of Normandy had inflicted upon his forces at Arques and Mortemer. During that time he watched as William and Geoffrey Martel of Anjou fought an endless series of petty skirmishes, jockeying for power in the borderlands between Normandy and Maine. All the time he was waiting for an opportunity to intervene once again: a moment of vulnerability when the duke might be taken off guard. Then, in the early summer of 1057, he tired of waiting and began negotiations with Martel, and as July became August and the farmers and landowners of Normandy turned their minds away from war and towards their harvests, the allies struck.

The Franks and the Angevins thrust deep into the underbelly of Normandy, bypassing the strongholds of Domfront and Alençon, marching through the land known as the Hiémois and making for the towns of Caen and Bayeux, and the coast beyond them. By doing so, they cut the duchy in two, separating the western counties and the Cotentin peninsula from the rest.

William let them come. He based himself and his army in his birthplace, Falaise, and seemed reluctant to emerge and fight. He sent messengers to the invaders, pleading with Henry to negotiate, repeatedly emphasising how reluctant he was to attack his own liege lord. At Arques, the Normans had defeated Enguerrand of Ponthieu; at Mortemer their opponent had been the King's brother Odo. But never had the duke done battle with the king himself.

Henry took this as a mere excuse for cowardice. 'You see!' he crowed. 'He doesn't dare confront us. This Bastard's not so brave after all.'

Martel, being by nature cunning and even deceitful, was not so sure. 'I do not doubt for a second that Your Majesty is right. But we must consider the possibility that he is just biding his time. He may even be hoping to lull us into a false sense of security, so that we lower our guard and can be taken unawares.'

'Then we shall not lower our guard. We shall be ready for Duke William at any time and in any place, and if he should suddenly rediscover his manhood and dare to engage us in battle, then he will swiftly regret his decision.'

It was, however, one thing to promise a policy of alertness and even to give the orders necessary to implement it, and quite another thing to maintain it. With every day that passed, the invading column of troops and camp followers became longer and more ragged, until it stretched almost a league from end to end. As the days dragged by, and the looting continued, and the soldiers became befuddled by wine and weighed down by booty, and the ox carts piled with plunder slowed the entire army to a crawl, so the invaders' discipline worsened and their vigilance was dulled. The heat did not help. The summer sun sapped men's energy and aggravated their tempers. Arguments flared up more quickly, like a parched forest caught by a stray spark. Niggling disputes soon became violent brawls, and where there had been two men disagreeing over some trivial matter, suddenly there might be a dozen, or even a hundred, punching, clubbing and stabbing one another without the great majority of them having the faintest idea why.

Finally, one day, as the sun was reaching its zenith, they came within sight of the coast, just by the estuary of the Dives river. There was a ford across the river by a small village called Varaville. Henry, Martel and a cluster of His Majesty's courtiers stopped by a low hillock just large enough to give them a broader view of their surroundings as they watched the army make the crossing.

As the men and carts passed across the ford in an indiscriminate jumble, Henry gave an exasperated sigh. 'Really! Can't the men go first and then all their loot? Surely that would speed matters up.'

'It would, Your Majesty,' Martel agreed. 'But you'd have the devil's own job persuading them to let their property out of their sight. We'd be here all day just trying to make it happen. Best to let them go as they are.'

The whole process ground on through the middle of the day until around half the army had made their way from one bank of the river to the other. The water level of the ford had dropped a little without anyone really taking notice of it amidst the dust churned up by the troops, the animals and the carts, and the noise of several thousand men all talking to one another and shouting commands.

Then the tide turned.

No one had paid any attention to the level of the water when it was low, but suddenly, having been barely high enough to cover a man's foot, it was halfway up his calves. And still it rose, up to knees and then waists, and the hillock on which the royal party was assembled was in danger of becoming an island and they were forced to retreat, the horses' hooves splashing as they went.

The problem now was to stop the column, for the sheer momentum of all the men and animals and vehicles trudging forward could not easily be halted, let alone reversed. What had been a ford across a shallow stream was now just one slightly less deep stretch of a flowing river, and men were being swept away and oxen were bellowing in fear until even they could no longer stay on their feet.

And still the army could not seem to slow its chaotic progress towards the riverbank, though orders to stop were being passed all the way down the line, and men by the water's edge were using whips and even lances to try to keep the oncoming mass at bay.

Suddenly King Henry's army had split in two, with the two halves, on either side of the surging river, entirely cut off from one other.

And it was then that Duke William struck.

Norman scouts had been observing the progress of the Franks and the Angevins for more than two weeks, sending regular reports back to Falaise. It had become obvious to William, who knew the land so well, that the invaders would have to cross the Dives, that Varaville was the only place where they could do it, and that it would be impossible to get the whole army across before the tide turned.

So he marched his men hard, as was his way, and took up a position on the far bank, out of sight of the enemy. And when the tide had done its work, he fell upon the unprepared, ill-disciplined rabble who had forded the Dives, while Henry and Martel watched helplessly from the other bank.

By the time the sun went down, the butchery was complete. Hundreds of Henry's men had been killed by Norman swords, lances and arrows. Many had drowned as they flung themselves into the river and tried to swim back to their comrades on the far bank. Others either found a means to run from the field or surrendered, along with all their ill-gotten possessions.

The following morning, Henry and Martel awoke to find the ford across the Dives so shallow that it was the work of a moment to ride across to the previous day's battlefield, where the bodies of French and Angevin men – or what was left of them after the crows and foxes had had their fill – still lay in droves upon rain-starved earth that had been watered by a storm of blood.

Now another Norman rider arrived at the king's tent with a message from Duke William. Once again he pledged his loyalty to the king, as a token of which he would take no further action against the remains of His Majesty's army, which he now greatly outnumbered. This pledge was made with just one condition. Every single living Frank or Angevin had to leave Norman soil, with no more than their horse and the clothes on their back, within five days. After that time, any found on His Grace the duke's land would either be killed or captured for ransom. His Grace regretted that he was not open to negotiation. Should His Majesty, however, refuse these terms, a state of war would exist and no quarter would be asked or given.

The king did not need any time to make up his mind. He was on his way at once.

23

The Palais de la Cité, Paris, residence of the kings of France, and the King of England's palace at Westminster

'I have such happy news, Your Majesty,' said Queen Anne of France, desperate to find some way to shake her husband out of the dismal gloom into which he'd been sunk since William of Normandy had defeated him yet again.

King Henry said nothing, as was his habit recently. Anne found it impossible to arouse his interest these days, let alone his enthusiasm. She had always known that he was irritated by her strong Kievan accent, which was why she had tried so hard, with such little success, to get rid of it since becoming a Frenchwoman. But he had always at least pretended to listen to her in the past, and even if he was really only paying attention to her breasts, well, that was a start. Now, though, he had even lost his appreciation for her physical charms. Still, Anne was nothing if not determined, and she had a naturally optimistic nature. She felt sure that her man would return to her if she just tried hard enough, so she ploughed gamely on.

'I have just had letter from my sister Agatha, who is wife of Edouard, Prince of England, now living in land of Magyars. She is so funny about her little boy, Yedgr. I tell you what she says . . .'

Anne stopped. Henry was looking at her with the air of a man emerging from a deep sleep. He grimaced as if trying to formulate his thoughts well enough to turn them into speech.

'My dearest . . . ?' said Anne, hoping to encourage him.

Henry frowned. 'Did you say that someone was the Prince of England?'

'Yes, that is Edouard, husband of my sister Agatha. We are all growing up together at court of my dear father, Grand Prince Yaroslav of Kiev and Novgorod, who is dead three years now.'

'Yes, my dear, I know who your father was. But who is this Edward, and why does he call himself Prince of England.'

Anne reminded herself not to sigh, or roll her eyes. She had told Henry about Edward on more than one occasion, but of course he hadn't been listening. 'Edouard is son of Yedmund, who is son of Yettlerid.'

'Yettlerid?'

'Yes, Yettlerid, King of England, who was by Khnut the Dane defeated. Yedmund, who was called Sides of Iron, was for very short time King of England. Edouard is his son. My father has married Agatha to him because he says he will have daughters who are queens of four countries.'

'Ah yes, now I understand. But I always thought that Canute had the sons of Edmund killed so that they could never threaten his throne.'

'You are quite correct, Your Majesty. Khnut was sending boys Edouard and also Yedmund to Otto, King of Sweden – this is my grandfather – for killings. But Otto was good, kind man and he is not killing boys. He sends them with his daughter Ingegerd who is going to Kiev to marry Grand Prince Yaroslav.'

'And so you knew Edward and Edmund?'

'Oh yes, they are like big brothers to me! Yedmund was special friend, but now is dead.' Anne sighed sadly, but immediately perked up. 'Edouard is very well still, Agatha is telling me. They have daughter Margaret and son also, he is Yedgr.'

'So let me just sum up to make sure that I have understood.

269

There is a man living in the land of the Magyars at this very moment who is a direct descendant of the royal house of England – the eldest son of an eldest son, all by legitimate marriages – and who thus has a perfect blood claim to the throne. And he has an heir of his own?'

Anne paused for a second to make sure she had understood, then nodded in confirmation. 'Yes, is correct.'

'So if anything were ever to happen to the current King Edward, this other Edward would have the best claim to succeed him . . . and I dare say the English would be delighted to have him because they would see him as one of their own.' Henry paused, and for the first time in a very long while, Anne saw a smile wreath his face. 'As opposed to, say, the illegitimate spawn of a murderous duke of Normandy, who doesn't have a drop of English blood in his body. Oh, but this is perfect!

'I shall have Agobert, Bishop of Chartres, write to Stigand of Canterbury, telling him all about this Prince Edward of England. I happen to know that Stigand is not at all keen on William of Normandy becoming his king. He fears for his position and his estates. But a prince who arrives in England friendless and in need of advice . . . Oh, I can see Stigand, not to mention all the English barons, being very happy about that.'

Henry's mood had been utterly transformed. The morose, self-pitying, defeated man who had been sitting before Anne just a few minutes ago had given way to a cheerful, self-confident monarch.

'Would you be so good as to pour me a goblet of wine, my dear? I would like to drink to Prince Edward's health.'

'Of course, Your Majesty,' Anne said. She filled the goblet with a delicious Burgundian wine and brought it across to Henry. As she stood beside him, he reached up with one hand to take the goblet and with the other he gave her bottom a hearty squeeze. 'You are looking particularly lovely today, my darling,' he said.

His queen blushed. 'Your Majesty is too kind.'

Stigand, Archbishop of Canterbury and Bishop of Winchester – a double appointment for which he had repeatedly been chastised by a series of popes – reacted to the news relayed to him by Agobert of Chartres in exactly the manner Henry had predicted.

The idea that William of Normandy might be King Edward's successor had been Champart's idea, yet another of the ways in which he hoped to infest England with his fellow Normans. Stigand, however, was an Englishman and therefore wanted an English king. He particularly did not want Duke William taking the throne, bringing all his cronies with him to England and giving one of them the archbishopric of Canterbury. Of course, it was wildly unlikely that William would ever wear the crown of England. But everything one heard about the Bastard suggested that he defied expectations. He could not, however, defy the claim of a man who was a grandson of Ethelred and the nephew of King Edward. If this exiled prince could be persuaded to leave Hungary and put down roots in England – learn the language, make friends and, more importantly, alliances and start raising his son as an Englishman – he would be perfectly positioned when the present King Edward died.

As Stigand well knew, Edward had not been best pleased by William's response to being named his successor. He had expected the young duke to be overwhelmed by gratitude, but Champart had instead reported that while the Bastard was sceptical about the sincerity of the king's offer, he was also determined to take it at face value. The combination of insolence and belligerence was something that Edward had noted in William when he was just a small boy. It was altogether disappointing that he had not grown out of those faults, but had instead entrenched them.

'What do you think, my dear?' Edward asked Edith when Stigand told him of his namesake's existence. 'Shall we ask this nephew of mine to visit us?'

'It is not for me to say, Your Majesty,' Edith replied. 'You might enjoy the chance to meet a long-lost relative, and if you do choose to invite him, my ladies and I will of course do everything we can to make the prince and his family welcome. Whatever you decide, I'm quite certain that it will be for the best.'

Edward beamed with pleasure at his wife's humble trust in his superior judgement. Her time at Wilton Abbey had done her so much good that he had quite forgotten the glee he had taken in hurting her, and had instead come to believe that he had devised the whole plan for her benefit. There were times when her subservience was almost enough to make him desire her. That feeling soon passed, but he was certainly far better disposed towards her now that the Godwin arrogance had been replaced by the Christian virtue of submission. It pleased him, therefore, not only to ask but occasionally even to take her advice, knowing that it was given with only his interests in mind.

'Very well then, that settles it,' he said, not noticing the shrewd glance Stigand had cast in the queen's direction, for the archbishop too had perceived the change in the royal couple's relationship and could see precisely how much more power Her Majesty had acquired by appearing to surrender herself completely to her husband. 'We must send an embassy to the court of Hungary to invite this young man to come here. Tell him to bring his family.'

As Stigand looked back towards the king and gave a little nod to signal his obedience to the royal command, he saw something that was entirely unfamiliar to him. King Edward smiled, and in a voice that sounded perilously close to someone who actually had a heart, said, 'So I have a nephew, do I? Goodness me. That is a pleasant surprise.'

24

Paris, Rouen and Alençon, autumn 1057

Montgomery's father had died in exile in Paris two years previously, and now, with William's permission, Montgomery had journeyed there to help his mother, who was returning to her estates in Normandy. As they were having dinner one night, she happened to mention that all Paris was filled with anticipation about the imminent arrival of a mysterious English prince.

'He must be a fraud,' said Montgomery. 'There aren't any princes of England. That's why King Edward can't find a successor of English blood.'

'You know, you can be just like your father sometimes,' his mother observed, knowing that this would irritate her son but feeling that he deserved it. 'He wouldn't take anything I said seriously either.'

'I'm sorry, Mother. Tell me about this prince.'

And so she did, with the precise understanding of genealogical detail that came so naturally to aristocratic women, and the longer he listened to her chatter, the more Montgomery's blood ran cold. If Edward the Exile ever became established at the royal court in England, that would put paid to William's ambitions. King Edward would have a perfect, indisputable justification for repudiating his promise to William, for that had been made before it was known that he had an heir of his own blood. And if William never became king of England, then Montgomery and Fitz and their friends would not have the country's earldoms to carve up between them. He was simply not prepared to accept that possibility.

'When is Prince Edward arriving in Paris?' he asked.

'I don't think anyone knows for sure, my dear,' his mother replied. 'Within the next month or two, I should expect. I dare say his wife will want to stay here for a short while. She is Queen Anne's sister, after all. But then they will be going directly on to England. I'm sure King Edward will be itching to meet his nephew. Though I fear young Edward will be disappointed by his uncle. I remember him well from when he lived in Normandy. Rather a nasty, mean-spirited boy, I thought. His brother Alfred was a far finer prospect, in my view.'

It was all Montgomery could do not to desert his mother and leave her to make her own way to the estate at Bures, not far from Alençon, that he and Mabel had made available to her. But he did his best to speed up the loading of her furniture and possessions, and had the drivers whip the beasts pulling their carts so hard that the blood streamed down their backs. Finally the caravan had crossed into Normandy and Montgomery bade his mother farewell, leaving several of his men to guard her safely home, before riding like a demon to the ducal palace in Rouen.

Duke William was no more pleased by the news than Montgomery had been. But he was surprised when Montgomery, instead of asking, 'What can we do?' said, 'Your Grace, with your permission, I believe that I can resolve this problem.'

'How, might I ask?'

'Your Grace, it might not be wise to tell you. There are times when a lord or a king may be grateful not to know precisely what is done in his name, so that he can honestly deny any responsibility should anyone try to claim that he has done wrong.'

'I don't like subterfuge. You know me, Montgomery. I like to look a man in the eyes.'

'Your Grace, you have no hope of doing that in this case. Prince Edward is travelling in peace. If he reaches England and satisfies King Edward that he truly is his nephew, then his claim is beyond dispute. I can't see what you could do to challenge it.'

'Unless he does not reach England . . .'

'Or does not manage to satisfy the king . . .'

Montgomery could see the duke struggling between his scruples and his ambition. 'You realise,' William said at last, 'that if anything should happen that might cause suspicion to fall upon the House of Normandy, I will disclaim all knowledge before assuring King Edward that I have unearthed the culprit. You will be that culprit. And if I have to execute you to clear my name, I will.'

'I understand that,' said Montgomery.

'And you're still willing to go ahead with what you have in mind?'

'Yes.'

'Then I hope to God that you know what you are doing.'

Montgomery did not even spend the night in Rouen. He rode like a madman through four nights and days to Alençon. There he ate like a ravening wolf before collapsing into bed. When Mabel joined him, he said, 'I have a task for you. Something on which the fate of Normandy itself may rest.'

'Really? What could I possibly do that would ever be that important?'

'You can kill an innocent man.'

She snuggled up against his body. 'Good boy,' she said. 'You're making yourself useful at last.'

276

25

Various locations in Hungary, France,
Normandy and England

All his life, Edward the Exile had been told that he was a prince of England, but he had never really been sure what those words actually meant. Having been exiled when still a babe in arms, he had no memory of England, nor of his parents, and had never spoken English. So while he knew that his was the blood of the royal house of England, his memories were all of Kiev, and he conversed in the Slavic dialect spoken by the people there, or the *donsk tunga*, or 'Danish tongue', preferred by many of the Norse members of the royal court. Since moving to the land of the Magyars he had picked up enough of the local speech to make himself understood to his staff. Having been raised in the court of a man who sought to make Kiev one of the great cities of Christendom, he had also been taught Latin, the common language of written communication across the Christian world. But he did not know a single word of the Anglo-Saxon tongue spoken by the English who might one day, in theory at least, be his subjects.

Nor did Edward enjoy the wealth or grandeur normally associated with a prince. Just as his namesake uncle had been looked down upon by his Norman cousins and mocked for the shabbiness of his appearance through all his long years of exile in Rouen, so Edward had always been dependent on the charity of others. There had never been anything wanting in the generosity of his surrogate father Yaroslav, nor his lifelong friend

King Andras of the Magyars, but still he lived in properties made available to him by them, and relied upon their stipends to subsidise his upkeep.

So when the small group of Englishmen sent by King Edward arrived at the court of King Andras, the Exile's immediate reaction was one of bafflement. He was summoned from his home at Castle Réka and, having exchanged his usual affectionate greeting with Andras, was introduced to four total strangers, who immediately bowed down before him and began conveying what were clearly feelings of both homage and delight in a tongue that sounded entirely foreign to him.

Gradually, as the pair of clerics who had been brought along to translate conferred back and forth, Edward understood what was being proposed: that he, his wife and his son (Margaret, his beloved daughter, was not mentioned) should travel with this quartet of Englishmen back to their homeland, which was one day to be his kingdom. For one of the messages the envoys were most keen to convey was that the aristocracy of England were just as keen as their monarch to see Edward installed as the acknowledged successor. And since, as was then explained to Edward, the accession of the monarch depended on the approval of a formal gathering of nobles, their guaranteed support removed any uncertainty from his claim to the throne.

For their part, the English seemed very well pleased by their newly rediscovered prince. During the days while they had waited for Edward to travel from his castle to the court, they had heard nothing but good reports from the Magyar king. Andras was unequivocal in his approval. Edward, he assured them, had fought bravely in the campaign that had led to Andras's coronation. He was a good and loyal friend, whose word was his bond. He was a devout Christian (this brought a broad smile to the face of the English priest, who knew how pious his own king was) and a dedicated husband and father.

Any suspicions that this paragon could not possibly live up to the expectations created by King Andras's descriptions were dispelled when he stood before them. Edward was a tall, fair, blue-eyed epitome of Saxon manhood: the nobility and common folk alike would easily be persuaded that he looked the part of their monarch. His modest clothes and absence of finery were also met with approval, for they all knew how suspicious King Edward would have been if presented with a man who set too much store by material wealth. But more than that, this exiled prince embodied all the qualities that Andras had attributed to him. He had the unmistakable, unfeigned air of a good and honourable man.

Edward accepted the envoys' invitation to return with them to England. Agatha, Margaret and Edgar were sent for and duly appeared at court, accompanied by their pitifully modest baggage. Edgar's sturdy, energetic presence produced still more approval, for he gave every sign of being the kind of lad who might one day grow to be a good king. And when Edward added, in passing, that his wife was in the early stages of a third pregnancy, the prospect of yet another string to the regal bow only added to the general air of good fortune.

They travelled westwards up the Danube to Vienna and from there across country to Linz and Nuremberg and then via Metz and Rheims to Paris. By the time they reached the court of King Henry of France, Agatha's pregnancy was more immediately evident and the necessity for her to travel at a leisurely pace more pressing. She was also, understandably, very keen to spend some time with her sister, Queen Anne. And there was something to be said, too, for giving the prince and princess a little time to learn a few phrases of French, a language with which the English king was more comfortable, after so many years in Normandy, than his native Anglo-Saxon.

It was therefore agreed that the English envoys would press

on to London. The king was waiting at his new palace on Thorney Island, somewhat to the west of the city, where he was building a new abbey, known as the West Minster. He would, it was generally agreed, want to hear the good news of his successor at the soonest possible opportunity. Meanwhile, Prince Edward would remain with his wife and children in Paris before travelling to England a short while later. He asked the envoys to assure their master that he was particularly keen to see the church that King Edward was building at his new abbey, for he had been assured that it was one of the wonders not just of England, but of all Christendom.

Queen Anne was thrilled by her sister's arrival. A month passed very agreeably as the women chatted, Agatha's belly expanded and Edward went hunting with King Henry and his nobles. Both Edward and Agatha did indeed master a few basic phrases – Edward was particularly proud of his ability to say, 'It is my great pleasure and honour to make your acquaintance, Your Majesty.' But there came a time when their departure could be delayed no longer and they took to the road once again, bound for Boulogne and a ship for Dover.

Montgomery had not been idle. Having told Mabel to prepare her poisons and then join him in Rouen, he rode to Bures and quizzed his mother about her contacts at the French court until they came up with one who might provide them with intelligence about the English prince and his movements. He then rode incognito and unescorted to Paris, where he contacted the man his mother had suggested, offering him a small purse of gold with the promise of a much larger one to come and telling him to find out all he could about this prince who had suddenly emerged from the other side of the world. 'The moment you know he is leaving Paris, and where he is going, ride to me. You will find me in Rouen, staying with Duke William. And make sure you ride fast. We must be ahead of the prince. That's absolutely vital.'

The man turned out to be an excellent spy. He arrived in Rouen late one night, insisted on being taken to the chamber where Lord Montgomery and his wife were sleeping and told them that Edward and his family would be leaving Paris the following morning, bound for Boulogne and thence to Dover, in England.

'And I have one piece of good news, my lord,' the man added. 'Prince Edward's wife, Princess Agatha of Kiev, is with child. She grows large and her time of confinement cannot be far away. So she will have to travel to the coast in a carriage, and that will determine the speed at which her husband travels too.'

'Slowly, in other words,' said Montgomery.

'Precisely, my lord.'

Montgomery handed over the promised gold and felt the money well spent. Mabel lay with him that night, but once she had broken her fast in the morning, she was away on horseback towards Boulogne, accompanied by men-at-arms to guard her, spare horses (for both Roger and Mabel knew only too well that when she left England, it might very well be as a fugitive, and she had to be able to move at speed), and generous funds to hire the fastest ship in the port and then procure anything she might need once she arrived in Dover.

The ship was secured and the captain was even able to tell Mabel about the vessel on which the prince and his family would be travelling. 'A Frank arrived in town a couple of days ago, and came down looking for a boat to carry a great dignitary and his family to England. But I'll tell you what, your ladyship, he didn't have the purse for a ship fit for a prince, I can tell you that straight up, no word of a lie, 'cause it was a pal of mine got the job and his boat, well, she's sturdy enough, I'll give her that, but I could sail an ale barrel over to England faster'n that tub'll go.'

When they arrived in England, Mabel told the captain to keep an eye out for his friend's boat and let her know the moment he caught sight of it.

'Don't you worry, m'lady, I'll have a boy up the mast. He'll see her coming a good few leagues off, you can count on that.'

Three mornings later, she was roused from her bed in a local inn by news that the ship had been spotted. She made her way at once to the port, expecting to see a party of English soldiers and a mighty noble leading them, all sent by the king to escort his new heir to London, along with as fine a carriage as Dover could provide for this Princess Agatha. But no such escort nor any carriage was there.

An hour later, the ship was a little closer, but there was still no sign of any of the king's men. It dawned on Mabel that she had just been provided with the most glorious stroke of luck. If she handled matters correctly, her victims would be delivered straight into her arms.

There were just a few details to arrange first. But she had gold in her purse. And in her experience, there was absolutely nothing that gold would not buy.

26

Dover and the road to London

'Is that England? Is that England?' Edgar asked as the line of white cliffs on the horizon, gleaming in the full light of the morning sun, drew ever closer.

Dear God, I hope so, thought Agatha, for she had spent a miserable, restless night. She had prayed for a calm voyage but instead a strong breeze had produced a heavy swell on the water and that had only worsened the sickness she already felt from being with child.

'I think so, yes,' his father replied. 'I couldn't quite understand what the captain was saying, but he was pointing in that direction and nodding a lot.' He turned to his wife and wrapped a consoling arm around her. 'Not long now, my darling. I'm sure you'll feel much better once we are on dry land.'

Yet even though they were soon able to see the harbour nestled at the foot of the cliffs, it seemed to take an age before the sturdy, broad-beamed merchant ship wallowed its way into port and finally docked. Edward, Agatha and the children disembarked. They assembled on the quayside, with Edgar longing to dash off and explore, Margaret looking around with a quiet, thoughtful air and Agatha trying to calm her stomach on land that somehow seemed to be almost as unsteady beneath her feet as the sea itself had been.

A couple of sailors unloaded their little pile of baggage and put it down beside them, and then stood in front of Edward, clearly expecting some kind of reward for their endeavours and looking distinctly unimpressed when he finally gave them a single, very small Magyar coin.

'Where are the English?' Agatha asked unhappily. 'There should be an escort.'

'Well, I'm sure there are people to meet us somewhere nearby. I can't believe His Majesty would simply leave us to make our own way to see him.'

Agatha frowned at her husband. 'You did send word that we were on our way, didn't you?'

'King Henry sent a messenger. He assured me that the news would be delivered well before we arrived in England and that King Edward would have plenty of time to send men down to greet us. He assured me that if he were in King Edward's position, he would make sure that his new heir was treated like a prince of the realm from the moment he stood on English soil.'

'I fear the King of England has a very different idea of hospitality to the King of France,' said Agatha, getting her first inkling of the kind of man they had come all this way to meet.

'He can't just expect us to make our way by ourselves, can he?'

Edward cast a despairing eye around the bustling port. All around him sailors were talking, shouting, joking and yelling abuse in a host of different dialects. Crowds of merchants mingled with the dockers, taverners and women of ill repute that gathered in any port. There were even a couple of men whose clothes and bearing suggested that they were of high birth or great wealth. But none of this multitude showed the slightest interest in the man who might one day be their king, or the family at his side.

Then a woman emerged from the throng and walked towards Edward. As she came closer, it was clear that she was no doxy looking for a man to pay for her company, but was as noble as any man there. She was also a woman of remarkable beauty, with slightly hooded eyes the colour of cool grey marble. Agatha tensed. The last person she wanted coming anywhere near her husband when she felt and doubtless looked as unwell as she did was a creature as ravishing as this.

But then the most extraordinary thing happened. As the woman came within a couple of paces of Edward, she stopped and said in French, 'Do I have the great honour of speaking to Prince Edward of England?'

Edward gave an enthusiastic nod. 'Yes, madam, you do. May I . . .' he searched for the right words, 'be asking who you be?'

The woman dipped into a deep curtsey. As she rose to her full height she said, 'Of course, Your Royal Highness. My name is Muriel de Poitiers. I am travelling to London. I wonder, may I be of assistance? I have a carriage. It would be my honour to put it at your disposal.'

Edward could hardly believe his luck. He wanted to shout out in delight and relief, but did his best to maintain an air of royal self-control as he said, 'Thank you, madam. That is most kind offering. We are very thank you, yes.'

'I am so honoured by your kind acceptance of my humble offer,' the woman said. 'Please be so good as to stay here while I fetch my carriage. And do not worry about your baggage. My men will take care of that.'

Oh dear, thought Mabel, he really is just as shabby as Roger's man said he would be. But I dare say King Edward would like that. Father always used to say he looked like a tramp when he lived in Normandy. The wife will be the problem. She's suspicious and she doesn't want me getting anywhere near her man.

Mabel stopped walking for a moment and laughed to herself. Maybe I should give him the same dose as Roger. At least his last nights on earth would be happy ones.

When the carriage was brought to the quayside, Mabel ordered one of the spare mounts to be untethered and saddled so that the prince might ride. Agatha and Margaret joined Mabel inside, while Edgar sat beside the driver, with the promise that he might, if very good, be allowed to take the reins. Mabel had made a point of ensuring that there were plenty of soft cushions to ease the bumping of the solid wheels on the uneven, potholed roads and tracks along which they were likely to travel. She had also prepared a potion that mixed calming herbs with a smaller dose of the poppy-based *afyun* that Roger liked so much.

'I could not help but notice that you are carrying a new baby, Your Highness,' she began once they were all installed in the carriage and finally under way.

Agatha looked uncertain. Her daughter said a few words, evidently translating Mabel's French into their mother tongue.

Mabel smiled sweetly at Margaret. You clever girl, she thought. You've picked up much more than your parents, haven't you? I bet those beady little eyes of yours don't miss much, either. I'll have to watch myself around you.

'Yes, am having baby . . . one more!' Agatha said, doing her best to make conversation.

Mabel laughed sympathetically. 'How brave you are! I have a son and a daughter, too. But of course, my husband wants lots more!'

She waited for Margaret to be her interpreter, then added, 'I always felt very sick when I was expecting, especially when I was travelling. I hope you don't feel too unwell.'

Agatha waited as her daughter explained, then smiled ruefully and said a few words to Margaret.

'My mother confesses that she has not been feeling well, especially on the sea.'

Mabel gave a sympathetic nod. 'My dear, could you tell your sweet mother that I have some medicine. My own mother gave it to me when I was expecting my first child. She said she used it when she had my brother and me.'

Mabel gave Margaret time to explain all this, then went on, 'It is made by an old lady who lives in the woods near my parents' castle. She uses herbs and flowers she finds among the trees. It works so well that I always carry some with me, just in case I feel sick . . . even though I'm not expecting a baby!'

Another pause, a polite laugh from Agatha, and then Mabel said, 'Would you like some?' She had brought a small wooden chest, decorated with carvings of animals and flowers, filled with all the things she might need on the journey. Now she reached inside it and drew out a little flask. 'Here,' she said, 'do try some.'

Agatha looked suspicious. I don't blame you, Mabel thought. But she plastered her sweetest, most encouraging smile across her face. 'Do you know what? I think I might have some too. The carriage is making me feel a little sick.'

Taking great care not to spill anything as the carriage lumbered from side to side, Mabel poured a little of the medicine into a silver spoon and drank it. 'I feel better already!'

That seemed to encourage Agatha. She had two spoonfuls. Within a few minutes she said she was feeling calmer than she had done in days. A short while later, she was asleep.

'Thank you, madam,' said Margaret. 'My mother was not able to rest at all last night. Now she sleeps. Is good for her, no?'

'It certainly is,' Mabel agreed. 'Very good.'

27

Edward was pathetically grateful for the change that a morning's rest made to his wife. When they stopped at an inn for their midday meal, Agatha's health and her mood seemed greatly improved. He noticed, too, that she had decided to set aside her initial suspicion of Lady Muriel. The two women seemed to be talking perfectly happily about the usual subjects that women seemed to find worthy of endless hours of discussion – babies, mostly, from what he could catch of their conversation – and Margaret was making herself useful as a translator. The knowledge that his womenfolk were happily occupied and had no immediate need of his presence, nor any demands for him to take action on their behalf, came as a great relief.

He was pleased, too, by the modesty with which the Frenchwoman carried herself in his presence. She very clearly looked up to him as her superior, both as a man and a prince, and it struck Edward that this might be the way he would be treated by the world in general in years to come. Being a man of heartfelt religious convictions, he truly tried to live in the belief that all men were created equal in God's eyes and that it therefore behoved those who had been blessed with good fortune on earth to behave with due humility. Still, as Muriel bent her knee to him, bowed her head and looked up at him shyly, Edward could not help but enjoy the effect that his new status was having.

They spent that night near the village of Charing, staying at the manor house of what the English apparently called a 'thegn', which seemed to mean a substantial local landowner. Muriel had sent one of her men on ahead to find suitable shelter for the night and explain Edward's significance. It transpired that the thegn, Aldwyn, was a liegeman of Leofwine Godwinson, Earl of Kent. The earl had mentioned to him that a scion of Edmund Ironside had been located in a faraway land to the east and was journeying to take his place at the court of his uncle, King Edward. The thegn had been overcome with joy at his master's news, for Ironside's memory was still treasured by the English for his courage and warrior spirit. The very idea that this new-found prince would even consider staying at his humble home was enough to send Aldwyn rushing to call for his wife, his stockman and his most trusted tenant farmers so that preparations could be made for the arrival of their king-to-be.

By the time the carriage trundled through Charing, with Edward and the French men-at-arms riding before it, the whole village was lining the road to greet the cavalcade. People had dashed from all the neighbouring farms and even other villages. Some could still be seen in the distance, racing across the fields to catch a glimpse. Charing was on the pilgrim road to Canterbury, so folk thereabouts were far more accustomed than most country-dwellers to the presence of strangers in their midst. But royal strangers, well, that was another matter altogether.

'I hadn't expected all this when I offered you the use of my carriage,' said Mabel as she and Agatha looked out at the groups of peasants clustered by the side of the road and the children running along beside them. Word of their coming seemed to have spread right across Kent, so that the scenes they had witnessed the previous night in Charing were now being repeated at every village and every farm they passed. News of Aldwyn's good fortune had also reached the ears of the nobility of the region, and many had sent messengers to intercept the royal party and offer the most lavish hospitality imaginable. Even monks were riding up to them to explain, on their abbots' behalf, the very great advantages of cleanliness, privacy and splendid catering that their monasteries could provide. The privilege of a royal visit was a great prize indeed, and no one wanted to pass it up.

'The peasants look very well fed, and the crops in the fields are all flourishing, have you noticed that?' asked Agatha. 'I think England must be a rich land. Look how green it is. The animals all grow fat. And I think it must be a very peaceful land, too.'

'How very interesting, Your Highness,' said Mabel. 'Why do you say that?'

'Because we have hardly passed a single castle since we left Dover, and your men are the only ones I have seen who have swords. The people here feel no need to defend themselves or live behind high stone walls.'

'That's very true. I had not been aware of those things myself, but now you mention them, of course you are quite right. England is rich and yet defenceless. Perhaps His Highness should build some castles when he inherits the throne, just in case anyone else should see what you have noticed.'

And perhaps I should tell Montgomery about this, Mabel thought. Duke William will love the idea of a country that has no castles to besiege.

'Well, we must not get ahead of ourselves with all this talk of thrones,' said Agatha. 'But I confess, I would feel honoured to be Edward's queen one day. There is so much good one could do if God blessed one with that position, don't you agree?'

'Absolutely,' said Mabel. 'And how gracious of you to think of this as a chance to do good for others, instead of thinking about yourself.'

She gritted her teeth. You ridiculous woman! What kind of a fool thinks that charity is the point of being a queen? Power, treasure, control, domination – that's what it's all about. That's why people put a crown on your head, because they want to be ruled, they want decisions to be taken for them, they want orders to obey. Oh well, what difference does it make? You're never going to be queen of England. You're never going to be anything at all.

Mabel kept Agatha talking about the duties and obligations of a good monarch, while turning over a decision in her head. She had narrowed the possibilities down to three before she even left Alençon, but had waited to get a sense of the victim and the circumstances before she made her decision. But just as Agatha was wittering, 'Endowments to religious institutions are so important, don't you think?' she made up her mind.

Hemlock, she concluded. It's going to be hemlock. And I think I'll wait till the very last day. Poor old Edward. You'll actually be in sight of London when you finally die.

As they ate their breakfast on the final day of the journey from Dover, Edward and his family were all in a state of high excitement. Even Margaret, who was normally so self-possessed for a girl of eleven, was giggling and squealing in anticipation of all the wonders that would await them at King Edward's court, and bombarding her parents with almost as many questions as her little brother. They had all been served with wooden bowls of meat and porridge when a servant ran into the great hall of Dartford Manor, where they had spent the night, and announced that a number of the king's own housecarls, his personal bodyguard, had arrived to escort Prince Edward and Princess Agatha to Westminster. Margaret and Edgar immediately jumped down from the table and dashed towards the door. Edward and Agatha looked at one another and wordlessly agreed that there was no point in trying to rein their children in, so they might as well follow them outside.

The other servants and members of the household were all a-buzz with conversation, plainly longing to follow the exiles out into the abbey courtyard but unable to do so without the permission of their lord, who was himself getting up to see what all the fuss was about. In the confusion, no one paid the slightest attention to Mabel as she discreetly sprinkled a fine powder of ground hemlock seeds onto Edward's porridge and stirred it in. Then she waited patiently for the family to return, the children in an even more exuberant mood and their parents walking arm-in-arm with a spring in their step and broad smiles on their faces.

As they all sat down again, Edward spoke in French, as befitted his new life. 'Eat up now, every scrap. We have a long journey ahead and you need to keep your strength up.' He looked at Edgar. 'Bet you can't finish before me!'

The boy immediately attacked his bowl with gleeful gusto. Edward matched him spoon for spoon until his bowl was half empty, then, seeing that his aim had been achieved and his son would be well fed before his journey, paused and took a drink of beer from the pewter tankard that had been set before him.

When he spoke again, it was with a much more serious expression. 'Lady Muriel, we will be leaving you here . . .'

'I quite understand, Your Highness. I wish you a very good journey to London.'

'Thank you. But before we part, I just wanted you to know how very grateful I and my wife and children all are for your kindness, your generosity and your delightful company.'

'You are too kind; it was nothing.'

'On the contrary, we arrived in . . .' he conferred briefly with Margaret, 'yes, a strange land, with no friends and no one to meet us. But you were our Good Samaritan. You showed us true Christian kindness. And I want you to know – in fact we all do – that you will always have a place in our hearts and . . .'

He leaned over towards Margaret again, and for a terrible moment Mabel thought he was about to say that he wanted to introduce her to the king. The arrival of the escort had been a godsend; the very last thing she wanted was to spend any more time than she absolutely had to in England. A dash for the coast and a swift boat home was what she had in mind. But then she relaxed as Edward said, 'If you should ever find yourself in England again, you will always be a welcome guest at our home.'

Mabel lowered her head, as if overcome by the honour the prince was bestowing upon her, and Agatha, thinking that her new friend was about to cry, reached out across the table and took her hand consolingly. 'Thank you with all my heart, Lady Muriel. I will never forget your kindness and I hope that you will honour me by allowing me to be your friend.'

'The honour is all mine, Your Highness,' Mabel replied, biting her lip to keep herself from bursting out laughing. Only one thing concerned her now: had he eaten enough of the hemlock powder?

But then Edgar called out, 'Father, I've finished my bowl – look! – and you've not nearly finished yours. That's cheating!'

Edward laughed and made a great play of eating every scrap of food in his bowl before holding it up and saying, 'See! All gone!'

The royal party had been travelling for about two hours when Prince Edward suddenly appeared to sway in his saddle. Asked by one of the housecarls if anything was troubling him, he said he felt a little faint in the head. He also reported that he felt oddly weak and that his joints were aching. 'I'm sure it's nothing to worry about,' he said, insisting that they should carry on.

A further hour passed and then Edward slumped forward in

his saddle, so that he was leaning against the neck of his horse. He was unable to dismount and had to be lifted from his mount and carried across to the carriage in which his wife and daughter were travelling. He seemed completely lucid and did his best to calm his family and assure them that he would soon be feeling better. But as the day went on, his condition worsened. He lost all feeling in his hands and feet and reported that his limbs seemed cold.

That combination of numbness and chill slowly spread up through Edward's groin and abdomen, and though he tried to maintain a cheerful disposition and was still able to think clearly, it gradually became apparent that he was in fact dying, inch by inch. As his last reserves of strength failed, he told Agatha, Margaret and Edgar how much he loved them, and instructed his son to look after his mother and sister and to be sure to be a good, wise and God-fearing king of England when his turn came.

Finally, when they were barely two leagues from London Bridge, the last spark of life left Prince Edward's body and, surrounded by his distraught and bewildered family, he died.

28

It fell to Stigand, as the man who had proposed sending for Edward the Exile in the first place, to tell the king that he had suddenly expired.

'What do you mean, he's dead?' King Edward replied with peevish irritation. 'I was told this morning that he would be here before sunset. I must say, this really is not good enough. Not good enough at all.'

'I'm sure he did not intend to die, sire,' said Stigand, who was struck by the king's instinctive air of resentment. Clearly he felt that the most significant aspect of his presumptive heir's death was the inconvenience it had caused him. 'I am assured that he was quite well this morning and greatly looking forward to meeting Your Majesty, but fell ill quite suddenly on the way.'

'Well, I still say this is most unsatisfactory. I went to a great deal of trouble to invite this purported nephew to my court, and now it has all been in vain.'

'Not entirely, sire. Your nephew's wife, or rather his widow, is here, as are her two children, who are also of royal English blood. I am sure they would be greatly comforted if you were to grant them an audience at this time of great loss. They have, after all, come a very long way.'

The king frowned and shook his head crossly. 'No, no, I really don't see any reason why I should put myself out on their account. Tell them to come back tomorrow. I may have time for them then.'

'Where are they to stay in the meantime, sire? Might I suggest that a room be found for them in the palace?'

King Edward sighed. 'Oh, I suppose so. I am retiring to my chamber now, Stigand. This business has quite exhausted me and I need a little rest. I do not wish to be disturbed.'

'Of course not, sire.'

The king gave a grunt of acknowledgement and wandered away, leaving Stigand to ponder the precise nature and significance of the day's events. The Exile's death might, of course, have been a simple twist of fate. One never knew when fevers or evil spirits might strike, cutting a man down in his prime. That was a matter for God to decide and humans did best to accept these things as part of His great plan.

But sometimes God acted through the agency of his human sons, and when considering who might have done what, and why, Stigand liked to recall the words an elderly bishop had said to him when he first became chaplain to King Canute almost forty years earlier: 'Always ask yourself one question, my boy: "*Cui bono?*"'

The words were Latin, and their literal translation was, 'To whose good?' In other words: who benefits?

In this particular case, the answer was 'Anyone who would lose by Edward the Exile's accession to the throne.' And the most obvious losers were those men who coveted the crown for themselves.

Stigand could think of two main candidates. One was William of Normandy. But he did not strike Stigand as a man who would resort to poison. If he had wanted Edward dead, he would surely have had him killed while he was still on the Franks' side of the Channel, and the means of death would have been a sword piercing Edward's guts, or slicing his head from his neck.

There was another candidate, and he was standing not far

away in the great hall of the palace. So Stigand went to talk to him.

'My dear Wessex, how are you today?'

'Very well, thank you, Stigand,' replied Harold Godwinson. 'Terrible news about Prince Edward, isn't it? I was looking forward to meeting him. My father told me so much about Edmund Ironside – he really admired the man – so I was curious to meet his son.'

'So was I. But still, his unfortunate passing is rather convenient from your point of view, wouldn't you agree?'

Harold was taken completely by surprise. For an instant he seemed startled, then a puzzled frown furrowed his brow before he said, 'I'm sorry, but I don't have any idea what you mean by that.'

Good Lord, Stigand thought, I almost believe that you don't. 'I merely observe that your interests might not, perhaps, have been well served by the arrival of an adult heir to the throne.'

'Why ever not?'

'Well, purely by way of example, he might have chosen his own courtiers and advisers and excluded the House of Wessex.'

'I suppose so, I really hadn't thought about it. But even if he did, would that really make much difference to me? He couldn't take away my title or my land. Not unless I committed an act of treason, and why would I want to do that? Anyway, there are all my brothers and their earldoms to consider. I can't imagine any king wanting to take on all of us.'

'Of course not, no, quite right,' Stigand said soothingly. 'But now, with our beloved king growing older, as we all do, and only a child of six carrying the bloodline of the royal family, well, you are very well placed, are you not?'

'Look, I'm not sure I like the tone of this conversation. Forgive me, Your Grace, I don't mean to be impertinent to a man of God, but the suggestion that I would harm a prince of England that I have never met, that I have no quarrel with, simply to make myself more powerful . . . well, I'm sorry, but I'm just not that kind of man.'

'No, of course you aren't . . . Please excuse the philosophical speculations of an old priest. I am afraid I think too much sometimes.'

Harold smiled, for it was not in his nature to hold a grudge. 'Well, no one has ever accused me of that, eh? Now, if you'll excuse me . . .'

Stigand thought about what Harold had said. He had absolutely no doubt that the earl had been telling the truth. Murder was simply not in his nature. Unlike his father, who had never shirked a stab in the back if he felt it was necessary. Godwin had not been as honourable a man but he had been much the harder. Harold Godwinson might just be too decent for his own good.

In Dartford, Mabel explained to her host that she had only travelled this far into Kent because she felt a duty to make sure that such a noble prince and his charming family should reach their destination safely. Now that she had accomplished that task, she was turning back towards the true reason for her journey to England, which was to visit her sister, the wife of an English noble, who lived near Canterbury. Accordingly, when she departed, a short time after Prince Edward, her party turned in the opposite direction to the one he had taken and started retracing their steps back towards the south-east. The lord of Dartford and all his household were agreed that this noble Frenchwoman was a credit to her race and a most gentle Christian soul.

At about the time that Edward felt the first symptoms of his hemlock poisoning, Mabel and her men were passing through a great expanse of forest. Mabel had the carriage driver take the vehicle as deep into the trees as it would go. He then loosened the horse and loaded it with sacks containing all the cushions and other possessions that had been inside the carriage. Mabel mounted the fresher of the two spare horses, while the driver took the one that had carried the prince from Dover to Dartford, tethering the packhorse behind him. Then they rode for the coast, not holding back on account of Mabel, for she was a fine horsewoman. They slept that night under the light of the stars, so that no innkeeper would remember them, and reached Dover just before sunset the following day.

The captain was waiting for them and had good news: the tide was ebbing but the water was still high enough in the harbour for the ship to sail without fear of grounding. The wind was blowing from the west and would carry them straight back home. And there wasn't a cloud in the sky, so that he would be able to navigate by the stars.

'God is looking kindly on your journey, ma'am,' he said.

'Then I thank Him for it,' Mabel replied, though the truth was that she had never really believed in God, or perhaps it was more that He simply didn't interest her.

The Devil, however, was another matter. Him she found entirely fascinating.

29

The ducal palace in Rouen

Herbert of Maine, son of the late Count Hugh, was not a particularly impressive specimen. A thin, pale, underdeveloped young man of sixteen, whose face was disfigured by cream-tipped red pustules, he made a poor contrast with William of Normandy, whose assistance he was now seeking. Nor did his nasal, somewhat whiny voice do him many favours. Then again, William reminded himself, the lad had spent the last six years locked up in a cell in Le Mans, ever since Geoffrey Martel had captured the city. His father had died before it had fallen. His mother had been banished. He had been left alone and defenceless.

My story could have turned out like his, William told himself. I was just luckier in my enemies. Ah well . . .

'So, how did you escape the Hammer?' he asked.

Herbert shrugged and wiped the back of his hand against his nose. 'My mother got someone to pay off the jailer. Took her long enough. Six years I'd been in that dungeon. She could have done it ages ago, but—'

'Enough,' said William, sharply, not wanting to listen to what was clearly a long list of complaints. 'Just tell me why you decided to come here.'

'For help, obviously . . . I mean, who else can kick that man out of my county?'

'Martel, you mean?'

Herbert rolled his eyes as if to suggest that he could not possibly be describing anyone else.

300

William fought back the urge to step down from his chair and clip the obnoxious youth around the ear. 'And what will you give me in return?' he asked.

'Well . . . I could be your vassal, I suppose.'

'Could you now? And how would I gain by that, eh? Are you any good with a sword?'

Herbert gave another shrug. 'I don't know. Haven't done it for six years, have I? I mean, I was a prisoner. I didn't exactly get weapons and training.'

'No, I don't suppose you did. Nor did you get any soldiers or militia, or any barons you could call upon to provide their men. So you'd be no good to me at all.'

'Well, it's not my fault!' Herbert protested. 'I can't help it! What can I do?'

'You can talk to me like a man, that's what. You can stand up and fight for your land and your title. If you came to me and said, "I have nothing. I can offer you no men, no money, no land. But I will stand at your side and fight till I drop to win back what is rightfully mine," then I would respect you.'

William leaned forward on the table and poked a finger in the youth's direction. 'Listen to me, I know what it's like to be alone and friendless in the world. Everything you see here – this palace, the tapestries on the walls, the horses in the stables, the men in the barracks, my wife and children – I fought for all of it. I risked my neck, spilled my blood and swam in my own sweat. And if you offered to do the same, I would help you without a second thought. But you won't make that offer. So we will have to do things differently.'

'How?' said Herbert, suspiciously and without the slightest suggestion that William's words had made him revise his attitude.

'Give me something in return.'

'Like what?'

'Well, some courtesy for a start. I am a duke. Even if you were truly the Count of Maine, I would be your superior. So you should address me as "Your Grace".'

'Oh . . . all right then . . . Your Grace. Anything else?'

'Oh, I would think so. Let's begin with the county of Maine. It is your birthright, after all. Once you retrieve it, you'll have plenty to offer me.'

'What? You mean I get my land back and then I have to give it to you? That's not very fair.' Herbert stopped, thought, realised he'd forgotten something. 'Your Grace.'

William took a deep breath. He could feel his temper rising, and if he wasn't careful, he was liable to do something he might regret, like removing Herbert's pimply head from his scrawny shoulders.

'Correct me if I'm wrong, but don't you have a sister?' he asked.

'That's right, Marguerite. Haven't seen her in years, mind you. Not since I was locked up. She could be dead for all I know . . . Your Grace.'

'Let's hope she isn't. How old would she be now?'

'I don't know . . . Ten? Eleven? Something like that.'

'And is she betrothed to anyone yet?'

'I keep telling you, I don't know. I've been in a cell!'

'Stop whining! I swear to God I will not be held responsible for my actions if I have to listen to one more second of your snivelling. Pay attention, Herbert of Maine. I am only going to say this once and I will not enter into any negotiations. Here is my offer. I will drive Geoffrey Martel of Anjou out of Maine and restore the county to you. In return, you will from this moment on consider yourself my vassal and swear absolute, unfailing loyalty to me. You will also, as of now, betroth your sister to my son Robert. If you die before you produce an heir – and heaven knows I can't imagine why any woman would wish to assist you in that activity – I will inherit Maine from you. If I am dead by then, it will pass to Robert. Any attempt by you to renege on any part of this agreement will result in my bringing the wrath of Normandy down on your head and taking Maine from you by force. Do I make myself clear?'

'Yes, but . . . I mean, what happens if you don't drive Martel out of Maine? Do I still have to—'

'Enough! Do you agree to my terms or not?'

'Oh . . . I suppose so.'

'Then get down on your knees, Herbert of Maine, and accept me as your lord.'

'Well, I've found Robert a wife,' said William as he walked into the solar where Matilda was passing the time in embroidery and conversation with a pair of her attendant ladies. The four children the duke and duchess had produced over the past six years were scattered about the chamber: Robert, who was now six, was playing a game of chase with his sister Adeliza, who, though a year younger, was already taller than her brother. The second of their boys, Richard, a stocky bundle of three-year-old energy, was desperately running after them, trying to join in the game. Meanwhile William, at eighteen months, was sitting on the ground amusing himself by bashing a wooden spoon against a small metal pot.

'Really, my lord?' Matilda replied. 'He seems a little young to be getting married just yet.'

William chose to take the reply as a joke rather than a criticism and laughed. 'True enough! The agreement has been made, but the ceremony can wait a few years yet.'

'May I ask whom you have chosen for his bride?'

As all three women looked at him, William suddenly became uncomfortably aware that the arrangement of marriages was traditionally an activity in which the lady of the house was at the very least involved, and more often than not the prime mover.

'Marguerite of Maine,' he said. 'Her brother Herbert, the rightful count, has managed to worm his way out of Le Mans. He says his mother bribed the jailer, but if I were Martel I'd have paid good money to get rid of the snivelling little rat.'

'Well then, we'd better hope his sister is nothing like him.'

'Oh, I'm sure she'll be fine. The main thing is, this is going to give us control of Maine. If Herbert survives, he'll know, because I'll remind him at every opportunity, that he rules at our pleasure. If he dies without an heir, which I would bet a purse of gold he will, because plenty of men will want to kill him and no woman will want to bed him, then Maine passes to our family and Robert will be its count.'

'Lord of Normandy and Maine . . . yes, that is quite a prize,' Matilda conceded. 'You did well, my lord.'

'Thank you, dear lady.'

William strode across the chamber, reached down and grabbed Robert as he raced across the floor. In a single movement he swept the boy off the ground and threw him squealing into the air, catching him a second later.

'Again! Again!' Robert demanded, but William ignored him and held him close, with the little boy's legs wrapped around his waist.

'Now, Robert, did you hear what I was telling your mother just now? I was saying that I have found you a nice girl called Marguerite to marry.'

'A girl? Ugh! I don't want to get married!'

William laughed indulgently. 'Well, not now you don't, no. But in a few years' time you will, and then you can meet Marguerite and fall in love with her, just like I fell in love with your mama.'

Robert frowned. 'But what happens if I don't love her? Maybe she's fat and ugly and smelly.'

'I'm sure she won't be any of those things.'

'But what if she is?'

'Then I suppose we will have to get sweet perfume and bags of scented herbs to make her smell better, and give her less food so that she's not so fat, and as for making her less ugly, well, she'll have to hide behind a veil or something. And in the meantime . . .' William held Robert out in front of him, 'you are going to have to grow. You are shorter than your little sister and Lady Marguerite is four years older than you. If you're not careful, you'll be so short she won't be able to see you.'

William put Robert down on the floor and started walking round the room with exaggerated steps, pretending to search for something. 'She'll be walking all around the palace going, "Where are you, Robert? I can't see you!" and you'll be saying, "I'm down here!"'

Adeliza was shrieking with laughter at her father's performance, and that set Richard laughing too. Robert, however, was red in the face with shame and humiliation. 'I'm not short!' he shouted. 'I'm not! I'm not!'

'Yes you are,' William continued, blind to the hurt he was causing his boy. 'In fact, I've got a new name for you. I'm going to call you Robert Shortpants.'

'Shortpants, Shortpants!' Adeliza joined in.

Robert ran weeping to his mother, who lifted him onto her lap and stroked his head. 'There, there. Papa didn't mean what he said. He was only playing.'

'Not short!' Robert insisted through his tears.

Matilda looked up at William. 'Perhaps your lordship should return to ruling the duchy. We women will get on with looking after the children.'

He stood for a moment looking furiously at his wife, then turned away without a word.

As he walked towards the door, Robert pulled away from his mother's grasp and shouted after him, 'I hate you! I hate you!'

30

As he stalked back into his council chamber, William saw Montgomery coming towards him, still in his riding cloak. He fixed him with a stony stare. 'Yes?'

Montgomery stopped short, taking in William's mood, then, with the practised air of a man well used to dealing with his master's ill temper, said, 'I have news, Your Grace. I feel sure that it will interest you and, perhaps, distract you from whatever troubles you.'

William's eyes narrowed, but there was curiosity in them now. 'And where does this news come from?'

'From England, Your Grace. I am informed that Prince Edward, son of the late King Edmund, returned safely to his homeland after many years of exile but was then, very tragically, taken ill. He died just a few miles short of his uncle King Edward's palace. He and the king never met.'

'I see,' said William. He looked around and saw that a number of the barons and hangers-on who had gathered in the chamber were now looking towards him, having overheard the news. 'Well, I'm sure that King Edward will be very sad to hear of his nephew's demise. We must send our condolences to His Majesty. I hope I can count on you to see to that.'

'Of course, Your Grace.'

'Walk with me a while, Montgomery. There are matters on which I would welcome your counsel . . .'

The two men strolled out of the palace into the gardens without the faintest suggestion of urgency. When he was sure that they were not being observed or overheard, William asked, 'Were you responsible for the Exile's death?'

'On my word of honour, I did not kill Prince Edward,' Montgomery replied. 'Save for my recent journeys to Paris on my mother's business, I have not left Normandy for a year or more. And I have never in my life been to England.'

The faintest flicker of a smile hovered briefly over William's expression. 'Neatly put, Montgomery. I'm glad we have settled that. Nevertheless, I realise as we speak that I may not have adequately rewarded you for the many services you have done me. Tell me, is there anything you desire that is in my power to give?'

Mabel had made sure that Montgomery was well briefed to answer just this question. 'As a matter of fact, Your Grace, there is. You may recall that Arnaud d'Echauffour died almost three years ago, intestate, since when his estates have reverted to your domain . . .'

'D'Echauffour's land borders on Bellême, does it not?'

'Quite so. It would be a very natural addition to my wife's own property. I know she would be delighted and deeply honoured if you could favour us in that way.'

William gave Montgomery a searching look. 'Arnaud died quite suddenly, did he not?'

'Yes, I'm afraid so. Very sad.'

'And not long beforehand, your brother Hugh also departed this world for the next. Tell me if I remember this incorrectly, but wasn't Hugh taken ill very suddenly at dinner?'

'I was not there, being on campaign with Your Grace at the time. But as I understand it, your memory is quite accurate. Hugh had consumed a gross quantity of food and drink in a very short time. Sadly, he was prone to that sort of indulgence and excess.'

'But your wife was present, was she not?'

'Indeed so, Your Grace.'

'And wasn't she offering the hospitality of her castle to Arnaud d'Echauffour at the time?'

'Yes, it was an occasion of reconciliation. Arnaud felt a need for recompense following the death of his father, William Fitzgiroie, who had suffered greatly at Mabel's father's hands. Mabel was going to satisfy this by endowing a chapel, to be built in Fitzgiroie's memory at the monastery of Le Bec.'

William nodded, 'Ah yes, that venomous old devil Talvas did terrible things to poor Fitzgiroie. Talvas's father was just as bad, apparently. Runs in the blood with those Bellêmes.'

'I wouldn't know.'

'Still, I'm sure your beautiful wife has inherited none of her father's, ah . . . poison, eh?'

For a second, Montgomery's mask slipped. He sounded like a man who had been verbally ambushed as he stumbled over his words. 'Ah . . . poison . . . no . . . not at all, Your Grace, absolutely not.' He gave a sudden nervous laugh. 'Very worrying for me if she had, eh?'

William had only mentioned poison because he'd just said that Talvas was venomous. It was intended as no more than a play on words. But now he realised he must have stumbled on the truth. Still, the rules of the game they were both playing forbade any suggestion of that.

'I'm sure the sudden deaths of both Hugh and Arnaud were no more than a tragic coincidence,' he said. 'Nor will I draw any rash conclusions from the fact that your mention to me of the need to do something about this possible heir to the throne of England was followed a short while afterwards by the unexpected news of his death.'

Montgomery had recovered his sangfroid. 'These mysteries are all part of God's plan, Your Grace. Who are we to say what the good Lord means by them?'

'Well said, Montgomery. And yes, Lady Mabel may have Arnaud's estates, by all means. I suspect that she has earned them.'

'Just as you, Your Grace, may now count upon the knowledge that England will one day rightly and properly be yours.'

'I do not count upon anything, Montgomery. Life has taught me that. But my experiences have also taught me that if I desire something, and put my mind to having it, then, rest assured, in the end it will be mine.'

Book Three:

The Pieces on the Board

Spring 1064–Summer 1066

1

The royal palace of Westminster

There were very few things that truly stirred King Edward's blood, but one that did was hunting. He had no interest in bedding men or women, and disapproved of excessive drinking. He cared not for war, or its spoils. The possession of treasure and gold was merely an unfortunate necessity for any monarch who needed to fund his court, reward his subordinates and finance the defence of the realm. But hunting . . . ah, that was different.

Over the years the unfettered right to chase wild animals wherever and whenever he chose had become the one great privilege of Edward's position. Every morning he would take Mass and give his confession. And when that was done, wherever he was in the kingdom, he would set off at once for the nearest forest, heath or moorland to pursue deer and boar, or the marshes and estuaries where wildfowl provided the game.

It was the sense of power he felt as a huntsman that intoxicated Edward: the knowledge that he had another creature's life at his mercy, to take or preserve as he saw fit. It seemed to him that this must be how God felt about every living soul on earth, and that in turn brought him closer to the Almighty. It made him feel as though they had something in common. The great drawback, of course, was that one had to hunt with other people. And men being men, the day would end with feasting and the drinking of wine and ale, which in turn would be followed if not by debauchery then, all too often, by boastful descriptions of it, provided by one man to the others. Edward found it all distasteful, not to say disturbing. Gross descriptions of the female form and the uses to which it could be put by a man enslaved by his animal lusts made his skin crawl with the horror of physical intimacy.

He far preferred it when, as now, he could use his palace at Westminster as his base and set out from there to the countryside round about before returning to inspect the day's work on the magnificent abbey church that was nearing completion beside the palace. Then he could return to court and concentrate on his other favourite pursuits. Such as, for example, making life just that little bit more difficult for Harold Godwinson.

Edward would never forgive Earl Godwin for his part in his brother Alfred's death, and Harold, as the head of the Godwinson family, had thereby inherited his father's guilt in the king's eyes. Harold was, of course, far too powerful to be challenged directly. In recent years he had even acquired the status of 'subregulus', or deputy monarch. But even so, Edward felt sure that there must be ways in which Harold could be undermined. As yet, he had been unable to come up with anything that had caused Harold quite the level of misery and, ideally, humiliation that was required. And then one day the king discovered that he had an ally in his cause.

Queen Edith had always had a special place in her heart for her brother Tostig. From her earliest girlhood she had got on with him better than any of her other brothers. He had always been more willing to talk and even play with her than Sweyn or Harold. She, in return, sympathised with him for having to put up with the two oldest boys. Sweyn was just a bully, always willing to kick or punch his smaller brother, while Harold could never understand why Tostig had to work much harder to be even reasonably good at things that came effortlessly to him.

So when Tostig told her that he was having a hard time maintaining control of his earldom of Northumbria in the face of relentless opposition from the regional nobility, and complained that Harold had not lifted a finger to help, Edith felt for him. How dare Harold be so arrogant, so dismissive of everyone else's problems? Why did no one ever take him down a peg or two?

The next time Edward launched into one of his bitter little speeches about the Earl of Wessex's lack of respect for the throne, Edith did not, as in the past, do her best to mollify her husband. Instead, to her own surprise, she found herself encouraging him.

'You are quite right, as always, my lord,' she said. 'My poor brother Tostig was saying just the same thing to me only recently. He looked to Harold for help and was dismissed without a shred of sympathy.'

Edward sighed. He had a great deal of time for Tostig, whom he regarded as a misunderstood soul, much like himself. 'I confess I worry about what will happen when I am gone,' he said.

Edith looked pleadingly up into his eyes. 'Your Majesty, I beg you not to talk of that terrible day. You know how it pains me.'

'I know, my dear,' he said, patting her hand, an act of extreme intimacy by his standards, but one which he had recently started to indulge in, and even enjoy. 'You will be lost without me, I know. But it is a king's duty to consider the consequences of his passing. Young Prince Edgar remains in England. He is of true royal blood. But if he takes the throne, Wessex will surely wield even greater influence.'

'What if Edgar does not take the throne?' Edith asked in a tone of sweet innocence.

Edward let go of her hand in alarm. 'You mean your brother might ascend himself?'

'Oh no, Your Majesty, please forgive me. I had not intended to displease you. I was thinking of a very different possibility. One that would prevent the very outcome you seek to avoid.'

'How do you mean?'

'Just that there is always the other heir, whom you, in your great wisdom, first chose . . .'

Edward smiled as he took his wife's point. 'So there is.'

'And if you should decide to reinstate him as your successor, perhaps it would be right for someone as senior as your deputy to impart the good news in person, rather than relying on a humble messenger.'

Edith saw the smile playing around her husband's mouth and the light of pure pleasure in his eyes and realised that she had not seen that precise expression since the awful day when Champart had come up with the idea for her own punishment. How ironic that all these years later it should be she, the former victim of the king's malice, who had become his fellow conspirator.

But then she saw a sudden doubt cross Edward's mind, and he frowned. 'I apologise, my dear, but I cannot help but wonder why you should be so willing to act against your own brother's interests.'

'Because I am a loving wife who cannot bear to see her husband suffer the slightest pain, and a loving sister who hates to see her favourite brother brought low. And if the same culprit is responsible for both of those crimes, then it matters not that he is my brother. He should be punished for his misdeeds.'

'Well said, my dear, well said!'

Edward was perfectly satisfied by the explanation, and rightly so, for Edith had been completely sincere. She had become so used to playing the role of the unquestioningly loyal, submissive

316

wife, and – just as the abbess of Wilton had predicted – gained so much from her subservience that it had ceased to be a role and become her true nature.

Much later that night, however, as she lay asleep, alone in her bed, the deeper, darker reason for her anger suddenly came to her in a dream. She found herself back at Wilton, in the arms of the reverend mother, with Harold hammering on the door. And when he smashed his way into the chamber and saw her there, with her mucky, tear-stained face, and her filthy rag of a dress, he took one look at her and then stood with his legs apart and his hands on his hips and laughed until he could barely breathe.

Edith woke with a start, and sat up in bed, sick to the guts with shame and humiliation. And she knew then why she was filled with rage and even hatred towards her brother. For he had seen her when she was less than nothing. That moment could never be wiped from either of their memories. And she would never, ever forgive him.

The following day, after a hunt that had seen the king bring down a particularly magnificent stag, he commenced his scheme to humble an equally splendid beast in human form.

'I have a commission for you, Wessex, and would be pleased for you to fulfil it at your very earliest convenience,' he began.

'Of course, Your Majesty,' said Harold with that blithe self-assurance that Edward found so intensely irritating, not least because he had never possessed such confidence himself. 'What do you wish me to do?'

'You may not be aware of this, Wessex, but I am sixty years of age and my lease upon life in this mortal form must soon come to its end.'

'Oh, I'm sure Your Majesty has no need for concern. You

are still at the very height of your powers. Why, your prowess on the hunting field this very day surely proves that point.'

'I'm sure it's very kind of you to say so, Wessex, but the fact remains that I must once again think about my successor, and who he might be.'

'I see . . .' said Harold, leaving the words hanging.

You want it so badly, don't you, Godwinson? thought Edward. He looked at Harold, inviting him to say more.

'Well, I just assumed that young Prince Edgar would be the natural choice, being descended from your father's line.'

'The boy is not yet thirteen. He is not ready to rule.'

'But Your Majesty will surely survive until he is. And if God takes you to join him in heaven, I'm sure a suitable regent could be found.'

And I wonder who you think that regent might be? fumed Edward. Well, I'd sooner hand the keys to the kingdom to a horde of ravaging Danes than let any of Godwin's boys near the throne. And now you must give it to someone else.

'That's all well and good, Wessex, but England needs a grown man as its king. You know as well as I do that Harald Hardrada of Norway and Sven of Denmark both have claims to the crown.'

'But surely, sire, those two men are too busy fighting one another to be able to attack England. The moment one of them sailed towards our shores, he would leave his own land vulnerable to attack by the other.'

'But what if they should make peace?'

'Those two? They've been hammering away at one another for as long as I can remember!'

'Nevertheless, the possibility of peace between the two Norsemen and thus the danger of war against England remains. Then there is the whole question of the Welsh. Whoever succeeds me will have to deal with them once and for all, or forever live in fear of invasion from the west. No, I'm sorry, Wessex, this task needs a man with a proven record as a leader in peace and war alike. As chance would have it, there happens to be such a man just across the water. And I know that the prospect of kingship is one that appeals to him.'

'So it's true . . .' Harold said, half to himself.

'What's true?' Edward asked.

'That the throne was once offered to William of Normandy, Your Majesty. My father was convinced that Archbishop Champart had visited the duke to pass on an offer while our family was, ah . . .'

'In exile?'

'I was going to say, while we briefly failed to satisfy our duties to Your Majesty.'

'Well, your father was well informed.'

'Might I therefore ask, Your Majesty, why, if that pledge to Duke William had already been made, you sent all the way to the land of the Magyars for your nephew Prince Edward?'

'The question is an impertinent one, but I will answer it nonetheless. My offer to Normandy was made when I was unaware of Prince Edwards's existence. Once I realised that there was a true scion of England to succeed me, naturally I preferred him. William would have appreciated that, I am sure. Circumstances change, and when they do, so do one's policies.'

'But there is still a true scion of England here in the country today, Your Majesty. Prince Edward's son Edgar.'

'Pah! He is just a child. And I, being king, have once again decided that circumstances have changed.'

'I see . . . and that being the case, might I ask what task you would have me perform?'

'Actually, the task is twofold. In the first instance, I would have you journey to Duke William in Normandy and assure him that my offer to him still stands.'

'Your Majesty is of course aware that the pledge of the throne means nothing without a formal declaration of support made by the nobles and bishops of the realm meeting at a Witenagemot.'

'Of course, which is why I also want you to give him your word that you and your brothers will stand before the Witenagemot and support his candidacy. You and your kin have done very well out of me, Wessex. You have your earldom of Wessex. Your brothers Leofwine and Gyrth have Kent and East Anglia respectively. Tostig has Northumbria, the largest earldom in the country. All the land between the Humber and the Tweed is his, from the North Sea in the east to the Irish Sea in the west . . . unless he loses it, of course, which I fear he may if matters continue as they are at the moment. You know how fond both Her Majesty and I are of your brother. It is therefore a matter of the greatest importance to me that you and I should find a way to reconcile Earl Tostig with the northern thegns . . .'

Edward had spoken as if he really meant what he was saying, but then, as if unable to summon up the necessary energy to follow his words with action, he paused and sighed. 'Though it will have to wait until your return from Normandy.'

'Sire, do you not think that Northumbria is the more urgent issue? The Scots are becoming bolder by the day. King Malcolm has already seized Cumberland and raided as far south as Durham. And as you say, Earl Tostig has not yet won the support of the Northumbrian nobility. Let me stay here and try to sort the matter out. He may listen to me. I am his older brother, after all.'

'Then talk to him this evening. He's here after all, though I wish he weren't. As much as I delight in his company, I am well aware that his attention should be directed elsewhere. You may tell him I said so. And when you have done that, be on your way to Normandy.'

'Yes, sire.'

'Very good then, Wessex. And there's no need to look so glum. I'm sure Duke William will be only too glad of your counsel and only too happy to maintain the Godwins in the manner to which you have become accustomed, just as so many of his predecessors have done.'

Harold nodded non-committally. 'I'll be on my way at first light tomorrow.'

'Good man.' Edward smiled with apparent benevolence, though his pleasure arose more from the way that his succession could be used as a way to manipulate the fortunes of other men, even after his own death. You'll have to use all that charm of yours on the Bastard if you're to keep any of your earldoms, Godwinson, he thought with satisfaction. I do hope it is possible to look down from heaven to the mortal world below. I feel virtually certain that you and Cousin William will have to fight it out. And I confess I am curious to discover who wins in the end.

2

Tostig Godwinson, Earl of Northumbria, was in the middle of a loud, ale-filled discussion of the day's hunting with a number of other courtiers and did not appreciate his older brother dragging him away for a lecture about the running of his earldom. His mood became even blacker when Harold told him that the king himself had suggested he would be better employed winning over his people in the north of the country than chasing deer in the south.

'So I'm not welcome here, is that it?' snapped Tostig, as ready as ever to detect a personal slight whether one was intended or not.

'Don't be ridiculous. His Majesty has never even hinted at any such thing. You're one of his favourites and Edith dotes on you. His point was simply that you might have better things to do with your time.'

'Like try and make the Northumbrians just the tiniest bit less stupid, pig-headed and unreasonable, you mean? It's impossible. They're a bunch of barbarians. And damned ungrateful ones too.'

Before Harold could reply, Tostig was off again. 'When I got to Northumbria, it was completely lawless. People couldn't travel anywhere without being attacked by gangs of thieves, and to make matters worse, most of the gangs were paying the local lords to turn a blind eye to the mayhem. I put a stop to all that, or tried to anyway, and people could finally travel with a bit more safety. But the thegns just resented me taking away the blood money they were getting from the damned outlaws.'

'I understand, but—' Harold began, only to be interrupted as Tostig continued his litany of complaints. 'The Bishop of Durham is conspiring against me. Then there's the House of Bamburgh. It's the oldest, most powerful clan up there and they're all just waiting for a chance to stab me in the back. There's a Bamburgh connection to what I call the Unholy Trinity: Gamel, Ulf and Gospatric—'

'I think I've come across Gospatric at court,' said Harold, trying to get a word in edgeways.

'Very possibly. His father's mother was King Ethelred's daughter Aelfgivu.'

'Which makes Gospatric King Edward's nephew.'

'That's right, though there doesn't seem to be much family feeling between them. Gospatric and his friends dream of re-creating the old kingdom of Northumbria, independent from England. But they want it both ways. I mean, none of the big families will pay their taxes, but then they complain if I don't protect their land against the Scots. They won't give me armed men like they've got a duty by law to do. So I'm obliged to hire two hundred Danish mercenaries as my housecarls and then they moan that I'm bringing in foreigners to lord it over their land.

'Do you know, they're still going on about having to pay tax to fund the war against the Welsh? All those months I spent freezing my arse off in Snowdonia, dealing with Gruffydd, and they have the brass nerve to moan about paying their share of the cost.'

For years, Gruffydd ap Llewellyn, the king of all Wales, had been a menace to England. Then the Godwinson brothers had set out to defeat him once and for all. Tostig had attacked Wales by land from the north. Harold had attacked by sea from the south. Together they caught Llewellyn in a pincer movement.

'Now that *is* ridiculous,' Harold said sympathetically. 'If we hadn't beaten Gruffydd, he'd have marched right into Northumbria, and with the Scots raiding England too, God knows what might have happened.'

Tostig fell silent, but it was only a short-lived pause. He took a step closer to Harold. 'Shall I tell you the real problem with Northumbria? They don't trust me because I'm not northern enough for them. They think they're better than us southerners, can you believe it? They sit up there on their freezing cold moors, where it's so impossibly bleak that even sheep hate it. They're miserable as sin because the sun never shines, and when it's not raining, it's snowing, and when it's not doing either of those things, well, it soon will. You can't understand a word they say and their idea of music is blowing into pipes that make a sound so vile it's like every tortured soul in hell wailing away in your ear. And yet somehow these damned Northumbrians have got it into their thick heads that they are better than us.'

Tostig's indignation was so extreme that Harold could not help but laugh. For a moment it seemed as though this apparent mockery would only infuriate Tostig still further. But then he cracked and laughed too. 'Honestly, Harold,' he said, 'if you were lumbered with that godforsaken earldom, you'd be down here too.'

'Well, be that as it may, you are Earl of Northumbria and it's still one of the greatest titles that England can offer. You'd be mad to throw it away.'

'I know that. And it's not as if I haven't tried.'

'I don't doubt it . . . Look, I know it must be frustrating dealing with people who won't be sensible and come to an understanding. But go up there and give it your very best, why don't you, there's a good fellow.'

'All right then, I will. But don't blame me if it all ends in disaster. I mean it. These people are impossible.'

3

Westminster, the village of Bosham on the
Sussex coast and the English Channel

Harold went off to make arrangements for the first leg of his journey. His first destination was Bosham, a two-day ride from Westminster. There he kept one of his finest residences and, not far away, a dock where his personal flagship, the *Stormrider*, lay at anchor, ready to take him at any time wherever he desired.

Tostig, for his part, was summoned by a royal page, who informed him that Their Majesties the king and queen would be pleased to grant him a private audience.

On his arrival at the chamber where Edward and Edith awaited him, Tostig was greeted with a warm hug and a scatter of kisses from his sister and a benevolent smile from the king, who seemed to regard him more and more as the son he'd never had.

'My dear boy, I do hope Harold wasn't too stern with you,' the king began.

'I wouldn't say stern exactly, sire, so much as condescending. He clearly thinks he would be able to run Northumbria without the slightest difficulty. I tried to point out that it is no easy task, but I'm not sure he appreciates the trouble I have to deal with up there.'

'Oh, poor you,' Edith sympathised. 'Still, Harold's not having it all his own way for once. His Majesty has just sent him off to Normandy, to confirm Duke William as the heir to the throne and pledge his allegiance to him.'

Tostig's mood lightened in an instant and a huge smile spread across his face. 'So he has to give another man the crown and then grovel to him. That's perfect!'

'I know, isn't it just?' Edward said. 'It was the queen's idea, I may say. She deserves all the credit.'

'Your Majesty is much too kind,' Edith said. 'I cannot possibly hope to match your wisdom. But even though a woman cannot reason like a man, she may have an intuition of how men will behave.'

'Does she now?' said Tostig. 'And what does your instinct tell you about Duke William and our brother?'

'That they may create an opportunity for you. But you must be patient, and you must be ready to seize your chance when it comes.'

'And, of course, you must still have the power of Northumbria behind you,' the king interjected. 'To that end, my boy, I have arranged a surprise, something to make your life as earl a little easier. It will await you, I believe, when you return to your earldom.'

'Might I ask what the surprise will be, Your Majesty?'

'You may—' Edward began.

Queen Edith interrupted him. 'But I think you should just be patient.'

'And seize my opportunity?'

'Precisely.'

Harold held a feast at his manor house in Bosham, but his sour mood was sufficiently ill-disguised that a number of his guests, unused to seeing their earl so lacking in his usual good cheer, asked what was troubling him. He fobbed them off by claiming that he was suffering a bout of indigestion, but the excuse was a poor one and few were fooled.

Afterwards he and Edith Swan-Neck retired to his chamber.

Harold's love for his wife had always been made manifest in the passion and attention that he lavished upon her in bed. His trip to France was going to keep them apart for weeks, and this would normally give him good reason to be even more attentive than usual to their mutual pleasure. But he was as half-hearted in his lovemaking as he had been at the dinner table. As she lay beside him afterwards, Edith propped herself up on one elbow and looked down at him. 'Well? And don't tell me it's your guts that are bothering you.'

He sighed. 'I'm sorry . . . It's just this task the king has set me. That self-righteous old hypocrite knew just how much it would stick in my craw to tell William of Normandy that he's going to be my king, and he just loved making me do it.'

'Why can't he just name Edgar as his heir?' Edith asked. 'His claim is much stronger than that Norman's.'

'He says it's because Edgar is just a child, but that's ridiculous. The lad's thirteen. He's old enough to rule if he has a good, strong regent.'

'You would be perfect for that.'

'Absolutely, and the role would be perfect for this family. We'd be stronger than ever. And if anything happened to the boy . . .'

Harold's voice died away. He did not wish to finish the sentence, since it was perilously close to treason, but Edith knew exactly what he was thinking. If for any reason Edgar's rule should either end prematurely or simply fail, Harold would be ideally positioned to step in as a strong, capable, experienced king. But William of Normandy would be very much harder to shift once he was on the throne.

Harold's discontent still hung over him like a thick fog as he kissed Edith farewell and stepped aboard the *Stormrider* at Bosham quay. But it was a miserable soul that could not be lifted by a voyage begun on a bright spring morning. There was just a hint of the night's chill still in the air, soon to be banished by the sun now glinting on the golden dragon of Wessex that stood so proudly above the prow. Harold breathed in the salty sea air. He closed his eyes and felt the sun's warmth against his face as he listened to the sound of the water rippling around the hull mingling with the creaking of the rigging and the rhythmic grunts of the sailors as they rowed out into Chichester harbour.

He stepped towards the bow of the ship to get a better view of his surroundings. He had known these waters since he was a small boy, and as he looked out at the salt pans of Hayling Island to starboard and the farmland of the Hundred of Manhood on the port shore, he could not help but smile. These were his lands, bequeathed by his father. One day he would pass them on to his own heir, and so they would continue, down through the generations. Kings might come and go, the family might prosper or struggle and other more distant earldoms and estates might be lost to them. But this was the heartland of the Godwin clan and so it would always remain.

As they came to the mouth of the harbour, where the long stretch of sheltered inland water met the open sea, the *Stormrider* began to strain against the rigging as it felt the first hint of the sea breeze, like a hunting dog tugging on its leash when it caught the quarry's scent. The oars were shipped, the sail un-furled, the wind caught the canvas with a loud crack, and the helmsman pulled hard on the steering oar as he set the *Stormrider* on its course to Normandy.

'God has blessed us with a fine wind, m'lord.'

Harold turned to see his captain, Aldred Kimballson. A lifetime spent with his eyes screwed up against the sun, the wind and the rain had left the seaman's face as tanned and cracked as an old pair of unpolished boots. But though he had deep criss-crossed wrinkles worthy of Methuselah himself, and his fingers were gnarled, with just a few cracked shreds of nails left at their tips, and palms that were nothing but twin expanses of calluses, his shoulders were still square and his back straight. For as long as Harold could remember, Aldred had been the senior captain in his family's fleet, and the man entrusted with bringing Godwin and his clan safely across the waters. There was no one on earth he would rather have skippering his ship today.

'Well, it's certainly good and strong,' Harold said. 'I don't claim to be a seaman like you, Aldred, but this feels just right. Enough wind to keep us moving at a fine pace, yet not so much that the sea is too rough or you have to take in your sail.'

'Aye, you got that about right, m'lord. And it's coming from the right direction too, that's the main thing. A nor'-westerly like this, if it's set fair, it'll blow us over to Normandy in no time. Can't promise to get you there by sunset, but if not, you'll be setting foot on Frankish soil first thing tomorrow.'

For the next several hours, everything went exactly as Aldred had promised. Harold had an excellent luncheon of cold chicken, a loaf baked that morning and a sweet honey cake, washed down with freshly brewed ale. He chatted to the sailors, for he always paid attention to the men under his command, whether on land or sea, believing that they worked and fought better when they loved their leader than when they feared him. Harold took his charm as much for granted as he did his strength and boundless energy. He could not have explained exactly how he made people feel better and happier and more confident, and thus much more willing to do what he wanted. That was just how things were. And now he came to think about it, there was really no reason why he could not win over Duke William of Normandy too. I'm going to make damn sure that if he does become king, I will be his right-hand man, he decided.

But maybe he won't become king. And if he doesn't, then I most certainly will.

Then every cheerful thought for the future was driven from his mind. And all that took its place was the desperate urge to survive.

4

It began with Aldred suddenly stopping in the middle of an order he was giving the helmsman. Harold glanced up and saw his captain looking through tense, narrowed eyes towards the western horizon, where the sun was already lower in the sky, as if the sea were about to swallow it up.

Now Aldred turned his attention to the ship's sail. Suddenly it was a fraction less full.

'What's the matter?' Harold asked. 'Has the wind dropped?'

Aldred shook his head. 'Changed direction . . . to the west.'

Even as he spoke, the sail snapped tight again as the wind gathered strength. Soon the first white wisps of cloud could be seen over their heads, while away in the distance much heavier grey and black masses of towering thunderheads were marching over the horizon like an advancing army of giants, hungry to feast on any humans in their path.

By Christ I hope this *Stormrider* lives up to her name, Harold thought.

Aldred was barking orders to change course and adjust the great sail, bringing the ship round, sailing closer to the wind so that instead of blowing at the boat from almost dead astern, it was now gusting at an angle from the side.

The wind rose and now the sea began to roughen so that the deck was bucking beneath Harold's feet as the shallow-drafted vessel skimmed up and down across the choppy waters. Whitecaps began appearing around them as the waves were whipped up still higher.

'Don't worry, my lord, this won't beat us,' Aldred said. 'We're still on course, just having to work a bit harder, that's all.'

Harold grabbed one of the stays that held up the mast to stop himself losing his balance. Rain began to fall, though the rising wind was now whipping so much spray into his face that it was hard to tell that there was water falling from the sky as well.

'Come on, my lovely, keep pointing that dragon nose of yours at Normandy, there's a good girl,' Aldred said. 'There you go . . .'

For a short while it seemed to Harold as though the ship were listening to her master. Although the crew were working hard, constantly adjusting the sail to meet the wind as it shifted to and fro, or using wooden buckets to bail water before it could pool too deeply beneath their feet, they were still cheerful enough.

And then, without warning, the full force of the tempest struck, battering the *Stormrider* and straining the sail so tight that it seemed that either its fabric would rend, or the whole boat would be blown right over.

Shouting to make himself heard over the howling of the gale, the thunder overhead and the crashing of the waves against the hull, Aldred ordered his men to furl the sail. There were two men now clinging to the steering oar, desperately trying to keep the ship on course, but it did no good. Harold was no seaman, but he could tell that the wind was now once again coming from dead astern. Aldred Kimballson was no longer in command of the *Stormrider*. Her course was being set by the gods of the sea and the sky, and they would take her where they willed.

Now there was an air of desperation about the men as they fought to keep their ship from being overwhelmed by the waters. Harold was no longer the mighty Earl of Wessex, just another pair of hands, a link in the human chain that passed full buckets from the bowels of the hull to the men standing hard against the side of the ship, throwing the water overboard.

Sometimes the wind would taunt them by catching the water and hurling it straight back into the hull. Then a mighty wave emerged out of the darkness like a ravening monster and crashed down onto the *Stormrider*, and when the ship finally managed to pull itself back up to the surface, two of the sailors were gone, swallowed up by the gaping black maw of the sea.

Harold lost all track of time, or place, or anything but the never-ending labour of taking a bucket in his bloodied and blistered hands and passing it on, feeling his back and his arms ache just a fraction more than they had before, then taking another . . . and another . . . until his whole world had reduced to this one repetitive ritual. The air was so thick with water that it sometimes seemed he might drown just by breathing. His body hurt in so many ways and so many places that it was a single sensation of pure agony.

Suddenly there was a sharp, startling noise, so loud that it cut through the cacophony of the storm like the cracking of a huge whip. An instant later it came again. Before Harold could work out what it was, a thick rope whistled past him, hit a man with pulverising force and clubbed him to the ground, stone dead.

The mainstays had snapped. Before any of the crew could react, the mast itself crashed down onto the deck. More men were caught beneath it, but there was no time to worry about them. The top of the mast, the spar and the sail itself were hanging over the side of the ship, pulling it down towards the water.

There was a chest towards the back of the vessel where the crew's weapons were kept. Aldred made his way back there, followed by a few of his men, returning with axes and swords. It was obvious to Harold that they were going to cut away the last pieces of wood and rope that still attached the mast to the ship. It was equally clear that not one of the sailors was as tall or strong as he himself was, or, he'd wager, as used to handling an axe.

'Here, give me one!' he commanded. Not waiting for anyone to obey him, he simply grabbed an axe from another man's grasp. Then as the others set to work on the ropes, he and Aldred took up position on either side of the mast.

On land, working on a fallen tree, the job of hacking away the amount of unbroken wood that was acting as a sort of hinge between the stump of the mast still standing and the much longer shaft that had fallen across the *Stormrider* and into the water would have been the matter of moments. But at sea, in the middle of a raging tempest, with the boat rearing and plunging with every passing wave and listing at an ever greater angle towards the water so that it was hard enough just to stand, it was a very different matter. The two men were both racked with pain, exhausted, their bodies drained of strength and energy. But they had no choice. If the mast wasn't cut away, the boat would capsize and they would all be drowned. So they swung their axes, even as the handles slipped in their blood- and water-slicked hands, their feet slid and their eyes were blinded with salt spray. The coating of water over the mast seemed to dissipate the force of their blows, and as the wood itself became soggier, so that too blunted the impact of the blades.

At first Harold and Aldred shouted encouragement at one another, chanting out a rhythm like oarsmen at their blades, but their voices soon petered away, for they had no breath to spare. They just worked on, each of them barely paying any attention to the other, so that on more than one occasion their axes hit the wood at the same time, butting the metal heads so hard that Harold almost lost his grasp.

The work was futile. More and more water was spilling over the side of the hull and into the ship's interior. The men still on the bailing chain were as shattered as everyone else and the passage of buckets to and fro had slowed to a rate that could not possibly cope with the deepening flood. The ropes, at least, were close to giving way under their assailants' blades, but the mast seemed unbreakable.

And then, out of the darkness, Harold sensed as much as saw a greater, deeper wall of black bearing down on them, rising in height as it came closer. Now the boat itself was being dragged towards it by the undertow.

'Mary, Mother of God . . .' Harold gasped as the wall drew closer and the paler battlements of foam atop it became clear, and he realised that this was a wave unlike any they had previously encountered: a single wave of unimaginable magnitude, higher than a castle keep, thundering towards the foundering ship.

One by one the men understood that this was death itself racing in their direction, claiming them for a watery grave. They stopped what they were doing and just stood, silent, immobile and helpless.

Then Aldred Kimballson at last found his voice. 'Hold on!' he shouted. 'Grab a rope, a spar, a bench, anything . . . but for God's sake hold on!'

There was a length of rope at Harold's feet. He had no idea what it was attached to, or whether it was just lying loose on deck, but he grabbed it regardless, coiled it around his right forearm and gripped it with both hands.

The onrushing wave was almost upon them. It towered above them and then unfurled over them, blotting out the sky, and then it broke and fell upon the *Stormrider* and its crew.

In the instant before the wave hit, Harold took as deep a breath as he could, but most of the air was immediately smashed back out of him as the huge weight of bitterly cold water, falling faster than any punch or swordsman's strike, crashed down onto the ship.

He was flung off the deck and into the ocean. A sudden fierce wrench pulled his arm half out of its socket as the rope went taut, and though the coils around his wrist suddenly tightened so severely he felt his hand might be cut off, he thanked God they were there, for his own grip would never have been strong enough.

Then he wished that he could just let go, for the force that was sucking at him, trying to swallow him, hungering to drag his body deep underwater, would not relent. The strain upon his wrist and shoulder increased with every second. The waterlogged woollen cloak on his back felt as heavy as the burden on an overladen mule, bearing down upon him. His breath had run out now and it struck him that it would be so much easier just to give up and make the pain go away.

Only the raw, unthinking, animal will to survive stopped him from giving into that temptation, and then, just as it seemed that it would make no difference, for he was going to die anyway, like it or not, the water let go.

Harold started rising towards the surface, and now, with the possibility of survival in his sights once again, he was for the first time struck by a desperate, panicky craving to live. He kicked and thrashed as he fought to speed his progress through the water, flailing his one free arm as if pushing the ocean itself out of his way. And then his head burst through the surface and he sucked sweet air into his lungs, hardly caring that he swallowed a mouthful of water as he did so.

He coughed and hacked and puked the water back out, breathed again . . . and again . . . and then looked around.

The *Stormrider* was nowhere to be seen. Harold darted his head from side to side, but it was impossible to know whether the ship had sunk or simply sailed away. Now a new fear clawed at his guts as he realised that he was alone in the middle of the open sea. He was no great swimmer, though he could just about keep himself afloat. But for how long?

Calm down, think, he told himself. The rope is attached to something that's floating. Follow the rope.

He pulled himself along through the churning water, trying to see where the rope was leading him but unable to make anything out until he suddenly banged his head on something very hard.

He reached up and touched wood: a planed shaft of wood. He pulled again and was dragged along to the point where the rope was attached.

It had to be part of the mast, or a spar. He felt around and discovered that the rope was wrapped tightly around it, just as the other end was wrapped around his own arm. By pulling himself along it, he established that the floating debris was about twice as long as his own height and thicker than his waist. He saw at once that if he could only drag himself up so that he was lying on top of it, it would easily support his weight.

First, though, he had to get rid of his cloak. But his fingers were numb with cold and could not undo the clasp that held it. So that dead weight remained on his back, adding to the difficulty of scrabbling for hand- and footholds as he tried to pull himself up with his arms or wrap a leg around the damn thing. He felt as though an age had passed before a wave ran under him at precisely the right moment to lift him level with the top of the spar. He threw a leg over it like a drunk trying to mount a horse, and then clung on tight to the rope as though it was the reins of this strange, ill-disciplined wooden beast.

As he lay along the spar, he lifted his head and saw, away in the distance, the first pale grey-blue strip of dawn light along the horizon. That's the east, he thought. There's land in that direction.

Then his head slumped down against the wood. His eyes closed. And he finally gave in to exhaustion.

5

The coast of Ponthieu, northern France

All morning, the debris had been washing up along the beaches on either side of the river's mouth. And as it did, more and more people came out to see what they could find, for who knew what rich pickings might come ashore when a ship foundered in a storm? The richest of all were people. The dead could be stripped of their clothes, their boots and, if fortune was smiling, their jewels, fine swords and purses. The living could be sold – into slavery if they were poor, or for ransom if they could fetch a better price from their families than on the slave market.

Today, though, the pickings were few and meagre. A dozen or more corpses had come ashore on the rising tide, but they were just common sailors, with no valuables whatever to be stripped from them. The scavengers began to give up hope of any reason to spend more time on the cold, windswept shore, until there were barely half a dozen hardy souls left, on one of the beaches to the left of the river.

Two of them, hardbitten men who made their living by fishing, smuggling and thieving, were at the far end of the beach when one of them screwed up his eyes and lifted a hand to shade them from the sun. 'What's that?'

'Where?' the other replied.

'Over there, right by those rocks, looks like a bit of mast.'

'Well, a mast's no good to us. Chop it up for firewood, that's about it.'

'Depends. If it's big enough, you can get beams out of it.

Good enough for building a house, or a new ship. Them's worth something.'

The other man sniffed sceptically and spat on the sand to emphasise his doubts, before relenting. 'Yeah, all right, s'pose it doesn't do any harm to take a look.'

As they walked on across the sand, the second man said, 'What's that on the mast – that big lump there?'

The first man stopped, concentrated and then gave a long, low whistle. 'That's a man.'

'Alive or dead, though, that's what I want to know.'

'I say he's alive. How else has he hung on?'

'Not moving, though, is he? I say he's dead.'

When they got there, the matter was still in doubt, for the man lay motionless, eyes closed, not apparently breathing, with strands of brown-green seaweed in amongst his fair hair. Then again, his skin, though very pale, lacked the waxy grey-white look of a recently drowned man.

'Hard to tell, innit?' said one of the scavengers.

The other pulled a dagger from its scabbard. 'Only one way to find out,' he replied, and advanced towards the body.

It took a second for the pain from his right buttock to penetrate the fog of Harold's brain. But then he yelped, 'Ow!' and the shock seemed to clear his mind, and in very quick succession he was awake, rolling down onto the sand and then getting to his feet looking for the source of his discomfort.

It wasn't hard to spot.

Standing opposite him were two of the mangiest, ugliest, meanest-looking individuals it had ever been his misfortune to encounter. Their clothing was little more than filthy, salt-encrusted rags. Their faces had the pinched, suspicious, shifty look of men who had been born to nothing and yet somehow managed to go down in the world. And in his right hand one of

340

them was holding the rusted but evil-looking blade that had just, if the trace of fresh blood at its tip was any guide, been stabbed into Harold's backside.

The man holding the blade poked it towards Harold and snarled some words he could not make out. The other man spotted a piece of driftwood on the sand, a shaft about as long as a man's arm that looked as though it might have snapped from one of the *Stormrider*'s oars, and picked it up to use as a club. He stared at Harold, waving his new-found weapon in what he clearly intended to be a threatening fashion.

Had he been in anything close to his normal condition and armed with a sword, Harold would have taken on the two of them without a second thought. But he was battered, exhausted and unarmed, and as he looked along the beach he could see another four men running along the sand towards them.

He held up his hands to suggest that his intentions were peaceful. There had been so many Normans in King Edward's court over the past twenty years and more that he had picked up enough of their language to be able to make himself understood.

'My name is Harold, Earl of Wessex.'

He might as well have been a barking dog for all the men seemed to understand him. They're the scum of the earth, he told himself. They don't know what an earl is and they've never heard of Wessex. Try again.

'My name is Harold. I am a mighty count. I have been sent by the King of England to visit William, Duke of Normandy.'

The two men looked at him with expressions that suggested a hint of comprehension, albeit mixed with loathing and distrust. They began talking between themselves and the debate expanded as the other men arrived.

From what Harold could gather, they seemed to be speaking in some kind of Frankish dialect that sounded similar but by no means identical to the Norman tongue. He caught the meaning of just enough words to understand that the argument centred on the issue of what would be the most profitable course to take with this new arrival, who they had decided must be a Dane, on account of his yellow hair. Two of the men wanted to take him off to their lord to get a piece of the ransom money. The other, majority group thought it would be simpler just to kill him.

Harold was appalled by both suggestions. He was a ship-wrecked traveller. Common decency demanded that he should be rescued, fed and given shelter until he could move on. Equally, it would be his duty to ensure that his benefactors were properly rewarded for their kindness. That, however, was not even an option, so far as these mangy curs were concerned. His only hope would be to appeal to their greed and then make their lord and master see sense.

'I am a great lord,' he said, speaking as slowly and clearly as he could in the hope that they might be able to understand him better. 'I am very rich. My family will pay a great ransom. And I give you my solemn oath that when they do, I will make sure that you men receive your fair share.'

One of the prospective killers seemed to have caught Harold's meaning. Evidently he found the argument persuasive, because he immediately rounded on his former allies and started berating them for their folly. They argued back at him for the sake of their self-respect, but swiftly conceded.

Harold gave a great sigh of relief. But his happiness was short-lived, for now one of the men suggested a cunning idea that brought the others out in broad, gap-toothed grins with slaps on the back all round for their cleverness. The one with the knife jabbed it at Harold's chest, with the blade at an angle, pointing up towards the base of his neck. For a second, Harold thought they were going to do for him after all, but then he realised that this scrawny ape wanted his cloak.

It was made of the finest Flemish cloth and held by a gilded clasp decorated with a dragon curved around a piece of scarlet carnelian. That alone was a treasure of unimaginable worth to men such as these. So too were the silver buckle on his belt and, even more so, the golden signet ring on his finger. Bit by bit he was divested of anything of value, right down to his tunic and boots, until he stood shivering in nothing but his hose. He had not eaten or drunk anything in many hours and it was all he could do to remain upright and moving forward as he was led away along the shore.

The ruffians' master was little better than his underlings. He resided in a single-storey wooden house, standing within a rough stockade not far from a quayside at which a few fishing vessels and small merchant ships were moored, none of them intended for anything more than short journeys upriver or along the coast. The house had one main chamber, and the man seated at its table, picking at a plate of grilled fish, introduced himself as Niblung of Montreuil.

'And who, might I ask, are you?' he enquired, in a marginally more civilised and comprehensible version of the dialect used by Harold's captors.

Harold did his best to stand tall, square his chest and hold his head high as he replied, 'I am Harold Godwinson, Earl, or as you would say, Duke of Wessex. I have been sent by King Edward of England on an embassy to Duke William of Normandy.'

'Prove it.'

'That man there,' Harold pointed at the knife-waver, 'has my signet ring. It will confirm my identity.'

Two of Niblung's men, who were little more than better-fed and better-armed versions of the ones from the beach, duly took the ring off its new owner, though not before he had protested loudly. Niblung looked at it blankly. Plainly he could not read.

'The inscription reads "Harold Dux". That's Latin for Duke Harold. I'm sure a priest would confirm it, if you asked. Now I insist on fair and proper treatment. I am a king's envoy. To harm me is to harm the king. And you would not be wise to make an enemy of the King of England.'

Niblung shrugged. 'What's he going to do to me? You are in Ponthieu, Duke Harold. We have our own customs here. And one of them is that people who are washed ashore are no different from any other kind of flotsam. They're ours to do with as we please.'

'So your master is the Count of Ponthieu?'

'That's right, Count Guy, brother of the late Count Enguerrand . . . who was killed by William the Bastard's men, so don't expect any sympathy from him.'

'Very well, I won't expect sympathy . . . but then again, nor should you.'

Niblung leaned forward with his elbows on the table. 'What do you mean, sympathy? What's that got to do with me?'

'Simple. I am a very rich and powerful man in England, the richest and most powerful apart from His Majesty, in fact. That makes me very valuable. Count Guy will take the view that I landed on one of his beaches, so any ransom I fetch should go to him first. If he hears that you had me but did not hand me over, he will be unhappy. If he hears about me, comes to get me and discovers that I am half dead of thirst and starvation and might not live long enough to be ransomed, he will also be unhappy. And if he is unhappy, well then, you can't expect much sympathy from him, can you?'

'Sit down,' said Niblung. 'Pour yourself some ale. Do you want some bread and fish?'

* * *

Niblung had no dungeons or cells at his disposal, so he gave Harold a jug of water, a rough woollen blanket to keep him warm and a pot to piss in, and stuck him in a dark, lice-ridden woodshed with a bar across the door and an armed guard to watch over the place. He had been there for two days, surviving on a few more scraps of bread and a couple of bowls of watery, fish-flavoured gruel, when there was a sudden commotion outside. He heard the sounds of horses, ridden by armoured men. Commands were shouted and then came Niblung's voice, now with a much more wheedling, obsequious tone.

'Oh yes, your lordship, absolutely. He's quite safe, I assure you.'

A few moments later, the door of the woodshed was flung open. Harold screwed up his eyes against the sudden dazzling light and saw a man's figure silhouetted against it. When the man spoke, it was in an educated, but unexpectedly effete drawl: 'Well, he doesn't look like the greatest earl in England, but the ring seems genuine enough . . . unless he stole it, of course. Did you steal that ring, Harold Godwinson?'

'No, I damn well did not, nor the cloak, the clasp, the belt, the buckle, the boots or any of the other possessions that were taken from me. Do I take it, sir, that you are Guy of Ponthieu?'

'You do, indeed, and I can tell just from your insolence that you must be genuine. No impostor would dare be so rude to his betters.'

'And no count with a shred of honour would countenance the imprisonment of a nobleman who has been washed up on his shores by pure chance. If you had taken me in war, that would be one thing. But I am a king's envoy. I deserve to be treated with respect, for to disrespect me is to mock my king.'

Guy of Ponthieu emitted a smirking, almost giggling little laugh. 'Well, I'm very sorry to disappoint you, but as I'm sure you've been told by now, the customs of Ponthieu are rather different. Still, I'm sure we can arrange a ransom soon enough, if you are as rich as you say.'

'You know that I am bound for the court of Duke William?'

'I had gathered that, yes.'

'As I recall, he has had the best of Ponthieu on more than one occasion.'

Any last trace of amusement disappeared from Guy's voice. 'Yes, what of it?'

'I would send a message to him first, if I were you, before you contact my family in England. He will want to hear what I have to tell him.'

'Which is?'

'For his ears only . . . But be assured, should he ever hear that you prevented me from speaking to him and that King Edward's message to him did not get through, well . . . You wouldn't want him beating you a third time, would you?'

'I'm not sure I like you very much, Harold Godwinson. In fact, I don't think I like you at all. I might have been inclined to treat you generously while you were my prisoner. But then you mock me and threaten me . . . No, I don't like that at all.'

Guy turned to face back into the dusty yard that lay between the woodshed and the main house. 'Take him away. And don't be gentle about it.'

Harold was bound hand and foot, blindfolded and thrown like a sack of turnips into the back of an open cart. For the rest of the day and into the evening he was bounced and jolted, adding even more aches and bruises to those he already had. At one point there was a prolonged downpour, accompanied by a strong wind, that left him sodden and chilled to the marrow. He was still shivering and so stiff in his muscles and joints that he could barely move when the cart finally came to a halt and he was pulled off it. The rope around his legs was untied and his blindfold was removed.

Once again the first person he saw was Guy of Ponthieu. 'Where am I?' he asked.

'My castle, Beaurain.'

'And will you tell Duke William that I am here?'

'I'll think about it. In the meantime, your quarters await you. I fear they may not be quite what you would desire. But they're exactly what you deserve.'

6

The Earl of Northumbria's palace, York

While his brother languished in the dungeons of Beaurain, Tostig was making his way to York. He had hardly expected to be greeted by beautiful maidens throwing bouquets of flowers as he and his retinue passed through the gate in the city walls, but the reception they received was worse than he had anticipated. The mood in the city was even more sullen and bitter than it had been when he left. He heard muttered curses coming from the townspeople lining the streets, and even a couple of shouts of 'Murderer!'

When he reached the former palace of the kings of Northumbria, from which he now governed, or tried to govern, the duchy, he summoned Reavanswart and Amund, the captains of his housecarls, the Danish mercenaries he had left behind to keep order in his absence.

'What the hell's been going on?' he asked. 'There were people calling me a murderer. Why would they be doing that?'

Reavanswart grimaced. 'It's Gamel Ormsson and Ulf Dolfinsson, those ones that keep stirring up the local folk about bringing back their old kingdom . . .'

'What about them?'

'They're dead,' Amund said

'How? What happened?'

'They were killed in a fight, in the hall here, just a few days ago.'

'You mean they died under my roof?'

'That's right, my lord. Just as they were eating their dinner.'

Tostig had the unnerving sensation of the ground giving way beneath his feet. He was struck by a sudden realisation: this must be the 'surprise' that Edward had promised him. And then, an instant later, the consequences of the king's actions became obvious. *The fool! All he's done is convince every man and woman in Northumbria that these deaths are my doing. And I had nothing to do with them!*

His only hope was to find the true culprits and have them punished as horribly and publicly as possible.

'Tell me what happened,' he ordered. 'I want every detail.'

'Don't ask me, I was with my men, guarding the town walls,' said Amund.

'What about you?' Tostig asked Reavanswart.

The housecarl captain shrugged. 'I don't rightly know. I wasn't in the hall at the time. I was, ah, taking my supper in town that night.'

'Just supper, was it?'

Reavanswart said nothing, but the look on his face made it plain that he wasn't about to discuss his private life. He was a hired mercenary, not a sworn liegeman. He had an obligation to fight for Tostig, but beyond that his life was his own.

'No matter,' Tostig conceded. 'Neither of you was in the hall. What have you heard from the men who were?'

'Just that there was an argument between the local lads and three or four other men,' Amund said. 'No one knew who they were, though they sounded like southerners.'

'What were they doing at dinner in my hall?'

'They demanded hospitality, said they were on an important mission to Scotland.'

'What kind of mission? Who sent them?'

'They wouldn't say. Just that the safety of the realm was at stake.'

'So they were the king's men?'

The two captains remained silent, but Amund grimaced as if to say, 'Maybe.'

'Very well, so this group of southerners had an argument with Gamal and Ulf. Did it turn into a fight?'

'Not right away,' Amund said. 'From what I heard, there were some serious words exchanged – insults, curses, things that would make a man think he'd been dishonoured, give him reason for wanting his own back – but it didn't turn violent. Not then, anyway.'

'But later?'

'No one knows. Dinner ended, everyone went off to find a place to sleep – all the usual places: the floor of the hall, the barracks, a guest chamber if they were lucky, or an inn somewhere in the city. No one thought any more of what had happened, but then the next morning, at first light, one of my lads finds Gamal and Ulf's bodies lying in the yard, right up against the walls, in a dark corner where no one would have seen them at night.'

'What about the men who'd been arguing with them?' Tostig asked, though he knew the question was almost certainly pointless.

'Gone. Vanished into thin air, no sign of them at all.'

'So they lured Gamal and Ulf outside . . .'

'Or just waited for them to come out, yeah.'

'Then killed them, dumped the bodies and left before anyone knew what had happened.'

'That's about it, my lord.'

'And this all happened under your nose.'

'Like I said, I wasn't there.'

'But you two are in charge. And your men are supposed to maintain the safety of my person and my property.'

'You weren't there either,' Reavanswart said, with an

insolence that reflected the offence he had taken at Tostig's attitude.

'But there were people under my roof. I had a responsibility for them whether I was there or not. So you had a responsibility whether I was there or not too.'

'What are you saying?' Amund asked.

'I'm saying someone needs to be brought to account for these killings or the whole of Northumbria's going to be up in arms.'

'I agree, my lord, it is. So you're going to want all the help you can get.'

'I am, am I?'

'Yes, my lord. And if you let this go – this whole responsibility thing – me and my men will be right here to fight for you . . . just as long as you keep paying us, of course. But if you try to punish any of us . . .' Amund sighed. 'If you're lucky, the men will just go away back to Denmark. If you're not, they'll get their revenge before they go.'

'Revenge against me?'

'You can't blame them, my lord,' Reavanswart said. 'I mean, if one of their comrades was made to take the blame for all this, let alone one of their captains . . . well, they'd have to avenge him, wouldn't they?'

Tostig was too angry to be frightened. 'You're lucky I don't just strike you down here and now for talking to me like that. And I'd do it too, by God I would, except that one of these days a very large, angry armed crowd is going to appear outside this building demanding restitution for those dead men. When that day comes, it will largely be due to you. So you and your men can damn well sort it out.'

7

Rouen and Beaurain Castle, Ponthieu

Two weeks went by before Guy saw fit to dispatch a messenger to the ducal court at Rouen, and another week passed as his man made his way to Normandy and waited there for William to return from visiting his half-brother Odo. The duke was intrigued by the news from Ponthieu.

'Harold Godwinson, eh . . . If Edward has sent him as his messenger boy, then the message must be worth hearing.'

William needed a man he could trust absolutely to go to Guy's court, extract Harold with the minimum fuss and bring him safe and sound back to Rouen. Montgomery was the cleverest diplomat among his close circle, but he was away in Bellême, getting up to God knows what with his useful but unnerving wife, and would not be back for at least a week. That left the staunchest, most reliable of all his friends. 'Fitzosbern . . . a word in private, if you please.'

'I demand to see Godwinson immediately,' Fitz told Guy of Ponthieu, having ridden to Beaurain on Duke William's command.

'Do you now? And what if I refuse?'

'King Edward sent the Earl of Wessex as his personal envoy to Duke William. His Grace is therefore responsible for the earl's safety and well-being. It is a matter of honour and propriety. I'm sure you understand.'

'I'm not sure that I do. None of us can be held responsible for what happens to travellers at sea.'

'The earl is not at sea, though, is he?'

'He was, that is the point.'

Fitz gave a brisk, frustrated sigh. 'No, with respect, my lord, that is not the point. Let me put this very clearly. It does not matter what you think, or I think, but what Duke William thinks. We are both his vassals. You pledged your fealty to him, did you not, as a condition of your release after the battle of Mortemer?'

'I did . . . but he kept me as his prisoner for two years first. I've only had Godwinson for a matter of days.'

'Days, years . . . what does that matter? It's our duty to obey our duke. His Grace wishes Earl Harold to be handed over to him immediately. If you act upon those wishes, you can be sure that he will remember the respect you showed him and reward you for it.'

'You mean he'll pay the ransom?'

'No, I mean that he won't march up here to Beaurain, raze your castle to the ground, kill you, exile your entire family and take Ponthieu for himself.'

'Don't you threaten me!'

'I am not threatening you. I am simply telling you the truth. Ask your two dead brothers how much good it did them to defy William of Normandy. Ask Martel. Ask the kings of France he has defeated and the rebels he has crushed. If you give us Harold, there will be no trouble and you can be assured that the duke will protect you if you should ever be harassed by your enemies.'

'I see . . . So why do you need to see Godwinson? All you need for his release is a yes or no from me.'

'The duke wishes me to see him.'

'And if I don't accede to that demand . . .'

Fitz shrugged.

'Very well,' Guy conceded. 'By all means meet the prisoner. Hold your nose when you go in there, that's my advice.'

353

The flickering flame of the torch Fitz held in his left hand was barely sufficient to illuminate the subterranean dungeon, but even its poor light was enough to cause Harold Godwinson to hold up his hands to protect his eyes. Fitz grimaced as he caught the full stench of the small, airless cell. He could see piles of human filth dotted about the floor, and there was a puddle of urine at his feet.

'My God,' he gasped. 'Your Grace, I had no idea . . . This is appalling.'

'Forgive me,' Harold replied, with a pained attempt at humour. 'I do not always greet my guests like this. Might I ask who you are?'

'William Fitzosbern. I have been sent by Duke William of Normandy to secure your release.'

'Oh, thank God . . .' Harold seemed overcome by the news. 'I . . . I was beginning to fear you wouldn't come. These people . . . they're barbarians.'

'I can see why you might think so, Your Grace. I will do my very best to secure your release from this torment as soon as possible. But His Grace Duke William has various questions he wishes me to put to you.'

'Questions? Why do you need questions? Just get me out of here!'

'Yes, absolutely I will, I assure you. But the duke was very insistent . . .'

'Very well, what does he want to know?'

'Firstly, is it the case that you are sent by King Edward?'

'Yes.'

'Might I ask what message you bring?'

'You may, but I will tell none but Duke William.'

'You may tell me. I am his representative.'

'So you claim, but how am I to know that? My king

commanded me to speak directly to the Duke of Normandy. That is what I will do. But if you are who you say you are, you can tell Duke William this much: he will be very glad of what I have to say.'

Fitz understood at once what that meant. He and William had of course wondered whether Edward was repeating his offer of the crown, or whether the presence of so senior an envoy was a sign of the exact opposite: that he was withdrawing Normandy's claim to England and wanted the message to come from a man who could not be doubted. It seemed there was no need now to worry about that possibility.

'Can I get out of here now?' Harold asked, struggling to his feet.

'One moment, Your Grace; there is another matter to be discussed . . .'

'Get on with it then.'

'It is Duke William's great wish to see you freed and restored to your rightful dignity. He has made that very clear to Ponthieu and let it be known that he is willing to go to whatever lengths are necessary to secure your release . . . by force, if necessary.'

'You may tell him that I am very grateful for his actions on my behalf.'

Fitz smiled. 'Ah! Then you appreciate the situation perfectly. You have a certain debt towards His Grace – a debt of honour, I stress: His Grace would never dream of asking for financial recompense . . .'

Harold nodded. He understood that every man's favour came at a price. 'And how does he feel this gratitude should be best expressed?'

'Simply through friendship, Your Grace. Duke William hopes very much that you will be able to offer him your support now and in the future, both in Normandy and . . . elsewhere.'

'And if I do not wish to be his friend?'

'Please, Your Grace, let us not even consider that possibility. The thought of you spending any more time in this vile purgatory . . . Who would want that?'

'Not me, that's for sure. You may tell your master that he will have my support.'

'Then we are as one. This is splendid! I shall convey the happy news to Duke William, and in the meantime, you may rest assured that Count Guy will treat you with the full respect your rank deserves . . . or be made to pay for his lack of manners.'

When Fitz sat down at the high table of Beaurain castle that evening, he found Harold Godwinson there too, freshly washed and dressed in what appeared to be Guy's own clothes, since they were of fine quality but rather too small for the tall, broad-shouldered Englishman.

In the morning, Fitz set off for Rouen. Within the week, Guy had brought Harold down to the castle of Eu, which stood on the northern border of Normandy. And Duke William himself was there to meet them.

8

Normandy

As Guy begged to be pardoned for any misunderstanding, William gave the merest nod of acknowledgement and then a flick of the hand to dismiss him. It was Harold Godwinson that interested him. The Englishman seemed fully recovered and a far cry from the piteous wretch Fitz had reported seeing in the dungeon at Beaurain. He was tall enough to look William straight in the eye and sure enough of his position to do so without flinching or giving any sign of subservience, though there was nothing aggressive about his demeanour. Harold was a man who smiled easily and, to judge by the way Fitz greeted him as a long-lost friend, found it easy to win men over. William felt a sudden sharp stab of envy and even resentment.

It's all come effortlessly to you, hasn't it, Harold of Wessex? he thought. You take your privilege for granted. You've never known anything else. That's why you can afford to be so damn casual. Well, we'll soon see about that.

Putting those feelings to one side, he met Harold's smile with one of his own and shook his hand warmly. 'It's very good to meet you at last. I have heard a great deal about you over the years. Now we must be on our way to Rouen. You will be my guest, Godwinson, my honoured guest. And as we ride, you can tell me what brings you here to Normandy. I am informed that your message is for my ears only. Rest assured, you will have my full attention.'

* * *

Harold was riding through northern Normandy alongside the duke, passing herds of well-fed cows grazing on rich grassy pastures, and orchards filled with apple trees coming into a blizzard of pink and white blossom. This land was really not so different from his own estates in Kent and Sussex. William will feel right at home in England, he thought acidly, as they made the polite political small talk that was the prelude to any serious discussion. Harold described life at the English court, doing his best to convey his own semi-regal status in a powerful, settled nation that was well able to defend itself without for a moment suggesting that England's strength might ever be turned against Normandy.

William, likewise, emphasised that with his old adversaries Geoffrey Martel of Anjou and King Henry of France both now dead, and the king's successor, his son Philip, still just a boy, he felt more secure in his dukedom than at any time in his life. The preliminaries thus concluded, Harold steeled himself and delivered King Edward's confirmation that his promise of the throne still stood.

Just as Champart had been almost fifteen years earlier, Harold found himself surprised by William's response to his good tidings. The duke barely cracked a smile, contenting himself with a brusque 'Good. He kept his word.' Then he thought for a second, narrowing his eyes like a man buying a horse from a trader he did not quite trust. 'What about Edgar, son of Edward the Exile? He has a better blood claim than me, don't think I don't know it.'

'His Majesty and I discussed that very question. The king was very clear that in his view the kingdom needs a grown man to guide it through what may be challenging times ahead.'

'The boy must be what – thirteen, fourteen by now?'

'Something in that region.'

'Then he's not far off being a man. I bloodied my sword

for the first time when I was fifteen. If young Edgar had a regent . . . I dare say you'd have fancied that job. Just the sort of thing your father would have jumped at.'

'The thought never crossed my mind.'

'Is that so?' For the first time Harold caught something close to genuine amusement in William's eyes, and noted that what had tickled him was not a witty remark, or a comical event, but the pleasure of thinking he had caught someone out.

'You have a very loyal companion in William Fitzosbern, if you don't mind me saying so,' Harold said, wanting to learn more about the man who might one day be his king. King Edward's views on William were hardly affectionate – not that he ever displayed much affection to anyone these days – but he had a grudging respect for his Norman cousin.

The duke grunted in agreement. Harold remained silent, sensing that the more he said, the less likely William would be to elaborate.

'We grew up together,' the duke replied eventually. 'His father was steward to mine. Good man. Murdered right in front of my eyes, when I was about the same age Edgar of England is now. I know I can trust Fitz, know he'd never let me down. Not many men I can say that about.'

The two men had been riding side-by-side, both mostly watching the path ahead of them. Now William turned his head to look at Harold as he spoke. 'Let me tell you something, Godwinson. You are a man who takes every man for a friend until he shows himself to be an enemy. I am a man who takes every man for an enemy until he has proved beyond any possible doubt that he is my loyal friend. I learned that lesson when I was a boy, betrayed too many times by people I thought I could count on. So if you want a place by my side when I am on the throne, you will have to earn it. And I can tell you right now, there aren't many men who have done that.'

'Still, you can trust your common soldiers, which many men can't. You have their absolute loyalty; it's obvious, just looking at them.'

William nodded. 'They know I'm one of them, an ordinary man, half duke half peasant. They know that if they serve me well, I will reward them, and if they fail me, I will punish them without mercy. And they accept that because I never ask them to do something I wouldn't do myself.'

'That's the golden rule,' Harold agreed. 'Lead from the front.'

'Done much campaigning, have you?'

'My brother Tostig and I spent two years fighting Gruffydd son of Llewellyn. He had made himself king of all the Welsh. That made him a threat to England.'

'And how did this war against the Welsh king end?'

'With me holding King Gruffydd's severed head in a leather bag. Now his kingdom is divided in two, England is safe . . . and I am here with you.'

'Then I may have another fight you will enjoy, for I believe the people of Wales are cousins to those of Brittany: black-eyed, black-hearted men who speak a language no one can understand and sing endless dirge-like songs to the accompaniment of a harp.'

Harold laughed, surprised but also pleased to discover that William did have a faint hint of bone-dry humour about him after all. 'That certainly sounds familiar. What trouble are they causing you?'

'None yet, and I intend to keep it that way. The Count of Brittany, Conan, is a cousin of mine. His father was one of my guardians when I was a boy. A good man. He was murdered just like all the others . . .'

'How many were there?'

'Four, all killed within the space of two years.'

'Good Lord! Was Fitzosbern's father one of them?'

'Yes . . . Anyway, Conan has been having problems with his lesser barons, minor rebellions and so forth. I've been encouraging them. Want to keep Conan occupied while I get on with my business elsewhere. Now one of the rebels, a man by the name of Riwallon—'

'You're right, he could be a Welshman with a name like that.'

'Well, right now Conan's got him besieged inside his castle at Dol, about half a day's ride across the border from Normandy. I'm minded to take that ride, relieve the siege and give Conan a good kicking; then, once I've made my point and stirred them all up, head back home. Why don't you come along? We can get to know one another properly. Nothing like going on campaign together for getting the measure of a man.'

'King Edward will be expecting me to return with news of your response to his renewed offer.'

'What does King Edward matter? He's yesterday's man. What matters now is how you and I get along. I need to know: can I count on you as an ally when I arrive in England, or will I have to deal with you as an enemy?'

'As you rightly said, I always prefer to be friends.'

'Good, I'm pleased to hear that. Now tell me, do you have any possessions at all with you, aside from those ill-fitting clothes on your back?'

'Not a thing. My baggage all went down with my ship, and the scum of Ponthieu took my cloak, my belt and my signet ring.'

'Really? And Guy didn't give it all back when he released you? We can't be having that. I'll send word to him at once. In the meantime, I'll make sure that you have everything you need. You'll need a stallion worthy of your seniority for the Brittany campaign, and another in case the first falls sick or is harmed in some way. A sword – the finest quality, of course – dagger, shield, armour, helmet and all that goes with them will clearly be essential. Then we must have some decent clothes run up for you and a proper cloak – even if Guy does manage to find yours and return it, God only knows what condition it will be in.'

William looked down at Harold's foot in its stirrup. 'We'd better add new boots too, by the look of those.'

'You are too kind, Your Grace,' said Harold, who had been strangely unsettled by what any reasonable man would agree was an extraordinarily generous offer on William's part. He could not quite shake the idea that there was a threat lurking beneath these honeyed promises.

'Not at all,' William insisted. 'All eyes will be upon you when you are presented to my court in Rouen. I would be a very poor host if I did not enable you to look your best.'

'I feel that I should offer something in return. What can I possibly give you in exchange for so many blessings?'

'Reassurance,' said William. 'Just give me a little reassurance.'

9

*The ducal palace in Rouen, and Brittany,
spring and summer 1064*

In the days after they reached Rouen, Duke William introduced
Harold to the men who formed his close-knit circle of
lieutenants, advisers and friends. Harold's first impression of
Roger Montgomery, Raoul de Tosny, the duke's brothers
Bishop Odo of Bayeux and Robert, Count of Mortain, and
the rest was that they were all very much of a muchness. For a
start, they were of a similar age to their master. They had
followed William since they were all barely more than boys, and
as a consequence, they owed everything they had to their duke
and worshipped the ground on which he trod. They all looked
the same too: strongly built, clean-shaven, wearing their hair
cropped very short at the back and sides, with just a patch of
thicker hair on the crown of their heads. The style, they
informed Harold, was designed to make it easier to don their
helmets as they went into battle and then cooler and more
comfortable once they were on.

'What do you do when you aren't at war?' Harold asked
Montgomery when he explained this reasoning.

Montgomery grinned. 'We're always at war.'

As the days passed, however, Harold began to pick out
individual characteristics. Fitz was clearly the duke's second-in-
command, absolutely trusted and absolutely reliable. He might
make a very occasional joke at William's expense, but that
privilege was earned by his unshakeable loyalty. Of the two

brothers, Rob was the eternal baby of the family, still full of boyish enthusiasm even as a fully grown man, while Odo shared, albeit to a lesser degree, William's hard-nosed, unflinching attitude.

Montgomery was the one who intrigued Harold the most. It was clear that he was just as much the duke's man as any of the others, but still, he was the least like the others, too. For one thing, he made no secret of the fact that his allegiance was founded on reason rather than sentiment. He had supported Duke William because it was the sensible thing to do, had been well rewarded for his decision and had absolutely no desire to change his mind.

Yet even if Montgomery's commitment to William was sure, there was something not quite settled about him. There were times when his charm, normally so smooth and engaging, seemed brittle, edgy, as if he might at any moment crack. Even his face, at first glance so handsome, was surprisingly drawn, his skin almost grey at times, as if he was nursing some hidden sickness. Instinct told Harold it had something to do with Montgomery's wife Mabel, who was titled the Dame of Bellême. She was lovely to look at, there was no question of that, but as with her husband, that beauty did not withstand close examination.

In Mabel's case, the unwelcome surprise lay in her eyes. When she wanted to make a good impression they were ravishing, almost hypnotic in their feline grace. But if Harold looked at her when she was not aware that she was being examined, those same eyes had a very different, cat-like quality: a cold, flat, predatory indifference to anyone or anything else in the world. Over time, Harold grew to like and even admire a number of his hosts. He certainly respected their military prowess.

The only one he feared was Mabel.

* * *

For their part, the Normans seemed to take to Harold. When a hunting expedition was organised, he very quickly proved his quality as a horseman and his skill with both lance and bow. He had a firm handshake, an easy smile and a ready laugh, and he held his drink like a good man should.

This latter ability was put to its greatest test when William held a feast in Harold's honour. He gave a speech praising his English guest as both the finest man that country had to offer and a good and noble ally of Normandy, and many a toast was proposed and sunk in honour of this new-found friendship.

Harold knew perfectly well that William's words were conditional upon him doing what the duke required. Still, he was suitably impressed by the lavish profusion of dishes and drinks that was laid before him. The food was better than any he had eaten in England. Every form of red meat was served, from well-fattened beef and pork to deer and wild boar from the hunting field. The poultry ranged from farmyard ducks, hens and geese to swan and heron, and there was a profusion of fresh fish and lobsters, shrimp and mussels, as befitted a maritime duchy. All these ingredients he was used to, but the food was enhanced by sauces and spices of a richness and savour far more subtle and delicious than any he had known in England.

Harold presumed that this was the Duchess Matilda's doing. William was a soldier. He would eat whatever was put in front of him, so long as it filled him up and gave him strength for the fight. She, however, had grown up in the famously rich court of Flanders, with a princess of France for a mother. Her tastes were bound to be more sophisticated and she would have seen to it that cooks would be hired who could satisfy those tastes. Harold saw her hand, too, in the lavish yet exquisite decorations that the ducal palace boasted. Ceilings were painted deepest blue, with the stars of the night sky, the planets, the constellations and the signs of the Zodiac all picked out in gold. In the duke's private apartments, to which Harold, as an honoured guest, was given access, he saw a floor painted with a map of the world, complete with rivers, lakes and mountains and all the strange men and wild animals to be found within them. The walls were hung with beautiful tapestries that showed scenes from the Bible, or the myths of Ancient Greece and Rome.

Matilda herself was strikingly beautiful. Unlike the noble-women of Harold's acquaintance, who would never be seen in public without a wimple covering their hair as modestly as a nun, she wore her long, dark tresses loose, so that they fell about her shoulders, covered only by a veil of a fabric so fine that it was virtually transparent. While her husband's conversation consisted of nothing other than politics, war and hunting, with the occasional nod to religious propriety (Harold was struck by the fact that a man who made no secret of the ruthless brutality with which he waged war never failed to attend both matins and evensong), Matilda was clearly a woman of high intelligence and considerable education.

Her greatest pride was the number of scholars who were now coming to Normandy. 'You will know, I'm sure, of the school that Father Lanfranc of Pavia has established at the abbey of Le Bec,' she said, as yet another lavish course was placed before them.

Harold nodded sagely, hoping to disguise his embarrassing ignorance of this establishment. His feeling of intellectual inadequacy only increased as Matilda went on, 'Some of the finest minds in all Christendom have travelled there to study under him. Why, even our Holy Father, Pope Alexander, was one of his students, although we knew him as Anselm of Badagio in those days. And of course, Lanfranc was tremendously helpful in obtaining the Pope's approval for my marriage to the duke.'

'I gather there were objections to it, Your Grace,' Harold said. 'Quite unfounded, I'm sure.'

366

'It was all just politics. You can't imagine the trouble William had to cope with when we were first married. There were so many enemies attacking him from every side. He defeated them all, of course.'

The sweet but pointed smile that accompanied those words made it plain to Harold that the diminutive Duchess of Normandy was in her own way just as tough and combative as her husband. They've each found the only person on earth who's strong enough to put up with the other, he realised. And they love one another, no doubt about that. William's a different man when she's beside him.

With the deftness of a practised hostess, Matilda, having made her point, changed the subject. 'Now, my dear Earl of Wessex, do tell me something about yourself. The ladies of my court are all very intrigued by you.'

Harold was an experienced swordsman in more ways than one. He felt sure he detected the very slightest hint of flirtation in Matilda's tone, and so he answered it with a little nod of acknowledgement, a smile and a fractional lean towards the duchess. 'Do they now? May I ask what, in particular, intrigues them?'

'Oh, just the usual questions that women ask themselves about a man who appears to be handsome, charming and desirable.'

'Ah, yes . . . Well, there's only one sure way to answer those questions.'

'All my attendants are ladies of exceptional virtue.'

'What a pity. Their questions will have to go unanswered.'

'Surely you would not be in any position to give the answer you suggest. Are you not married?'

'In a manner of speaking,' Harold replied. 'I've been with one woman for the past twenty years or more. She's my true love, Edith.' He smiled at the thought of her. 'The common

367

folk call her Edith Swan-Neck on account of her grace and beauty. She has borne me three fine sons and two beautiful daughters.'

'How charming . . . But are you saying that you and Edith have never exchanged vows in the sight of God?'

'No, but we consider ourselves married *in more danico*, as they say: in the Danish way.'

'Thank you, my lord, but I comprehend both the meaning of the Latin and the significance of the phrase. The key point about this *more danico* is that it is not recognised by the Church and thus you would be free to marry someone else.'

'Well, I have to say that I have never had any desire to do so, but yes, you are quite right that it might, in theory, be possible.'

The following morning Duke William approached Harold. 'You spent a long time talking to my wife last night,' he said, in a way that suggested he didn't appreciate another man paying such close attention to her.

'We were talking about her love of scholarship,' Harold replied. 'And that led us to the Church and its views on marriage. I was telling her about Edith, the woman I love.'

'Ah yes, the whole *more danico* business, she mentioned that. My ancestors were great believers in it. People call me the Bastard – though not to my face if they've got any sense – but most of the dukes of Normandy were the sons of their father's concubine, not his wife. Still, it's a good thing you've not had a church marriage. If I'm going to be King of England, I need to feel that my most senior earl is truly tied to me.'

'By way of, ah, reassurance, you mean . . .'

'Exactly that. Now there are a number of ways we can establish that sense of trust, and one of them is by joining the houses of Wessex and Normandy together by marriage.'

'That's a very interesting idea, Your Grace. None of my boys has yet been betrothed, nor my daughters, come to that. I would be honoured if one of them were to marry a son or daughter of yours.'

William grimaced. 'It wasn't actually your children I was thinking of. It was you.'

'I'm sorry?' Harold could scarcely believe his own ears.

'When I am king, I shall require you, as a sign of your loyalty and commitment to my cause, to be married to my daughter Adeliza.'

Harold had been introduced to William and Matilda's older children. He had a dim recollection of a shy, plain child who had the misfortune to have inherited her diminutive size from her mother and her looks from her father. The very idea of marrying her was absurd, but it clearly wasn't wise or even safe to say as much to the duke. Instead he merely observed, 'She's very young to be a bride . . .'

'Twelve,' William snapped back. 'A little young now, perhaps, but I dare say she'll be ready for the marriage bed by the time I ascend to the throne.'

Twelve? My own daughters are older than that! Harold thought, but again managed to bite back the words before they were spoken.

'So you don't require an immediate marriage, then?' he asked.

'No, but I want a betrothal. And if you agree to marry my girl then you'd damn well better do it, because I always hold a man to his word. Always.'

'I see. Did you have anything else in mind?'

'Yes. There will be a service in the cathedral tomorrow, asking God for his blessing for the Brittany campaign. A large number of my most important men will be there. I want you to swear your fealty to me, in the sight of God, and of all those men, so that they can bear witness to your promise.'

'Fealty to you . . . now?'

'That's right.'

'But you and I are of equal rank. I am the senior earl of England, the official subregulus to the king. I don't know how far Normandy extends, but I should be surprised if its size exceeds Wessex and all my other lands. I don't know how many men you can put in the field, but I'd wager I would have as big an army at my back. I'm damned if I'll get down on my knees and be your vassal.'

'You will be my vassal when I am king.'

'And if you are king then of course I will be your subject. But you hold no royal rank now, and until you do, we are equals. If anything, I am your superior.'

The muscles of William's jaw bunched as he clenched his cheeks. His eyes narrowed. Harold was suddenly very aware that this was a man in whom fury was seldom very far from the surface.

'I will be king. And I need to know now – not when I am crowned: now – that I can count on you. Because if I can't, well let's just say you were very lucky to survive the journey to Normandy. You may not be so fortunate on the way back.'

'So . . . if I promise to marry your daughter and pledge fealty to you, I'll be your companion in arms and be showered with gifts and favour, and if I don't, I run the very strong risk of being killed. Well, you don't keep your threats veiled, I'll say that much for you.'

'You call that a threat? From the age of thirteen I never ate a bite of food or swallowed a single drink without wondering if it was poisoned. I never went to bed at night without wondering if I would wake up in the morning. If anyone wanted to be my friend, I asked myself how long it would be before they too betrayed me. If anyone protected me, I feared that they would be killed like all the others. And you say I'm threatening you?

I'm telling you the simple truth, Harold Godwinson. You are either on my side, completely on my side, or you are my enemy. And I always destroy my enemies.'

'Then I'd better be your friend.'

Harold duly betrothed himself to poor Adeliza, who was clearly terrified by the whole idea of being his wife. He swore the sacred oath to be William's vassal with his hand on a box of saintly relics, just to make the sin he would commit by breaking it even greater. For his own part, however, he felt certain that God, who knew all things, would recognise that he was acting under coercion and relieve him of any obligation to stand by his word.

William, however, seemed satisfied. Harold understood that from the duke's point of view, the sincerity of a vow was irrelevant. The very fact that it had been made gave him the right to act upon it. So now he was perfectly content to revert to the role of generous host and military comrade.

William had been fighting for more than twenty years to secure control of his duchy, fight off aggressors and expand into neigh-bouring counties. His victories had won him a great reputation as a warrior and commander, and the Brittany campaign gave Harold a chance to judge him at close quarters. As the duke had said on the road from Eu, he never asked his men to brave any danger that he was not willing to face as well. Indeed, he made a point of going where the action was fiercest, with a bannerman beside him bearing his standard, so that no one on either side should be in any doubt as to his location.

As William himself had suggested, however, this wasn't much more than an extended raid, conducted with the aim of keeping the domestic politics of Brittany sufficiently chaotic that no challenge could be made to Normandy. They relieved the castle at Dol, then chased Conan's forces off, fighting occasional engagements that were really little more than skir-mishes between groups of horsemen. A few men were wounded, some even killed, but to Harold's eye the action seemed mostly to consist of knights charging at each other, shouting, waving swords and jabbing lances, but as much for display as any deadly intent. Certainly there was nothing to compare with the months he had spent fighting the Welsh, where the bitter weather and mountainous terrain could be as deadly as any enemy soldier, and the combat was on foot, toe-to-toe, face-to-face: brutal, bloody and to the death.

Still, there was no doubt that you got to know people when you marched, fought, slept, ate and pissed beside them. Harold came to understand why the men, of all ranks, were so devoted to William. Whatever his faults, he possessed a remarkable com-bination of physical strength, sharp intelligence and implacable will. More than that, he clearly believed that he had a destiny that would raise him above other men, and that inner conviction was so palpable that it made other men believe that William of Normandy was somehow marked out by God to do great things.

But did that make him invincible? Harold thought not. It was one thing for William to make himself the dominant figure among a small group of Frankish lords. It was quite another to rule England. And what if it was not handed to him on a plate? What if he had to conquer the entire country to win its crown?

That could be done. Fifty years earlier, Sweyn of Denmark had invaded England and his son Canute had made himself king. England, though, had been weaker then, and Ethelred had not been man enough to keep the Danes at bay.

But I'm not Ethelred, Harold told himself. I have proved that I can fight, and win, and that men will follow me into battle. Your lords may worship you, William of Normandy, but I don't. Oh, you're good all right, that's obvious. But I can beat you. I have no doubt about that.

10

'Do you think he will keep his promises?' Matilda asked. She and William had made love a short while earlier. Experience had taught her that the calm after the passion had ebbed away and her man was at his most relaxed, as close as he ever came to being unguarded, was always the best time to have the most open conversations with him.

William answered one question with another. 'No, but does it matter? The important thing is that he made them and everyone saw him do it. No matter what he does now, I will always be able to call on that. In the eyes of the world, it will put me in the right.'

'But he will say that he acted under duress, that he was alone, as much a hostage as a guest, and he had no choice but to make those oaths.'

'Of course, and he'd be telling the truth. The English will certainly see it that way. So he will be justified in defying me, just as I will be justified in fighting to assert my right to the throne.'

'Does it really have to end in bloodshed?'

'Yes. That's the only way this can possibly end.'

'Harold is a good man, you know.'

'I agree. But look at this from his point of view. One day King Edward will die and Harold will be at his deathbed. In that instant, Edward's wishes will die with him and Harold will be the obvious choice to rule England. Whatever differences he may have with other lords will be forgotten, because they will all agree that they would rather have another Englishman as their king than some Norman that none of them has ever met, who has never even set foot in England before. And when they all say to Harold, "Be our king," he cannot possibly reply, "No, I made a promise to serve William of Normandy." No man with ambition could possibly say that. I wouldn't, and I would have no respect for Harold if he did.'

'I understand that, but I think it's a pity. After all, he would be no worse off as Earl of Wessex if you were king than he is under Edward.'

'But he cannot be Earl of Wessex if I am king. He cannot be anything at all.'

'Why not?'

'Because I could not be king knowing that Harold and his family were still as powerful as before, with the whole country looking to them to support the English cause, every man just waiting for the moment to rebel. He would be a hundred times more dangerous to me than Martel or Talou ever were.'

'Even without Harold, the English will be no happier to have you as their king.'

'That's true. I will have to rule by fear; to make them understand that any resistance will be met with reprisals that will make the butchery at Alençon seem like a mother's gentle touch.'

'Must you do this, my love? Can't we be happy here in Normandy? We are secure at last, with no enemies to fear. We can give our children the kind of life you never had, growing up in peace, knowing that they are safe, and loved . . . a good life . . .'

William held Matilda tighter as her voice drifted away. 'But there is no good, safe life, my darling. There is only struggle, all the time. The peasant has to work himself to the bone just to survive, and one bad harvest or a rampaging army that takes all

374

his crops can leave him penniless and starving. The minor barons fight with one another over scraps of land. The viscounts dream of becoming counts. The counts have to keep these lesser barons happy or destroy them if they rebel, all the while fighting with their neighbours to defend their own lands against attack or go on the offensive themselves. Kings fight other kings, or form alliances against the Holy Roman Emperor. Christendom fights the Saracens. The world is filled with blood. That is just how it is.'

'No, that is how men make it. And we women just have to watch the sons we bore in our wombs and suckled at our breasts go off to kill one another, and there is nothing we can do about it.'

'Ssshhh . . .' William comforted her. 'Don't be upset. This is just the way the world is, the way God has made it. If we live and die the way we do, that is because He has planned that for us. It's in heaven that we will find peace.'

Matilda fell silent for a while and just tried to believe that the feel of her husband's arms around her and the strength of his body next to hers was enough to protect her and her children from all that the world could throw at them. Finally she said, 'Well, at least one person will be happy if Harold Godwinson breaks his word.'

'Who's that then?'

'Adeliza. The poor child has been walking around in a state of terror at the very idea of being married to "that ugly old English giant".'

'Ugly? I got the impression all you women were swooning over him.'

'Not me. I have an ugly old Norman giant of my own.'

William laughed softly. 'So that's what I am, is it?'

'Mmm . . . Anyway, our little Liza's not ready for any man just yet, big or small, handsome or ugly.'

'Then it is your job, as her mother, to make her ready. For we must all do our duty to Normandy. And that is how she will do hers.'

11

Norway, autumn 1064

The conflict had been going on for so long that neither side could now remember what it was they were fighting for, nor why they should be such enemies. It was just what they did every summer, sailing off to do battle against one another, their journeys as predictable as those of migrating birds. But nothing was ever resolved.

Sven of Denmark could never win a battle.

Harald of Norway could never quite win the war.

'The people of Denmark will never accept you as their king, Harald, no matter how much you might wish to conquer them,' Sven told him when he finally sued for peace.

Harald could not deny the truth of that statement. Nor could he pretend that he, or anyone else, could suppress a nation of rebellious Norsemen who were determined to rid themselves of an unwanted monarch. He had enough trouble controlling unruly barons and warriors in his own lands. He had been ruthless in removing any man who defied him. He took the view that a single act of treason was the acorn from which the oak of full-scale rebellion would grow, and so crushed even the slightest sign of dissent. Yet even now he could never feel entirely safe in Norway. How much worse would it be if he were trying to root out Danish acorns too?

So the two kings made peace and accepted the existing boundaries of their respective realms. Harald's oldest daughter Ingegerd was betrothed to Sven's son and heir Olfa, though their marriage was delayed on account of the groom-to-be's youth. He was yet to celebrate his fourteenth birthday. Once he turned sixteen, however, the wedding would take place. With the decision, the enmity between the two kings and their nations was brought to a close, and now Harald was faced with a problem.

He had led an extraordinary life, piled up riches and made himself a king. When not fighting Sven or his own nobles he had travelled to the furthest extremities of the known world: into the far ice-trapped north to Svalbard and beyond; and west, past Iceland and Greenland, to the newly discovered territory of Vinland, beyond which the lands seemed to stretch on forever, as infinite as the oceans themselves.

Along the way, he had found himself not just one wife, but two. Thanks to the second, Tora Torbergsdatter, he had two fine sons, Magnus and Olaf. From the time they were small boys he had prepared them both for kingship by sending them with his fleets on military expeditions into the Orkneys and Hebrides, down into the Irish Sea and even on raids against the Scots and northern English.

Harald Hardrada's dynasty was therefore established, his greatest enemy neutralised, his legacy secured. Now just one question remained: what could he possibly do next?

12

Westminster

In the final week of Advent 1064, Gospatric, scion of the House of Bamburgh and nephew of the king, left the snows of Northumbria and rode south to spend the Christmas season at the royal court. His intention was both to establish his standing as a man of royal blood and plead the cause of the north. By the time the twelve days of celebration concluded with the feast of the Epiphany, Gospatric was dead. Word was that he had been murdered, and opinion varied as to who might have ordered the killing. Tostig was an obvious suspect, though he swore most vehemently that he was innocent. Gospatric might, for all anyone knew, have had enemies among his own people who would profit by his demise. But a few more daring souls, speaking only to those they trusted absolutely, pointed the finger of blame at the king, or even the queen, conspiring on behalf of her brother.

Gospatric's demise, following less than a year after the murders of Ulf and Gamel, only added to the loathing and mistrust with which Tostig was regarded in Northumbria. Men were talking openly now about the possibility of an uprising against their hated earl. Conspiracies were being hatched. Hundreds of miles to the south, however, in the very different world of the king's court, the troubles of a distant earldom were of far less concern to most courtiers than the apparent certainty that William of Normandy would be their next king. Harold found it all but impossible to impress upon his fellow earls and thegns the way in which the duke would rule them. Far too many were steeped in complacency.

'Oh, he may be a half-decent soldier,' one would say, 'but that doesn't mean he's ready to rule a country.'

'The man's not born for it,' another would agree. 'Damn tanner's boy, what does he know about being a king?'

'Mark my words,' the first would conclude, 'he'll need us more than we need him. How else is he going to keep the country in one piece? He may arrive thinking he can do things his way, but he'll soon learn that there's an English way, and if he doesn't respect it, he'll find himself out on his ear.'

Again and again Harold found himself saying, 'You don't know the man. I do. And if you think William of Normandy will stand aside so that we can keep on just as we always have done, as if he's hardly our king at all, then you're in for a nasty surprise. He'll rule England the same way he rules Normandy. He'll have his oldest, closest allies beside him. They'll follow him to the ends of the earth and he'll reward them accordingly. And everyone else will be given a very simple choice: do exactly what he says, or live to regret your disobedience.'

To Harold, this was just a simple statement of fact. But it appalled him that no one else seemed to accept it as such.

'Oh come now, that's a bit of an exaggeration,' they'd say. 'Look at Canute. He was a foreigner, just like this Duke of Normandy. God knows he wasn't lacking in arrogance, ambition or will – the man ruled an empire far, far larger than Normandy. But he could see there was no sense in changing things. He let us keep the earldoms, let the thegns hang on to their estates. As long as everyone did what was expected, he was happy to let things carry on as they always had done. This Norman will be just the same.'

But as time went by, the mood began to change. From every

380

traveller who brought news from Normandy the message was always the same: the whole duchy was abuzz with talk about William the Bastard's impending succession to the throne of England. The duke was making no secret of his conviction that whatever the customs of England might dictate, and however much the English nobility might treasure their age-old right to select their king, he was going to rule them whether they liked it or not.

Norman nobles were openly talking about the land and titles they hoped to receive in England when the duke came to reward the men who had served him the longest and most loyally. Soldiers who had spent years and even decades seeking their fortunes in the Norman enclaves in Sicily and southern Italy, fighting the Byzantine Empire, the papacy and the local people alike as they carved out a new kingdom of their own, were now returning home. There was more to be gained by following their duke into England, just across the water, than by putting up with the heat, the flies and the homesickness on the other side of Christendom.

Now the mood in England changed and a new argument began: was it best to accept the reality of Norman rule and find a way to survive and even thrive within it? Or should they just accept that they could never allow William to be crowned king, and if that meant fighting him off when he arrived, so be it?

For his own part, Harold was now certain that his only possible course of action was to claim the crown for himself and then defeat William when his inevitable response – an invasion of England – took place. He was still sure that the war could be won. He would be fighting on his own home ground: literally so, since William was almost bound to land somewhere on the south coast, along a shoreline that fell within Harold or his brother Leofwine's earldoms. That meant he would have easy access to supplies and reinforcements. He could pick the

381

best battlegrounds. And he should surely be able to call on overwhelming superiority of numbers.

But it all depended on unity. At the very least, the Godwinson brothers had to stick together. If Edwin, who had succeeded his father Aelfgar, son of Leofric, as Earl of Mercia, brought his forces to the battle, victory would be all but assured. But then, as the autumn leaves began to redden, the unity that he was so desperately seeking faced the most serious possible threat.

13

The manor of Britford, Wiltshire, October 1065

The storm in the north had been years in the building. And then, quite suddenly, it broke. Rebels marched into York, led by Gamelbearth, a cousin of the murdered Gamel, and two other Northumbrian nobles: Dunstan, son of Aethelnoth, and Glonicorn, son of Heardulf. They slaughtered any officials – the tax collectors in particular – they saw as guilty of collaborating with Tostig, and plundered the Northumbrian treasury. The earl's housecarls were massacred. Their commanders, Amund and Reavanswart, managed to escape the city, only to be cornered in a barn on a nearby farm. The rebels surrounded the barn and burned it to the ground, with the two housecarls still inside. Then, with their immediate enemies dead, they held a gathering attended by every significant thegn in the north-east of England, at which they formally declared that Tostig had been deposed and called for the appointment of Morcar of Mercia, brother of Edwin, as the new earl of Northumbria in his place.

For that, though, they needed the king's approval. So the men of the north had decided that they would march south and demand an audience with His Majesty in person.

Harold and Tostig were hunting near Salisbury in Wiltshire when news of the uprising reached them. Tostig paled at the news, reduced to shocked, helpless silence. Only as he and Harold rode to the nearby manor of Britford, where the king and queen were in residence, did his rage explode. As he ranted at the rebel thegns for their disloyalty, their thieving, their slaughter of his men, he was so caught up in his own misfortune that he did not notice Harold's stony silence and the absence of the slightest sympathy. Even when his older brother very pointedly said, 'I told you to win your people over. You couldn't even be bothered to live up there,' it barely interrupted Tostig's self-pitying monologue.

At Britford, more bad news awaited them. The rebels, now with Morcar and Edwin at their head, were encamped less than three days' ride away, in Northampton. Furious that the town's citizens had not seemed sufficiently enthusiastic in supporting their cause, the Northumbrians had run wild: killing the men, raping the women and enslaving anyone who remained alive when their frenzy abated. They set fire to the reserves of grain that had been put aside to feed the townspeople through the coming winter and had their cattle driven back towards Northumbria.

The Godwinson brothers found King Edward consumed with fury at the rebels' impertinence, terror at their looming presence and resentment towards Harold for not preventing this outrage from occurring in the first place. Tostig was greeted with tearful hugs from Edward and Queen Edith, both of whom took his side, sympathising with his complaints and assuring him that they would see to it that his earldom was restored to him and all who were responsible for usurping him were put to death.

Harold, meanwhile, rode to meet the rebels, measure their strength and hear their case. He took just three men to guard him against the normal dangers one might meet upon the road, reasoning that if he was accompanied by enough men to keep him safe against the Northumbrian army, they would constitute sufficient threat to provoke that army into battle. As it was, he was plainly no more than an envoy and thus entitled to safe passage.

One look at the size of the northern host and one hour spent gauging the seriousness of its leaders was enough to persuade Harold that Tostig stood no chance of winning back his earldom. Morcar had accepted the rebels' offer and Edwin was prepared to put the whole weight of Mercia behind their cause. Together the two brothers now controlled all of England north of a line drawn between the Bristol Channel to the west and the Wash to the east. They represented a very real threat to the House of Godwin's domination, but that was a problem for another day. For now, Harold had to find a way to persuade his brother, his sister and his king to accept the reality of the situation.

'We face a simple choice,' he said on his return to Britford. 'Either we give them what they want, in which case they will return the way they came, without a drop of blood spilled in anger. Or we do not, in which case I fear . . . no, I am certain that they will keep marching towards us and only force will stop them. Your Majesty, we face the prospect of civil war.'

'No, we do not!' Tostig protested. 'We face the prospect of anarchy. Because that's what we'll get if we give in to these people. Once one upstart mob has had its way, there will be plenty more, believe me. And all of you . . .' he jabbed his finger at the other nobles, 'every single one of you will be in danger of suffering the same fate as me: a legitimate earl, appointed by the king, turfed off his land by outlaws.'

'Earl Tostig makes a fair point, Wessex. We can't allow the people to decide who rules them. The whole country would descend into chaos.'

'Your Majesty, the chaos will surely come if we attempt to impose an earl upon them by force who has already proved unable to rule by consent.'

'You treacherous bastard!' Tostig shouted.

'That's no way to speak of your own brother, Wessex,' said Edward, like a disapproving parent.

'I'm simply stating the truth,' Harold insisted. 'Earl Tostig has had ten years in which to find a way to rule Northumbria. I am very well aware of the difficulties he has faced, not least because he has told me about them in great detail. And I know that the local nobility has done nothing at all to help him. I sympathise with his situation. I do not claim that I would have done any better. But the truth is, Northumbria will not have him back. Any attempt to impose him by force will lead to conflict, bloodshed and division. That in turn will leave England weaker and more vulnerable. Our enemies will see a perfect opportunity to strike. Harald of Norway, Sven of Denmark, for example . . . both men have made claims upon our throne. Now they may try to seize it. If that should happen, William of Normandy will not stand idly by and watch another man take the crown he regards as his by right.

'Do you really want that, Your Majesty? When you were a boy, you saw what devastation an invasion could wreak on your family and your country. Can you bear to witness that again, in the autumn of your days?'

'No . . . that would be too ghastly to contemplate,' the king admitted.

Harold could see his brother still glaring at him with undimmed defiance. 'Tostig, please, I beg you, as your brother who loves you, give up your claim to Northumbria.'

'Never!'

'But it needn't be the end of the world. We all know how the fortunes of men, and of their families, ebb and flow. We've all seen men be granted titles, lose them, then return again in even greater glory. We saw it happen to our own father, for heaven's sake. Even if you are not earl of Northumbria, you still have estates aplenty. You'll always be a man of wealth and influence. And I'm sure His Majesty could bestow another title upon you . . .'

'Oh yes, I'm sure that would be possible,' said the king, grasping at the straw of a possible way out of the crisis.

'I am very grateful for your kindness and generosity, Your Majesty,' Tostig said, 'but this is a matter of principle. I have a right to be earl of Northumbria and I will not abandon it.'

'There are other principles at stake here, brother,' said Harold. 'The safety of the realm, for example. Are you putting your self-interest above that?'

'How dare you!' Tostig shouted. 'This isn't about keeping the realm safe from civil war, or foreign invasion. It's about your endless lust for power. I'll bet you planned the whole thing. I know you. You're conspiring with Edwin and Morcar, admit it!'

'Don't be ridiculous. Why in God's name would I conspire with another family against my own? You can take it from me that I had nothing to do with this. I'll swear to it on oath if that would make you feel better. The simple truth is that there is a large army of rebels no more than three days' march from here. And we either give them what they want, or prepare for war. And it will be a war in which the enemy is already in the field, while we have not yet even recruited our forces.'

'Really, Wessex, I refuse to believe that the prospect is really that bleak,' the king insisted.

Unable to convince Edward by himself, Harold had a handful of his own and the king's most senior military commanders summoned for a council. They were unanimous: if Edward wanted to oppose the rebels by force of arms, it would lead to full-scale war, which would require levies to be raised across the entire country. By law the king could call upon the fyrd, the army of England, and every community in the land was obliged to supply its quota of men. But that could not be accomplished before winter weather made campaigning impossible.

'In short, Your Majesty, we would have to recruit in the new year with a view to going to war in the spring against Northumbria and Mercia, if the two brothers are still allied. Even if we win, there is still the question of how to force Tostig upon the people against their will . . .'

Edward looked around at the men ranged against him. He felt hemmed in, more like a cornered animal than a king. He had never wanted this council. Harold of Wessex had pressed it upon him, and now Wessex and his cronies were ganging up to force him, their monarch, to accept the consequences of a rebellion against his favourite earl. Edward could see them all looking at him, waiting for him to back down, as if they were the ones who gave the orders and it was his duty to obey. But he was the King of England, consecrated by God, and they had no right to tell him what to do, no right at all.

'But we must win, I insist upon it!' he raged, and the blue veins were so swollen and visible beneath the skin of his forehead that those around him actually feared for his health. 'Tostig must be given his earldom back, and I don't care if every earl and thegn and peasant in all Northumbria is slaughtered in the process. I will not see him deposed!'

'May I suggest a compromise?' said Harold as Edward subsided, exhausted, onto the wooden chair that was serving as his throne. 'Why don't you call a Witenagemot to debate this entire issue? Let all the nobility and senior clergy of England decide what is right. That way, whatever the outcome, it will have been decided by a majority vote and you will be sure that the nation supports it.'

Edward looked at Harold through rheumy, baleful eyes. 'Oh

well, if you insist, have your damned gemot. But let all who attend it know that their king supports the rightful cause of Earl Tostig and will never be swayed from it.'

14

Oxford and Westminster

The assembled magnates and clerics of the Witenagemot were clear in their decision. They were not prepared to see the kingdom torn apart just to put Tostig back in an earldom he had, in their eyes, forfeited by his own inability to govern it. To that end, no charges were brought against the perpetrators of the despoliation of the treasury at York, the killing of the housecarls or the ravaging of Northampton.

The king had raged against his people as they debated Tostig's fate. But once the decision was made and both the earl and his king defied, Edward's strength deserted him. He was a broken man, physically and mentally diminished and enfeebled as he pleaded, 'Please, Tostig, my dear boy, try to see sense. There is nothing we can do for now. But you can count upon my good will and favour. Just relinquish the title of Northumbria and I assure you another will be found.'

Tostig remained defiant to the last. 'No, I won't do it.'

'You are aware, Tostig, that you're defying the will of the King of England,' Harold said. 'If you continue to refuse to obey him, you will make yourself an outlaw. You will either face imprisonment here, or exile overseas.'

Tostig stood alone, looking around at his tormentors like a bear about to be brought low by a ravenous pack of hounds. 'How can I be outlawed for holding on to what is rightfully mine? This is not justice. This is conspiracy.'

He turned to Harold with hatred in his eyes. 'You have

betrayed me, brother. You have betrayed our family, too, and our father's memory, and you will be cursed for it, that I know.'

Then he shook his head and heaved air into his chest. 'I won't rot in any cell. I choose exile. But I will be back. By God, I will be back.'

Within days, Tostig and his family were setting sail for Flanders, where his wife, Judith, was always assured of a loving welcome at her brother's court. They took with them Tostig's personal treasure, which he had never taken up to the treacherous north, and a few loyal retainers, including a northern thegn called Copsige, who had been Tostig's deputy in Northumbria and was therefore no longer welcomed north of the Humber.

Morcar was duly appointed earl of Northumbria and travelled up to York alongside the rebels who had just deposed his predecessor.

The king set off for Westminster, where his magnificent abbey church would soon be consecrated. But he seemed an old man now. His strength was gone and there were times when he barely seemed aware of his surroundings, so deep was his gloom and so great his confusion.

Edith's grief at her husband's decline and her fear of losing him were profound. But the realisation that her marriage was coming to its end only made her aware of how much she had sacrificed for its sake. She had no children to share her loss, no grandchildren to comfort her with their laughter and love. For all her machinations, Tostig was in exile and Harold was barely bothering to conceal his intentions. He wanted to be king. And as if to prove that there was no length to which he would not go to achieve that ambition, he finally did the one thing he had always done his best to avoid. He agreed to a marriage.

His bride-to-be was not Edith Swan-Neck, for dearly though he loved her, and as much as he swore to her that her place in his heart could never be taken by another, she had no political

391

influence of her own. Instead he chose Ealdgyth, the daughter of the late Aelfgar of Mercia and widow of the Welsh king, Gruffydd ap Llewellyn. Harold had, in fact, played a large role in making Ealdgyth a widow, but that was a subject they both tacitly avoided. There was a union to be made and no need to disturb it by going over past conflicts, for what good could possibly come of that?

In betrothing himself to Ealdgyth, Harold became the prospective brother-in-law of Edwin of Mercia and Morcar of Northumbria. All the major earldoms of England were now tied to him by blood or marriage. And even if he was never likely to win the Welsh over to his side as allies, he might at least be in a better position to persuade them not to support William when the war between them came. For come it surely would, and soon.

15

The palace of Westminster, 25 December 1065–
6 January 1066

The succession to King Edward had been a talking point for fifteen years or more. And then quite suddenly it became a reality. The greatest men in all England had gathered at Westminster for the Christmas celebrations. But with every day the king seemed more poorly. He managed to make a brief appearance at the Christmas Day Mass and the feast that followed, though he seemed unaware of where he was or what they were all doing. After three days in bed, he raised himself for long enough to attend the consecration of the church that had been his passion for the past twenty years, but it took all his strength even to stay awake during the ceremony, and the effort left him utterly exhausted.

He retired again to his bed and for the next week lay there drifting in and out of consciousness as it became ever more apparent that his end was near. Queen Edith, Harold, Archbishop Stigand and Robert FitzWimark, the Norman-born Sheriff of Essex, who was one of the king's closest courtiers, maintained a vigil at his bedside. Finally, on the fifth day of January, Edward awoke and gave Edith a smile more loving than he had ever bestowed upon her when in his prime. Then he did his best to stretch out his right arm to grasp Harold's hand and whispered his *verba novissima* – the final declaration of will that in Saxon law took precedence over any previous wills or bequests. 'I commend this woman and all the kingdom to your protection,' he said. 'Remember that she is your lady and sister and serve her faithfully and honour her as such for all the days of her life. Do not take away from her any honour that I have granted her.'

He spoke a few more words granting Harold command of the royal housecarls and asking him to give safe conduct and fair pay to any of the king's servants, many of whom were Norman – for Edward, having lived for so long in Normandy, had never ceased to be, at heart, more Norman than English. Then his feeble grip relaxed, his eyes closed and a few minutes later he gave a final rattling exhalation and did not breathe in again. The king was dead.

Harold moved fast. There was a sufficient quorum of nobility and clergy at Westminster to constitute a Witenagemot that could name a king of England. No sooner had Edward been buried than the debate began.

They met in the great hall of Westminster palace, throwing out the servants who had been preparing for the memorial feast that was due to follow the king's funeral. There was only one candidate as Edward's successor. Harold put himself forward. 'I make no claim on the grounds of blood, for I shared not a drop of it with our late king. Instead I make the claim that I am the man best suited to be the king of this realm. Firstly, I am English, which none of my likely rivals can claim. Secondly, I am the senior of all the earls, both older and more experienced than any other man who shares that title. I can govern this country in peace and lead it in times of war, which there will be soon enough, you can all count on that.

'You know, I hope, that I am a decent man, and that my nature is both fair and generous. If you anoint me as your king, I will respect the lands and titles of every man here, for as long as he is loyal to the Crown. I will govern according to the laws and customs of England. In short, I offer the rule of an

Englishman, in the English fashion, for the benefit of all England. On that I give you my word.'

'You gave your word to that Norman bastard that you would be his vassal . . . aye, and marry his daughter too,' one burly thegn shouted from the back of the hall, provoking a rare burst of laughter on this solemn occasion. 'You're breaking your word to him by standing here saying you'll be our king. How do we know you won't break your word to us too?'

'That's a fair question,' Harold replied, squinting to see who it was that had spoken. 'You're Eldred, aren't you . . . Eldred of Buxted.'

'Aye, that I am,' the man said, puffing out his chest as befitted a man known by name to the next king of England.

'Trust one of my own Sussex thegns to ask the trickiest question,' said Harold. 'And no, before anyone suggests it, I did not put him up to it.'

Harold looked around the hall. He was winning them over, as he had known he would. But the matter would not be concluded until he had addressed Eldred's question, for no man could expect to be king if he was known to be untrustworthy.

'I will answer you, Eldred of Buxted, for you are right, I did make a vow to serve Duke William, and with my hand on a saint's holy relics, in a church and in the sight of God.'

There was a collective intake of breath at that, for there could be no more binding circumstances in which to make an oath.

'But the laws of God and man alike are very clear that an oath made under duress or threat can never be truly made. An oath must be given freely, of a man's own will. His word cannot be taken from him by force.

'Now, when I went to Normandy, on an embassy from our late, beloved King Edward, I was shipwrecked. And when I came ashore I was seized by brigands, who stole all my possessions. By and by I was claimed by the Count of Ponthieu, on whose shore I had landed, and thrown in a dark, stinking dungeon, as if I were a criminal, or a prisoner captured in war, rather than a desperate, helpless traveller.

'I was rescued from that dungeon by an envoy from Duke William of Normandy. But that rescue was made on condition that I would offer the duke my friendship and support. If I did not, I would simply be left to rot. What could I do? I told the envoy I would support Duke William. So I was taken from the cell and thence to the border with Normandy, where William the Bastard himself was waiting to meet me.'

Harold paused. He was coming to the key point in his story. The other character in this tale was a man who was telling all Christendom that he would be England's next king. Everyone gathered here at Westminster wanted to hear what kind of a man this William was.

'I will say this for Duke William. He doesn't mince his words. He doesn't pretend to be any better than he is. He gave me a very simple choice. I could either swear to be his vassal, in which case he'd treat me with honour, afford me every possible hospitality and give me whatever I wanted, from a horse to a sword to a new set of hose. Or I could refuse to make that oath, in which case I'd find that I might have had a lucky escape on my journey to Normandy, but I'd be a lot less fortunate on my way home.

'He threatened me with death, my lords. And you may be sure that William of Normandy does not make idle threats. If he says that he's prepared to kill a man, he means it and, by God, he'll do it, too.

'So I made that oath. But as I did so, I made another promise to myself: that I would rather die than see William of Normandy become king of England. For if he does, he will take your lands, he will strip you of your titles and he will govern by his laws, not England's. And so, with that in mind, I ask you this: who would you rather have as your king?'

The answer was instant and unanimous. The following morning, just a day after Edward had died, and hours after he had been laid to rest, Harold was crowned king of England in Westminster Abbey.

A few days later, the news reached William's ears.

16

Rouen

'How is he, Your Grace?' asked Fitz, standing outside the door of Duke William's bedchamber.

'Still the same,' Matilda said. 'I don't think he's changed out of his hunting clothes yet. He hasn't even pulled off his boots.'

'I don't understand why he's so upset. We all knew Harold would do this.'

Matilda smiled ruefully. 'A man can know something in his head, but in his heart . . . I think William hoped that Harold might not, in the end, let him down. You know how he is. He pretends he doesn't care when people disappoint him, but he still does. He can't help it. He's like a little boy again, abandoned by someone he trusted.'

'But he didn't trust Harold. He told me so. Didn't he say that to you too?'

'He did, yes . . . but that was his head talking.'

'And his heart . . .'

'Exactly.'

Fitz sighed impatiently. Several hours had passed since he and William had heard the news from England, delivered by a messenger while they were hunting in the duke's parkland of Quenilly, outside Rouen. William had not said a word. He had simply turned his horse and galloped away towards the city, with Fitz in pursuit and the rest of the hunting party wondering what on earth was going on. Even when Fitz had caught up with him, William had remained silent, not replying to any

398

questions until Fitz had given up, accepted his duke's wishes and ridden wordlessly beside him all the way to the palace.

The moment he reached home, William had dismounted, not so much handing the reins of his horse to his groom as throwing them, and stalked away upstairs. The heavy oak door of the chamber had slammed shut behind him and there he had remained, refusing to see or speak to anyone. Matilda had been rebuffed. Even Robert had knocked on the door and called out, 'What is it, Papa? What's the matter?' The boy had swallowed his pride and used the nickname he hated: 'It's Shortpants here, your son. Can I help?' but there had been no response.

Now the sun had set and the servants were preparing the great hall for the night's meal.

'If he doesn't come out soon, he'll miss dinner. I've never once known him refuse to eat a meal before,' Fitz said.

To his surprise, Matilda giggled, putting a hand across her mouth to stifle it.

Fitz looked at her enquiringly.

'I'm sorry,' she said. 'I just remembered the last time I behaved the same way His Grace is doing now. It was the day William rode back to Bruges, after you had all left, and . . . well, you know.'

Fitz smiled. 'How could I forget?'

'I was so angry. I went up to my room and slammed the door, just like His Grace this afternoon. My poor father was standing outside in the passage, shouting at the top of his voice that he would avenge this appalling insult, this shameful disrespect that had been shown to me, our family and all Flanders. "I will go to war for you, my little one!" And then he stormed off to call a council of all his generals, and I was lying there, and as time went by and I calmed down, I realised that I didn't feel at all insulted or disrespected. I felt loved. But I didn't know what to do . . . I mean, once one shuts a door, it can be very hard to open it again. So I just lay there until my mother came in. She didn't knock, she just let herself in very quietly and waited until I noticed her. Then she talked to me and of course she understood exactly how I felt, and she made me go downstairs to ask my father not to go to war and . . . well, here I am.'

'Perhaps you should go in now, Your Grace, just as your mother did.'

'Yes, perhaps I should . . .'

Matilda opened the door just far enough to let her slender little frame into the room, slipped in and closed it silently behind her.

A few minutes passed. Fitz could hear nothing from inside the chamber, but he told himself that this was a good sign. After all, the walls were made of massive stone blocks and the door was thick, so the duke and duchess would have had to be shouting and screaming at one another to be heard. Silence was far preferable to that.

Eventually Matilda reappeared at the door. 'His Grace the duke will see you now.'

Fitz walked in. William was sitting on the edge of his bed, leaning forward, his elbows on his knees. He looked up. 'I'm going to make that treacherous shit-head Englishman pay for what he's just done,' he said.

Fitz grinned. That was more like it. 'Absolutely, Your Grace.'

'Starting tomorrow, we are going to work out how we raise an army big enough to beat the English, build enough ships to carry it, and then get it across the sea to that godforsaken island. Summon both my brothers, as well as Montgomery, Giffard, my cousin Richard of Evreux, Beaumont, Grandmesnil, de Montfort, Warenne . . .' The duke named his entire inner circle. 'How soon can you get them all here?'

'Most of them are already at court. Those that aren't I can reach in two days, at most, and have here in three or four.'

'Good. We will meet in four days then. In the meantime, you and I will keep talking. I want to know what we are going to say before we step into the council chamber. I'm also going to send an embassy to Harold . . . and he will never, ever be referred to as "King Harold", by the way. Make sure everyone knows that.'

Fitz nodded.

'Our envoys will point out that Harold has broken his word twice over – apparently he is marrying some Englishwoman, the sister of two of his earls, so he has also rejected and humiliated my darling Adeliza. They will give him the chance to keep to the terms of his agreement with me and will say that all will be forgiven if he does.'

'Do you think there is any chance of persuading him?'

'No, but I want to be seen to have tried. I want all Christendom to know that I have right on my side.'

'Perhaps we should get God on our side too, Your Grace,' Matilda said.

'I have no doubt that He is on our side already,' William replied. 'I shall, of course, continue to pray for His support in our endeavours.'

'Forgive me, but that wasn't quite what I meant. I was referring to the support of the Church.'

William's eyes narrowed. 'Continue . . .'

'Thanks to Lanfranc, we have influence in Rome with the Pope. And Lanfranc is also close to Hildebrand, the papal archdeacon. He might be able to persuade them to put the weight of the papacy behind us.'

'On what grounds?' William asked. 'Harold broke an oath made on the relics of a saint. I suppose that might give us grounds for saying that he insulted the Church. But Rome is likely to regard this as a quarrel between two men seeking power here on earth. There is no reason for the Church to get involved.'

'Actually, Your Grace, there might be,' Fitz broke in. 'The senior churchman in England is Stigand, the Archbishop of Canterbury. Am I not right in thinking that this Stigand has offended the papacy by holding more than one bishopric? I believe he retained his last post when he accepted Canterbury.'

'That's right,' Matilda said. 'He holds Winchester as well as Canterbury. It's quite wrong. If you were to promise the Pope that you would strip Stigand of both his posts and appoint them to two individuals . . .'

'. . . then Rome would have reason to support us,' William concluded. 'That's very good. And if I also promised to make Lanfranc archbishop of Canterbury, then he would be sure to support our efforts too.'

17

England, early 1066

Harold married Ealdgyth. He bedded her repeatedly, enjoyably and with any luck sufficiently to have sired an heir. Then he went north.

Tostig's usurpation had precipitated the king's death. Harold did not want it to cause his own downfall too. Both Morcar and Edwin had voted for him at the Witenagemot and could be counted on for some support. But the fact remained that the great bulk of northern gentry and senior magnates had been opposed to Tostig and were likely to look on his brother with suspicion. The churchmen of the north, particularly those from Durham Cathedral, had also been vehemently anti-Tostig. So Harold brought one of his closest allies, Bishop Wulfstan of Worcester, with him to act as a go-between.

Another gemot was called at York, and Harold stood before it knowing that he had one chance to win the men there over to his cause. He emphasised that while William based his claim on an old promise made by King Edward, he himself could claim the king's blessing, made with his dying breath, in front of witnesses, and backed up by the vote of the Witenagemot.

'I am an English king, rightfully chosen in the English way, as our law and custom demand. William is a foreigner with no claim at all apart from his greed and his hunger for power.'

He pleaded with them to understand the seriousness of the peril facing England. He repeated the point he had made so often at court in Winchester or Westminster: this was more than a battle between contenders for the throne. 'William will not just make himself king. He has men around him who will demand rewards for their services. He will give them land and titles: your land, your titles. He will rob your sons of their inheritances, and give them to the sons of Norman invaders. I say this because I know the man and I know the men who surround him. They are not just coming for me . . . they are coming after you, and your land and your heritage too.'

He warned that they had to be wary of treachery from within. 'For centuries our kings have made Winchester, the traditional capital city of Wessex, the seat of royal power. I was Earl of Wessex and now I am king, so of all men I might have been expected to have my court at Winchester. Yet I will rule the country from London. Why? Because I do not trust my own city. My sister, Queen Edith, lives there. She has always been close to Tostig and wants more than anything to see him reinstated to rule over you here in Northumbria. If she has to make common cause with William of Normandy and see the downfall of England in order to secure Tostig's return, believe me, that will be a price well worth paying in her eyes.

'My sister puts her love for her brother ahead of her love for her country. I love my brother and my sister too. But I love my country more. My duty is to England. I will fulfil that duty to my dying day, to the last drop of blood in my body, to my very final breath. Now I call upon you to stand beside me.

'If we fight among ourselves, we will soon fall prey to our enemies. But if we unite, if we stand together, if we set aside any differences we have in favour of the greater cause that binds us all – the cause of England – then we can never be defeated. Never!'

Harold rode back to London with the cheers of the northern thegns, earls and bishops still ringing in his ears. When he reached Westminster, he was met by the embassy from Normandy, who told him that if he gave up the throne and accepted William as his rightful king, then his position as Earl of Wessex would be respected and he could expect a place among the king's most trusted advisers. If he did not, he could rest assured that Duke William had no fears about fighting for what was rightfully his. The ambassador added, 'His Grace has instructed me to tell Earl Harold that he will soon make his presence felt in England. Furthermore he says, "If you do not see me before the year is out, then you may spend the rest of your life in peace, for I will not be coming any later."'

Harold had no intention of giving up anything. Nor did he have the slightest confidence that William would ever allow him any power or influence should he become king. He told the Normans that their duke's claim to the throne was entirely invalid. He, Harold was the rightful king, chosen in the proper way and supported by his people.

When the embassy had been sent on its way, Harold summoned all the senior earls in the land to a council in London. 'Duke William will be coming for us this year. We must be ready for him. Let your thegns know that I will be calling upon the fyrd. I need the mightiest, most numerous army these islands have ever seen. And with it I will throw that Norman braggart right back into the sea.'

18

Bruges and Rouen

Tostig had spent three months with his father-in-law Count Baldwin in Bruges. He was so immersed in his own problems, and his need for retribution against those he felt had wronged him, that he had barely registered any of the events in England. The only significance of Harold taking the throne was that it proved to Tostig that his older brother had never cared about anything other than making himself king, no matter what the cost.

Baldwin had not given Tostig a huge amount of encouragement. 'You have my permission to build or buy ships here. You may recruit as many men as are willing to fight for you. What you do with those ships and those men is entirely your concern. If you are successful in regaining your earldom, I will be happy for you. But I am regent of France and as such I cannot be seen to do anything that might involve the king in war against another nation. So no, I cannot give you direct help in any fight against your brother. Why don't you try Duke William? I am sure he will be glad of an ally. And Matilda adores Judith, so she will certainly speak up for you with her husband.'

So Tostig and Judith travelled south to Rouen. Matilda's grandfather, the previous Count of Flanders, had taken a second wife, Eleanor of Normandy, late in life, when the children of his first marriage were already grown up. Judith was the child of this second marriage. So while she was younger than Matilda, she was in fact her aunt. The two women had grown up together and greeted one another like sisters, with hugs and kisses and laughter and tears of joy, before going off for a heart-to-heart conversation that would continue virtually uninterrupted for the whole time Judith was in Normandy, for they had so much of the past to catch up on and so many plans and hopes for the future to discuss.

William, who was only a year younger than Tostig, took a certain gruff pleasure in pointedly greeting him as 'My dear uncle . . .'

Tostig was struck by the fact that even as the duke made what was clearly intended as a pleasantry, still there was an undertow of menace. He felt like a farmer standing beside a prize bull: no matter how docile the beast might seem, it was at any moment capable of goring or trampling him to death.

'Or should I call you "cousin"?' William went on. 'For Lady Judith's mother Eleanor was my great-aunt, and sister to Queen Emma of England.'

'Who was, of course, mother to our late, lamented King Ethelred,' Tostig observed, understanding full well where this was going.

'And there you have my blood claim to the throne of England.'

'Which my damn usurping brother cannot match.'

'Precisely so.'

William celebrated Tostig's visit with as lavish a feast as had been accorded to Harold. Matilda insisted upon it, if only for Lady Judith's sake. But Tostig was not as charming a guest as his brother had been. Though he was good-looking enough, and not without intelligence or even a certain distinction, he lacked Harold's charm, and his resentment at being ejected from his earldom was too close to the surface. William and his barons found themselves publicly sympathising with Tostig over what was clearly an illegal act of rebellion, while privately thinking that no true leader would ever have allowed it to occur in the first place.

'Can you imagine what William would have done if we'd marched into Rouen while he was away, said we were stripping away his title and invited someone from Flanders, or Brittany, or God knows where to take his place?' Fitz asked Montgomery after the feast.

Montgomery winced. 'It doesn't even bear thinking about. I mean, we all know what he did to those poor bastards at Alençon, just for mocking his family. If we took his duchy . . .'

'Ouch.'

William, meanwhile, was deep in negotiations with Tostig, but to the latter's disappointment he seemed in no mood to be generous. 'I'm more than happy for you to make life as difficult as possible for your brother, and I wish you well in that. But I can't offer you any direct help, and I'll tell you why.

'In the first place, I will need every man, horse, ship and gold piece I have for my own invasion. Secondly, it would not help me to be seen alongside a man who has been outlawed by the previous king. One of the overriding aims on which all my plans are based is the need to present myself as the legitimate king of England. I intend to get the backing of all Christendom, right up to the Holy Father himself. It would do me no good to compromise my cause by association with you. And finally . . . what can you offer me?'

Tostig made as if to speak, but William held up a hand to stop him. 'Hear me out. If you were still earl of Northumbria and could promise me the north and all the men in it, then I would forget my previous objections in an instant. But you can't, because you have no friends, or power, or influence in Northumbria. That, in fact, is precisely why you are here. So I cannot help you, and that decision is final.'

Tostig pleaded in vain for the duke to change his mind.

Judith, who was outraged that William should have been so dismissive, promised to intercede with Matilda on his behalf. She poured out her heart to the woman who was both her relative and her closest, oldest friend. Matilda listened to what she had to say, then she took Judith's hands and looked into her eyes. 'I will write to my father, making your case and pleading with him to offer you more open support. As for my husband, I fear there is nothing I can do. I flatter myself to think that no one is closer to Duke William than me. He loves me very deeply, as I love him. But when he says that his decision is final, he means it.'

Tostig and Judith decided to return to Bruges the following day, for there was nothing to be gained by staying any longer in Normandy. Just as they were leaving, and the last of their baggage was being loaded onto a covered wagon, the embassy that had been sent to Harold returned. By the time they went to say their farewells to William and Matilda, the duke was in a foul temper.

'Do you know what your brother has said? I did my best to be fair. I said that if he gave up his throne he could keep his earldom and have an honoured place at court.'

'That's certainly more than reasonable,' Tostig said, sensing a faint glimmer of hope for his own ambitions.

'That's what I thought . . . much more than reasonable. But he has thrown that offer back in my face. And not only has he gone and married some old widow when he could have had my daughter, he's . . . he's . . .' William was so outraged that for once in his life he could not find the words to express himself.

Tostig said nothing, knowing that it would be unwise to butt in when the duke was in this mood.

William took a couple of deep breaths to gather his wits, and then spoke very deliberately and with an obvious effort to control himself. 'Listen, I meant what I said yesterday. I cannot help you. Not openly, at any rate. But I will make this commitment. If you help bring down your brother, I will be truly grateful for that help and I will reward you for it. I cannot say now what form that reward will take. But I am a man of my word. If I say I am going to be your friend, then a friend I will truly be. So, Tostig of Northumbria, you can count on my friendship and appreciation.'

'And my brother?'

'I will kill him. And you can count on that too.'

19

Denmark and Norway, early spring 1066

If there was one lesson Tostig had learned from his recent experience, it was that he was powerless unless he had the military might to promise assistance to his allies and destruction to his foes. And so, rebuffed in Flanders and Normandy, he left Copsige in Bruges to look after his family and start putting together a fleet of ships and an army to man it, then headed north to Denmark, where he hoped for better luck.

King Sven was his first cousin, and had a legitimate blood claim to the English throne through his mother Estrith, who was King Canute's sister. He was also among the many men to whom Edward had at one time or another promised, or affected to promise, the succession. Tostig therefore felt confident that he would support an attack on England.

Once again, however, he was disappointed. Sven still hoped for a chance to press his claim to England, but for now both he and Denmark itself were exhausted and impoverished by the wars against Norway, and there was no appetite for any further bloodshed. He allowed Tostig to recruit a few Danish boats and crews to fight with him as mercenaries, wished him luck and even offered him a position of honour at his court. Tostig paid for the ships and men, but took the offer as an insult, rebuking Sven furiously for his lily-livered cowardice and storming out of his palace.

There was now just one place left for him to go, one man who might help him: King Harald Hardrada of Norway. The

411

king greeted him at Sarpsborg, a city founded by his half-brother King Olaf in the county of Viken on his kingdom's south-eastern shore. At first Tostig feared that he was in for another cold shoulder, for Harald was suspicious. 'Sven of Denmark is your kinsman, not I. Why have you not found the ally you seek in him?'

Tostig answered one question with another: 'Sven is a broken man, Your Majesty. You were the one who broke him. Why would I not prefer you?'

Hardrada appreciated wordplay, and all the more so when it flattered him. 'Come then. We will eat and drink and listen to bards' tales and minstrels' songs. Then we will talk, and if you are very lucky, I may even write a verse to celebrate the occasion.'

The food at the court of Hardrada was less fancy than that served at the ducal palace in Rouen, and the drink was rougher on the tongue, but the men who presided over the two tables had a great deal in common, starting with their sheer physical presence. Tostig had been impressed by William of Normandy's stature, but Harald Hardrada was a good head taller still, even broader in the shoulder and massive through the chest and waist. Like William, he was completely frank about his capacity for violence, admitting to the murder of more than a dozen of his own nobles and boasting, 'I kill without a second thought and remember all my killings.'

By God, this is another wild bull, thought Tostig as Harald went on, 'Consider the battleaxe and its curved blade. It looks like the curve of a smile, don't you think?'

'I confess, sire, I'd never thought of it quite like that.'

'Well, I have, and I can tell you that I have carried my axe through more battles than I care to remember, and many a man has felt the steel kiss from those thin lips.'

Harald looked at Tostig, who felt as though he were being sized up for the next swing of Harald's deadly smiler. 'Now tell me why I should wield my axe for you. What would be the purpose of our campaign, and what would I stand to gain from it?'

'As to the why, we would be fighting to recover my earldom of Northumbria.'

'What is your earldom to me?'

'It is in the north of England, with harbours on both the east coast and the west. At the moment, the Norsemen who settle there are all Danes. But I would open it to your people: tradesmen, farmers, merchants, all would be welcome. I would grant your ships the right to moor along all my coasts. You would have access to supplies, safe havens in time of war and shelter from any storms. And from the north of England your warships could strike wherever they liked: plundering the fat, defenceless south; venturing across the sea to the Low Countries or the lands of the Franks; regaining control of the Scottish islands.'

'I do not need England for any of that. My forefathers have ploughed those seas since time out of mind, and reaped rich harvests from them too.'

Tostig quickly switched his point of attack. 'Forgive me, Your Majesty, if I underestimated your ambition. It was remiss of me, for of course you have a right to far more than mere access to Northumbria. You have a just claim to the throne itself. For did not your predecessor Magnus enter into an agreement with my more distant cousin Harthacnut, son of Canute? And did they not agree that whoever died first, if they had no son to take their place, would bequeath his throne to the other? For years we in England nervously awaited the first sighting of Magnus's fleet on the northern horizon. I heard tell that His Majesty died when, having finally mustered the ships he needed, he fell overboard and drowned.'

Harald nodded in agreement.

413

'Very well then,' Tostig pressed on. 'Are you not the rightful inheritor of Magnus's claim to all England? I can help you secure it.'

'And if you did, what would be your reward?'

'No more than what is rightfully mine: the earldom of Northumbria.'

'Hmm . . .' Harald considered the matter. Tostig could see that his vanity and ambition had been tickled by the idea of becoming king. And there was something else, too, some deeper emotion that Tostig could sense but not quite identify. One thing he was sure of, though: the Norwegian was more interested than anyone else he had approached. The fish had swallowed the hook. The trick now was to reel him in.

'Your argument is a good one, Tostig Godwinson,' Harald said, 'but I would be a fool not to think about its possible flaws. For example, how would the people of England respond – the ones that matter, I mean, the men with power and influence? It would be a hard task indeed to rule a kingdom as large as England if the thegns and earldormen were against me. As I understand it, your brother Harold won their votes. They have pledged themselves to him. Why would they turn around and follow me instead?'

'Because my brother is a treacherous, deceitful liar,' Tostig replied, unable to keep the bitterness out of his voice. 'Oh, he has a way about him all right. If he were here now, you would think him a fine fellow, even if he was charming your woman into his bed behind your back. But as time went by, you would see with your own eyes that he is two-faced, a man who makes and then breaks oaths without a second thought.'

'William the Bastard would agree with that,' Harald observed.

'He does, believe me. I spoke with him barely a month ago, and his fury at Harold was terrible to behold. He feels betrayed

414

and double-crossed, just as I do, and my beloved sister Queen Edith. Soon the men of England will understand why we who know Harold best hate him the most. And when they do, they will revoke their pledges of loyalty to him, just as he did to Duke William. Then you will be able to win them over. There is no doubt about that.'

Harald was half persuaded, but he still needed the support of his magnates. They would be the ones who would have to captain the ships and lead the companies of soldiers in any expedition against England.

A council was therefore called the following morning, with the leading men in Norway in attendance. Tostig presented his case, moving from the legitimacy of King Harald's cause to the chances of success and the great benefits that would follow from a conquest. No one disputed the final point. England was famously prosperous and well organised. As for legitimacy, the men in the council chamber didn't really care about the finer details of Harald's claim. If the invasion was successful, what would it matter whether it was justified, and if it failed, all the justification in the world would make no difference.

The key point was the single question: can we win?

Among the older men in the room, warriors who had spilled enough blood and lost enough friends to know the real cost of war, there was an air of caution. The English fyrd system would make tens of thousands of men available to Harold, more than could ever be carried over the seas from Norway.

'Pah! I don't care about the fyrd,' said Ulf Ospaksson, Harald's right-hand man. 'They are just peasants with a club or a rusty sword in their hand.'

They're a bit better than that, Tostig thought, but kept his mouth shut.

'It's the royal housecarls that worry me,' Ulf continued. 'They are brave beyond reason. They fight equally well with sword or axe. Any one of them is worth two ordinary fighting men.'

There were nods of assent from those who knew of the housecarls' fearsome reputation, or had seen them fight, and a few murmurs of alarm from those who were hearing about them for the first time.

Now Tostig felt it prudent to step in. 'I am surprised at you, sir,' he said. 'I thought it was the English who feared the mighty Norsemen and not the other way around. Believe me, I know all about the housecarls. Yes, they are good. Only the best men are chosen to be the king's guards. But they are still men. They bleed like anyone else, piss like anyone else and shit like anyone else.'

'Aye, and I'll wager they shit twice as much as any normal man too,' Ospaksson muttered.

Then someone called out from the back of the chamber, a much younger man by the sound of him. 'May I speak, Your Majesty?'

'You are not a true member of the council, Skule Konfostre. I only allowed you to attend for my son's sake.'

'Please, Father, let him have his say,' said another youthful voice.

'Very well, Olaf . . . but he had better talk sense or I will hold you responsible.'

'Thank you, Father,' said Prince Olaf. 'Now speak, Skule, and make our case well.'

Skule Konfostre stood, a tall, golden-haired youth, on the very cusp of true manhood. He looked around, meeting the eyes of all those who stared at him, and took his time to collect his thoughts. 'Your Majesty, I was raised on tales of your daring: how you fought at Stikelstad where old King Olaf met his maker when you were still just a boy, even younger than I am today . . . how you journeyed to Kiev and thence to

416

Constantinople . . . how you made a fortune worthy of the gods in the service of the emperor, fighting in every corner of his far-flung lands. And I know the stories of your valour and your hard-won battle scars, Ulf Ospaksson. The men who gave you those scars are but dust and bones now, for you repaid them in full measure and more. And I am sure that all you great men gathered here have stories worthy of the poets and the sagas from the days when you were young and Norsemen roamed the whole world, fighting, trading, exploring.

'What fine days they were. But what do we young men have to stir our blood? There are no new lands left for us to discover, no wars in which we can prove our courage, earn our glory and write battle stories of our own. Yet we are as hungry as you once were. We hunger for the sound of steel upon steel, for the ship's prow furrowing through the churning waves on the way to the farthest horizon, for women to have in our beds and gold to put in our treasure chests. And where are we to find these things, eh? Here in Norway? We all know that the Norseman has always roamed because he has had to, because there is so little wealth to be had here.

'And now, like a messenger from the old gods, the gods of thunder and war, comes Tostig Godwinson. He is half Norseman himself, as his name and ancestors testify. And he comes with a challenge fit for heroes. "Come with me," he says. "Avenge the wrong that was done to me. And in doing that, seize the richest kingdom this side of Byzantium itself." But then the naysayers speak up. "Oh, but there are so many soldiers guarding this kingdom! They are so big! They are so strong! They are worth any two of us."'

Skule's words were delivered in the voice of a frightened old woman, and his play-acting was so well done that even Ulf Ospaksson could not help but laugh. Now he let the last chuckles fall silent and pointed at the king with a look of

417

absolute seriousness on his face. 'What man on earth is worth two King Haralds? Surely His Majesty has proven time and again that no five men on earth together could defeat him? And when did you, Ulf, encounter an opponent on the field of battle and say, "I am only half the man he is"?

'We are Norsemen. We are the greatest warriors and sailors and traders and explorers in the world. We bow to no man. We do not run away from a battle, we run towards it. We do not duck a challenge, we embrace it. Thanks to one man, this man Tostig Godwinson, we have the chance to conquer England, to create an empire Knut the Great himself would have envied. I ask you, my fellow Norsemen, will we accept that challenge?'

For a moment there was silence. It continued for what seemed to Tostig like an age, until he could hardly bear it any longer. He could see that Skule's nerve was stretched to the limit. For a while he had made himself an orator; now he seemed more like a frightened boy. But then he was struck by one last gasp of inspiration. 'Raise the Landwaster, Harald Sigurdsson!' he cried. 'Raise the raven banner on English soil, bring its magic to bear upon the battlefield and nothing can stand in your way. Show us, your loyal warriors, the Landwaster and we will follow it to glory!'

That got the nobles cheering. Of all his countless treasures, none was as precious to Harald as his war banner. Landwaster was a simple enough thing. It was woven of plain white silk and was roughly triangular, with one straight edge up the pole from which it hung and another across its top, but a quarter-circle curve along the longest edge. The only decoration was a single black raven, the symbol of Odin, lord of the old gods. Yet not a man there doubted that the banner had mystical powers, for it had never once failed to bring victory. So long as Landwaster flew, they could not be defeated.

Suddenly there was a crash that echoed around the hall as

Harald Hardrada slammed his fist onto the wooden table before him. At once the other men fell silent.

'Yes, by God,' growled the king. 'I will accept your challenge, Skule Konfostre.'

'Yes!' shouted another man, and at once the rest joined in with a chant of 'Yes! Yes! Yes!'

Olaf, his brother Magnus and all the younger men gathered round Skule, slapping him on the shoulder and praising him for his eloquence.

Having said his piece, Harald did not join in the shouting. He simply leaned over towards Tostig. 'Congratulations. You got what you wanted. We're going to war.'

20

William summoned a full gathering of all the noblemen who would be called upon to serve in the attack on England. They would also provide the bulk of the men and ships that would be required for the campaign. His inner circle all made public pledges of support. Fitz declared that he would pay for the construction of sixty ships, as did Roger Montgomery and a handful of the other heads of the great Norman families. William's brothers were even more generous. Bishop Odo promised one hundred ships and Rob, most lavish of all, declared that the duke could count on one hundred and twenty vessels to be funded from his personal treasury.

But though the very greatest men in the duchy were unanimous in their support for William's cause, the lesser nobles were much harder to persuade. They had all fought for Duke William in counties and duchies that lay immediately beyond Normandy. But England was another matter altogether. It was across the sea, a long way from home, and would be very hard to escape if anything went wrong.

Militarily they were taking on far more than ever before. The armies of Brittany, or Anjou, or even the King of France himself were not remotely as large as the one that could be mustered by King Harold. Furthermore, he could easily call up reinforcements, whereas they would have a much harder job.

They didn't like the thought of funding William's foreign adventure either. Men whose estates were of modest size, barely big enough to support them and their peasants, lacked the means or the desire to pay their duke the levy he was demanding, and could see no chance of getting any return for their money, even if they did stump up. One cynic, a minor landowner from the Cotentin called Etienne de Brix, told his drinking partners, 'It's all very well for the duke's brothers and his little pets to throw their money around. Mark my words, that lot'll have land as far as the eye can see. They'll give themselves fancy new titles, build massive great castles and help themselves to everything England's got. And the likes of us'll be living off scraps, same as usual.'

As the first day of the council drew to a close, William dispatched Fitz to meet the objectors, listen to what they had to say and assure them that their duke was more than willing to address all their concerns. Fitz spent several hours having his ear chewed off by angry men who thought they were being asked to risk their necks on a fool's errand, and promised them that he would represent their case in council the following day.

The new morning came, the gathering reassembled and William called upon Fitz to report on his talks. Fitz stood up. 'Your Grace, I have splendid news. The men to whom I spoke last night were absolutely united. With one voice they all said the same thing. They are Your Grace's loyal and devoted servants, they would follow you to hell and back and they are absolutely set on coming with you to England, sure in the knowledge that our cause is just, that Your Grace will be triumphant and that we will end the year crying, "Long live King William of England!"'

If he had hoped that this blatant deceit would be enough to shame the objectors into silence, he was sorely mistaken. The hall descended into a cacophony of shouted oaths, complaints, insults and ill will. Finally William got to his feet and roared, 'Silence!'

He stood, legs apart, hands on hips, glaring at his vassals

until they quieted. 'If any man objects to anything I have proposed, let him come and see me in my private council chamber and say his piece. You may speak your minds openly and without fear and I will listen.'

Then without another word he turned and walked away to his chamber.

No one moved a muscle. Suddenly all the men who had been shouting and waving their fists a few moments earlier found themselves with nothing to say. Finally Etienne de Brix muttered, 'Well, if no one else has got the guts to do it . . .' and went off in the same direction as the duke.

When he entered the chamber, de Brix found William sitting on a chair in the middle of the floor. He looked around. There was no other chair provided. The duke did not greet him, but simply gestured to him to step forward. 'Well?'

As he had walked down the passage, de Brix had rehearsed all the points he intended to make. Now, though, as he looked into the duke's cold blue basilisk eyes, and saw the furrow of his brow and the hard set of his jaw, he found that the words that had sounded so fluently persuasive as he was saying them under his breath now vanished from his head and stuttered on his tongue as he tried to speak them. He just about managed to express a vague sense of unease about the cost and risk of the invasion, to both himself and Normandy as a whole, before he came to an unconvincing conclusion.

The duke let the silence linger until de Brix's nerves were stretched almost to breaking point. At last he asked, 'Have you finished?'

De Brix nodded, managing a feeble 'Yes, Your Grace.'

'Did I hear you out, as I promised?'

'Yes, Your Grace.'

'Good. Then we are agreed. Tell the next man to come in.'

About a dozen men had summoned up the courage to follow

de Brix and were waiting outside the chamber when he emerged.

'Did he let you speak?' one of them asked.

De Brix nodded.

'And he let you say whatever you wanted?'

Another nod.

'He didn't shout at you or anything?'

De Brix, who was now more in need of a large tankard of wine than at any previous moment in his life, said, 'No, no . . . nothing like that. He . . . he just sat there,' and fled away down the corridor.

Three more men had the nerve to follow de Brix into the room. Each emerged more flustered than the last. By the time the third man was through with his audience, the corridor outside was empty. Every other objector had fled.

William waited a while to see if anyone else was going to appear, then got up, walked to the door and peered out into the passageway. There wasn't a soul in sight.

'Good,' he said.

The invasion was going ahead.

21

The palace of Westminster

'I presume Your Majesty knows that Harald of Norway is mustering troops and building boats. He makes no secret of his intention to invade England, nor his ambition to be king,' said Morcar of Northumbria.

'This is your brother's doing,' said Edwin of Mercia, only adding 'sire' as an afterthought.

'I am well aware of Hardrada's plans and of the man who put the idea into his head,' Harold replied. 'My brother . . . our brother . . .' he looked across the council chamber at Leofwine and Gyrth, 'has been a traitor to us all. He's gone looking for help from any man he thinks might be this country's enemy. He has betrayed England and our father's memory and now he's so eaten up with bitterness and jealousy that he's put himself on a course that can only end in his death or mine. He cannot have his duchy back unless I am dead—'

'And I too, don't forget that,' Morcar observed.

'Aye, and every other noble or thegn who wanted an end to his time in Northumbria.' Harold shook his head sadly. 'It's madness, sheer madness. He simply would not accept that no one but him was responsible for his failure as an earl.'

'No point fretting about it now, though,' Gyrth Godwinson pointed out. 'Tostig is like Sweyn. He's got himself into trouble and now the rest of us will have to deal with it. The question is: how do we stop him and Harald, and William of Normandy?'

'There's going to be a river of blood spilled this summer,' said Leofwine.

'But we will ensure that it is their blood, not ours,' said Harold. 'I rule England, but we five control it: Godwinsons in the south, you sons of Aelfgar in the north. So that is how we shall deal with the two main attacks against us. I am going to call out the fyrd. If necessary, I will also draft more men beyond the standard levy. The danger we face will be so obvious, no one could possibly protest. Even if Hardrada and William both come against us with ten thousand men—'

'Ten thousand? That many?' Leofwine could not hide his alarm.

'My spies in Normandy say that the Bastard is calling for a thousand ships to carry ten thousand men, their horses and all their camp followers. I'm told Harald is planning on a mere three hundred vessels, but they will be bigger and carry far more men. So yes, we assume that they will each have ten thousand fighting men. But we can split the fyrd in two and still outnumber them on both fronts. And we are on our own soil, with all the kingdom to call upon. They will be far from home, with an ocean to cross for reinforcements. God forbid we lose a battle, but if we do, we can fight another. If they lose one, they are done for.'

Harold turned to Edwin and Morcar. 'Can I count on you? Will you stand firm against Harald, and Tostig if he fights beside him?'

The two brothers nodded. 'Ten thousand Norsemen, twenty thousand, it makes no difference to me,' said Morcar. 'We will master them.'

'Will you stand at my side in the south?' Harold asked Gyrth and Leofwine.

'You know we will,' Gyrth replied. 'As loyal subjects and loving brothers, you can count on us to the death.'

'Then we will win, I'm sure of it. The north can be defended from York. We will have a fleet based on the Isle of Wight patrolling the Channel. There will be men keeping watch along the shoreline from Portland Bill to Ramsgate. William will not set foot on English soil unseen or unmolested. I will remain here in London with the royal housecarls, ready to move north or south, wherever we are most needed.

'Now go back to your earldoms. Get every last man you can find and press him into your service. And may God be with you.'

The men made their farewells and went on their way, leaving Harold alone in the chamber, deep in thought. A short while later there was a tentative knock on the door.

'Come!' he called out.

His wife Ealdgyth entered the room and approached. She was not a bad-looking woman, he supposed. Her face was somewhat careworn and her body past its prime, but no more than was to be expected of a woman who had already been married once and borne her husband three children. But the contrast between his queen's homely appearance and the beauty of Edith Swan-Neck, who would always, in Harold's eyes, be the ravishing young girl who had captured his heart all those years ago, was too pronounced for him to ignore.

As she reached him, Ealdgyth curtseyed. 'I hope I am not disturbing Your Majesty,' she said.

'Of course not, no . . . my dear,' Harold replied. 'I was just in council with your brothers. I'm sorry that you missed them.'

'I thank Your Majesty for your concern, but I saw them as I was coming here and we were able to exchange farewells.'

'Good, good.' Harold wished that he and Ealdgyth could be more like a loving husband and wife. Theirs was a marriage of political convenience and neither of them knew how to make it anything else. I'm hardly any better than Edward, when all is said and done, he realised. He refused to bed poor Edith, but I've not done much better by this poor woman.

'I know that Your Majesty is very burdened by the troubles of the kingdom at the moment and has no need for the distractions of woman's talk, but I bring news that I hope may lift your spirits when they are oppressed.'

'You are quite right, my dear, I am in some need of good cheer.'

'Then it may please you to know that I am with child.'

Harold was taken completely by surprise. He sprang to his feet, a smile wreathing his face, and was about to wrap Ealdgyth in the sort of warm hug that he had always given his beloved Swan-Neck, but something stopped him dead in his tracks, as though there were an invisible but unbreachable wall between them. 'Well, ah . . . you are quite right, my dear, that really is excellent news. Let us pray God that He has blessed us with a son.'

'That is, of course, my most heartfelt prayer, Your Majesty, for I very much want to do my duty to you and the kingdom. And I hope . . .'

She looked at Harold, and her eyes were so forlorn, and so filled with the want of everything she did not possess, that it cut him to the heart. 'I know Your Majesty does not love me . . . not as a man loves the one who is truly dearest to him.'

He did not even pretend to deny it. For the sake of her self-respect, he would not insult her with a lie.

'But I hope that if I do give you a son, then you will at least be able to love him. And if you do, I will be content with that.'

'Oh Ealdgyth . . .' Now Harold did bridge the gap between them. He placed one arm around her waist and with his other hand gently wiped away a tear that had fallen down her cheek. 'If you present me with a son . . . with an heir to my crown . . . then I promise you this. I will love the child, and the woman who gave him to me. You have my word on that.'

22

The ducal palace, Rouen

William was sitting alone, composing his thoughts. He was about to conduct what promised to be a very delicate and potentially difficult private audience with Roger of Montgomery. They would then be joined by Fitz for a discussion that would be less politically sensitive, but even more mentally taxing. He had therefore given strict orders that he was not to be disturbed until he was ready. So he was not best pleased when his preparations were disturbed by the sound of an argument outside his door.

He heard a high-pitched, educated, priestly voice insisting, 'I demand to be let in!' followed by an indistinct sound in a lower register that was undoubtedly the voice of the soldier on sentry duty in the passage saying that he was under orders not to let anybody in.

'But I have news His Grace will want to hear, news from Rome!'

That was enough to get William out of his seat, across the floor and opening his door in an instant.

Lanfranc of Pavia was standing outside next to a soldier, who turned at the sight of his commander-in-chief. 'I'm sorry, Your Grace, but—'

'Doesn't matter,' William assured him. He looked at Lanfranc. 'Come in.'

When the door was closed behind them, William simply asked, 'So?'

Lanfranc was a monk and a scholar. He was not given to unbridled emotion of any kind. But on this particular occasion he could not restrain himself. A huge grin crossed his face.

'Good news?' William asked, trying hard to keep his own feelings in check.

'The very best, Your Grace,' Lanfranc replied. 'I have just had word from Rome. His Holiness the Pope has given his personal blessing and the unqualified backing of the Church itself to your expedition.'

'That's wonderful!'

'And that's not all. The Holy Father will be sending his banner, with the crossed keys of St Peter woven in gold upon it, and a ring containing a hair from St Peter's head. You will march into battle under the protection of the greatest of all saints, whom Our Saviour called his rock. He will be your rock too, Your Grace.'

William was dumbstruck. The politician in him saw at once how the Pope would now become his best recruiter, for any soldier who fought with Normandy against England could expect a reward in heaven to go with his gains on earth. But his profound Christian piety was even more deeply touched. The crossed keys of St Peter were no mere symbol to him any more than the hair was just a tiny fragment of a corpse. He felt that the man who had stood at Christ's right hand would be standing by him too.

There was a knock at the door, which then opened without waiting for a reply. Montgomery came in.

'Roger, my dear friend!' William exclaimed with an open affection so rare that Montgomery was taken completely un-awares and stopped dead in his tracks. 'Come in, come in! Do you know Prior Lanfranc of Bec Abbey? He has just arrived bringing the most splendid news. Go ahead, Prior, tell Lord Montgomery . . .'

Lanfranc explained about the Pope's decision, to which Montgomery reacted with the same mixture of delight and awe as his duke had done.

'Now, Prior Lanfranc, you must excuse us. Montgomery and I have business to conduct. But I absolutely insist that you stay to dinner. I will ask Duchess Matilda to get the cooks to lay on a special feast in your honour. And Lanfranc . . . ?'

'Yes, Your Grace?'

'You have done me a very great service. Be sure that I will not forget it.'

'Thank you, Your Grace,' Lanfranc said, with a modest bow of the head.

William waited till the door had closed behind the departing cleric then turned to Montgomery. 'This news may just have earned Lanfranc of Pavia the archbishopric of Canterbury . . . and the wily old fox knows it too.'

'He was wily enough not to make it too obvious.'

'Of course. He will play the role of the poor scholar right up to the second he has the archbishop's mitre on his head and the crozier in his hand.'

'Ha!' Montgomery laughed. 'Those churchmen like to act so pious and pure, but they're just as hungry for all the good things in life as any of us sinners.'

'True enough.' William waved towards a chair. 'Sit down. Can I get you anything . . . some wine, perhaps? A pastry?'

'No thank you, Your Grace,' said Montgomery. He took a deep breath as if gathering his strength. 'May I ask why you have summoned me?'

William sighed, frowned, and hesitated. 'I might as well tell you now . . . you're not coming with me to England.'

'But Your Grace!' Montgomery protested. 'How can that be? Have I done something wrong?'

'Not at all . . . quite the contrary, in fact. It's precisely because I trust you so much and have such great faith in you that I want you here in Normandy.'

'But—'

'Don't worry, you won't lose out. If you carry out the tasks I am about to set you as well as I expect, you will be rewarded as richly as any man who fights at my side.'

'But it's not a matter of reward. It's . . . it's . . .'

William had not bothered to pay much attention to Montgomery's appearance. Like most men, he took the way his friends looked for granted. But there was something in Montgomery's voice, a tone that was less disappointed than desperate, that made William pause now and examine him more closely. As he did, he realised that the gradual, almost imperceptible sickening that, now that he came to think about it, seemed to have gripped Montgomery for years had reached some kind of a crisis.

Montgomery's skin was sallow, his cheeks hollow and his eyes lifeless and exhausted. The day was not particularly warm, and no fire burned in the chamber, yet there was a light sheen of sweat on his forehead.

'Are you all right?' William asked. 'Here, have some wine . . .' He poured the drink himself and handed it to Montgomery, who gripped the goblet with whitened knuckles and sipped at it listlessly.

'You don't seem yourself,' William said, still trying to get an answer. 'Tell me what ails you. That's an order.'

Montgomery managed a wan, exhausted smile. 'You know I always obey those.'

'So . . . ?'

Montgomery finished his wine. He knew what he wanted to say. He had rehearsed the words so many times: the confession he longed to make, the one that would begin with the two words *It's Mabel.*

He had every word he wanted to say memorised, beating at his brain to be let out: *When I married her, I sold my soul to the Devil. She killed Prince Edward the Exile. She did for my brother Hugh as well, and Arnaud d'Echauffour, poor bastard. And I think she's been poisoning me too, little by little, all these years.*

She makes these potions. God knows what's in them, but when we fuck . . . I can't describe it . . . it's like going to the stars . . . and then afterwards she gives me one that brings the deepest sleep I've ever known. And once you've tasted these things, you have to have more of them. And when you don't have them, you're so sick and desperate . . . Mother of Christ, my head aches, my guts ache, I puke all the time, I can't sleep . . . But that passes, just as the way I feel now will pass. I'll feel better. I'll be my old self. Then I'll go back home and . . . I'm so ashamed, so weak . . . then I give in to her again, because I just can't resist. And she knows it.

All this he longed to say, and then to plead with the lord he had served so well for so long: *You've got to let me come with you! I've got to be kept away from her! She's going to poison me one of these days, I know she will. I'm a dead man if I don't stay away from Alençon.*

But he knew that this was not the time to show such weakness, not now, with the invasion on the horizon, when William needed his closest allies more than ever and when there was so much for them all to gain. So he simply groaned and said, 'Just my damned guts playing up again. I don't know what it is. Maybe it's the water in Alençon, or the food they cook down there. Don't worry, I'll be fine.'

'Huh,' William grunted. 'You'd better be. I need someone I can count on absolutely, without the slightest doubt or hesitation, to do vitally important things. The first is to organise the quartering, equipping and supplying of all our troops and ships as we prepare for the invasion. You're the perfect man for that, Montgomery, because you've got the best mind of any of us. You think of details, you see ahead, you plan for every possibility. I don't know anyone better than you at that . . . when you're well.'

'Will I be based on the coast?'

'Yes, with the invasion force and the fleet.' William leaned forward and squeezed Montgomery's shoulder affectionately. 'A long way from Alençon and all that bad water.'

This time Montgomery's smile was more like the man William knew. 'And the second thing?' he asked.

'I need a man to look after Her Grace the duchess and my son while I am gone. Robert is my heir. When I am away, he will be the acting duke.'

'He's very . . .' Montgomery searched for the right word, 'inexperienced, Your Grace.'

'Indeed he is, and also very young, very hot-tempered, very capricious and very reckless. That is why the Duchess Matilda will be his regent. She will take effective control.'

'That's very wise.' Montgomery had known Matilda for fifteen years. He knew as well as anyone what a tough, intelligent mind was contained within that tiny frame.

'I have no doubt that the duchess will cope admirably with the demands of running the duchy,' continued William. 'I will be leaving your namesake Roger de Beaumont as an adviser. He's been around forever; nothing will surprise him.'

'Good choice.'

'And you will be there to add your wise counsel, which I know Her Grace will value as highly as I do; but also, more importantly, to take command if anyone should decide to take advantage of my absence and attack Normandy.'

'Is there anyone who could do that?' Montgomery asked. 'Surely none of our neighbours would dare make a move against us.'

'In theory, no, they wouldn't. And I'm going to do everything

I can to neutralise every county and duchy from Flanders down to Aquitaine by signing up their best fighting men for my army. But you never know . . . The point is, any potential enemy will be much more cautious if he knows that you're here, with plenty of good men at your disposal, to meet him head on and send him packing. Your job will be to deter invaders as much as it is to defeat them. Will you be up to it?'

Montgomery drew himself up straight. 'Yes, I will. Thank you. I'm deeply honoured and grateful for your trust.'

'Good man. Fitzosbern should be with us soon . . . Ah, here he is. Excellent. So, my lords, let's begin . . .'

23

The first words out of Duke William's mouth were enough to make his loyal lieutenants gasp. 'I intend to take a fighting force of between eight and ten thousand men across the water to England. And at least three thousand of them will be mounted. That is, as you will both immediately realise, a bigger force than this duchy has put into the field in living memory. And I very much doubt any of my predecessors commanded its like in days gone by.

'I will come to the issue of getting this number of troops to England in a moment, but first let's deal with what we're going to do with them all before they even set foot aboard a ship. My plan is to assemble the army at the mouth of the Dives, on the shoreline close to the fishing village of Cabourg.'

Montgomery's ears pricked up. 'The Dives? That's on my family's land,' he said.

'Strictly speaking it's all my land,' said the duke, 'but yes, the Montgomerys have held it from my father and from me. That's one of the reasons I wanted you here today. You see, I don't intend to supply the army in the usual way, just stealing everything it needs from the surrounding country. That's all very well in enemy territory, but I'm not going to ravage my own duchy . . . or your estates, Montgomery. That means we will have to make sure that everything the army needs is purchased and brought to it from elsewhere.'

'I'm sure my people could be persuaded to sell you their produce,' Montgomery said, with a wry smile.

'And I'm sure that would keep about one in a hundred of my men well fed. But we need to think about the other ninety-nine. And consider this, my lords: for every ten fighting men there will be at least six non-combatants who will also have to be taken care of.'

'That many, really?' Fitz asked.

'Absolutely. The men need cooks, armourers, fletchers, carpenters, blacksmiths, servants, laundry women, labourers, priests, monks . . . As for the horses, they must be fed and groomed and shod. And we need carters to bring all the feed and bedding and shoes and nails for those horses, quite apart from the meat, bread and wine for the men.'

'My God, where do we even start?' gasped Fitz.

'With some basic calculations,' Montgomery replied. 'Let's just think about the horses, for example. If we have three thousand mounted knights, then we need six thousand horses, because every man will need a spare mount. Plus hundreds more held in reserve, here in Normandy, ready to be shipped to England to replace those lost in battle. Let's call it seven thousand horses in all.

'Now, every horse needs four shoes every time it is re-shod, and every shoe needs four nails . . . Don't ask me to tell you how many nails and shoes that is for all the horses we're going to need, but a monk with a counting board could tell us soon enough.

'Then we do a similar calculation for the hay and grain the horses will eat – we can put them out to pasture for some of the time we're on this side of the Channel, which should help – and the straw they'll need for bedding. The amounts will seem huge, but at least we'll know what they are. And the same will apply to the men. We just work out how much bread and meat a man needs to eat in a day, how much wine and ale he needs to drink, and then calculate the number of men and the number of days.'

'So far as possible, we need men to provide for themselves,' William said. 'Every lord will have to be responsible for his men's weapons, tents and mounts . . . and for the horseshoes and nails, come to that. We'll still have to have everything they need, just in case, but the more help we can get, the better.'

'It's a lot to ask of men who are already responsible for providing ships,' Fitz pointed out. 'Like us, for example.'

'They don't have to be great ships,' said William. 'We'll need some true warships to guard the rest of the fleet, but the rest can be very simple. We're not going on a great voyage here. We just need to get our army one-way across a short stretch of water. Just build me wooden tubs that will take twenty or thirty men, or ten horses. If they have a hull, a mast, a sail and a steering oar, that will do the job.'

'Unless we run into a storm, or Harold's navy,' said Fitz.

'Well, we'd better make sure we don't then, hadn't we?' William snapped. 'What's got into you, Fitzosbern? You're fussing and fretting like an old woman.'

'I'm sorry, Your Grace.'

'Very well then, put your mind to better use. Think about every single thing we could possibly need when we get to England. We'll live off the land, of course. I don't care how much we plunder and scavenge over there. And think about castles; we're going to need at least six of them.'

'I don't quite understand . . .'

'The English don't appear to have castles. So we will have to build our own. It's like the boats – we won't need full-scale copies of Domfront or Falaise. But I have to be able to put up basic wooden forts, with a palisade, a gateway and a keep, to establish our presence when we land, like the Romans did. We won't have time to build them from scratch, but if we had sections of wall or tower that we could assemble quickly and simply, that would be a great help.'

437

'Sections small enough to fit in a ship?'

'Exactly . . . and Montgomery, you must think about the problem of human shit.'

'The shit humans produce, or humans who are shitty?' Montgomery enquired, getting a gruff laugh out of William.

'The shit that comes out of their arses. We're going to have the best part of fifteen thousand men, maybe more, in camp for several weeks before we make our move. I don't know why it is, but whenever there's crap lying about the place, people seem to get sick. Maybe it's the smell of it, or the flies and rats it attracts, I don't know. But I don't want sickness in camp. If we're right beside a river, just as it joins the sea, let's use that to take our mess away: build latrines over the water or something.'

'Like a bridge with a bench along one side with holes in it . . .'

'That's the sort of thing.' William paused and looked at the two men. 'Listen, this is a huge undertaking. But it won't all be a matter of cost. Think of the shipbuilders and boat merchants who'll get rich supplying our fleet, the farmers whose crops will be sold to feed the army and horses, the blacksmiths and farriers who will be kept in work through the whole spring and summer, the butchers who'll provide the meat for the army and the skinners making the leather for tents and boots and men's belts and horses' tack.' He stopped and laughed to himself. 'My uncles kept the family tannery business. At last it pays to be a tanner's boy!'

24

The port of Barfleur, Normandy

The shipyard was virtually deserted, for the workers had not yet arrived. But two people had risen early to examine the vessel that was being built there. Just the keel, the stems and the frame had been completed, so that the hull looked like the bones of a giant ribcage, yet the scale of the construction was already apparent, for it measured almost forty paces from stem to stern and its imposing, intimidating scale was exaggerated even further by the long black shadows cast by the early-morning sun.

'You won't see a finer ship than this anywhere, Your Grace,' said Haimo the master carpenter, whose yard this was. 'You could go to Denmark, Sweden, Norway, speak to every boatwright in all the northlands, there's none of them building anything better than this. Now, you see those timbers across the hull, that's where the rowing benches will go, all thirty of them. When they're fully manned she'll race across the water faster than a man can run. Even with her sail up she'll make good speed. But there's still room for ten fully armed knights and their horses, as well as the crew. And she's solid, too, nothing but the finest oak, and I picked every piece of it myself.'

Haimo paused and looked up at his creation, basking in his achievement. 'So, Your Grace, what do you think?'

Beneath the shelter of her hooded cloak, raised to keep her identity hidden, the Duchess Matilda smiled contentedly. 'It is magnificent, Haimo, well done. This was just what I wanted. How is the sail coming along?'

439

'Oh, the women are working hard at that, ma'am, don't you worry. They're spinning and dyeing and weaving like you wouldn't believe. With the size of it, and that bright red colour you asked for, men'll be able to see this ship coming for leagues in every direction.'

'That's the whole point of it. I want the world to know whose boat this is.'

'Oh, it will, Your Grace, don't you worry about that. Now, just one thing . . . Are you sure you want a figurehead of a child on the front? Only, with a ship like this . . . I mean, the flagship of a great war fleet . . . well, you'd normally have something a bit more . . . I don't know . . .'

'Menacing?'

'Exactly, Your Grace, that's the word . . . menacing. I mean, you want to scare the enemy, that's the idea.'

'No, I'm quite sure, thank you. His Grace will understand why I've chosen the child. It is being carved at the moment. Once it has been gilded and decorated, it will be sent to you. And speaking of His Grace, he is not to find out about this ship until I give it to him. Do you understand?'

'Absolutely, Your Grace. I've not told a living soul, not even my foremen. Of course, people are trying to guess who it's for and the lasses in the sail loft have been gossiping about it for weeks. I'll be honest, some of them have guessed, but I just tell them they're talking nonsense and order them to pipe down and go back to work.'

'Quite right. Now, there is one thing upon which I insist. The ship must be ready – completely finished in every respect – by a particular date. And on that date, at midday, it must be precisely where I want it to be.'

'What day and place did you have in mind, Your Grace?'

'I cannot tell you, not yet. But I will say this: if you have not finished your work by the middle of June, the fifteenth at the very latest, then I will make you regret your tardiness.'

'Yes, Your Grace,' said Haimo. He was a big man and the top of the duchess's hood did not even reach his shoulder. But when this tiny woman gave an order, he knew he had better obey it. He told himself that it was because she was the Duchess of Normandy and he just a humble tradesman. But he had a feeling that it really would not have mattered what station Matilda of Flanders had been born into: big strong men like him would still have been doing exactly what she told them.

25

Bosham and the south coast of England

Harold rode out of London with his two brothers and their retinue to make a tour along the south coast, scouting for the best places for their lookouts. He spent one night in his house at Bosham. Edith Swan-Neck was waiting for him there. Harold looked at her now and saw that she had aged, just as they all had. There were lines on a face he remembered so well in all its untouched loveliness, and many silver threads in her once-golden hair. But somehow he forgave those flaws that seemed so glaring in Ealdgyth and cared only about the beauty that was still there: the clear blue of her eyes and the love he saw in them, the sweet touch of her lips upon his, the way her body seemed to mould itself to his so that the moment they embraced it was as if they had never for a single moment been apart.

They made love together and it was a gentle rapture, a welcome homecoming more than a thrilling new departure. Afterwards, Edith asked, 'How is Her Majesty? I hope she is keeping well.'

'She is with child,' Harold replied.

'Oh . . .' Edith seemed to shrink away from him a fraction, retreating into herself as she digested this news. 'I imagine you are hoping for a son,' she said.

'Yes, that would be good . . . for the kingdom.'

'Of course, yes. A son born in wedlock would be the proper heir to the throne.'

'Yes, but you know that I will not love our sons any the less.

442

They will still inherit estates and have titles of their own and—'

'I don't care about that. I care that another woman will be having a son that should have been mine.'

'Oh my darling, you know that I wish we could have been king and queen. And I wish it was you that was carrying my heir. But a king has to marry for the good of the kingdom, whatever his heart might desire.'

Edith gave a sad, bitter laugh. 'Poor Harold. You finally get what you and your father always wanted, only to lose what you already had . . .'

Harold felt a terrible sense of dawning loss. Something very bad was happening here, in his bed, an ending that he had never for a second anticipated. But his melancholy thoughts were interrupted by the sound of scurrying feet outside, followed by the slamming of the bedchamber door as it was flung open and then the excited squeals of their two young daughters, Gunhild and Gytha, as they raced in and flung themselves on the bed.

'Mummy, Daddy, come quick!' Gytha exclaimed. 'There's a beautiful new star in the sky with a long silver tail behind it.'

'It's not a star, silly, it's a comet,' Gunhild corrected her, in true older-sister style. 'But it does look beautiful. You must come and look.'

'I'm the King of England. No one tells me what I must or must not do, particularly not cheeky little girls,' said Harold.

'Sorry, Your Majesty,' said Gunhild, swiftly followed by Gytha.

'Very well, then, I accept your apology.'

'You really should see the comet, though, Daddy,' Gunhild persisted.

Harold and Edith wrapped themselves in their cloaks and walked barefoot out of the house and down towards the shore. There they stopped and gazed up at the night sky, just as men and women all over Christendom were doing that night, marvelling at the heavenly apparition.

'I've heard that comets are supposed to be omens,' Gunhild said. 'They're a sign that something terrible is going to happen.'

'Or something very, very good. After all, there was a comet in the sky when Our Lord was born in Bethlehem. That's what the Wise Men followed when they made their way to the manger. And there was never any news better than the birth of Jesus.'

'Yes, but Jesus was crucified. That's not good,' piped up Gytha.

'Oh stop it, just stop it!' snapped Edith. And before anyone could reply, she had turned and run back up to the house.

'What's the matter with Mummy?' Gunhild asked.

'I made her upset. I didn't mean it!' wailed Gytha, starting to cry.

'No, you didn't,' said Harold. 'Just go back to bed, both of you. It will all be fine in the morning.'

He watched them race away up the path, then stood listening to the creak of boats against their moorings and the lapping of water against the shore. He glanced up once more at the comet, then turned and followed his children.

When he reached his chamber, Edith was sitting up in the bed with her arms around her knees, pulling them tight to her chest. He went to hold her, but she was like a hedgehog, curled up against its enemy, and there was no way he could get to her.

'Gunhild was right. That comet is a sign. This is the end.'

'What do you mean? The end of what?'

'Of you,' she said, 'and me; of us, of our family, of England . . . It's the end of everything. I know it is.'

Of all the men threatening England, Tostig was the first to set foot on its soil. He sailed from Bruges with a fleet of sixty ships, most of them Flemish, with a few Danish and a dozen of his own and Copsige's personal vessels, crewed by their liegemen. The fleet headed west towards the Isle of Wight, long a stronghold of the House of Godwin, where he had estates of his own. He arrived while Harold's fleet was at sea, patrolling the south coast, leaving the island undefended. He ordered the tenants who worked his own lands to supply him with provisions and men for his force. Burghers and landowners who did not owe him anything were also forced to hand over money and goods. Tostig's offer was very simple: 'Give me what I want or my men will take it from you. And they'll burn down your houses and barns while they're at it.'

He slipped away before the English fleet could intercept him, sailing back along the Sussex and Kent coasts, all the way past Dover and round to the port of Sandwich. There he stayed a while, recruiting as many local butecarls – boat soldiers trained in the art of maritime warfare – as could be persuaded to fight under his colours.

Harold heard that his brother had come ashore and marched with his royal guard to do battle with him. But when the king arrived in Sandwich, all he saw of Tostig was the sails of his ships disappearing out to sea.

26

The ducal palace, Rouen, and the east coast of England

The Duchess Matilda consulted the list on the parchment she was holding. 'Splinters from Christ's manger . . .'

A woman in a nun's habit looked around a selection of magnificent gold, silver and carved wooden reliquaries arranged on the table before her, finally found the one she wanted and pushed it to one side. 'Yes, Your Grace.'

'Splinters from the Cross . . .'

The process was repeated, as was the response: 'Yes, Your Grace.'

'A morsel of bread touched by the hand of Our Saviour, and a strand of the Virgin's hair . . .'

And so the list went on, as various saintly body parts were duly ticked off: a hair from the head of St Denis, a finger belonging to St Cecilia, and a number of entire saintly corpses, housed in much bigger containers lined up to one side of the chamber in the ducal palace where the duchess was conducting her business with a seriousness befitting the importance of the occasion.

There were three great passions in Duchess Matilda's life. The first was her husband, the second her children, and the third her new abbey. When she and William had finally been granted papal approval for their marriage, they had decided to give thanks to God for their good fortune by building two monastic houses on either side of the massive castle that William was constructing at Caen: one for monks and the other for nuns. The duke had been responsible for St Stephen's Abbey, or the 'men's abbey' as it was usually known, while the duchess devoted her full attention to the women's Abbey of the Holy Trinity.

The consecration of Matilda's abbey was taking place in June, a suitably auspicious time, given the importance of retaining divine support for the invasion of England that would follow soon afterwards. To make sure that her abbey had a fine reputation from the very start of its life, Matilda had donated a remarkable collection of relics that was sure to attract the attention of churchmen and pilgrims from all across Europe. These were worth more than any gold or jewels and so their transport from Rouen to Caen was a matter to be handled with the greatest possible care.

Matilda did not rest until the carriage carrying the relics was on its way out of the palace, escorted by a company of ducal guardsmen. Then, having dealt with one of her passions, she turned her mind to the other two. 'Would you please find Count Robert and tell him his mother wishes to speak with him? I will be in my solar,' she informed a lady-in-waiting, who at once scurried away on her errand.

Some while later, Matilda looked up from the volume of Latin verse that she was reading to see her oldest child striding into the room. She sighed inwardly. Robert was a young man of fourteen, with his whole life ahead of him. His father had already made a public declaration that he would be his heir, so by the end of the year, if all went well, he would be next in line for the throne of England. Most young men would be thrilled by that prospect. Indeed, Robert could have been forgiven for being a bit cocky, a little too pleased with himself at the prospect of all he might become. Instead, he seemed to walk around with a hard-done-by air of wounded pride and even resentment. He was forever complaining about the lack of respect he was shown by his father and brothers. It was true that Richard and William were forever teasing him, but he was their big brother. He should have been able to slap them down himself.

It didn't help that he was much shorter than his father and rapidly being overtaken by his brothers. His nickname of Short-Pants, so casually, thoughtlessly bestowed by his father, had stuck with him ever since. He was a good-looking boy, and far from puny, and he had inherited his father's talent for swordfighting. Nor was there anything wrong with his courage, from what William related of his exploits out hunting. But somehow none of that seemed to count in Robert's favour, in the world's eyes or his own.

'Sit down, my darling, we need to talk,' Matilda said, patting the embroidered cushion on the wooden settle next to her.

'Must we?' Robert fumed.

'Yes, we must. You have a very important day coming up and I want it to go well. I certainly don't want to see the two men I love most in the world arguing with one another again.'

'Can you blame me? I'm fourteen, Mother. I've been Count of Maine for four years. I'm perfectly old enough to look after Normandy while Father is away in England. Indeed, I'm old enough to go with him, if he ever asked me to come.'

This time Matilda did not bother to suppress her sigh. She knew there was no point getting cross with Robert, even if he could try the patience of a saint sometimes. It was best to begin, at least, by being sympathetic.

'I understand, my darling, really I do. But I honestly think he's trying to do the right thing for you.'

She waited a second for a rebuttal, but none came. Encouraged, she pressed on. 'With him in England, this is a great chance for you to gain some experience helping to run the duchy.'

'So why can't I run it by myself?'

'Well, no one does that.'

'You know what I mean. I've been trained to rule Normandy since I was tiny. Why do I have to let a whole crowd of other people do it for me?'

'Hardly a crowd, Robert. I will be your regent, because I'm your mother and I've attended council meetings and signed your father's ducal decrees since before you were even born. Then there's your cousin, dear old Roger de Beaumont. He'll be your adviser, because he's always been utterly loyal to your father and has more experience than you and me put together. And Roger Montgomery will also advise us, because he's got as sharp a mind as any man in Normandy, he's a good soldier if there should ever be a need for it and your father trusts him absolutely.'

'Montgomery's wife is really odd.'

Matilda knew that for form's sake she should tell her son he was talking nonsense, insulting a woman as grand as Mabel of Bellême, but she could not resist asking, 'Why do you say that?'

'Just something about her. She's very beautiful, you know, for an old woman—'

'Old? She's about the same age as me!'

'You know what I mean . . . Anyway, she looks really nice until you get close to her and she looks at you. Her eyes are just . . . I don't know . . .'

'Cold? Unfeeling?' Matilda saw a chance to be on the same side as her son. She leaned over and spoke in a conspiratorial murmur. 'I'll tell you a secret. I agree with you. I think she's a very strange woman; quite frightening, actually.'

'People say she poisoned Hugh Montgomery.'

'Oh come now, I'm sure that's not true,' Matilda said, thinking just the opposite, because she had heard the stories too. Everyone had.

'Now, let's forget all about the lady of Bellême and think

about the way you and I and the others will run Normandy. It's really not so different from the guardians your father had when he was young.'

'What, are you all going to be murdered, then?' asked Robert, and this time there was the hint of a grin on his face.

'No! But I'm sure your father is remembering his early days, and trying to do for you what his father did for him. We aren't there to boss you around. You are the heir to the dukedom, so you will be in charge. We're just there to make sure that everything goes well while Papa is away and that he comes back to find Normandy just as he left it. And if he does, I promise you, he will be so pleased and proud of you.'

'Then why won't he say that to me?'

'Because, my darling boy, he knows how hard it is to be duke and how tough a man has to be, and so he's hard on you because he wants you to be that tough.'

'I suppose so . . . But you tell me you love me, Mama, why can't he?'

'I'm your mother; of course I tell you I love you. But listen, you've heard me say that if one of my children died, I would give all the blood in my body if it would make them rise again.'

Robert nodded.

'Your father would do the same. I just know he would.'

Robert chewed his lip and looked at the floor.

Matilda rubbed his bent back.

'A few days from now, Papa will summon all the noblemen who aren't going with him to England to a meeting at Bonneville castle. They will swear an oath of loyalty to you as the heir to the dukedom, and to me as your regent. You must make sure that you act like a man who is worthy of their devotion. Do you understand me, Robert?'

'Yes, Mama.'

'Promise not to let me or Papa down?'

'Of course not! You can trust me all right. I'll act like the next Duke of Normandy, I promise.'

'Good boy . . . thank you.'

'But the fact is, if it comes to a choice between me and you, Papa trusts you more.'

'Shh . . .' Matilda reached up to give her son a hug. 'He trusts you, he really does . . .'

But you're right, my boy, he trusts me more. And the terrible thing is, I agree with him.

The Flemish and Danish mercenaries who made up the bulk of Tostig's men were getting restless. They wanted to get some blood on their blades, burn buildings, steal treasure, fuck women. In short, they needed some action. Tostig duly gave it to them. He sailed the fleet up to the Isle of Thanet, on the very easternmost tip of Kent, where the farmland was rich, the population large and the pickings plentiful for any man bent on theft and ravaging.

From there he sailed north across the Thames estuary and past Essex, Suffolk and Norfolk. From time to time they would stop, like travellers looking for an interesting or attractive spot at which to take a break in their journey. Except that these men were more like locusts, dressed in chain mail and armed with swords, axes and clubs, stripping any place on which they landed of all its valuables, as a swarm devastated a cornfield, leaving smouldering ruins and dead, wounded and raped human beings in their wake.

Tostig had no great plan, other than the inchoate desire to get his own back for the wrongs he had suffered and destroy the property of the men he held responsible for his plight. If that meant wrecking his own family's holdings, he did not care. In fact, his rage demanded that those who had been closest to him should now be the ones who suffered the most.

'We had too many sons,' sighed Gytha when she heard of Tostig's acts of spite. 'There wasn't enough of England to satisfy them all.'

Gytha had gone to Bosham to see Edith Swan-Neck. The two women had known one another for twenty years or more, and the fact that Harold had married Ealdgyth for political reasons made no difference to Gytha's affection for Edith, who was the mother of five of her grandchildren and would always be Harold's true partner in her eyes.

'Did they need to be satisfied?' Edith asked. 'Please forgive me for saying this, but the longer I live, the more I wonder whether Godwin's legacy to them wasn't more of a burden than a blessing. His sons have everything men desire. They have more power, more land, more wealth than anyone else in all England. But what good does it do them – or us? I would be so much happier if Harold were just an ordinary thegn, with a single estate, and we could live there together with our children.' She gave a rueful smile, 'Let some other woman's husband worry about ruling the kingdom.'

Gytha said nothing and Edith tensed, for Harold's mother had always been just as fierce and strong-willed as any of her menfolk, all of whom had gone in fear of her anger or disapproval. But that had been when her hair was golden rather than silver, and age had yet to line her face and stoop her shoulders.

Finally she nodded sadly. 'I used to urge Godwin on. For years, he barely put one foot in front of the other without asking my advice first. We wanted all the things you talked about. We dreamed of the House of Wessex being the mightiest in the land. We hoped that one of our boys would one day be king of England. And now it has happened, and it brings me no pleasure at all. Godwin has gone. My poor, foolish, wrong-headed Sweyn is dead. Tostig is in exile. And Harold . . .' Gytha's voice died away.

'I fear for him so much,' Edith said. 'The night the comet appeared in the sky, I felt such dread, such a premonition of loss. I can't help it. I think we're all doomed.'

Gytha did not even try to argue. She just held out her arms. Edith walked to her and the two women hugged one another, seeking strength and reassurance. Then Gytha leaned back a little, looked at Edith and wiped a tear from her eye.

'We must try to be strong,' she said. 'For our children's sakes. What else can we do?'

Tostig and his ships had reached the Isle of Lindsey, in northern Lincolnshire, close to the mouth of the Humber. This was part of the earldom of Northumbria, the very land that Tostig claimed to hold dear. But once again he let his men loose to steal grain from barns, gold crucifixes from church altars and women from wherever they could find them.

This time, however, he made a miscalculation, staying too long in one place. Edwin and Morcar came down from the north with the levies they had raised, and struck with over-powering force. Tostig and his band were routed. They fled back to their vessels, and when they took to sea, Tostig discovered that the men from Denmark and Flanders had had enough. They set their courses for home, leaving behind just his and Copsige's personal ships and men. He was down to a mere dozen vessels. If he was going to have anything at all left by the time Hardrada came down from Norway, he had to find somewhere safe and out of the way to lay up for the rest of the summer.

'Scotland,' he told Copsige. 'Order your captains to set a course for Scotland. King Malcolm's always telling me what a great friend he is to me. Time he damn well proved it.'

27

The Dives estuary, summer 1066

Two days had passed since the consecration of the women's abbey, but instead of going back to Rouen, Matilda had insisted on accompanying William to his army's encampment. When they got there, she even stayed the night in his tent, and seemed particularly amorous, making love with greater than usual passion.

'What's got into you?' William asked as he recovered after their third bout of lovemaking, feeling very well satisfied, exhausted, but a little puzzled.

'I don't know,' she replied. 'It's exciting being in the camp, I suppose, seeing this huge army gathered here just for you. And it's cosy snuggling up in this tiny camp bed. And I love you very much.'

'I love you too, my darling,' said William, meaning it with all his heart. But as he lay there on his back, with Matilda's sleeping head nestled between his shoulder and his chest, he smiled in the darkness and murmured, 'You're up to something, my clever little wife, I know you are . . .'

The next morning, Matilda toured the camp, speaking to the soldiers, taking a keen interest in the work of the countless men and women required to keep the troops and their animals fed, watered and properly equipped. She was awed by the sheer scale of the enterprise that was being assembled. There were huge numbers of men from every corner of France, all with their different dialects, their myriad colours and emblems.

At one point she saw a banner bearing the three red

circles on a bright yellow background. 'Those are Eustace of Boulogne's colours,' she said sharply. 'What's he doing here?'

William laughed. 'Getting ready to invade England, like everyone else.'

'Yes, but why?'

'Mostly because he thinks he'll do well out of it. But also he likes the idea of dragging Harold through the dirt. Eustace has never forgiven old man Godwin for refusing to back him in some quarrel he got into with a bunch of Englishmen . . . I think it was in Dover. I'm sure he'd be only too happy to tell you the details.'

'I'm not going to start having nice little chats with Eustace of Boulogne! He's been at daggers drawn with my brother Baldwin for years. You should know that.'

'Of course I know that.'

'So why are you siding with him?'

William sighed. 'I'm not siding with anyone. I'm looking for men to help me conquer England. The moment they are disloyal to me, or argue with me, or set themselves up against me, I'll make them regret it. But until then, what arguments they have with people outside of this campaign are none of my concern. Is that a satisfactory answer, my lady?'

'Yes, my lord,' Matilda said. Then she wrapped both her arms around one of William's. 'I'm sorry. I really don't want us to argue. Not today of all days.'

Her husband was about to ask what was so special about today, but stopped himself, reckoning that if peace had been made, there was no point doing or saying anything to jeopardise it. Instead he said, 'Come on, let me show you how we supply this place. It's something to behold.'

The roads and tracks for leagues around the camp were jammed with an endless stream of carts and wagons, pulled by packhorses, donkeys, mules and oxen, each of which had to be directed to the precise spot where its cargo was to be unloaded. Matilda was struck, too, by the health of the men and the cleanliness of the camp. William had advised her not to go too near the river. 'There's a reason it's running brown,' was his less than delicate way of phrasing it. But the main encampment, though it covered an area as large as either Bruges or Rouen, and contained more people than either, was actually less filthy and malodorous than any normal town.

Matilda and William spent all morning inspecting the preparations for the invasion. Then, just as the sun was approaching its zenith, she pointed to a high dune that rose over the site. 'Let's go up to the top of that dune, just the two of us, and look at the view.'

William smiled indulgently and shrugged his shoulders. 'Why not?'

They wandered over to the dune and went hand in hand up the sandy slope like a couple of young lovebirds. When they reached the top, Matilda said, 'It's such a lovely day. Let's just sit down over there and look at the sea.'

The sun was shining and the sea was all a-glitter with its light. The air was balmy, with just a gentle breeze to prevent it feeling too hot. It was in every respect perfect, but William could never bear to be inactive for long, and was soon itching to go.

'Just a little longer,' Matilda said. But soon she could feel his impatience rising again, even when she tried to distract him by kissing him. He had actually got to his feet and was about to turn away down the dune when she called out, 'Wait! Just a second, my lord, I pray you . . . Look out to sea.'

'What am I supposed to be looking at?' William asked irritably.

'Over there, coming round that headland, there's a ship . . . do you see it?'

'There are several hundred ships.'

'No, the one further out to sea . . . the big red sail.'

William frowned, screwed up his eyes and looked where she was pointing. He nodded. 'Huh, nice ship.'

'Watch her a little longer, my darling. Look . . . she's larger than any other ship in your fleet.'

He looked again, darted his eyes back and forth a few times between the one ship on its own and the densely packed vessels crowding the bay closer to shore.

'So she is . . . Who owns that damn ship? By God, I'll teach him a lesson. Coming up to my fleet like that as if he's mightier than me . . . Why are you laughing?'

'Because I know who owns it.'

'Who?'

'You, my lord. You own that ship. She is called the *Mora*, and she is my present to you. I ordered the builder to give me the biggest ship on the seas, because my man deserved nothing less.'

'My God!' gasped William. 'That's why you were in such a good mood last night, isn't it?'

Matilda gave him a huge smile. William reached down, lifted her up off her feet and hugged her close to him. 'You are the finest wife that any man ever had. I don't care if I become king of England, or king of the whole world, I will never do anything half as great as marrying you.'

He kissed her with a passion so overpoweringly intense that Matilda all but swooned in his arms like a foolish maiden rather than a grown woman. Then he put her down and asked, 'Is she coming in to shore?'

'Of course. I want you to go aboard your new possession at once.'

'Then what are we waiting for?'

They descended the dune as fast as they could, jumping and

sliding and laughing. When they reached the bottom, William said, 'I think we should conduct ourselves like a duke and duchess now, don't you?'

'Of course, my lord.'

They walked on a little in silence before he said, 'Why did you call her *Mora*? The only thing I can think of is that *mora* is the Latin word for "delay", which doesn't sound like much of a name for a ship.'

'Well remembered,' she said.

'I wasn't a total dunce in class, you know, though I didn't enjoy memorising endless bits of Latin any more than Robert does.'

You should tell Robert that, Matilda thought, but she didn't want to spoil the mood by saying so.

'Well, it is Latin,' she replied. 'But it's an anagram.'

'Oh Lord, I'm no good at word games.'

'Well, it's a very easy one: M-O-R-A. Just put those letters in a different order.'

William stopped, concentrated hard and then grinned. 'A-M-O-R . . . *amor* . . . the Latin for "love".'

'Exactly, and that's our little secret. There's another mystery too, which only you and I will know.'

'What's that?'

'The figurehead . . . It's a golden child, a boy, looking out across the water with an ivory horn in his mouth.'

'A child? Shouldn't it be a dragon or a lion?'

'That's what the boatbuilder said. But it's a child because of the story you told me about your mother and her dream.'

'The one she had the night I was conceived?'

'That's right, the dream that prophesied you becoming a king across the water and starting a great dynasty. That child is you, the baby in your mother's womb, leading your manly, grown-up self across the sea . . .'

'To become a king,' William whispered.

'Yes, my darling lord . . . to that.'

Book Four:

Three Battles, Three Kings

Midsummer–mid-October 1066

1

From Normandy to Norway, and on to York

Week by week, month by month the summer went by. On the coast of Normandy, Duke William had now assembled a fleet to match the thousand ships with which the Greeks set off for Troy. His men had all the weapons, tents, horses and sections of castle towers and walls they could possibly require. They had been trained and exercised until they were sick of the endless practice and longed to be fighting for real.

All they needed was a south wind to blow them over the sea to England.

Across the water, the English fleet maintained its patrols up and down the south coast, while the bulk of King Harold's army waited, and waited, and waited for their adversaries to arrive. The lookouts posted atop every chalk-white cliff, every high, grassy hill along the shores of Hampshire, Sussex and Kent kept their eyes fixed to the southern horizon, searching in vain for an enemy that never seemed to appear.

Far away to the north, however, another man was on the move.

Harald Hardrada had completed his preparations by visiting the tomb of his half-brother King Olaf of Norway, whom people were already beginning to venerate as a saint. He looked upon Olaf's miraculously uncorrupted body, and then, following a Norse custom that had survived from the days of the old gods to those of the single God Almighty, he snipped some hair from the dead king's beard and cut clippings from his fingernails.

These he would keep when he went off to war, as both saintly relics and tokens of good fortune. That task done, he threw the key to the tomb into a river so that no other, lesser man could remove any part of Olaf's remains.

Harald was almost ready to sail. He had one last problem to sort out: his two wives. He summoned Elisaveta and Tora to see him. The two women greeted one another with great shows of affection. They embraced, they kissed, they each said how lovely the other looked, and yet the honeyed words were laced with venom and there were daggers in the eyes that gazed with such apparent fondness.

Both as a king and a man, Harald saw no need to consult his women when he made his plans for their futures. He simply told them, 'The time is fast approaching when I go away to war. The winds have been steady from the south, but as soon as they turn northwards, I will put to sea. I have more than three hundred fighting ships under my command, the biggest and fastest these waters have ever seen. I have twelve thousand men, as strong and brave as any that have ever left the lands of the Norse, with thousands more coming from the Orkneys, Iceland and Eire. I am confident of victory. I have no doubt of it at all.

'But what is to become of you, my two queens, while I am away?'

He intended the question to be rhetorical. He was going to supply the answer. But before he could, Elisaveta said coolly, 'Only one queen, Your Majesty, and only one true wife.'

'And only one true mother,' Tora retorted. 'Isn't that so, Your Majesty?'

Harald was well used to his womenfolk's arguments. He let their barbs bounce off his massive frame and smiled broadly. 'How well you both define our situation. Each of you has a special claim to higher standing. Neither will acknowledge the other's position. Clearly I would be a fool to leave you both in the same place while I am away fighting for my future, and yours, and those of all our children. Who knows what chaos would greet me upon my return?

'I have therefore decided upon the following course of action. You, Elisaveta, will follow me, bringing our daughters with you. You will leave the fleet when we reach the Orkneys and will reside in Kirkwall at the home of Pal Thorfinsson, Earl of Orkney. He will be coming with me to England. I dare say his wife will be glad of your company while her man is gone.

'When I defeat Harold Godwinson and take the throne of England, I will send for you, and you will be my queen in England.'

'Thank you, Your Majesty,' said Elisaveta, bowing her head modestly as she spoke. 'I am humbled and deeply touched by the honour you so graciously see fit to bestow upon me.'

She stood up straight and flashed a triumphant look at Tora, who very pointedly did not turn her head to catch her rival's eye.

'As for you, Tora, you will remain in Norway, as will Prince Magnus, whom I will appoint king in my absence. Prince Olaf will come with me to England. It will do him good to see his first proper fighting.'

It was Tora's turn to smile. She could now claim the status of king's mother, and would stand at her son's right hand as he ruled the kingdom.

'There now, you both have reason to feel well satisfied, since you will both be queens, but in different countries, a very long way apart,' Harald concluded.

He did not wait for replies, let alone arguments. He merely told Elisaveta, 'We will be leaving the minute the winds change. That could happen at any time. You and the girls should start packing at once.'

Barely two days later, with the queen and princesses still

465

deciding which gowns to take with them and how best to transport them, the weathervane atop the cathedral tower of Nidaros, capital of Norway, swung round on its axis, pointing in the opposite direction to the one in which it had been stuck for weeks upon end. Within the hour, Harald had given the order to sail. By sunset, they were on their way, streaming out of Nidaros and down Trondheim Fjord on their way to the open sea.

Harald had captained the fleet past the Shetland Islands to Orkney. There he met with Pal and Erlend, sons of Thorfin the Mighty, Jarl of Shetland, who had held sway over the waters from Shetland right round to the northern shores of Eire before his death a twelvemonth earlier. Another man seeking to equal his father's greatness joined them: Gudröd, son of Haraldr, King of Islay, Hebrides and Man. Finally there was a Norwegian warrior, Ostein Orre. Tall, handsome and renowned for his daring in the Danish campaigns, Ostein bridged the gap between the camps of the two royal wives, since he was the brother of Tora, and was betrothed to Elisaveta and Harald's daughter Maria. Ostein was the king's favourite commander, Maria his favourite child. Their wedding, when it came, would be a celebration worthy of the feast halls of Valhalla.

These men sat with Harald and listened while he described his plan of campaign, which differed little from many another invasions carried out by Vikings over the centuries: 'Land in the north, establish ourselves around Jorvik,' Harald still used the traditional Norse name for York, 'and head south from there. If anyone stands in our way, we will destroy him. That was how Sweyn Forkbeard destroyed the English, and left the country for Knut to inherit. That is how I will do it too.'

'Hear, hear!' Ostein slammed the table in approval. He had been among those urging the king to take up Tostig Godwinson's challenge when it was first discussed in the council at Sarpsborg. The others were more sceptical.

'I have heard that William of Normandy is massing a great army to strike against England too,' said Gudröd. 'What if he is the one we meet on the road to the south?'

'I have heard that too. But it matters not to me. William will surely arrive in England before us. He will therefore fight King Harold's army before us. Only one of them will win, but whoever it is, they will be exhausted and depleted by the time they meet us. We will be like a pack of wolves confronting two mighty bears. Together they would be too much for us. But if only one bear is left standing, and he is already bloodied, then we will rip him to pieces.'

'There is another bear,' said Erlend Thorfinsson. 'You forget Edwin and Morcar. They have the armies of Mercia and Northumbria. We will meet them before we reach that final battle with Harold Godwinson or William of Normandy.'

'Tostig Godwinson, brother of Harold, assures me that they will not be a problem. The sons of Aelfgar have no great skill as generals, nor do they command the loyalty of their people. If we are a wolf pack, they are two aged rams leading a herd of sheep. And never forget that the lands around Jorvik are home to countless men of Norse extraction. True, most of them are Danes. But we're at peace with them now, and whatever our past quarrels, they'll still side with us rather than the English.'

'Might I ask Your Majesty, what makes you trust Tostig Godwinson? He's lost his earldom and fallen out with his own brothers. I for one would not seek out an ally like that.'

'He sought me, Erlend Thorfinsson. And now that we're on the move, I no longer care in the slightest whether he is reliable or not. I trust in myself, my people and my friends. We are bound by common blood. We are a match for any fighting men on earth, and I've seen enough of the earth to know this for a fact. So long as we hold firm and stay true to our cause, all will be well.'

The arguments over strategy meant nothing to Harald's daughter, Princess Maria. She only cared that she would soon be saying farewell to her father, her brother and the love of her young life, not knowing if she would ever see any of them again. Her father, of course, had been going off to war for as long as she could remember, and he had returned so often, completely unscathed, that she hardly gave a second thought to his leaving.

But she had never before been in love, and the loss of her man was another matter altogether.

'Promise you'll come back to me,' she pleaded with Ostein Orre, fighting back the tears.

Ostein felt immortal, as so many young men do. He laughed as he said, 'Don't worry, my love. Of course I'll come back. I can't be so sure about your brother, though. I've practised swordfighting against him and I honestly think that you could beat him. So we just have to hope that Englishmen are worse warriors than pretty Norse maidens.'

Olaf cuffed him on the shoulder. 'Hey! You can't talk about a prince like that.'

'You may be a prince, but I'm the senior officer. So I can say whatever I damn well please.'

Olaf twisted his face into an absurdly serious frown and stroked his chin. 'Hmm, this is a very tricky constitutional problem. It can only be resolved over a tankard of ale.'

'Several tankards, I'd say.'

'Then we'd better get started.'

The two men walked off, loudly bantering with one another. Only later, when his friend was not watching, did Olaf go to his sister, much more seriously now, and say, 'My father loves Ostein like another son, so he will protect him. I love Ostein like another brother, so I will protect him. He will come home to you safe and sound and make you his wife. I promise.'

Maria hugged him with a whispered 'Thank you.' The following day, just as the fleet was preparing to set sail for the Scottish mainland, Ostein came to her too, and, just like her brother, showed a different face when there were no other young men watching him.

'Can I have a lock of your hair?' he asked.

Maria nodded and held out a long wheat-coloured strand. She watched in silence as her love took out his dagger, folded her hair over its blade, flicked the sharp steel upwards and sliced through the strand, cutting off a lock as long as her little finger. Then he reached inside his shirt and pulled out a silver locket on the end of a chain. He opened the locket, curled up the hair and placed it inside, then closed the locket and slipped it back inside his shirt.

'Now you will be next to my heart wherever I go. I swear I will not take this chain from around my neck until I come back to see you again.'

'Cut some of your hair for me,' she said.

Ostein did as she asked.

'I have a little chest where I store my most precious possessions,' Maria said. 'I will keep this there until you return and I will pray for you every day . . . no, every hour that you are gone.'

They held one another close and kissed. Then there was a shout from the corridor: Olaf's voice. 'Ostein! Time to go! The king is calling for you!'

Ostein took a half-step back, breaking the physical bond between them. 'I love you.' And he was gone.

Then the waiting began, and Maria understood what it was to see a man go off to war, and knew that she would never be fully alive again until he came back to her.

Harald's fleet sailed south, coming ashore from time to time on the east coast of Scotland and Northumbria to replenish the huge quantities of food and water required by so vast an army. On some occasions the transactions were peaceful, on others not so. The Norsemen descended on the small town of Scarborough and destroyed it utterly. The men were killed, the women and children taken into slavery (for human beings were among the most prized and easily traded spoils of war) and all their possessions, food stores and livestock stolen, butchered or destroyed. Along the way Harald's men encountered occasional detachments of English forces. Some were no more than pitiful groups of local farmers, levied into service and barely capable of even a token resistance. Others were more serious companies of trained men, sent as scouts and skirmishers by Edwin and Morcar. They were dispatched with barely more difficulty than the farmers.

By the time the Norsemen sailed up the Humber estuary, where Tostig had agreed to meet them, the fact that he arrived with a bare dozen ships, instead of the sixty he had promised, was more a subject for amusement than anger, let alone despair. Still, Hardrada accorded him the status of an honoured ally, the equal or greater of the lords of Orkney and Islay.

Edwin and Morcar had sent a fleet to meet the invaders in the Humber, but it was far smaller and no match for Hardrada's. So the English retreated along the River Ouse towards York, riding the Aegir, the tidal bore that made the river flow upstream. A few miles south of the city, the Ouse was joined by the waters of the River Wharfe. The English slipped up the Wharfe, hoping that the Norse would carry on up the Ouse.

When the last of Hardrada's fleet had passed the junction of the two rivers, the English planned to sail back downstream, re-enter the Ouse behind their enemy and block their way to the sea. On a narrow river, where only a few ships could be brought to bear on one another, the disparity in numbers would be far less significant. And if the Norwegians could be bottled up until Edwin and Morcar's armies arrived on the scene, they might be wiped out before they had reached any distance at all into the heart of England.

That was the plan, but Hardrada was too old and wise a soldier to be so easily deceived. He halted his fleet by the village of Riccall, less than half a day's march south of York. There the river curled round upon itself in an oxbow shape, creating an area in the middle of the bend like a flat sandy island on which most of Harald's ships could be beached, while the rest were strung out across the water. Now it was the Norse who were blocking the river and the English who could not get out.

That evening Harald sent scouts up ahead of them to spy out the approach to York, which he planned to seize the following day. They reported large numbers of English troops in and around the city, under the banners of both Mercia and Northumbria.

'So both the sons of Aelfgar want to do battle with me, eh?' Harald said to his commanders when he held a council of war that night. 'Very well then, we must not disappoint them. Olaf, Ostein, you will stay here with the fleet and one third of the army, just in case the English fleet is foolish enough to attack. The rest will come with me. We will march on Jorvik, and whoever we meet along the way will die regretting their decision.'

2

Foul Ford Gate, Yorkshire, 20 September 1066

The Norsemen marched before dawn, so that the sun was only just rising through the morning mist when they came to a place beside the River Ouse, less than two miles from York, known as Foul Ford Gate. There the road crossed a stream – or beck, as the local people called it – just before it flowed into the river. And there it was that they found Morcar and Edwin waiting to give battle.

The beck ran along a ditch, with higher ground on either side. Harald and Tostig stopped their horses on their side of the ditch and looked at the forces arrayed against them.

The English had lined up along the far side of the beck, atop the ground beyond the ditch. Their right flank, commanded by Edwin, rested on the banks of the River Ouse. Morcar's men were stretched out along the left of the English line.

'How many of them would you say there are?' Hardrada asked Tostig as they surveyed the field.

'No fewer than five thousand, no more than ten,' Tostig replied. 'In numbers, at least, we're evenly matched.'

'I agree . . . But what's over there, where Count Morcar's line ends?' Hardrada pointed away to his right. 'I can't see through this damn mist.'

A rider was sent off to investigate. A few minutes later he returned. 'The land up there is marshy, very wet, impossible for any soldiers to march across.'

'So they've got the river on one side and the marsh on the other. They can't be outflanked,' Tostig observed.

'True,' Harald agreed. 'But they're also trapped.'

The mist was clearing now and visibility was gradually improving. 'Look beyond the Mercians,' Harald said, pointing at a causeway that ran along the riverbank, bearing the road to York. 'See where the road is. I'll bet the land on the other side of that causeway is as bad as the marsh. If we can get them on the run, Edwin and his men won't all be able to take the road at once.'

'Then the river and the marsh will kill them for us.'

Harald nodded. He briefed his commanders on what he planned to do, sending Tostig to take charge of the Norwegians' right front, opposite Morcar. Then they all dismounted, for Norsemen did their fighting on their own two feet.

The start of the battle was as ritualised as a gigantic military dance. Both sides sent their bowmen forward, and arrows flew in great swarms across the sky until everyone had emptied their quivers.

The bulk of the two armies was lined up in shield walls. They fought in a way that dated back to the Roman legions, and before them the Macedonian armies of King Philip and Alexander the Great. The men were lined up in closely packed ranks. The front rank held their shields upright ahead of them, so close together that they overlapped like the scales of a gigantic snake. The ranks behind held their shields over their heads, to protect the entire body from arrows falling from on high. A shield wall was virtually impregnable as long as it held together. But if one rank, or even a part of a rank, broke and a hole opened up in the wall, then the enemy could flood through it and wreak havoc.

The archers forced no holes in either line. Now the Norwegians advanced across the beck and another exchange took place at closer range as the two armies hurled spears. Still there was no decisive break on either side.

Undertaking any physical activity in a coat of chain mail and a heavy helmet, while carrying a large wooden shield was physically taxing. So there was a brief pause in the action while the two sides got their breath back, had a drink and prepared for the next phase of the battle. It began with Tostig, on the right of the Norwegian line, closing on Morcar's Northumbrian forces. The two bodies of men tangled and fought without either side gaining any clear advantage. But then Morcar formed a section of his line into a wedge shape and drove them forwards, with the point of the wedge cutting into Tostig's line.

Tostig did not wait for his wing of the army to be cut in two. He ordered an immediate withdrawal. The Norwegians disengaged and retreated over the beck to the position they'd held at the start of the battle.

The English paused again, re-formed their wedge and advanced once more. Again Tostig retreated. Again the English followed him. They were jubilant, shouting out their battle cries and singing a war song in time with the marching of their feet and the slashing of their swords.

Harald Hardrada had not committed his full force to the battle just yet, sending just enough men forward against Edwin's Mercians to keep them tied down. He and his finest troops were held in reserve. The king watched as Tostig's men retreated and the English followed them. He did nothing, just waited and watched. For with every step Morcar's men took forward, their line curved and stretched a little more.

Then came the moment Harald had been waiting for. A gap opened up in the middle of the English line between Morcar's men, who were moving forward against Tostig, and Edwin's, who had stayed where they were. And it was when he saw that gap and knew that the centre of the English line was now at its weakest point that he ordered Frirek, his bannerman, to raise the Landwaster high.

A huge roar went up from the Norwegian ranks as they saw the black raven fly above them. Then Harald ordered the blowing of the war blast on a hollowed-out cow's horn that signalled the advance. He led from the very front, towering over every other man on the battlefield as he ran at the English, swinging his mighty battleaxe and cutting down his enemies like a farmer scything corn.

The heart of the English army disintegrated under the impact of the Viking charge. Edwin's forces were cut off from Morcar's.

Now Tostig and his men suddenly switched tactics, attacking Morcar's men from the front, while Harald swung round and took them in the flank

The Northumbrians, who had been so confidently anticipating victory just a short time earlier, were taken completely by surprise. The enemy that had been falling back before them was now attacking from every direction. Men began to panic, but there was nowhere to run because their escape was blocked by the marsh. The English were cut down in their droves, forced into the gully where the beck flowed and slaughtered in such numbers that the stream ran red with their blood. Now men started plunging into the marsh, willing to risk the water rather than face certain death on dry land. But weighed down by their armour and exhausted by the hours of fighting, they were trapped by the mud and sucked down into the boggy swamp.

Tostig, meanwhile, had fixed his attention on Morcar's personal banner. Wherever it was, there Morcar would be too, and Tostig wanted the satisfaction of killing the man who had usurped his dukedom. He led his own men, together with Copsige and his retainers and a detachment of Norwegians, against Morcar's housecarls, who were guarding the banner, and their earl, with their lives. They died to a man, and when the banner finally fell, it seemed that Morcar must have perished too. But as Tostig looked around, his sword, his face and his armour drenched in the blood of the men he had slain, he could see no sign of his hated enemy. Tostig screamed obscenities into the air. Somehow Morcar had smuggled himself out of the battle. 'The cowardly bastard's escaped!'

Once Harald was sure that the Northumbrian flank of the English army was routed, he turned his attention to finishing off Edwin's Mercians. They made a fighting retreat, backing away along the causeway, but as Harald had predicted, the sheer press of men was so great that many lost their footing and fell to their death in the river or the marsh.

The battle had been as deafening as all combat was, with the shouting of fighting men, the screaming of the wounded and the constant hammering of weapons against shields and armour. But as the day drew towards its close and dusk began to fall, a quiet came over the killing ground and the only sounds to be heard were the last cries of men in their death throes and the murmuring of the victors. They were too exhausted for any wild celebrations and too awed by the scale of the carnage they had wreaked.

The English bodies lay so thick along the beck that men could walk across them from one end of the stream to the other without getting their feet wet. Then the water began to rise, for the Ouse was a tidal river, and the dead were suspended in it in great shoals, like an army of the drowned, shrouded in the mist that was now falling again as the chill of evening set in.

3

York, 24 September 1066

Harald took his time. He had hundreds of dead men to bury on the field of battle and many more wounded to tend to once they'd returned to the fleet. There was in any case no need for an immediate advance, for no matter when he made his move, no one was going to stand in his way.

In the end, it was hunger that forced the Norwegians to march on York. Their supplies were running low and the city was the best place to find the provisions they needed.

Some of his men argued that they could satisfy their hunger for more than mere food if they ravaged the city and either slaughtered or enslaved its people. Harald would have none of it. Many of York's citizens were Norsemen, just like them, he said. Far better to win them over with mercy. And if that mercy were made conditional on a very large payment of gold, and every coin in York's mint, then so much the better.

So it was that four days after the battle at Foul Ford, Harald led his troops like a conquering Caesar through the gates of York and into the city. He had sent envoys ahead, ordering a gemot to be called, and all the significant burghers of the city and thegns from the countryside thereabouts had duly assembled on the greensward outside York Minster.

So too had Edwin of Mercia and Morcar of Northumberland. Having taken such a merciless beating, they had no desire to remain Harald's enemies and so begged him to accept their pleas for peace.

'How do I know you won't take up arms again the moment my back is turned?' Harald asked.

'How could we?' Edwin replied. 'We have no army left to fight with. My brother and I are agreed. We have done our duty by Harold Godwinson. We fought in his name and paid for our loyalty in the blood of our retainers. He can expect no more of us.'

'And we want no more to do with him,' Morcar added.

The two earls swore allegiance to Harald, and when the same was asked of the men at the gemot, they too agreed without protest.

'You were right,' said Harald to Tostig, not bothering to conceal his surprise. 'These people don't love your brother and they were hardly begging me to reinstate Morcar, either.'

Tostig shrugged. 'They're northern. You're even more northern. They'd rather have you than any man from the south.'

Harald had three further demands, in exchange for his guarantee of mercy towards the city and safe conduct for Edwin, Morcar and their few remaining men. First, he wanted every scrap of gold and silver that the city and its mint contained. Second, he demanded hostages to act as surety, just in case the people of Yorkshire should be tempted to renege on their vows of loyalty. And finally he needed food, a great deal of it, for his army.

The men of the gemot agreed to the surrendering of treasure that day. They discussed the precise number and nature of hostages with Harald and agreed that one hundred and fifty children from the leading families of the city and shire would be appropriate. They also agreed to the handover of food in principle, but pointed out that Edwin and Morcar's army had already stripped the city granary bare and killed all the livestock for their own use. It would therefore be necessary to send out into the country for more supplies.

Harald gave them one day to find the children and the provisions and bring them to him. There was then a discussion about the best location for this delivery. His own camp at Riccall, to the south-east of the city, was far from ideal, for the best farmlands, and thus the richest sources of flour, meat and ale, were to the north, in the Vale of York, and beyond that to the north-east in the Vale of Pickering.

A point was therefore chosen that was conveniently placed for farmers from the two districts and accessible by both land, for a number of old Roman roads converged there, and water, along the River Derwent. Its name was Stamford Bridge, and Harald agreed with the men of the gemot that he would be there the following morning. He warned them that their food and hostages had better arrive on time and in full measure, or he would take his revenge on the city of York and every single man, woman and child it contained.

The Yorkshiremen were in no doubt that Harald Hardrada would carry out his threat. They were only too happy to assure him that when he arrived at Stamford Bridge on the morrow, he would not be disappointed.

4

Stamford Bridge, Yorkshire, 25 September 1066

The early autumn in England can often be warmer than the summer that preceded it, and sure enough, the morning of 25 September brought clear skies, a sun that soon burned off any lingering shreds of mist and the promise of a hot, dry day once the cool of the dawn had gone.

Harald had decided to take one third of his full army to Stamford Bridge. It would be at least three, maybe four hours' march each way, and there was no point tiring out any more men than was absolutely necessary. Ulf Ospaksson was sent to select the units that would be making the journey, and as he was doing so, some of the men pleaded with him to beg a favour from His Majesty. Ospaksson had been at Harald's side through more campaigns than either man could count. If he asked for something, the king might not agree to it, but he would at least give it serious consideration.

Ospaksson listened to what the men had to say, decided that their request was reasonable and put it to his king.

'The men want to march to this meeting without their armour and shields,' he said. 'They say that it's going to be a hot day. They have a long way to go and may have to carry supplies on the way back, if there aren't enough wagons. Why be weighed down by shields and mail as well?'

'And what do you say?' Harald asked, knowing that his old friend was a stickler for doing things properly and, as his initial scepticism about this very campaign had shown, averse to taking unnecessary risks. The fact that he had survived so long only proved the wisdom of his approach.

'I say that I never, ever like to see soldiers go anywhere without their proper equipment,' Ospaksson replied. 'But they have a point. It will be hot, and they may need to carry sacks of grain, or barrels of ale. It would be foolish to deny ourselves goods that we badly need because men haven't the strength to transport them.'

'I don't see why a man can't sling his shield over his back and still have two hands free for carrying a bit of corn or a drop of ale.'

Ospaksson chuckled. 'That's because you could carry two barrels and barely even notice the weight. But most men are not like you . . . no men are, in fact.'

'I suppose so. But I don't like the idea of them marching unprotected through hostile territory.'

'Nor do I, sire. But then, is this hostile territory? Your enemies are defeated. Their leaders have pledged their allegiance to you, and the local people are only too happy to give everything you ask. What threat do we actually face?'

Harald thought carefully, for this was a serious question. 'We face two possible threats,' he concluded. 'The first is the threat of hunger, and that is a certainty unless we are properly supplied. The second is the threat of ambush, or some other attack, and that chance strikes me as very small. As you say, old friend, who is there to attack us? It follows, therefore, that it is more important to avoid the first threat than the second. Thus the men need to carry as little as possible on the way to Stamford Bridge, so that they can carry more on the way back. Very well then, they can leave their mail here, but they must have their shields and helmets and their swords, axes or bows. If the worst comes to the worst and we encounter trouble, then at least we shall have a shield wall to shelter behind and weapons to fight with.'

481

And so the orders were given. As before, Olaf and Ostein Orre were left to guard the ships and watch as Harald and his chosen men set off for Stamford Bridge. They left in high spirits, with the king and his lieutenants on horseback at the head of the column, accompanied by a company of mounted troops, and the bulk of the foot soldiers marching behind. Who could not feel happy to be alive on such a perfect autumn day, with the countryside lush and verdant and the blackberries so thick on the bramble hedges beside the road that many men stopped to pick handfuls as they marched by? Barely ten days had passed since they made their first landfall in England, but already their ships were laden with treasure and soon their bellies would be filled with fresh food.

Stamford Bridge lay across the River Derwent, which flowed south from there until it joined the River Ouse a short way downstream of Riccall, where the Norse fleet was beached. So Harald and his men marched north to their rendezvous, with the Derwent to their right, until they came to the village of Gate Helmsley. It stood atop a low ridge, and from there they could look down on Stamford Bridge itself. Just upstream of the bridge, on the far bank from Harald's approach, there was a semicircular bulge in the river that created a small bay, providing a natural harbour. Any boats bringing supplies would unload there, and so it made sense for Harald to march the bulk of his men across the bridge and set up camp on the far side of the river, leaving a detachment to guard the bridge and wait for the first of the provisions to turn up. Other men were set to work rounding up cattle grazing on the meadows that ran along the riverbanks.

They had not been there long when a man stationed on the far side of the bridge ran back across it and approached Harald. 'There's a cloud of dust, Your Majesty, coming up from the south. Lots of men and animals, I reckon. It looks as though it's the same road we marched on when we came here.'

'I imagine that's farmers bringing their herds,' said Harald.

A moment later another man ran up. 'Soldiers, sire! We can see soldiers.'

Harald turned to Ulf Ospaksson. 'It must be more of our men. Olaf or Orre must have sent them.'

'Why would they do that?'

'Heaven knows. I suppose we'll find out when they get here.'

By now the dust cloud was clearly visible from Harald's side of the river, and with every second the shadowy shapes concealed within it were becoming more distinct, revealing themselves as men in full battle armour, carrying banners.

'My God,' Tostig gasped, 'the wyvern!'

'What are you talking about?' Harald asked.

'That banner over there, in the very centre. That's the dragon of Wessex. We call it the wyvern. It's the flag of the Earl of Wessex.'

For once in his life, Harald Hardrada was rendered speechless. 'You mean . . .' he began, and left the words just hanging.

'Yes, that's my brother. King Harold of England is here. And he's brought his army with him.'

Tostig paused for a moment, looked around at their position, then glanced back at the approaching army. 'We're outnumbered, Your Majesty, and the men have no mail coats. Wouldn't it be wise to withdraw towards the fleet? If we had the whole army, we'd outnumber them.'

'Withdraw?' Harald boomed. 'I have never fled the field in my life and I'm not starting now.' He looked at Ospaksson. 'Send word to Riccall. Say we need every man who can walk. Tell them to wear their armour. And tell them that if they want any glory, they'd better hurry up or else we'll have killed all the English before they get here.'

Then he turned back towards his English ally. 'You run from your brother if you want to, Godwinson. But I'm going to stand and fight.'

5

Bosham and Westminster, August–September 1066

Harold had spent the summer at Bosham, going half mad with the waiting. By custom, the men of the fyrd owed him two months' service. By early August, most had served their time and were desperate to get back to their homes. They had heard no word of their families and villages. They had harvests to gather and fattened pigs to slaughter. It had taken all Harold's charm, persuasion and regal authority to keep them at their posts. And all the while, the land where they were stationed, on the Isle of Wight and along the south coast, had been stripped bare of supplies, so that the local people wanted rid of the soldiers as much as they wanted to go.

To add to that, as August gave way to September, the owners and captains of the ships that made up most of Harold's fleet began to worry that they would not be able to return to their home ports before the storms of autumn and winter made navigation impossible.

'God bless Your Majesty, but we can't stay beyond September Ember Week, we just can't,' the leader of one mariners' deputation told him, referring to the three days of fasting at which, according to the church calendar, the season of autumn began. 'It's the equinox on the Saturday after Ember Friday, and you ask any captain in your fleet, Your Majesty, there's always gales on the equinox. Any seafarer that knows his business, doesn't matter where he comes from, he wants to be safe in harbour by then.'

'So when do you propose taking your ships away?' Harold asked.

'The Nativity of St Mary would be favourite, Your Majesty. That's on the eighth of the month. Gives us a good week to make our way home. If it please you, sire, you should do the same with your own ships. Otherwise the autumn gales'll have 'em, you can be sure of that.'

'That's all very well, but it's not the equinox, or gales, or Ember Days that I'm worried about. It's Duke William of Normandy. If the fleet disperses, who'll stop him sailing over to England, completely unopposed?'

'Begging your pardon, Your Majesty, but he sails by the same winds we do. And gales'll sink his ships just like they'll sink ours. Mark my words, he'll be hearing the same from his captains.'

'He may not be as willing to listen to his as I am to mine.'

'That's very gracious of you, sire. But if it eases your worries, we all reckon that Master William will have been packed off back home to Normandy by the time September comes around. I mean, the wind's blowing from the north now. But it won't keep blowing that way, not in high summer. Southerly winds, that's what you get in summer, and that's what we'll get soon enough. Then the Normans'll sail and you can rest assured, Your Majesty, we will be more'n ready for 'em.'

But the southerly winds did not blow. All through August, the northerly winds trapped William on his side of the Channel and left Harold kicking his heels and struggling to keep his forces together in England. Then September began, the Nativity of St Mary came and Harold had no option but to dismiss his soldiers and let his fleet disperse.

The decision came not a moment too soon, for the storms that the captain had predicted came shortly before the equinox, on the night of 12 September, into the morning of the 13th. A gale blew in from the far Atlantic, bringing surging seas and driving rain. Harold's own ships were thoroughly battered by the wind and waves before they arrived in the port of London.

Later that same day, once the weather had calmed, he took his housecarls up to Westminster, marching over London Bridge to be welcomed by cheering crowds of city folk.

People thought the danger had passed. The fighting season had come and gone and all the men had gone back home safe and sound. But then, out of the blue, there came the news of an invasion: not Normans, attacking from the south, but Vikings, sailing down from the north, led by King Harald Hardrada of Norway. And Tostig Godwinson was marching at his side.

'There we were thinking the north wind was keeping us safe, but all the time it was blowing the Norsemen down from their fjords,' Harold said, as he met with his closest councillors at Westminster to hear the news that the messenger had brought. 'So, what have you to report?'

'The Norsemen have ravaged the coast from Berwick to Spurn Head, Your Majesty,' the messenger replied. 'His lordship Earl Morcar sent troops to confront them, but all were slain. The Norsemen have a mighty fleet, with many hundreds of boats, some so big they are said to hold three hundred men.'

'Impossible!' Harold scoffed.

'Sire, the report I give you is true. Many eyes have looked in wonder on these ships.'

'So where are they, then, these giant ships?'

'When I left, Your Majesty, the Norse fleet had rounded Spurn Head, entered the Humber estuary and were sailing up the River Ouse towards York.'

'Is the city still in our hands?'

'Yes, Your Majesty. I believe it is.'

'Very well then, you may go.'

Harold waited until the man had left the chamber. 'We need to move north right away, to deal with Hardrada.'

He did not sound as though the matter was open to debate. His brother Leofwine looked around at the other advisers. He saw from their hesitant expressions and evasive eyes that none of them wanted to support the king's plan, but equally none dared oppose it. Very well then, the duty fell on him.

'Let Morcar and Edwin do it, Your Majesty. They wanted their family to control the north. Time they showed they're up to it.'

'They aren't. They won't beat Hardrada. He was fighting battles and winning most of them when they were just babes in arms. If his fleet is half as big as that messenger suggested, he's brought a massive army with him. Clearly the troops that have been sent against them so far have been pitifully inadequate. We'll need reinforcements up there, and I should be there too. A king should defend his country.'

'Defend it down here, Your Majesty. What if Duke William should land? The winds can't keep him in harbour forever.'

'Maybe he isn't coming. What kind of general begins an invasion just as winter is starting?'

'Hardrada, for one.'

'He's a Norseman. We all know they don't give a damn about the weather or the seasons. What difference does it make if William does come? I'll have to meet and defeat them both. One of them is here, on English soil. Fine, I'll deal with him first.'

Finally another man summoned the courage to try and dissuade the king. Stigand, Archbishop of Canterbury, gave a thoughtful little cough and then spoke.

'Your Majesty, I am no soldier, I admit, but it seems to me that even in winning a battle, a general will suffer losses, and even those men who survive will be exhausted by their effort. So it seems to me that in this war of three kings—'

'Two kings,' barked Harold, 'and one pretender.'

Stigand nodded his head and in his most emollient clerical tones said, 'Indeed, sire, how right you are . . . I shall instead refer to this as a war of three sides, but the point I wish to make remains the same. The winner will surely be the general who fights the fewest battles. If you march north now and defeat the Norsemen, as I have no doubt Your Majesty will do, then you will have to come all the way back to the very southernmost shore of England to confront the threat from Normandy. Duke William and his men will neither have fought, nor marched. Surely they will be the fresher for it.'

'Damn Duke William!'

'The good Lord may very well do that, sire, whatever his Holiness the Pope may say to the contrary. But consider this. Suppose Harald of Norway marches down from the north, and William of Normandy marches up from the south . . .' he paused a beat to let that thought sink in, and then added, 'and you are not waiting in the middle for either of them. Suppose instead, you and all our forces retire westwards, to Winchester, say, or even Worcester. Why, then our two enemies would be obliged to fight each other, for neither can even attempt to steal your crown while the other is alive, with an army in the field. I am sure that any clash between two great armies led by two such stubborn, warlike commanders would be a fierce, brutal, bloody affair, and that both would be badly mauled. Whereas you, sire, by standing aside, with patience, wisdom and majestic indifference to the squabbles of lesser men, would then be able to swoop down, like an eagle from the heavens, and pick off your battered and depleted enemies entirely at your leisure.'

Stigand fell silent, looking rather pleased with himself. Leofwine evidently felt he had every right to feel smug, because he burst out, 'My oath, Your Grace, you picked the wrong profession. You should have been a general, for your grasp of strategy and—'

'No,' Harold interrupted. And now all the tension and anxiety that had built up in him since the day he became king poured out. 'I won't do it! I can't stand back and let other men fight over my country while I do nothing to stop them. I just can't bear it any longer. My stomach is in knots every day. My body aches for no reason. I barely sleep. I've had enough. And I would remind you all that the threat from the north does not come just from Hardrada. My brother rides at his side. And I can't stand for that, either.'

Leofwine sighed. 'Your Majesty, may I speak to you as a loving brother now, as well as a loyal subject?'

Harold nodded.

'I'm sick of waiting, too. And I'm angry, bitter, disgusted . . . I don't even have the words to describe all my feelings about the way our brother Tostig has betrayed us. But we mustn't let our anger and our emotion confuse our thoughts. We can't let him affect our judgement.'

'I'm not letting my emotions affect my judgement, brother,' Harold said, more calmly, as he regained his self-control. 'This is a matter of strategy, a matter of necessity. We all know that without the Norwegians, Tostig would be powerless. But he gives them something too. Ask yourself, why has Hardrada shown him such favour? Because he knows that without Tostig he would be just another raider come to ravage this country. But with the King of England's brother, a Godwinson, an earl, at his side, he may be able to persuade the people that his is a cause worth following. And if he defeats the earls of Mercia and Northumbria, then his appeal will be all the greater. I have to show the people that I am the true king, and that I can defeat all who come against me. If they see a coward sitting in his palace, afraid to come out and face the enemy, well, then I have lost without a blow being struck. I must fight.'

He looked around the room, inviting, or rather daring anyone to contradict him. 'Very well then,' he went on. 'We march north in the morning. Gyrth, you are coming with me. We'll take your men and the royal housecarls with us. I want messengers sent out now to go ahead of us to sound the alarm and summon the fyrd. That way we can pick up more troops along the way.

'Leofwine, you will stay here and command the south. If the Normans land while I am gone, watch them, contain them, harry them if they march towards London, but don't come to battle. And cheer up. The worst of it is over. We know what we have to do, and that in itself is half the battle won.'

6

Tadcaster to Stamford Bridge, 24–25 September 1066

Harold marched hard for the north. He expected to meet Edwin, Morcar and their armies along the way, but when he reached Tadcaster, late on 24 September, he received the disastrous news of the battle of Foul Ford. Hardrada, he was told, had even marched into York and extracted promises of gold, provisions and hostages in return for not sacking the city and slaughtering or enslaving its inhabitants.

'Where's Hardrada now?' Harold asked the messenger.

'He's returned to his fleet at Riccall, Your Majesty.'

'So York has not been occupied?'

'No, Your Majesty.'

'York has high walls, built by Romans,' Gyrth said. 'No matter how many men Hardrada has, we can hold the city till more help arrives.'

'And then what do we do when William the Bastard lands in the south? How can Leofwine hold him off, with Edwin and Morcar's men cut to ribbons and us cooped up in York?'

'There's no food in York, sire,' the messenger pointed out. 'Hardrada discovered that for himself when he came asking. That's why he had to go away again. They're gathering the food now to give to him tomorrow.'

'At York?' Harold asked.

'No, Your Majesty, at a village called Stamford Bridge.'

'So Hardrada will have to split his forces: some to go and get the food, the rest to guard his fleet. Tell me, how badly were the

Norsemen bloodied at Foul Ford before they won their victory?'

'I was not there, sire. But by all accounts, the men of Mercia and Northumbria fought hard. They took a heavy toll of the Norsemen before their line was breached.'

'If we can do battle tomorrow, we can catch Hardrada with his army split and still tired and battered from its last fight.'

'But Your Majesty, which half of his army should we attack?' Gyrth asked.

'The half Hardrada is commanding. Wherever he goes, that's where we'll be.' Harold thought for a second. 'If I were Hardrada, I wouldn't spend all day sitting on my arse, waiting for someone else to go to Stamford Bridge. I'd go myself. I'd want to see what I was getting, make sure that the people of York had kept their side of the bargain. I'd reckon that if I wasn't there, they'd be more likely to go back on their word.

'We're going to Stamford Bridge. Gyrth, pass the word to all the company commanders. We march at dawn.'

In the first hour of the afternoon, the English marched through Gate Helmsley and looked down from the ridge towards Stamford Bridge, just as Hardrada had done earlier. Harold saw that the Norsemen were split, with the smaller part of their force on the near bank and the majority across the river. None of them were in battle formation.

For as long as anyone could remember, Anglo-Saxon armies had ridden to battle, but then dismounted and fought on foot. But that wasted time, and seeing his enemies scattered and vulnerable, Harold had no intention of giving them any opportunity to sort themselves out.

He rode to the front of the line, stood up in his stirrups and shouted his army's battle cries: 'Holy Cross! God Almighty!' And then, 'Charge!'

The mounted men fell on the Norse like hunters on a herd

of deer, impaling them on their spears, cutting them down with their swords, then chasing down any who tried to turn and run.

For a moment it looked as though the battle would be over before Hardrada's men had even formed into a proper fighting formation. But these were hard, experienced men. Impelled by instincts honed over years of campaigning against the Danes, enough of them retained their composure to form a shield wall in a semicircle around the near end of the bridge.

Behind them, the rest of the survivors dashed across the bridge to join Harald's main force on the far bank.

The king himself was composing a short verse, as was his habit before he went into combat. He summoned his scribe and declaimed:

> 'Arrayed for battle, we have no armour as the enemy
> we meet.
> Helmets gleam, but no mail can be seen
> We left it all at the fleet.'

He looked at Tostig. 'What do you think?'

The earl was baffled by the very idea of churning out doggerel with just moments to go before battle. His own mind was completely focused on the coming engagement and he could not think of a suitable response.

'Not good enough, eh?' said Hardrada. 'You're probably right. Let me give it another try . . .'

As his scribe looked on attentively, the king rested his chin on his fist, then squared his shoulders, stuck out his chest and started declaiming in a style that was half spoken, half sung, line after line, until he concluded:

'Long ago from war goddess Hilde did I the
command receive,
And since then
My head is held high as the weapons clash and my
axe cleaves
The skulls of men.'

A ragged cheer rang out from the men close enough to hear
the performance, and Hardrada nodded his thanks for their
appreciation. Satisfied now that due ceremony had been
observed, he turned his attention back to the bridge and the
small circle of Norse shields facing the full might of Harold's
army.

Hardrada grunted. 'Huh! Your brother's sent a herald out to
meet us. I imagine he's offering terms. Go to the man, Tostig,
and tell him to inform his master that I graciously consent to
accept his surrender and spare his life, provided that he gives me
his crown and throne.'

Tostig looked more closely. 'That's no herald. That's my
brother, the king.'

Hardrada raised a single eyebrow. 'Is that so? Well, he sits
well on his horse for such a small man.'

Tostig fought back the last remnants of his family pride. It
would do no good to point out that Harold Godwinson was a
notably tall man by normal standards. Hardrada was not
normal. Everyone looked small to him.

'Do you still want me to go to him, Your Majesty?' Tostig
asked.

'Of course. And on the terms I gave you.'

King Harold was not giving anyone his crown: not until it was
ripped from his cold, dead skull. He told Tostig as much when
Hardrada's offer was made. But he was prepared to make a deal

of his own. Reminding himself of how devastated their mother would be if she heard that either of her sons had died fighting the other, he had decided to make one last attempt to get Tostig to change his mind.

'We can't go into battle against one another. We're brothers. For God's sake, man, think of our mother. Imagine her tears if she hears that one or both of us is dead. Think of our father, looking down from heaven. He raised us to control England, not to fight over it.'

Tostig did not respond. Mentally cursing his brother for his limitless capacity to bear a grudge, Harold said, 'You know that you're outnumbered. I can see that none of your men is wearing armour. You can't possibly win. But if Hardrada concedes defeat and promises never to return, he and his men can have safe passage back to their boats. And if you come over to my side, to your own kingdom's side . . . if you will be my friend again, I will give you back Northumberland. A third of England will be yours.'

Now Tostig answered. 'You offer me generous terms, so why be so niggardly towards King Harald? He destroyed Edwin and Morcar's armies. He has not been defeated. It seems a strange time to surrender. Surely he should get some land at the very least.'

'All right then, he can have land . . . six feet of good English soil in which to lay his bones. No, wait, he's a big man. Make it seven feet.'

'You mock me, Harold, and you mock the king. Be careful, brother. One of these days your arrogance will get you killed.'

Tostig rode back to where Hardrada was waiting and relayed the conversation.

'Cocky bastard. I would have killed him there and then,' Hardrada said.

'He had come to parley, so to kill him would have been

murder,' Tostig replied. Then a piercing sadness seemed to cut deep into his soul as he finally accepted the truth of what Harold had said. Their parents would be mortified to know that they were about to fight to the death. He sighed and glanced at Hardrada. 'If one of us has to die, then I'd rather Harold killed me.'

Across the river, Harold had returned to the main body of his army.

Tostig saw him conferring briefly with his senior commanders and noticed that his younger brother Gyrth was among them. Gyrth had turned his horse so that he was looking directly across the river.

He's looking for me, Tostig realised.

Then the moment passed as an order was relayed through the English army and they started moving, slowly at first but with gathering speed, charging towards the river and the Norwegian shield wall guarding the bridge.

7

The fighting was hard, the casualties numerous. The Norsemen held their ground and fought with unstinting courage. But the sheer press of numbers was just too heavy, the odds too great. The wall cracked and then broke. Suddenly the Norse soldiers who had stood firm for so long were running for the bridge.

The first English horsemen were close on their tails. One man urged his mount onto the narrow wooden roadway and began to make his way across, eager to get at the fleeing Norsemen in front of him.

But then one of the Vikings, a huge man who wore no helmet, so that the tattoos on either side of his shaven skull could be seen, turned and faced back the way he had come. He let the last few of his comrades dash past to either side of him, like twigs in a stream racing by a large rock. Then he grinned, revealing a row of teeth filed to pin-sharp points. He carried no shield, for he needed both hands for the battleaxe he held in front of him, between his legs, with its head resting on the bridge floor and its handle reaching up past his waist.

He squared his shoulders, raised the huge axe behind his right shoulder and waited until the English horseman was practically upon him, then swung the double-headed blade at the horse's legs.

A terrible scream of animal agony pierced the clamour of battle as the swinging blade cut into the flesh and bone of the horse's left foreleg, snapping it in two.

The wounded beast collapsed onto the bridge, trapping its

rider beneath it as it thrashed about in a frenzy of pain and confusion.

More Englishmen rushed forward, on foot now. Taking care to stay away from the wildly kicking hooves, two of them dragged the badly wounded rider clear while a third ran to the back of the horse's neck, crouched down so the beast itself was acting as a barricade between him and the giant Norseman, and sawed through the dying animal's throat, spraying blood across the planking, until the horse was finally released from its anguish and the flailing legs fell still.

More Englishmen advanced across the bridge. For a moment there was a stalemate as the massed attackers confronted the single Norseman over the horse's corpse. Together the English would surely be a match for one man, no matter how fearsome he looked. But every soldier there knew that the first one who made a move would almost certainly be throwing his life away.

Then one of the Englishmen muttered, 'Fuck this,' clambered up the animal's flanks and literally threw himself at the Norseman.

Everyone could see that he was trying to get right up close to the Viking before he had time to swing the axe, for once men were fighting hand-to-hand and there was no room to swing a fist, let alone a long-handled weapon, an axe became worse than useless.

It was a perfectly reasonable idea. It just happened not to work.

The Norseman moved far too fast. His axe flashed through the air in a blur of cold blood-coated steel and left the Englishman on the floor, screaming almost as loudly as the horse had done as his guts spilled out of the great rent in his belly onto the wood beneath him.

But his sacrifice was not entirely in vain. For the time that it took the Norseman to kill his attacker, though no more than a couple of heartbeats, was enough for another three or four men to get over the horse and advance on him, forcing him back across the bridge.

Two more Englishmen went down beneath the scything axe, but still the rest pushed forward. Then a fourth man died and the Norseman picked up his body, lifted it over his head and threw it at the oncoming English. For a moment their advance was halted as they disentangled themselves from the dead man's arms and legs, and that gave the Norseman time to steady himself, take a side-on position, with his left shoulder facing the enemy, raise his axe and then swing it backhanded round in front of him. As he did so, he moved his right foot forward, bringing his other shoulder round, so that now he was side-on again, leading with the right leg this time, and bringing the axe back the other way.

The English fell back as the Norseman advanced, his axe and body and feet moving in the rhythm of a dance of death.

In the meadow on the far side of the river, Hardrada had finally formed his shield wall and was taking advantage of the delay to Harold's advance by bringing its two ends round to meet one another in a circle. He planted the Landwaster banner at the centre and stood beside it, with his finest axemen all around him.

Tostig stood at Hardrada's left, so that if they found themselves in hand-to-hand combat, he would be guarding the king's blindside.

'So now there is nothing for it but to stand and fight,' said Hardrada. 'We will stay here, and may all the gods, ancient and Christian, grant that we will still be here when the reinforcements arrive.'

* * *

500

On the riverbank where the English were now massed, unable to get across the bridge, a crafty soul spotted a small rowing boat, little more than a coracle, pulled up onto the bank. He gestured to one of his comrades to come over to the boat with him, and they launched it into the river and headed towards the bridge.

Up above, two men forced their way through the press of bodies carrying spears, thrown earlier by the charging horsemen, that they had picked up from the battlefield.

Now they could jab at the Norseman from beyond the range of his axe, and the English could gather themselves and move forward again behind the stabbing spears . . . until the Norseman snapped both their shafts within a matter of seconds, reducing them to kindling and regaining the upper hand.

Underneath the bridge, the man who had spotted the boat started hacking away at the plank above his head, while his pal used the oars against the stream to keep the little craft in place.

More men with spears came forward. The Norsemen could not break them all and was forced to inch backwards. Even so, none of the men confronting him had yet got past the relentless swing of his blade, and plenty more had died trying or been horribly maimed.

'Almost there,' the man beneath the bridge muttered. He could see a chink of daylight through the planking. A few more scrapes and there was a definite hole. He started jabbing the point of his sword directly upwards, trying to force it all the way through.

The Norseman took another step back, turned his left shoulder to face the enemy and planted his right foot behind him . . .

. . . just as the jabbing sword burst through the last splinters of wood that had been restraining it, pierced the planking and kept going upwards, planting itself in the Norseman's heel and cutting right through his Achilles tendon.

The giant warrior howled in agony almost as loudly and piercingly as the horse he had butchered. His leg gave way beneath him. He fell to the ground. The English leaped forward, piercing the Norseman's unprotected body with a dozen spearheads.

The bridge was taken. The dead horse was unceremoniously dumped in the river. The entire English army made its way over to the far side, where the remains of Harald's force awaited, a fraction of the full army with which he had first landed on English soil.

8

The riders sent by Harald Hardrada arrived at Riccall and gave the news of their countrymen's plight. Ostein Orre at once took command.

He shouted orders to the men to put on their armour and start running.

'Don't wait for anyone else. The moment you're ready, just go!'

Prince Olaf turned to get his gear, but Orre grabbed him by the shoulder. 'No, my lord, you must stay here.'

'I have to go. I have to be by my father's side.'

'No, you have to guard your father's bloodline. You are his legacy. Whatever happens to him, he has to know that you are alive and well. And someone still has to guard the ships. You keep five hundred men. I will take the rest.'

Olaf could not argue. He knew that Orre was right. And so he had to stand and watch in impotent frustration as one after another, thousands of desperate Norsemen ran down the road, praying that they would not be too late.

Hardrada knew that his men could not go on the attack. Their only hope was to remain where they were, a bristling mass of shields and spears, like a giant human hedgehog. So they waited as the English formed up opposite them in a configuration like a crescent moon that curved around the front half of their circular arrangement.

In truth, both sides were glad of a break. The English had

marched from dawn to early afternoon and then gone straight into battle. The Norwegians had suffered for their lack of armour. With no bodily protection against blades, clubs or arrows, far more men had been killed or seriously wounded than if they had worn their chain-mail coats. Even men who had received glancing blows to their limbs or torso were bloodied and bruised.

Finally the battle resumed. The English advanced, on foot this time, marching right around Hardrada's men to completely encircle them. Now the killing began again, a brutal accounting of men slaying and slain. But with a larger army to begin with, and his men all fully protected, Harold knew that the tally would always be in his favour.

As the Norse dead piled up, their circular shield wall constricted and the remaining men were crammed into a tighter and tighter space.

Through it all, Hardrada's impatience grew. It was against his nature to stand anywhere but the front line when the fighting was at its height. Nor could he bear to do nothing as his enemy inexorably tightened its grip.

It was a hot day, and even strong, fit men found it hard to run in full armour. But Ostein Orre would not let them rest, or even stop for a moment to catch their breath. He drove them on mercilessly, shouting that however much they might be suffering, their comrades at Stamford Bridge were surely suffering more. They could still save the day. But they had to get there in time.

One man simply collapsed from heat exhaustion, and was left lying by the side of the road as the others kept going. Another man dropped . . . and another, but still Orre would not allow them any respite.

They had to get there in time.

Harold had brought a small number of archers with him. There were not enough of them to fill the air with the deadly swarms that could stop an entire army in its tracks. But they maintained a steady stream of arrows that picked off one Norseman here, another there, and affected and distracted far more than they hit, for every man looking up at the sky knew that without any armour to protect him, he had to raise his shield against the falling arrows or risk a dart that cut deep into his flesh.

Harald's shield was already studded with feathered shafts, whose points were buried in its wood. He was infuriated by the drip, drip, drip of death from the sky, as a great bull might be enraged by wasp stings in his hide. Finally he lost patience. He felt the berserker spirit rising in him, that fighting madness so glorified by the Vikings, for it was displayed by a man who had thrown away the caution and calculation of everyday life, abandoned himself entirely to the Fates and wanted only to kill his enemies until they were all defeated, or they had killed him first.

With a wordless roar of defiance, he threw away his shield and plunged into the melee in front of him.

Hardrada cut a swathe through the enemy host. His axe decapitated with a single blow, lopped limbs off bodies, left men clutching at great blood-oozing rents in their bellies through which their intestines slithered. His one-man charge was so devastating that his enemies backed away. English soldiers who had marvelled at the Norseman on the bridge now discovered that even he was dwarfed by his king. For an instant Hardrada found himself alone and isolated, with no one in range of his axe.

He looked around. He saw the fear in the eyes of the men who confronted him. He knew that every one of them dreaded the possibility that he might be the next to stand in the giant king's way. Hardrada squared his shoulders, puffed out his chest, raised his chin and was about to shout out once again when he saw a flicker of black in the corner of his eye.

The arrow struck him in the throat. It tore through blood vessels and windpipe. He fell like a great oak, crashing stone dead to the ground.

Now it was the English who roared. The enemy's king was dead. There could only be one outcome now. The killing intensified until the only men left were the remnants of Hardrada's elite corps of axemen, grouped around Landwaster with Tostig at their centre.

Harold strode forward to the front of his line. His coat was torn and bloodied, his face smeared with gore and grime. He called out, 'Lay down your arms, I beg you. You have fought with honour. No man on earth can say that you did not acquit yourselves well. Yield now and I promise you safe passage to your ships. You too, brother. The king you swore to follow is dead. Your duty dies with him. Yield, please, I beg you.'

No one said a word as all eyes turned towards Tostig. He looked at Harold. 'God bless you, brother. Send our mother my love. But my answer is no. I will not yield.'

Thus they fought, and died, every man of them.

Tostig was among the very last to be killed, fighting till his dying breath.

When it was over, the English slumped to the ground, shattered, or stood bent over, their hands on their knees, trying to regain their breath.

And then a cry rang out.

'More of them . . . Christ Almighty, here are more of them!'

If Ostein Orre had been able to get his men just a little closer to the battlefield before they were spotted, he might have taken

Harold's army completely by surprise and turned a total defeat into a stunning victory.

If they had not had to run quite so far, Orre's men might have had the energy to fight with even greater determination.

As it was, their first frenzied assault, which wreaked havoc among men who were themselves giving in to their fatigue and feeling the sudden loss of power that came when the fear and excitement of battle had ebbed, almost carried the day. But Harold rallied his men for one last, gargantuan effort. The hastily assembled English line bent, but it did not break. Then the English established parity, which became superiority and that only renewed the letting of Norwegian blood. Orre was killed, as were most of his senior officers.

An English soldier caught a glimpse of a silver chain around the neck of Ostein Orre's corpse. He reached down and revealed the silver locket in which the lock of Princess Maria's hair had been placed. The soldier took the trouble to take Orre's helmet off, so that he could ease the chain over his head without snapping it. No sense in damaging valuable property. There'd be a woman somewhere willing to trade her body for that bauble, he was sure of it.

Only when night fell were a few survivors able to flee away under cover of darkness, and with them ended two hundred and fifty years of Viking invasions.

Tostig's body was recovered from the heaps of corpses that scattered the killing field and taken to be buried in honour at York.

Hardrada's corpse went with Harold and his men to Riccall. It was given to Prince Olaf, who was also allowed twenty-four of his father's three hundred ships in which to take his men back to Norway. So few had survived that the ships were quite sufficient for the task.

507

Hardrada's treasure, however, stayed in England and was taken to York to be kept in the safe keeping of Archbishop Ealdred. The decision caused outrage among Harold's men, who felt that they had fought long and hard and deserved their share of the booty.

Many deserted the army there and then. Others drifted away, arguing that they had served as much as their duty required and it was now time for other men to take their turn.

The army that Harold set marching back to the south was thus smaller and in less good spirits than it should have been, given the scale of the triumph of Stamford Bridge.

Nor did it have any support from Edwin or Morcar. Their forces had been torn apart at Foul Ford, of course, but Harold had pleaded with them to raise more. Mercia and Northumbria comprised half of all England; there were plenty more men to be had.

The two brother earls, however, dragged their feet. They promised that they would come south with reinforcements as soon as they could, but refused to specify a date.

'They're not coming, are they?' said Gyrth to Harold as they rode their weary horses down the road from York.

'I'm not sure,' the king replied. 'They're trying to play this to their best advantage. I dare say they reckon they'll win whatever happens. If I beat William, everything carries on as before, although they will do better if they've been part of the victory. If I lose and they haven't fought alongside me, they probably think they can make a deal with William. He can have the south of England if they have the north – something like that.'

'Will he agree to that?'

'Never. William will take one look at those two sons of Aelfgar and know that they'll never be a match for him. He'll crush them without a second thought.' Harold managed a weary smile. 'Unless we crush him first, of course.'

'I just wish he'd get on with it and invade. He must be as sick of waiting as we are.'

Harold did not reply. But in the end he did not need to. They were still a day north of London when the message reached them.

'The Normans have landed at Pevensey, Your Majesty. Duke William is in England.'

9

The Dives estuary, the port of Saint-Valéry and the English Channel, August–September 1066

The waiting had been no easier for William than Harold. The majority of his men were not Normans, bound to him by oaths of fealty, but mercenaries attracted by the booty that could be had by ravaging a kingdom as rich as England. William found himself promising more and more land to the commanders of the various groups within his army. Soon it was clear that it would not be enough just to take the crown from the English. He would have to take all their estates and everything in them as well.

Finally, with the summer over and William fearing that he might have to face the unconscionable humiliation of disbanding his invasion force and beaching all his ships without so much as seeing the shoreline of England, the wind changed.

It was the morning of 12 September. William was woken by Fitz dashing into his tent shouting, 'Come outside!' and then, as the duke was still struggling to his feet, 'Look at the banners, Your Grace. Just look at the banners!'

It took William a second to get the point. Banners, flags, pennants, even laundry pegged to the washerwomen's lines that had been blowing in one direction for weeks on end had suddenly, as if by magic, turned round the opposite way.

'Dear God,' he gasped. 'A south wind.'

His first reaction was to fall to his knees and offer up a prayer of thanks. Then he got up and immediately started barking orders. The ships had to be manned and fully loaded with crews, soldiers, animals, supplies and all the baggage that was going with them to England, so that when the tide turned, the ebbing waters would help carry the fleet out to sea.

The men set to work with a will. At long last the endless weeks of delay and inactivity were over. Everyone was filled with optimism, excitement and energy as they packed up their gear, lowered their tents and started the tricky business of getting every single human, animal and piece of baggage onto the correct vessel.

Somehow the task was accomplished. The fleet set sail, aiming for Bulverhythe, the port that served the town of Hastings on the Sussex coast. Both port and town stood on land that King Edward had given to Fécamp Abbey, in Normandy, so William would be landing on the safest, or rather the least unsafe, ground in southern England. The monks had also been able to provide him with advice about the local coastline, describing prominent landmarks and other harbours to aim for if he could not for some reason land at Bulverhythe.

First, though, his navigators had to find their way across the water. Their first target was the headland of Cap d'Antifer, just beyond the mouth of the River Seine. If they aimed for that landmark and then just kept going on precisely the same bearing, they should hit the shore of England very close to Hastings. Now that they were at sea, William was struck, and made a little uneasy, by the extreme contrast between vessels such as the *Mora* that were built along Viking lines and could, if required, cover the vast expanses of ocean over which the great Scandinavian explorers had roamed, and the very basic transport ships whose sole purpose was to make this one voyage, from Normandy to England.

He looked up at the blue sky and felt the fresh southerly breeze on his face. As long as the weather stayed this balmy, all would be well.

But God preserve those floating buckets if the wind started to really blow.

And then the wind shifted from the south to the west. It rose in intensity. It whipped up the waves and drove rain into the faces of mariners, passengers and animals alike. For this was the storm that hit the English ships that were heading for home just as the enemy they had so long awaited was heading for them.

There was nothing to do but run with the wind. It was every man for himself, for when a gale like this blew, a fleet ceased to be a cohesive unit and became a collection of individual ships, each fighting its own battle for survival.

Many a vessel did not survive. Some were lost at sea. Many were driven back to Normandy, to founder on rocks and beaches. Others searched for safe havens along the coast. And some, whose captains had the same low opinion of voyages in autumn or winter weather as their English counterparts, just cut and ran for the ports of northern France or the Low Countries from which they originally came.

At daybreak, the scattered fleet began to reassemble itself at the harbour of Saint-Valéry, the largest and safest haven on that stretch of the coast, which lay at the mouth of the Somme. Hour by hour they came in dribs and drabs as William stood at the water's edge desperately hoping that the pitiful tally of ships with which he had begun the day would be much greater by the close.

In the end, it took three days for the final stragglers to arrive. By that time it was clear that William had lost around one in four of all his ships. The one crumb of comfort was that most of the losses had been inflicted on the smaller boats, which carried fewer men and horses, so that his army was less reduced than it might have been.

'We've still lost as many men as we would have done in a major battle,' said Fitz, who had barely slept in three days and nights as he tried to create an orderly encampment at an entirely unexpected location.

'Yes, we were beaten by King Neptune,' William agreed. 'But we'll still beat King Harold.'

As the next week went by, William began to wonder whether he had not tempted fate with such blithe confidence. The weather that had been so benign during the long weeks on the River Dives now turned decisively for the worse. It rained incessantly, and the damp was made even worse by the chill wind that blew, once again, unceasingly from the north. The colder and wetter his men became, the more miserable they felt and the lower their morale dropped.

Matters were only made worse by the evident truth that there were fewer men and horses now than there had been before the storm. William sent parties of his most trustworthy men foraging up and down the coast, searching not for food or wine but for dead bodies, washed ashore along with the wreckage from their ships. It was bad enough for the army to know that men were missing, but if there were bloated grey corpses in clear sight of the survivors, discontent might turn to outright mutiny.

In desperation, he sought divine assistance. The local church contained the mortal remains of St Valery, a monk who had travelled to the area centuries earlier to convert the local people from their pagan beliefs to Christianity. William ordered the casket containing the saint's relics to be brought out of the church and placed upon a mat outside. He then called for charitable donations to be made in the saint's honour, leading the way with a purse of his own gold. Fitz, Odo, Rob and the other members of the ducal entourage made equally splendid, very public contributions. Soon soldiers of every rank were flinging coins onto the mat, until it was entirely covered in money.

The following morning, 27 September, the weathervane on top of the church tower had turned. The wind was once again blowing from the south, ready to carry the fleet to England.

William went back into the church for one last heartfelt prayer. 'Dear God, who has through His Holiness Pope Alexander given me, your servant, your divine blessing for this expedition, please grant that by your divine providence we may sail safely to England. Keep the storms at bay and distract the English, so that they may not be aware of our coming, or attack us while we are at sea. For thine is the kingdom, the power and the glory. Amen.'

He crossed himself before the altar and left the church. Barely had he stepped back out into the open than he was barking orders. 'Fitz! Tell the captains there has to be at least one lantern on every ship. They're to hang it from the mast so that we can spot one another. We're going to be at sea all night. I don't want our ships losing touch like they did during the storm.'

All the vessels were reloaded and for a second time the fleet set sail on the ebb tide. This time William's prayer was answered, for the wind blew steadily from the south, providing enough breeze to keep the ships moving, yet not so much that the sea was made rough. The *Mora* in particular made good speed, for she had the biggest sail in the fleet and her hull was well shaped and finely crafted. Though he had never before undertaken a voyage of this length, William found that the sea held no fears for him, nor did the motion of the boat make him as ill as it did some of his companions.

He would not, in truth, have cared if he had spent the entire voyage spilling his guts over the side of the boat. They were on the water, sailing for England, and that was all that mattered.

10

The Channel, and Pevensey, Sussex, 28 September 1066

Duke William slept well and woke just before dawn, looking forward to his breakfast. Glancing around, he saw that the sail had been furled and the boat was virtually motionless. That was to be expected. There was no point sailing hard through the dark. There was no knowing what one might hit. He contentedly turned his thoughts back to what he wanted for breakfast. But his good mood was short-lived.

The ship's captain, Stephen FitzAirard, hurried over as soon as he saw the duke opening his eyes and propping himself up on his elbows. 'We have a slight problem, Your Grace,' he said.

'What kind of problem?'

'We can't spot the rest of the fleet. In fact, we can't find any of it.'

'That's impossible. There's a lantern at the top of the mast. It must have been visible for leagues in every direction.'

'Yes, Your Grace, I'm sure it was. But no one else is anywhere near us now.'

'Have you sent anyone up the mast? You'd see a lot further from there.'

'I was waiting for first light, Your Grace.' FitzAirard looked towards the eastern horizon, where the grey clouds were being lit by the first pink rays of the rising sun. 'I'll send someone right away.'

An oarsman shinned up the mast, clung to the very top and looked around. 'Nothing!' he shouted back down.

'What about England?' FitzAirard shouted back. 'Can you see the coast? Look for a line of white cliffs.'

'No . . . just water everywhere, and nothing else but us on it.'

William could sense the nerves tightening around him. There was nothing whatever he could do to make ships appear out of nowhere, but he could at least set the other men an example. He ordered a hearty breakfast and plenty of spiced wine to warm him on a chilly morning at sea. The sight of their duke appearing so untroubled seemed to calm the other men, and they ate and drank too.

When William had finished his meal, he ordered the lookout to be sent back up the mast. At first he reported the same as before: 'Nothing!'

But then, just as even William was beginning to feel anxious, the man called down, 'Hang on . . . think I see something. Wait . . . Yes! I see ships . . . four masts to the south-east.'

A cheer rang out from the men massed on the deck down below. Then the lookout said, 'I can see more masts now . . . Great God Almighty, there's a whole forest of them!'

Soon the *Mora* had resumed her position at the head of the fleet, leading the way to England. A short while later, the long-awaited white cliffs were sighted.

'The monks at Fécamp say that we should make for the tallest of all the cliffs. There is a large beach to the right of it, as we are looking from the sea, and a peaceful bay beyond,' William said.

'They're talking about Beau Chef, Your Grace,' said FitzAirard. 'Every man who sails these waters knows it. There's a little town thereabouts called Pevensey.'

'Big enough to have a garrison?'

'Lord no, Your Grace. There's a lot of marshland round here that they use for salt pans. So there's a few salt merchants, and

516

cattle farmers too. But you won't get any trouble. A nice little spot to come ashore, I'd say.'

'I'd rather land at Hastings. Can you get us there?'

FitzAirard looked up at the sail, which was nicely filled by a decent breeze, then back at the coastline. He was obviously trying to work out how long it would take to get there at their current rate.

'No, reckon not,' he said, as much to himself as William. 'High water's at noon, and if we don't come ashore today as the rising tide's carrying us in, we'll have to wait for the next one tomorrow.'

'Can't you reach the shore if the tide's going out?' William asked.

'Not without risking every ship in the fleet, Your Grace. Steering's much harder against the tide. And there's a lot of nasty rocks around these cliffs. Even the best skippers could easily founder. Should get you into Pevensey all right, though, provided the wind doesn't drop or change direction.'

'Then I'll let you get back to work. The hell with the wind, FitzAirard. Get us on land today . . . or be ready to face my anger.'

FitzAirard was spared his duke's wrath. The fleet rode in on the tide and landed on the long shingle beach. As they were approaching landfall, William could see a sandy spur that projected out into the natural harbour, from which rose the semi-ruined walls that had once surrounded a massive ancient fort. With water on three sides, it made a perfect defensive position, so by the time he came ashore, William already knew that his first new wooden castle would be erected within the outline of the old one. And as the sun set on the first day of the invasion, a low mound had been raised and the first beams and palisades of the new fort, pre-fabricated in Normandy, were already in position.

The army feasted that night on cattle, swine and sheep that foraging parties had killed, and seafood of all kinds seized from the local fishermen. The army had also raided the village of Pevensey and every farm in the local area and seized all the girls and women to be used as servants. 'But not whores,' William insisted. 'There aren't nearly enough of them, and it will only cause trouble if one man in a hundred has had his way with a woman and the other ninety-nine have not.'

Scouting parties had been sent out and reported that there was a Roman road, presumably laid down as the castle was being built, that headed westwards to a town called Lewes. Other than that, there were tracks that wound around the shoreline of Pevensey harbour, which comprised two separate inlets, one much wider than the other, cutting into the coastline like two arms of a capital letter V.

The smaller, but similarly shaped Bulverhythe harbour lay to the east of Pevensey, with Hastings beyond it.

'I want to get us to Hastings as fast as possible,' William said.

'These harbours are a damn nuisance,' said Fitz. 'It's no distance at all by sea, but the tracks around the harbours wind around so much that they're three or four times as long.'

'Then we should get started as soon as we can. Tell the men that they are free to take whatever they want or need from whomsoever they choose. We need every scrap of food we can get. So take the animals from every field, empty every barn, strip every vegetable patch.'

'The people will suffer terribly.'

William glowered at Fitz. 'Yes, that's the point.'

11

*The Essex village of Waltham, the Sussex town
of Hastings and the royal palace of Westminster,
early October 1066*

King Harold was shattered. He had reached that point of
exhaustion when sleep becomes impossible, for the mind is so
agitated that it cannot allow the body the rest it so desperately
needs. His was more than physical fatigue, however. His nerves,
stretched almost to breaking point by the unrelenting tension of
the weeks spent waiting for William, had been tightened still
further by the sudden shock of Hardrada's arrival.

The king had bullied and cajoled his men into covering the
distance between London and York at extraordinary speed. He
had then flung them, without any break from their march, into
one of the bloodiest battles that Britain had ever seen. The
victory over Hardrada had been a triumph that should have
been followed by feasting, jubilation and celebration in every
corner of the realm.

Instead, all Harold could offer his loyal, equally bone-weary
housecarls was more marching and the prospect of even heavier
fighting to come.

He had to find some respite, just a short, blessed interlude
between one fight to the death and the next. So while his army
marched on into London, he stopped for a few hours' prayer
and contemplation at a church in the Essex village of Waltham
that contained an ancient stone statue, encased in silver, of Jesus
on the Cross. It was known as the Holy Rood and was said to

have miraculous powers, and Harold had grown up with the story of how, when he himself was a very small boy, the statue had cured him of a paralysis that had gripped his entire body.

In one of their periods of friendship, King Edward had given Harold the estate of Waltham and Harold had then paid for the rebuilding of the church, and staffed it with a dean and a college of twelve priests. The Holy Rood took pride of place above the altar, before which he now knelt to pray.

When at last he had finished, he got to his feet and bowed to the altar. As he turned to walk back down the aisle, with his eyes now fixed on the door, the statue bowed its head in turn.

Harold did not see what had happened. But as soon as the door had closed behind him, the priests who had been in attendance as he prayed gasped in awe and rushed across to look at the statue. Its head was still bowed, and miraculously, the silver was as smooth as if it had always been shaped that way.

'It's a miracle!' breathed one of the priests.

'It must be a good omen,' said another. 'Our Saviour is acknowledging the king and giving him his blessing.'

'You think it good?' asked a third, sceptically. 'If Our Lord hangs his head, surely he does so in sorrow. I fear he is bidding him farewell in this life, to meet again in the next.'

While Harold was marching south, a Norman resident of England had been writing to William. Robert FitzWimark had come to England with the future King Edward in 1041, and his many years of loyal service had been rewarded with a fine estate at Theydon Bois and the posts of Sheriff of Essex and High Officer of the Royal Palace of Westminster. The truest sign of FitzWimark's status as a favourite of the king had been his presence at the royal deathbed, but his career had not died along with his royal patron, for his evident decency and good sense had made Harold trust him and rely on his council just as much as Edward had done.

FitzWimark was also a distant kinsman of William of Normandy, and so, fearing the bloodshed and public disorder that a war on English soil would surely bring, he took it upon himself to act as an honest broker between the two warring sides by writing to the invader. And as Harold was praying in Waltham church, William, who had by now based himself in Hastings, along with his army and fleet, was reading that letter.

'He bids me good health and so forth,' said the duke, scanning the text while Fitz and the other close advisers looked on. 'Huh! This is interesting . . . He says that the Norsemen invaded the north of England, that Harold marched up there, fell upon them, taking them completely by surprise, and won a mighty victory.'

'When was that?' Fitz asked.

'About ten days ago, by the sound of it. Anyway, Harold is now feeling buoyed up by his success and is marching south with a massive army, all well equipped for war, and I have no chance because – damn FitzWimark for his impudence! – my army is nothing more than a pack of mongrel dogs. So, he says, I should stay behind my defences, because if I don't, I'll get into trouble that I can't get out of. Well, I'm not standing for that . . . Someone fetch my scribe.'

Moments later, a monk was busy setting up a folding table and stool. He laid out his pen, a bottle of ink and a roll of parchment, and William began. 'Tell my kinsman that I thank him for his advice, but wish that he had not put it with such rudeness and disrespect. Tell him further that I do not intend to follow that advice. I am not going to hide away. I intend to fight Harold – and make that plain "Harold", not "King Harold" – at the soonest possible opportunity. I have an army of sixty thousand men, but I would be just as eager if I only had ten thousand . . . That'll do it.'

He leaned over the monk and looked down at the parchment. 'Now, where do I sign?'

'But we have only got ten thousand men,' said Rob, when the monk had taken the signed letter away to give to FitzWimark's messenger.

'Absolutely,' William agreed. 'But there's no need for Godwinson to know that.'

The following day, still unaware that FitzWimark was corresponding with William, Harold briefed a courier with a message of his own.

'You may tell the Duke of Normandy that I cannot think of any just or lawful reason why he should be in my kingdom. Remind him that any claim he may have had to the throne disappeared when King Edward named me as his successor on his deathbed. Inform him that ever since St Augustine first arrived on English soil, a deathbed bequest has been considered sacred and unbreakable. Say that the right of the Witenagemot to choose the King of England is equally sacred, and that in naming me, the assembly overruled any previous claims to the throne by the duke or anyone else. Express my sorrow that he should have broken our pact of friendship by landing here. Tell him of my outrage and fury at the devastation he is wreaking on my land in Sussex. Farms have been utterly destroyed, herds wiped out, buildings torn down or burnt. Within the past few days I have heard of castles being built by him on my land. Assure him that I will insist on due reparations for the damage he has caused and that all his castles will be demolished. In short, I give him this simple choice. He must leave this kingdom with all his followers at once, or face the consequences. It's up to him.'

On hearing Harold's message, William appointed a personal envoy, a monk called Hugh Margot, who, though Norman, spoke fluent English. He dictated a long reply to Harold, pointing out yet again that Edward had made him his heir, in front of witnesses, and that Harold himself had sworn to uphold that claim and be William's vassal. 'If he thinks he's in the right, let him test that belief in court. I am willing to have this whole matter judged and I don't care if it's in Norman or English law. And if he fears to stand and make his case in court, let him stand and face me on the battlefield, in single combat. I will fight to the death knowing that God is on my side and will give me the strength to win.'

'Will he accept either of those two offers?' Bishop Odo asked.

'Of course not, brother. But they will make me the man who was willing to put his reputation on trial in court and his life on trial in battle, and Harold will be the coward who ran away from both. Oh, and Margot, there is something else you should tell this English pretender . . .'

12

The royal palace of Westminster

'You're lying . . . you have to be.' Harold's voice, normally so confident, was little more than a croak. His face was white with shock. 'Excommunication? Are you sure?'

'Yes, Your Majesty, there is no doubt about it. The Pope issued a papal bull some months ago, excommunicating you, Archbishop Stigand and all who follow you. This means that you are shut out, exiled from the community of Christ, which is to say the Church and all true Christians. You are forbidden from administering or receiving the sacraments, so that you may not attend Mass, still less take Communion. Should you die, you may not receive a Christian burial, not be laid to rest on hallowed ground.'

Harold stared at Margot through bloodshot eyes set in the deep black hollows of extreme fatigue. 'But how could I be excommunicated without even knowing about it? Why was I not allowed to mount a defence?'

He reached for a nearby flagon of wine, and as he filled his goblet, his hands were shaking.

Margot watched the king's nerves fraying before his eyes. 'That is not for me to say, Your Majesty. As to why you did not know, I imagine that the events of recent months have made it very hard to bring news to your country. But you should not be in any doubt as to the truth of my story. Should you ever face His Grace the Duke of Normandy on the battlefield, you will see that he fights beneath a sacred papal banner emblazoned with St Peter's keys. On his finger His Grace wears a ring containing a hair from St Peter's head. His brother, Bishop Odo, is in possession of the papal bull itself.'

'Then the bull is not valid,' blustered Harold, desperately trying to regain the upper hand. He took a hefty swig of wine, wiped his mouth and pointed his finger at Margot. 'Why, I was praying for hours in church – a church I endowed, mark you – just a few days ago. God did not strike me down. In fact, I've heard tell that as I left, the sacred statue of Jesus that hangs above the altar bowed its head to acknowledge me.'

'Was that what it was doing?' asked Margot. 'I should say Our Redeemer was hanging His head in shame to have the sanctity of His church defiled by your presence.'

'Get out!' roared Harold. 'Get out!'

As Margot turned and walked away, Harold shouted after him, 'And you may tell your master that my faith in God's mercy is unbroken. He will have his battle, and it will be between armies, not single men. I will bring my might to bear against his, in the sight of God, and let God decide whose cause is most just!'

Once again, Gyrth found himself cast as the naysayer. It went against his nature. Of all Earl Godwin's sons, he had always been the one who got on with everyone, without becoming involved in the arguments and trials of strength that split the other brothers. He did not particularly seek the power that Sweyn, Harold and Tostig had all craved, and so none of them saw him as a rival, let alone a threat to their ambitions. Now, though, he had to find a way to rein Harold in and dissuade him from acting rashly and leading them all to disaster.

'Harold, Your Majesty, please . . . don't rush into anything. Take your time. You're tired. The army – what's left of it – is exhausted. The horses are all on their last legs. There's nothing to be gained by charging off to fight the Bastard. Let him sweat. Let his men get hungry – they must have stripped the country around them bare by now. And let us get more men, fresh men, and make sure that when we go to meet William, we do so with overwhelming force.'

Harold laughed as he poured more wine and drank it greedily. Gyrth was reminded of someone. It took him a second to realise that he was thinking of Sweyn, and then he felt a stab of fear in his guts. If Harold was heading down the same road as their eldest brother, his journey would have no happy ending.

'Poor old Gyrth,' Harold mocked. 'When did you suddenly become a coward?'

Gyrth took a step forward, but Leofwine restrained him as Harold went on, '"Don't go! Don't go! It's bound to be a disaster!" That's what you said before we marched off to face Hardrada. And what happened?' He stroked his chin in an exaggerated imitation of a man searching his memory. 'Oh yes, that's right . . . We won the greatest victory this kingdom has seen since the days of Alfred the Great.'

'We were lucky,' Gyrth said. 'We surprised Hardrada with half his army missing and his men not wearing their mail coats. If he'd faced us with his full force, properly armed and prepared, God knows what might have happened. As it is, we left four thousand men lying dead in a field in Yorkshire. We won't get away with it a second time.'

'Get away with what?' asked Harold, advancing to within a couple of paces of his brother, leaning his head forward aggressively as he approached.

'Rushing things, not planning or preparing, just marching into battle hoping for the best. Look . . . Your Majesty . . . time is on our side. The longer we wait, the stronger we become and the weaker William's position is. We should take the Roman general Fabian as our model. We can defeat the Bastard without fighting a battle, or weaken him to the point where he is bound to lose.

'If he marches north, towards London, we strip the country ahead of him of every grain of corn and every fish, fowl or four-legged animal. We harass him all the way, constant raids and skirmishes, whittling down his army in ones and twos. If he wants to sail away, well, good luck doing it at this time of year. And in any case, we've got a fleet of our own. If we—'

'Enough!' Harold slammed his fist onto the table, knocking his goblet over in the process. 'I don't need a lecture on Fabian. Nor do I have any intention of letting those damn Normans cause more damage to my kingdom. In any case, there's a better option. We all know the land around Hastings, God knows we have enough estates in that part of the world. Look . . .'

He dipped a finger in the wine that he had just spilled and drew a rough triangle. 'The sea is here,' he said, pointing at the bottom edge of the triangle, 'with Hastings just here.' He jabbed a finger onto a point about one third of the way along that line.

'Then you've got Bulverhythe harbour on one side and the Brede estuary on the other. So their position is virtually surrounded by water except for a narrow neck of land at the top, with hills and woods on either side and only one road – one! – leading out towards the rest of England. If we put a decent force of men across that road, they'll be like a cork in a bottle. William will know he can't go back to sea, for the reasons you've just given, Gyrth. And he can't stay where he is, because his army will starve if he does. So he will have to attack. And that's when we'll beat him.

'And apart from all that . . .' Harold took a deep breath, eyes closed, as he fought to keep his mind on track. 'Apart from that, he's destroying all the land for miles around: my land, with my people on it. If I'm not seen to be doing something to stop him, they will lose faith in me. What kind of a lord can't protect his own people? No, I have to fight him now.'

'*You* don't have to fight him. Even by your logic, all that matters is that someone has to bloody his nose, weaken his army, kill enough men to make a difference and leave the rest feeling more tired and bruised and hungry. I can do that. Let me go in your place.'

'You couldn't fight a battle against William of Normandy, brother. Well, you could fight him, but you couldn't beat him.'

'I know how to marshal a shield wall and I know how to wield a sword, and that'll be enough. It won't even matter if he wins the battle. So long as we kill one man of his for every man he kills of ours, we will win the war. We can always get more men. He can't. And even if he killed me, that wouldn't matter. All that matters is that he doesn't kill you.'

Harold said nothing. He took another drink.

'This is a game of chess,' Gyrth went on. 'The pawns can be sacrificed. The bishops, castles and knights can be sacrificed. Even the queen. But if the king dies, the game is lost.'

It was a powerful argument and every man in the chamber knew it. One did not need a deep knowledge of military strategy to appreciate Gyrth's argument. Common sense was enough.

Harold shook his head. 'You think time is on our side, eh, brother?'

Gyrth nodded.

Harold gave a rueful smile. 'I wish you were right. But sadly, you have left one crucial element out of your calculation.'

Now Gyrth frowned, trying to work out where he had gone wrong.

'Excommunication,' Harold said, providing the answer to the puzzle. 'If that blasted monk is right – and he sounded like a man who was entirely confident that he was telling the truth – then William has the blessing of the Pope.'

'Well, of course he does,' Stigand interjected. 'Pope Alexander – Anselm of Badagio as he used to be – studied under Lanfranc of Pavia at Bec Abbey in Normandy. Lanfranc poses as an academic, with nothing on his mind but the glory of learning for its own sake, but trust me, he's as greedy for power and glory as any man in Christendom. He would have no trouble persuading Alexander to show favour to Duke William, if William had shown favour to him first . . . Ha!'

Stigand gave a dry, sardonic cackle as a thought occurred to him. 'I'll wager he's promised Lanfranc the archbishopric of Canterbury. That conniving monk is coming after my job.'

'Much as William is coming after mine,' observed Harold pointedly. 'If the Normans break out from Hastings and get into the heart of England, carrying their papal banner and telling the people I've been excommunicated, then William will have God on his side, and that's worth another ten thousand men in his ranks. Men won't be willing to fight for me, because then they'll be excommunicated too.'

'It isn't quite that simple,' Stigand observed.

'It will seem simple enough to the common man. He'll see William on the side of God and me cast out of the Church altogether. I won't be able to fight that. You know I'm right, don't you?'

He looked around the room. 'Well, is there anyone here who disagrees? Do any of you think we can fight the Duchy of Normandy and the Kingdom of Heaven at the same time? No . . . ?'

'Good. Then we march south, we fight that usurping bastard and we show him who really has God on his side.'

13

The road to Hastings, 12–13 October 1066

Harold left London on Thursday 12 October and marched south-east. He had sent word out to the able-bodied men of Kent and Sussex, summoning them to present themselves on the evening of Friday the 13th at the hoar apple tree at the top of Caldbec Hill, a well-known landmark that stood at a junction where several tracks met, and beneath whose spreading branches sessions of the local court were sometimes held.

Beside the king rode his brothers Gyrth and Leofwine, but few of the other great nobles of England had made their presence felt. Edwin and Morcar had not come south, nor even sent any men in their place. The Godwinsons had their own troops, however, and the ever-reliable royal housecarls provided the army with the reassuring presence of men whose whole lives were dedicated to professional soldiery. Alongside them were levies of the fyrd from corners of the kingdom as far afield as Devon and Cornwall on the one hand, and London on the other, alongside fighting monks from abbeys in Peterborough and Winchester. There were Danish mercenaries too, sent with the blessing of King Sven, who took the view that any enemy of Harald Hardrada was a friend of his.

By now, Harold knew of the correspondence between Duke William and Robert FitzWimark, but all the duke's talk of an army that was sixty thousand strong had not concerned him in the slightest.

He reassured his brothers, 'If William says he'd be willing to fight the battle even if he only had ten thousand men, then you can bet that's how many he's got. We have as many as that, we know the lie of the land, and all we have to do is hold our ground. He has to come and take it from us. In the end, that's what will make the difference.'

They stopped for the first day on the edge of the Andredesweald, the untamed forest that stretched across a vast expanse of Sussex and Kent. Patches of land had been cleared within it to allow for farms, villages and even a few small towns. But for the most part it was a wild and dangerous place, in which outlaws, wild beasts and who knew what evil spirits dwelled, and the land it covered was hilly, with rough tracks that turned and twisted up hill and down dale. But late on Friday night, having covered sixty miles in two days, Harold and his army arrived at the hoar apple tree and set up camp for the night.

Some of the men were so tired out by the march that they simply collapsed onto any spare patch of ground they could find. Others were either unable to sleep, for fear of the battle ahead, or reasoned that since this might be their last night on earth, they might as well spend it drinking, talking, singing songs and playing games of chance.

Harold walked through the camp, talking to his men, always delivering the same message. 'You're fighting for your freedom. You're fighting for the right of free-born Englishmen to live as they see fit and be ruled by a king appointed in the English way, by Witenagemot. If William has his way, you'll have a foreign king, imposing foreign laws, taking away your English rights. This is for you, your families, your children and grandchildren not yet born. You're fighting for their freedom. You're fighting for their England.'

His orders for the battle to come were very simple. 'We are going to take our position and hold it. If we end the day exactly where we started it, then we'll win. Just last out this one day, and then, with every day that follows, more troops will join us, and the stronger we'll become. So stand your ground. Don't go forward. Don't go backwards. Stand your ground.'

No man in the army needed to be told why the English way was worth fighting for. Their nation was peaceful, prosperous and governed by laws that seemed fair and properly applied. Nor was there any confusion about their task. The Bastard of Normandy wanted to march up the road to London. They were going to stand in his way and not let him past.

But there was something missing, and the men who had been with Harold at Stamford Bridge knew it. There, he had been bold, decisive, moving at speed and throwing himself and his men into the battle at a moment's notice. They had been on the attack from the moment they first spotted Hardrada's men. Of course, there was nothing wrong with fighting a defensive battle, but the king seemed oddly listless. His usual charm – the ready smile, the jokes with the men, the sense that he was full of spirit and vigour – had dimmed to the point where it had all but disappeared.

'Dunno what's got into him,' one veteran said to another as they sat by their campfire, sharing a skinful of ale. 'It's like he's going to turn up at the battle, line us all up and then just see what happens.'

'He'll get his arse kicked, that's what'll happen if he waits around doing nothing,' his comrade replied. 'I mean, even if you're just standing in the same place, you've still got to be doing something, if you know what I mean.'

'Yeah . . . Here, give us some more of that beer.'

Harold returned to his tent and sat down with his senior men. 'For those of you who don't know the area, let me explain how the ground lies. Just below us, about a third of the way down the hill that we're on now, there's a ridge that sticks out from the slope, with a track running along the top of it. That's the road to Hastings. On either side of the ridge, you've got two valleys, each with a stream at the bottom, running away from the ridge. One stream flows into Bulverhythe harbour, the other into the River Brede. And the land down there in the valley bottoms is marshy. You can't get armed men across it. That's important. It means William can't attack up those valleys. With me?'

The men around him nodded and gave grunts of assent.

'Very well, then . . . At the end of the ridge, the land spreads to either side into a cross-ridge, about eight hundred paces across. The Hastings road goes straight over that ridge and down the hillside in front of it. We are going to stand along the whole width of that cross-ridge.'

'It'll be a tight fight,' observed Leofwine. 'We won't get much more than a thousand men in a line across there. Not if you want them to have any room to swing their weapons.'

'Maybe,' said Harold. 'But the Normans like to fight on horseback, and they won't be able to get more than a few hundred horsemen up against our line. And they'll be coming uphill towards us.'

'What about the sides of this cross-ridge? Can't they outflank us?' asked another man.

'Not on the left; the land below the top of the ridge is too heavily wooded for that. And there's another marsh, with a stream running through it, in front of our right flank. The people round here call it Santlache. There's a small hillock just off the main ridge to the right. We'll put men there to guard it. Then the only way William can come is to follow the line of the road straight up the hill towards us.

'Now, I'm the only man here who's seen these people fight, so let me tell you, Duke William of Normandy has never faced a battle like this. I went on campaign with him to Brittany two years ago, and I doubt there were more than two thousand men, if that, in his whole army. They fought the way we did in Wales. You know the kind of thing, lots of little skirmishes and ambushes spread across a wide range of country. He's never faced a shield wall. And not too many of his men have ever used, let alone felt, a battleaxe.

'On the other hand, his army has things we don't. This won't be like Stamford Bridge. We're not going to go charging into battle the way we did there. We'll stand on our own two feet. But that's not how the Normans fight. Most of their men are mounted knights, backed up by far more archers and crossbow-men than we'll have, but a lot fewer foot soldiers.

'So the whole battle rests on one simple question: can the bowmen and the knights break our line? If the shield wall holds, we cannot lose. And that is all we have to do: avoid defeat and hold the position. It's William who has to beat us. So I want our best men in the front of that line.'

'Are you saying you want my housecarls spread right across the front, Your Majesty?' asked their commander.

'Most of them, yes. I'll have a core of them by me, but the rest should be dispersed evenly along the line. They know how to use their shields as a defence against arrows, and they'll hold their nerve when the mounted knights come charging up the hill. Their example will keep the other men's morale up and encourage them to fight.'

'And where will you be, sire?' asked Gyrth.

'Obeying my younger brother's orders,' replied the king with a tired attempt at one of his old light-hearted smiles.

'A few days ago, my brother the Earl of East Anglia offered to fight this battle on my behalf,' he went on, addressing those who had not been at the war council at Westminster. 'He pointed out that if he died, the kingdom would be none the poorer, whereas if I died, the consequence would be a kingdom that had no king. And in that event all would be lost.

'It was a powerful argument, and while I believed then, as now, that it was my absolute duty to my troops to be present at this battle, it seems to me now that I have an equal duty to my country to survive it. So I am obliged, most reluctantly, to conclude that I will remain behind the line, while my brothers represent me in it.'

There was not a man in the tent who could argue with the king's logic. But not one of them felt inspired by it. Harold Godwinson had always been a warrior. His personal banner was called 'The Fighting Man', and less than three weeks had passed since he had led it into the heart of the battle at Stamford Bridge. Now he was proposing to stand behind the line, not lifting his sword in anger.

Harold knew he was letting them all down. It was evident in the listless way he dismissed them without the slightest word of encouragement. Gyrth did not follow the others out, but waited until he and Harold were alone.

'You are my king and my older brother,' he said. 'You would never obey one of my orders. What's the real reason you're not leading from the front?'

Harold said nothing. He clearly wanted Gyrth to leave him alone, but the younger man stood his ground. Finally Harold was forced to reply.

'God,' he said simply. 'This battle will not be decided by me, or by William. It rests in the hands of God. If I am truly excommunicated, then there is no hope, no matter how hard I fight. But if I still have Our Lord's blessing, then He will take pity on me and grant us His favour. So I will throw myself at His mercy. I will offer Him my life, my crown and my country. He can decide what to do with them.'

14

The Norman camp, Hastings

William was in much better spirits as he made his final preparations for the battle. 'Do you remember when we were boys together in Brother Thorold's classroom?' he asked Fitz as they inspected the sentries that he had posted to ensure that Harold could not make a night attack and take a second enemy by surprise.

Fitz grinned. 'That poor monk. Was there ever a teacher who had three less willing pupils?'

'Just think of everything that has happened since then. Think of everything we've been through, you and I . . . all the losses we've suffered, all the challenges we've had to face. And here we are, with the crown of England in my grasp. It feels like my whole life has been leading up to this moment, as though it's all been part of God's plan, and now I will reap the reward.'

'He's certainly been watching over us so far,' Fitz agreed. 'Even things that seemed like setbacks have turned out in our favour.'

'Exactly!' William agreed. 'Take that damn north wind, for example. It drove us mad, keeping us stuck at Dives and Saint-Valéry for so long. But by the time we were finally able to cross over to England, the English navy that might have destroyed our fleet were nowhere to be seen. We sailed across without the slightest trouble.'

'And the Norwegians invading when they did – they've softened the English up nicely. We'd have a far harder task tomorrow if we were facing every man they had, and all of them still fresh.'

'Robert FitzWimark can say what he likes about Harold and his army. But I doubt he's ever been to war the way we have. He doesn't know what it takes out of you. Harold has gone up to York, then back, then down here. He must be out on his feet.' William slapped his friend on the back. 'We're going to win. I can feel it. Now go and get some rest. I'll be counting on you to be fighting fit in the morning.'

When dawn came, William had his men up early, ready to march and fight. But before they moved, he stood atop a cart and called them all to gather round him. He knew that as strong as his voice was, it might not carry to the very back of the crowd, but that did not matter. The men there would hear the cheers of those at the front, and word of what he had said would have spread through the entire army by the time they were on the move.

'Normans!' he began, for wherever his men came from, they would all be Norman today. 'The bravest of all nations! I have no doubt of your courage, and no doubt of your victory, either, because you have never, ever been defeated.'

A few men at the front gave the first ragged cheer of the day.

That's a start, William told himself. Now I have to warm them up a little.

'If you had failed to conquer your enemy, even once, then I'd need to raise your spirits and try to give you courage by the power of my words. But I don't need to do that, because you . . . yes, you,' he pointed at a soldier in front of him, 'and you,' he added, pointing at another, 'you all have all the courage you need, all by yourselves.'

This time the applause was a little louder.

537

'Just think of Rollo, my ancestor, the bravest of all men,' William went on. 'What could the King of France, ruler of peoples from Lorraine to Spain, do against my predecessor? Nothing! Whatever Rollo wanted, he took, and he only let the king have what he was pleased to give him. He conquered the French at the gates of Paris. The king was so scared, he begged Rollo to take his daughter and all the land that is now known as Normandy . . . named after you, the brave Northmen.'

That got a cheer.

'Then the King of France tried to steal Normandy from Duke Richard the Fearless, when the duke was just a boy. Well, your forefathers – men of honour and pride, who bowed their heads to no man who was not worthy of their loyalty – they captured the king and kept him imprisoned in Rouen until he gave the duchy back.'

William did not wait for a response this time, but kept his recital moving on.

'And when the daughter of Duke Richard the Good was being mistreated by his son-in-law, Hugh of Chalon, Normans just like you, from your very families, marched hundreds of leagues across France, right down to the southern foothills of the Alps, and forced this Burgundian man to submit himself to the rule of his Norman wife . . . because even our women are stronger and braver than the men from anywhere else!'

That got the Normans shouting and cheering, and the men from other parts of France calling defiantly that their women were even tougher. William saw a couple of arguments breaking out, even a punch being thrown, but he didn't care. The men were waking up, feeling the sap rise, building up their fighting spirit.

'But why am I telling you stories about the old days? How many of you were at Mortemer? You saw with your own eyes how Normans made the pride of France turn tail and run.

'Now you're up against the English. These men are your exact opposites. You have never lost a battle . . . and they have never won one.'

Here was a subject on which every man in the ranks could agree, for only William's most trusted confidants were aware of the news from Stamford Bridge. A volley of catcalls and boos derided the useless English.

'If any Englishman – you know, the kind that Danes and Normans have defeated in a hundred battles – can come here and tell me of one battle – just one – that the race of Rollo has ever lost, I'll admit defeat and walk away. But they can't, can they?'

'No!' came the roar from the crowd. Now William let anger enter his voice, and it was with genuine outrage that he asked, 'How dare they – these people who are used to being conquered, who are completely ignorant in warfare, who don't even know how to shoot arrows properly – how dare they try to do battle against you? How shameful is it that King Harold, a perjurer who has broken the oaths he made in your presence, should even show his face to you?

'These criminals murdered my kinsman Alfred. They beheaded your relatives who were with him, and yet their heads are still on their shoulders.'

William paused, his chest heaving with effort and emotion. Then he took a deep breath, and this time shouted loud enough that every man could hear.

'Raise your standards, my brave men! Set no limits to your righteous fury. May the lightning of your glory be seen, and the thunder of your presence heard from east to west . . . And be ye the avengers of noble blood!'

The army clapped, cheered and stamped its approval. William stood to take the applause for a few seconds and then jumped back down to earth. The men who would be his key lieutenants – Fitz, Rob, Bishop Odo, Eustace of Boulogne, Walter Giffard and Raoul de Tosny – were waiting for him.

'Go!' William said. 'Sound the advance and take the army off to war.'

15

*The land around Caldbec Hill and the valley
of Santlache, Sussex, 14 October 1066*

Scouts had been sent ahead of the army, and as William rode
along the road out of Hastings, they returned to report what
they had seen.

'There's a host of them, Your Grace, coming out of the
woods and down the hill. They're carrying spears, all glinting
in the sunlight . . . thousands of them. And banners everywhere.'

'Yes, thank you, but I don't need the poetry. Just tell me, are
they in formation yet?'

'No, Your Grace. Just a great mass of men, thousands of
them.'

William looked pensive. He and his lieutenants had scouted
the land around Hastings looking at possible battlefields and,
like Harold, had spotted the potential of the cross-ridge below
Caldbec Hill as a defensive position.

'Now think carefully,' he told the scout. 'You saw them
coming out of the trees and down the hill, yes?'

'That's right, Your Grace.'

'Now, there's another, lower hill, just in front of the big one,
with a ridge between them. Were the English on the lower hill
yet?'

'Some of them, Your Grace, but most weren't. Though they
were heading that way, I reckon, now that you mention it.'

'Damn it!' William muttered. His cavalry had ridden out of

Hastings without putting their chain-mail coats on, to lessen the weight that their mounts had to carry until it was absolutely necessary. So there was no way that they could dash for the hill and seize it before Harold had time to get his men organised. But they could at least make that process a great deal harder for the English.

'Send the archers and crossbowmen ahead of us!' William ordered Fitz. 'Tell them to fire on the enemy, but don't get too close to them. Just harass them. Make life hard for them. If possible, keep them off the hill until we can mount a proper attack. But don't engage them in serious combat. If the English threaten them, they're to retreat. Do you understand me? I don't want them taking any risks. Not yet.'

'Faster!' Harold urged his men, shooing them down the slope. He could see what William's intentions were and he couldn't afford to let the Normans keep his army off the ridge. That position was the key to the battle.

The housecarls rushed ahead, forming an impromptu shield wall at the front of the ridge so that the fyrd men could line up behind them. Now another advantage of the ridge became clear. The Norman archers, shooting from down in the valley, either fired their arrows harmlessly into the shield wall, or sent them flying way over the entire army.

On the other hand, there was a disadvantage to the position too. It was so crammed that the English army ended up assembling in a muddled crush of men that was seven, eight and in some places ten men thick. They were so tightly packed that many of them could not even raise their arms to wield a weapon. Not that it would make any difference, because there were hundreds of men between them and any possible enemy.

The crowding was so great that some of the volunteers, who had arrived from Kent and Sussex the previous evening, simply turned round and walked away, reckoning that they would not be needed.

Harold had another problem. In order to see and be seen – for his men needed to know that he was there on the field, even if he wasn't in the midst of the crowd – he and his personal force of housecarls had to stand some way back from the main body of the army, where the hill was slightly higher. From there, he could survey the entire field.

The main Norman force had appeared atop of another high point, Telham Hill, directly opposite his position, and made their way down into the valley between that hill and the ridge. Harold felt his spirits sink as he caught sight of the white papal banner and realised that Hugh Margot had been telling the truth: William had indeed received the Holy Father's blessing for his invasion.

That doesn't mean that God agrees with him, Harold told himself. Forget about that. Concentrate on the battle.

The Normans, he saw, were forming up in three blocks, with the papal standard, next to which William would surely place himself, in the centre. Each block of men was divided into three lines, with archers and crossbowmen at the front, foot soldiers behind them and the mass of cavalry in the rear. William's tactics were immediately clear. He would soften up the English with arrows, use the infantry to prise openings in the shield wall and then send the cavalry to wreak havoc once the first cracks in the line appeared.

Then something entirely unexpected occurred.

A single rider detached himself and rode through the Norman lines into the no-man's-land between the two armies. A cheer went up from the enemy ranks that drifted across on the wind so that Harold could catch a faint echo of it.

The man, who appeared to be some kind of minstrel or fool, rode up and down the Norman lines, making his horse perform trick steps and throwing his sword high into the air, spinning end-upon-end, then catching it by the hilt when it fell back down towards him.

Harold heard another cheer and realised it came from much closer: even his own men were applauding the performance. A few broke ranks, pushing through the line of housecarls and stepping out in front of the line to get a better look.

Then, without warning, the rider suddenly turned his horse to face the English, kicked it into a gallop and raced up the hill.

The spectators who had come out to watch him suddenly realised that he was heading straight for them. They raced back for the safety of the shield wall, but their comrades were crammed so tightly that it was almost impossible to push their way in.

Some managed to squeeze to safety. But three men did not. As if to prove that his skills with a sword extended to more than juggling, the rider cut them down, then kept going, hurling himself at the shield wall. He and his horse were swiftly skewered by spears and then butchered by axes, but his death seemed to spur his countrymen into action, for as he fell, the entire Norman army started moving across the valley, towards the foot of the ridge on which the English were massed and then on up the slope towards the waiting shield wall.

William had chosen a mace as his weapon for the day. Not only did this blunt but brutal instrument seem like the best way to smash his way through the English defensive line, it also resembled a royal mace and underlined his claim to kingship. He could not use it, however, until the archers and foot soldiers had cleared the way for the mounted knights. So for now, all he could do was watch as the archers fired volley after volley without any apparent effect on the mass of English atop the hill.

This was a battle unlike any he had ever known. Not only

was it on a far greater scale, but the notion that one side would simply stand there, in an immobile mass, and let their enemy come on to them was entirely new to him too. The English barely even bothered to shoot back at the bowmen attacking them. So far as William could tell, they themselves had no more than a smattering of archers dotted amongst their ranks, and they let loose their arrows in ones and twos, with no attempt at the kind of volleys that filled the air with raining death and made the bow such an effective weapon.

The duke was not the only Norman to be baffled by what he was witnessing.

'Why don't they do something?' asked Rob, who was positioned directly next to his brother, with Odo on William's far side. 'Why are they just standing there?'

'They remind me more of a castle than an army,' Odo observed. 'Those shields serve as walls for the rest of them.'

'Well, we've taken plenty of castles in our time,' said William grimly.

But this one did not seem to be yielding. When the foot soldiers marched up the hill, they were met with a hail of missiles: spears, hatchets and rocks – some attached to pieces of wood to make them easier to hurl – flew out from behind the impenetrable line of interlinked shields. Then, as the Normans came within a few paces of the wall, it opened enough to allow the housecarls to swing their axes, while the yeomen of the fyrd jabbed spears at the approaching foot soldiers.

The infantry came on up the hill, wave after wave, but they could make no impression on the wall. Meanwhile, the bodies of slain Normans, French and Bretons lay ever thicker on the thin strip of ground between the front lip of the ridge and the English line.

William waited for an eternity before he accepted that the initial assault had failed. No cracks had appeared for the cavalry to exploit. Very well, they would have to prise open the line for themselves. He stood up in his stirrups, raised his mace in the air, then swung it downwards, shouting, 'God aid us!' and spurred his horse into the charge.

16

Leofwine was on the right of the English line, facing the Breton wing of the Bastard's army. He had discovered the identity of his opponents from a Cornishman standing near him.

'I can understand every word they say,' the Cornishman marvelled. 'How do you suppose that is, eh?'

Wherever they came from, they had not managed to do any damage to the English line. And if Gyrth was right and all they had to do was make sure that at least one of William's men died for one of theirs, then the battle was going exactly to plan, for the tally of casualties was well in favour of the English.

The archers and the infantry had both been seen off. Now it was time for the horses. Neither Leofwine nor any of his men had ever faced a charge by horsemen before, and as the mighty beasts came up the hill, with their armoured riders raising spears to hurl at the English line, it took all his self-control to stand his ground and shout to his men to do the same.

The housecarls did not move an inch, and just as Harold had hoped, their example gave courage to the less experienced men around them. Then the horses arrived and the housecarls set about them with their axes, just as the Norseman had done on the bridge at Stamford, and the men saw how vulnerable the unprotected animals were to the cruel blades of the twin-headed axe.

Now it was the Bretons who were afraid. The massed phalanx of axemen was as new to them as cavalry were to the English, and as their mounts were slaughtered, so their nerve faltered and they cracked. Their foot soldiers had made an orderly retreat, but the cavalry were routed. Those who still had horses under them turned tail and galloped away. The ones who had lost their mounts did their best to run with their mail coats flapping around their legs.

Harold's orders had been very clear: don't move. The housecarls obeyed that command, knowing that this was only the start of the battle. But the men of the fyrd, unversed in military strategy, saw a fleeing enemy and could not resist chasing it. They barged their way past the housecarls and hurtled off down the hill, pursuing the Bretons.

Leofwine hesitated, not sure what to do next. But then he saw that the entire left flank of the Norman army was in disarray. If the English army went onto the advance – all of it – he could turn the enemy's flank and attack them from the side while the rest of the army advanced on them head-on.

Come on, Harold. Sound the charge! he thought. Then, not waiting for his brother, he set off after his men, racing away down the hill.

Harold saw the right flank lose its shape as half its men ran after the fleeing Bretons. His first reaction was one of fury: By Christ, Leofwine, you idiot. How often did I tell you: don't move?

But then he spotted the same thing as Leofwine. This was an opportunity to roll up the entire Norman left flank and destroy William's army before the battle had barely begun.

Maybe God is on my side after all!

He called to the most senior member of his housecarl guard. 'Get word to the rest of the army. Tell them to attack now. Head straight for the Norman lines. But for God's sake, hurry!'

* * *

Duke William was at the very front and centre of the cavalry charge, smashing his mace down on the enemy all around him. But then he heard a whinny of pain, a sound he recognised at once as that of a wounded animal, and a moment later his horse buckled at the knees and began to fall.

He leaped from the saddle before the horse hit the ground. Landing on both feet, he saw an English soldier advancing towards him and felled him with three sharp blows of the mace. Then, hearing the cheer from the English, who thought that their enemy's commander was dead, and knowing how bad this would be for his own men, he forced his way back through the press of bodies until he found a young knight on the fringe of the battle who was still trying to make his way to where the actual fighting was taking place.

'Give me your horse,' William commanded.

The young knight was so shocked to see his duke standing in front of him that he could not speak. Instead he just nodded, dismounted and helped William up into the saddle. William rode closer to the heart of the fighting, took off his helmet and waved it over his head.

'I'm alive!' he shouted. 'I'm alive!'

A few men who had seen and heard him cheered. Then more looked to see what the fuss was about and roared their support too. William was about to charge back into the fray when he felt a tugging on his sleeve.

He looked around to see Eustace of Boulogne. His eyes were wide with panic, and there was real fear in his voice as he pleaded, 'For God's sake, Your Grace, retreat, I beg you. The Bretons are fleeing. The English are advancing. We must retreat, before it's too late!'

Come on, Harold, come on! thought Leofwine as his men became ever more detached from the rest of the army.

If everyone else followed their lead and advanced, the battle could be won. If they did not, he and his men would be caught out in the open and slaughtered.

Harold was looking on in horror as he saw the chance of victory turning to disaster on the right.

Why wasn't the army moving?

Just then the housecarl he had sent to pass on the order to advance returned. 'It's no use, Your Majesty,' he said. 'There's that many men, I can't get through them. And even if I could, I can't find anyone to tell. I mean, I know there's thegns and abbots and earls in there somewhere, but I just can't find them.'

'Retreat?' roared William. 'Are you mad? Come with me and I'll show you what I think of anyone who retreats.'

Just in front of the duke's horse stood a knight who had lost his mount. There was a spear lying on the ground in front of him.

'You there! Pass me that spear!' William ordered. He looked at Eustace and shouted, 'Come on!' then rode away towards the left flank.

When he came across his first Breton, riding away from the English line, William swung the spear horizontally, like a fighting stick, and knocked the man from his horse. Then he rode into the confused, milling, panic-stricken mass of Bretons, waving the spear, hitting horses on the rump and shouting, 'Turn around! Turn around!'

The Bretons looked at the frenzied duke, one of the finest warriors in all Christendom, who was clearly ready to strike them down rather than let them run away. They looked at the attacking English, who were, now they came to examine them more closely, mostly just farmers running down a hill. It wasn't a difficult choice. They regathered, turned and rode back up the hill.

'To me, men! To me!' shouted Leofwine.

He had scrambled up the hillock Harold had described that rose a little way from the right end of the English line. There he planted his standard.

As the men of the fyrd ran towards him, Leofwine assembled them into a rough approximation of a shield wall.

'Hold steady, lads!' he called. 'Hold steady!'

And then the Breton cavalry were on them, attacking from all sides at once, stabbing lances, swinging swords. But this was no housecarls' wall. This was just honest yeomen – farmers, fishermen, blacksmiths and carpenters – decent, brave men doing their duty for their country.

And it wouldn't be long before their wall cracked.

Up on the hill, Harold could see his brother desperately rallying his men, hurling himself into the fight wherever the line was about to break. But Leofwine was only human. He only could be in one place at one time, and there were just too many cracks.

Then the wall broke and the knights were in among them. Harold saw Leofwine fighting right to the very end. He was the last man to fall.

But fall he did. The little hillock was lost.

And so, Harold feared, was the battle.

17

Now it was William who saw a chance to break the deadlock. The English shield wall had fractured of its own volition. If he could attack it now, with everything he had, it might just break apart completely.

Shouting and gesticulating at the mass of Norman horsemen who were milling around on the fringes of the fighting, trying to find a gap in the melee that would allow them close enough to get to grips with the enemy, William signalled to them to follow him, then spurred his horse and rode back up the hill, right into the heart of the battle. He battered his way through the apparently impenetrable press of fighting men, just as he had done at countless skirmishes, sieges and even pitched battles. And always the result had been the same: the enemy broke and fled. It was as if his will created his destiny, as if he could destroy his enemies by the sheer power of his determination, so that they were persuaded that there could only ever be one outcome and gave in to that inevitability.

The English, however, were different. They did not accept that they were beaten. On the contrary, they simply filled the gaps in their shield wall, shortened their front so as to keep it as deep and strong as before, and fought with an even greater intensity.

There was a crude, barbaric power to the way that King Harold's army fought. The housecarls were grim-faced slaughterers, trained to wield their battleaxes with brutal efficiency.

A few of them would step in front of the wall and set up a terrifying rhythm, so that the steel blades of their axes moved with the same unified beat as the wooden blades of a warship's oars. Horses reared in terror as they came near the housecarls, seeing other beasts lying crippled all around them, hearing their whinnies, smelling their fear and sensing that their limbs could be next on the butchers' blocks. Their riders were no less petrified. Once their lances had been thrown, they had no way of closing on the enemy without taking their chances with those axes; and all the time there was another, less experienced or well trained, but equally deadly peril confronting them.

The levies of the fyrd fought with the unschooled savagery of men who feared that their country, their way of life and everything they held dear was about to be ripped from their hands. They threw whatever weapons, implements or natural objects they could find at the Norman soldiers. Some wielded swords, but many just had wooden clubs or long-handled lead mallets with which to batter their opponents, with an assortment of daggers, carving knives and scythes with which to finish them off. Many were not as well protected as the Normans. They could not afford finely made hauberks of chain mail and made do with padded leather jerkins. But this made them lighter and more nimble, and they seemed to fight in swarms, at close quarters, where the crush of men was so thick that some of the dead remained on their feet, propped up by the mass of living bodies all around them.

The Normans were used to battles of movement, free-wheeling exchanges between groups of mounted men riding across broad stretches of open country. But this was war at its most confined, and there was something almost intimate about the individual contests between warriors who could look one another in the eye and smell the other man's sweat and shit and foul breath.

William had no fear of that. He plunged into the blood and guts of the fight with a cold-eyed savagery to match any house-carl. He understood now that this was a battle of attrition, in which the side that was most efficient in its killing would win, and he set about reducing the English numbers with a will.

And then one of those axes found its mark and a second horse went down under him, and suddenly William found himself struggling to free his feet from his stirrups and pull himself out from under his writhing charger. He saw an Englishman, one of the common soldiers, point in his direction, shouting at three of his comrades who were near him. Of course, they knew who he was. He had always made sure that everyone on a battlefield knew that. The English soldiers came towards him across a small patch of the battlefield that suddenly seemed to have emptied.

William's right leg was still trapped. He couldn't get up. The men were drawing closer, and none of his own men seemed to have noticed the peril he was in.

Is this how I die? Trapped beneath my own horse? Killed by English peasants? Is this how it all ends?

He refused to accept that. He fought against the grip of the stirrup and the weight of his horse as death drew ever closer.

They were almost on him now, and all he could do was prop himself up on his right arm and feebly wave his mace with the left.

And then a figure appeared out of nowhere, a nobleman on his charger. He skewered the Englishman closest to William with his spear, flinging it into the middle of the man's chest as if he were pig-sticking a wild boar on an afternoon's hunting. Then he drew his sword and cut down the second man, and rode hard at the remaining two, who turned and fled back to the relative safety of their line.

Only when the knight dismounted and came to help his duke disentangle himself did William realise who it was.

'Boulogne!' he said, unable to keep the surprise from his voice. 'You saved my life. Thank you.'

Count Eustace grimaced. 'I let you down once today. I wasn't going to do it again.'

William nodded. A knot of men was forming around him now, and as he got to his feet, he saw Fitz and his brother Odo, their faces caked in blood and grime, the skin only visible along the thin tracks washed clean by rivulets of sweat.

'Withdraw,' he told them; then, seeing the looks of concern on their faces, 'The battle's not lost, but it isn't won, either. We have to regroup. The men need food and water.'

'What if the English quit?' Fitz asked. 'We can't let them get away.'

'They won't. They're not going anywhere. Not unless we make them. Now . . . I've ordered an orderly withdrawal. Make it so.'

A third horse was brought up for William, and he rode back to the bottom of the hill. On his way, he sought out the commanders of his archers and crossbowmen and gave them fresh orders. 'Maintain a steady rate of shooting. Don't let the English rest. And tell your men not to fire directly at them. Aim for the sky. Send their arrows and bolts up over the shield wall so that they drop down onto the men beyond.'

'An arrow loses a lot of its force if you shoot it like that, Your Grace,' said the master of archers. 'The flatter it flies, the harder it hits.'

'Aye, Your Grace, same with crossbows,' the other man agreed.

'I don't care. I want them having to look up, thinking about your attack, raising their shields to protect themselves.'

The master of archers grinned. 'Because if they're holding their shields up against the arrows . . .'

'They can't use them to keep our knights at bay.' William finished the sentence.

'There's just one problem, Your Grace . . .'

'What is it now?'

'Well, I know this sounds mad, but they're not shooting enough arrows back at us. Normally my lads can use everything they've got in their quivers because they know they can gather up all the enemy arrows that have come at us and shoot 'em right back again. But there's hardly any come at us, so we're running low.'

'Then shoot sparingly. It won't matter. You don't have to kill the English; you just have to distract them.'

'Like a fly buzzing around their faces, eh?'

'Exactly like that.'

The Normans withdrew, tended to their wounded, wetted their parched throats and restored their strength with whatever was left of the food their scavengers had been able to strip from the surrounding countryside over the past few days.

Up on the ridge, the English were trying to do the same, but their efforts were hampered by the steady fall of arrows from the sky: not sufficient to cause serious casualties, but enough to mean that no man could ever relax or feel safe. The result was a sense of uneasiness, even irritation, that spread through the ranks. Men started muttering about the wisdom of just standing still and making themselves easy targets.

'We should either go forward or go back,' one man muttered, and his comrades nodded and grunted their agreement. 'Just standing here like sitting ducks, well, it's driving me mad.'

'Dunno what the king's doing, neither,' a second man chimed up. 'He's not himself. I was at Stamford. You should have seen him; fighting like a man possessed, he was. But here, he's just standing around like he doesn't care.'

'Why does their king not fight?' Odo of Bayeux asked. 'Whatever his sins might be, I had not thought cowardice could be numbered among them.'

'He's no coward,' William said. 'I saw that when he was with me in Brittany.'

'So why doesn't he fight now?'

'I don't know. Maybe he thinks it's not worth taking the risk. Why let himself be killed here? As long as he's alive, he's still king. And as long as he is king, England belongs to him.'

'Hmm, yes, I see that . . . Of course, there is another explanation.'

'What's that, brother?'

'The Church has cut him loose. He does not have God's blessing. Without that, what point is there in fighting?'

Before William could answer, Fitz cut in. 'What are your orders for the rest of the battle, Your Grace?'

'Exactly the same as before. We will keep attacking them until they break. And mark my words, if night falls before we've finished the job, and Godwinson withdraws in good order, our men will think we've won. But we won't have. The English have got a whole country to call on. If they just fight us and withdraw, fight and withdraw, over and over, they will grind us into the dust.'

William looked around, searching for any sign of doubt in the eyes of those around him. Then, with his exchange with Odo still fresh in his mind, he said. 'We have to kill their king. That matters more than anything.

'Giffard, Boulogne, take a small group of men, hold yourselves in reserve. Stay close enough to the fighting that you can move fast when you have to. Just keep an eye on Harold

Godwinson. And the second you see him leave the protection of his guards, hunt him down and kill him. We'll take care of the rest.

'We finish the job today. We destroy them all before sunset.'

18

And so it started all over again: the relentless assaults of the Normans and their allies, the unbroken resistance of the English. Thousands of men on both sides had died, or been so severely wounded that they might as well be dead. There were far fewer knights in the Norman charges. The English shield wall was barely half the length it had been. But the carnage did not cease.

It was Gyrth Godwinson who led and rallied; encouraged and cajoled; commanded his men and killed his foes as a true king should. He had offered to take Harold's place and command the army in his absence, and though his brother was present in body at least, it was Gyrth who showed the character of a true leader. He strode up and down the line, picking the spots where his presence could make a difference, stepping in to rally the men when their resistance seemed to be waning, or shoring up the shield wall when cracks started to appear.

He fought with unrelenting courage and vigour, taking on one man after another and besting them all. And then there came one of those sudden moments of calm and space, as if the battlefield were a forest and all the men on it trees, and an open glade had appeared by magic. Gyrth lowered his sword and steadied his breathing. Then he lifted his head and took a look around to get a sense of how the ebb and flow of the battle was going.

Maybe we can do this, he told himself, trying to maintain his own faith. We might just beat them yet.

And it was at that precise moment that a lance, thrown by a Norman Gyrth had not even seen, caught him side-on on the very top of his shoulder. The spearhead skimmed over the steel links of Gyrth's hauberk like a stone skittering across an icy pond, and embedded itself in his neck.

The impact of the blow knocked him off his feet. He could not shout in pain, for breathing was impossible. His own blood was pumping into the air around him. A pack of Norman foot soldiers raced towards him. But he did not feel the blades that hacked at his arms, his legs and his torso.

He was dead before the first blow was even struck.

Harold did not see Gyrth die. But as the afternoon drew on, he knew the battle was lost. The Normans had worked their way around his right flank and were now coming at his army from the side as well as the front. The shield wall was disintegrating and the once solid, impenetrable mass of the army had been broken down into smaller groups, one or two of them sizeable enough to maintain a meaningful degree of resistance, but others just knots of ten or twenty men who were soon washed away by the Norman tide.

'Flee, Your Majesty,' the commander of the royal house-carls begged him. 'If you leave now, we can be miles away by sunset.'

Harold shook his head. 'No, it's all lost.'

'The battle may be. But not the war. Not the country!'

Harold said nothing. His eyes were empty. His spirit was broken.

The housecarl grabbed his king by the shoulders and shouted at him as if he were a raw recruit. 'For God's sake, be a man! Your troops need you. England needs you. If you won't run, then for fuck's sake fight!'

Harold nodded listlessly.

And then, before the housecarls could stop him, he was walking towards the fighting, hardly seeming to care where he went.

He wants to die, the commander thought. Should I even try to stop him?

Down at the base of the hill, just beside the marshland of Santlache, an archer was looking at his quiver. There was just a single arrow in it. He glanced around at his mates.

'Anyone got any more?'

'No, I'm all out,' replied another man, and the rest agreed. 'Reckon we're done for the day.'

The archer shrugged. He and his friends had shot every arrow they had and had come through the day unscathed. That constituted a victory so far as he was concerned. He took out the final arrow, raised his bow and fired, just as Duke William had commanded, high into the late-afternoon sky.

'It'll be dark soon,' he said conversationally, as he turned back to the other men.

Harold was in a daze, hardly able to comprehend what was going on around him. All he knew was that God had deserted him at his moment of greatest need. That could only mean that he had sinned in some way, he knew not how, and was now being punished. It was William who had the support of God and the angels, while he himself was not only going to die, but faced an eternity of damnation, denied salvation, cast off forever from the Church.

He looked up at the sky, as if searching for God in the heavens.

The arrow hit him in the right eye. As the master of archers had suggested, it lacked the force to kill him instantly, but it did enough to obliterate his eyeball and lodge in the socket behind it.

Harold doubled up, consumed by excruciating agony. His hand clutched desperately at the shaft of the arrow, but the more he tried to pull it from his head, the more terrible the pain became.

The housecarls saw the king fall and rushed towards him.

The Normans saw the same thing and came riding the other way.

The Normans got there first.

Harold was hacked to death by the men William had set aside for that specific purpose.

The main body of the Norman army surrounded the housecarls, who refused to surrender but fought to the very last man. The rest of the English army either fled for their lives or were cut down by the victorious Normans.

The battle of Hastings was over.

19

The field of battle, Hastings, 15 October 1066

William camped on the battlefield that night and ordered his army to remain there too, surrounded by the bodies of their fallen comrades and enemies, with the moans of the dying still hanging in the air. 'We're not taking a backward step,' he told his men. 'Not one.'

The following morning, the open-air charnel house was filled with people picking through the corpses that lay as thick as new-mown hay across the ridge where the fighting had been. Some were scavengers; others were just gripped by ghoulish fascination. But most were women looking for the bodies of their men.

One wore a fine woollen riding cloak, with the hood up to hide her face.

There had been a time, not so long ago, when her beauty had been famed throughout the kingdom, but now her face was ravaged by exhaustion and grief. Her bones stood out against hollow cheeks, her eyes were red with weeping, her lovely mouth cast down by her despair.

She saw a group of Norman soldiers who were watching proceedings. One of them was mounted on a fine stallion. His mount, his clothes and his bearing all suggested that he was of noble rank. The woman approached him and spoke in French. 'What have you done with the king?'

The nobleman replied with another question: 'Did you know him?'

The woman did not answer at once. She just nodded, then looked the nobleman in the eye. 'My name is Edith. His Majesty was the father of my children.'

'Come with me,' the nobleman said.

Edith Swan-Neck was taken to a pile of bodies that had been collected from the area where Harold was known to have died. His face was unrecognisable and his corpse more a collection of parts than a coherent body, but she was able to identify him by various marks on his torso that only she, as his lover, could possibly have known.

Later in the day, Gytha Thorkelsdottir, widow of Earl Godwin and mother of four sons killed within the space of a month, was brought before Duke William. As she approached, she appeared to be a pitiful old woman, moving slowly and with some difficulty, leaning on her stick, her grey hair poking in bedraggled strands from the veil around her head. When she first looked up at the duke, it was clear that she, like Edith, had been weeping, her face haggard and etched with loss and pain. But this was the widow of the most powerful man in England and the mother of earls and a king. She was the sister-in-law of Canute the Great, the warrior ruler of England, Norway and Denmark. She had been seated at power's right hand since before this new arrival on England's shores had even been born, and she was certainly not going to be intimidated by him now.

She summoned up all the strength her mind and body possessed, willed herself to stand tall and looked William square in the eyes. 'You have His Majesty King Harold's body.'

William nodded in confirmation of the statement.

'I am sure you know that my family is very wealthy,' Gytha continued. 'I earned a lot of that money myself. I used to be a merchant, you see. I bought and sold people. I know that everybody, alive or dead, has a value, and every man has a price at which he is willing to sell. So here is my offer. If you return the body of my son Harold, I will give you his weight in gold.'

William's favoured nobles were standing nearby. They could see that he was, for a moment at least, taken aback. It was no secret to them that he was badly in need of gold. The expedition had been hugely costly and there was still more fighting to be done. Even now, they only had a toehold on English soil. And every man in the army cost money. Every day of campaigning drained the ducal treasury further. But to take that gold would be a sign of weakness, and William was no more willing to give an inch to Gytha than she was to him.

'You dishonour both yourself and me, madam,' he replied. His voice was flint-hard, without a trace of sympathy or an iota of human feeling. 'I am not a trader and I do not sell my good name for gold. You may see your son's body if you wish. It has been wrapped in purple cloth, as befits a king, even one who treacherously usurped a throne that had been promised to me, and broke the oaths of loyalty that he swore to me.

'But you cannot have the body, nor may you or anyone else bury it, nor will any monument, not even a headstone, be raised in his memory. I will not have shrines erected to my enemies. There will be no pilgrims to Harold Godwinson's tomb.'

The tears in Gytha's eyes had given way to blazing fury. 'Listen to you . . . William the Bastard. I suppose I should not be surprised that you lack the grace, the breeding and the bearing of a true king. You come from the filth of a tannery after all. Ah well, I suppose I should be grateful you haven't skinned my boy and used him to make new boots.'

A cold, tense silence fell. Rob was standing close to his brother. His mind flashed back to that morning at Alençon, and the grisly reprisal William had ordered against the Angevin soldiers who had mocked his parentage.

'Mind your tongue, madam,' the duke said. 'I've killed men for less than that. I would not hesitate to kill a woman too.'

'As if I'd care. My boys are all dead . . . my lovely boys. Go ahead and kill me, William of Normandy. Kill a mother as she grieves. Let the whole world know that you are nothing but a monster.'

William sighed and gave a shake of his head. 'Do you really think your words make any difference to me? All my life I've had to deal with people's contempt. People who thought they were better than me, who wanted what I'd got. I've had friends turn on me, members of my own family. I've had kings break solemn vows and then try to break me too. Your precious son perjured himself because he wanted the crown that was rightfully mine. And not one of those people – not one – has ever beaten me.

'Why did your son think he would be any different? All my other enemies are dead or exiled. Why would he have escaped?

'Look at all those dead Englishmen. It was their destiny to die here, just as it was mine to defeat them. I was born for this. I will take the crown of England and place it on my head, because that was what God planned that I should do. That was what my mother prophesied.

'You may call me a monster, madam. Others may call me the Bastard. But I am neither of those things.

'Look around you, see what I have done.' He waved a tired arm towards the battlefield. Then, summoning up his last reserves of energy, he clenched his jaw and looked directly at the mother of the king he had vanquished and would soon replace. 'I am William, Duke of Normandy.

'I am the Conqueror.'

Postscript

After the battle of Hastings, William took a circuitous route up to and then around London before crossing the Thames at Wallingford in modern-day Oxfordshire, eleven miles up the River Thames from Henley. He approached London from the north-west and met a deputation of English nobility at Berkhamsted, where he accepted their offer of the throne. He was finally crowned king of England in Westminster Abbey on Christmas Day 1066. Charlemagne, the Holy Roman Emperor and founder of an empire that stretched across the Low Countries, France, Germany, Austria and northern Italy, had also been crowned on Christmas Day, in the year 800. It is reasonable to assume that the coincidence was entirely intentional.

Matilda was crowned Queen of England, also at Westminster, in May 1068. She bore William four sons and at least five daughters (chroniclers were apt to ignore the births of female offspring), of whom two, William and Henry, succeeded their father as king of England. She died in November 1083 and was buried at the Abbaye aux Dames, which she had founded, in Caen. Though false rumours were spread of her alleged infidelity, her marriage to William appears to have remained close and loving to the very end.

Robert, the eldest son of William and Matilda, led a life that was far from happy. Frequently mocked by his younger siblings, he seemed to be both hot-tempered and ineffectual. This led him into numerous quarrels with and even wars against his father and brothers, which Matilda did her best to resolve. Having spent years in exile, wandering Europe, he was named duke of Normandy at his father's death in 1087, but within a dozen years had so mismanaged his inheritance that he had to mortgage the duchy to his younger brother William to pay for his participation in the First Crusade.

Robert returned from the Holy Land to find William dead and his youngest brother Henry crowned king. More family feuds ensued until Henry finally defeated Robert and imprisoned him in Devizes Castle and then Cardiff Castle, where he finally died in 1134.

William Fitzosbern flourished mightily after the Conquest. He was named earl of Hereford, Gloucester, Worcester, Oxfordshire and Wessex. He built numerous castles across his vast expanse of estates and was also responsible for extending the conquest of England into Wales. But his greed for more land proved the undoing of him. In 1070, following the death of Matilda's brother, Count Baldwin of Flanders, Fitz was promised the hand of his widow Richilde, and with it the chance to rule Flanders. Other men, however, coveted the same territory, and Fitz died in battle in February 1071, fighting for one conquest too many.

Roger Montgomery may not have taken part in the battle of Hastings, but he was rewarded for his loyalty to William by being named the first earl of Shrewsbury and also earl of Arundel, in Sussex (his land included the town of Chichester, where the newly arrived Normans built a castle . . . and where this book was written). He and Mabel had at least ten children; the eldest, Robert of Bellême, married Agnes of Ponthieu, the daughter of Guy of Ponthieu, joined Robert of Normandy in his rebellion against Henry and was described by the chronicler Orderic Vitalis as 'grasping and cruel . . . unequalled for his iniquity in the whole Christian era' – a chip off the old Bellême block, in other words. Roger and Mabel's daughter Matilda married Robert of Mortain, bearing him a son and three daughters.

Mabel of Bellême came to a sticky end. In 1077, after years of conspiring to acquire land that belonged to other noble families, she took control of estates belonging to a knight called Hugh Bunel. Two years later, on 2 December 1079, Hugh and his three brothers entered the castle of Bures, a little way north-east of Alençon, where Mabel was spending the night. They broke into her bedchamber, where she was relaxing after a bath, and Hugh cut off her head with his sword. The intruders then escaped unharmed.

Well, she had it coming.

Timeline

This timeline relates to events as they occur in this book. I have tried to stick as closely as possible in my writing to known historical chronology. But – as I have remarked in previous volumes – Norman chronology is often inexact, even assuming that events reported by chroniclers actually occurred at all. And of course, this a work of fiction in which events sometimes have to be manipulated somewhat to create a more condensed, coherent narrative than pure history can provide. So a certain latitude can, I hope, be forgiven. That said, I have placed asterisks by events that I have knowingly shifted, if only marginally from their actual dates, or to which I have given a date where none is precisely known. There may be other, unintentionally misplaced items. If so I apologise profusely for any mistakes – D.C.

1044
- Harald Hardrada returns to the court of Kiev after twelve years fighting for the Emperor Michael in Constantinople and imprisonment
- Marriage of Harald Hardrada and Elisaveta of Kiev*

1047
- Harald Hardrada becomes King of Norway

1051
- Geoffrey 'Martel' of Anjou takes Maine and Chateau-du-Loir
- Duke William of Normandy is named heir to the English throne by King Edward the Confessor
- Godwin, Earl of Essex, and his sons are exiled
- King Edward sends his wife Edith to a convent
- William retakes Alençon and Domfront from Martel

1052

- Queen Edith is permitted to return to court
- Sweyn Godwinson is murdered while returning from pilgrimage
- Hardrada raids Hedeby and defeats Sven of Denmark*

1053

- Death of Godwin of Wessex
- William successfully lays siege to his uncle Talou's castle of Arques; Talou is exiled

1054

- Mabel of Bellême attempts to poison Arnaud d'Echauffour and kills Hugh Montgomery instead by mistake. She later bribes Arnaud's chamberlain to poison him*
- William's men take Mortemer castle

1056

- King Edward the Confessor learns of the existence of Edward the Exile and makes him his heir, recalling him to England *

1057

- Sudden death of Edward the Exile within days of his landing in England
- William defeats Martel and King Henry's armies at Varaville on the River Dives

1064

- Harold of Wessex travels to Normandy and meets William, swearing an oath of fealty to him
- Truce between Sven of Denmark and Harald Hardrada of Norway

1065

- Rebellion in York against Tostig Godwinson, Harold's brother
- Tostig is deposed as Earl of Northumbria and sent into exile

1066

- Death of Edward the Confessor (January). Harold of Wessex is crowned King of England
- Marriage of convenience between Harold and Ealdgyth of Mercia
- Tostig recruits Harald Hardrada to help him fight in England to get back his earldom and the crown
- Halley's comet appears in the night sky
- Tostig returns to England with an army, but he is defeated and driven back to sea by Edwin and Morcar's forces
- Harald Hardrada sets sail from Norway to support Tostig and take the English throne
- Hardrada and Tostig's forces defeat Edwin and Morcar at Foul Ford Gate
- William and the Norman army set sail for England
- Battle of Stamford Bridge (25 September). Harold of Wessex defeats Harald Hardrada, who dies in battle
- Harold marches south to meet William. En route he learns he has been excommunicated by the Pope
- Battle of Hastings (14 October). William defeats Harold, who is killed in battle
- Duke William of Normandy becomes King of England